THE MIGHTY ENGINE

THE PRINTING PRESS AND ITS IMPACT

# NIGHT THOUGHTS

## ON

## LIFE DEATH and IMMORTALITY

*by the late* Dr. YOUNG

to which are added

*The Life of the Author and a*

## PARAPHRASE

on Part of the

## BOOK of JOB.

*Wait the great teacher Death.*

London.

Printed for Toplis and Bunney in Holborn, and J. Mozley, Gainsborough.

MDCCLXXX.

# The Mighty Engine
## The Printing Press and its Impact

Edited by
Peter Isaac and Barry McKay

ST PAUL'S BIBLIOGRAPHIES
WINCHESTER

OAK KNOLL PRESS
DELAWARE

PRINT NETWORKS

This series, edited by Peter Isaac and Barry McKay, publishes papers given at the annual Seminars on the British Book Trade

1. *Images & Texts*
2. *The Reach of Print*
3. *The Human Face of the Book Trade*
4. *The Mighty Engine*

© St Paul's Bibliographies and the Contributors 2000

First published 2000 by
St Paul's Bibliographies
West End House
1 Step Terrace
Winchester
Hampshire SO22 5BW

Published in North & South America and the Philippines by
Oak Knoll Press
310 Delaware Street
New Castle
DE 19720
ISBN 1 - 873040 - 61 - X (UK)
ISBN 1 - 58456 - 024 - X (USA)

British Library Cataloguing in Publication Data
available from the British Library

**Library of Congress Cataloging-in-Publication Data**
The mighty engine: the printing press and its impact /
edited by Peter Isaac and Barry McKay.
p. cm -- (Print networks; 4)
Includes bibliographical references and index.
ISBN 1-873040-61-X (UK)
ISBN 1-58456-024-X (USA)
1. Printing -- Great Britain -- History. 2. Publishers and publishing -- Great Britain --
History. I. Isaac, Peter C.G. II. McKay, Barry. III Series.
Z151 M64 2000
686.2'0941 -- dc21
00-040656

Composed in MONOTYPE *Bulmer* by Peter Isaac & Barry McKay
Printed in England by St Edmundsbury Press, Bury St Edmunds

# Contents

List of Contributors       vii

Editorial       ix

RHEINALLT LLWYD    'Worthy of the poets and worthy of a gentleman':
Publishing *Gorchestion Beirdd Cymru* (1773)       1

CHRIS BAGGS    The Potter Family of Haverfordwest,
1780–1875       13

RICHARD SUGGETT    Pedlars & Mercers as Distributors of Print in
Early-Modern Wales       23

PHILIP HENRY JONES    'Business is Awful Bad in these Parts':New Evidence for
the Pre-1914 Decline of the Welsh-Language Book
Trade       33

AUDREY COOPER    George Nicholson and His *Cambrian Traveller's
Guide*       43

BRENDA SCRAGG    William Ford and Edinburgh Cultural Society at the
Beginning of the Nineteenth Century       57

IAIN BEAVAN    Advertising Judiciously: Scottish Nineteenth-Century
Publishers and the British Market       69

STACEY GEE    The Coming of Print to York, *c*1490–1550       79

MAUREEN BELL    Sturdy Rogues and Vagabonds: Restoration Control of
Pedlars and Hawkers       89

DAVID STOKER    Printing at the Red-Well: an early Norwich Press
through the Eyes of Contemporaries       97

DAVID J SHAW    Canterbury's External Links: Book-Trade Relations at
the Regional and National Level in the Eighteenth
Century       107

SARAH GRAY    William Flackton, 1709–1798, Canterbury Bookseller
and Musician       121

MARGARET COOPER    Books Returned, Accounts Unsettled and Gifts of Country Food: Customer Expectations around 1700    131

DIANA DIXON    Newspapers in Huntingdonshire in the Eighteenth and Nineteenth Centuries    143

JIM ENGLISH    Chapbooks & Primers, Piety, Poetry & Classics: the Mozleys of Gainsborough    153

BARRY McKAY    John Ware, Printer and Bookseller of Whitehaven: a Year from his Day-books    163

JOHN HINKS    Some Radical Printers and Booksellers of Leicester *c*1790–1850    175

JOHN R TURNER    Book Publishing from the English Provinces in the late Nineteenth Century: Report on Work in Progress    185

Index    197

(*Frontispiece*) Engraved title-page of Young's *Night Thoughts* (London, 1780) – reduced to 92% (see pp 153 sqq) Rteproduced by kind permission of N J L Lyons

# Contributors

**Chris Baggs** lectures at the University of Wales Aberystwyth. His research concentrates on reading and library history, but walking the Pembrokeshire Coast Path has aroused an interest in the county's book trade.

**Iain Beavan**, Senior Curator (Projects) in Historic Collections, Aberdeen University, is a member of the University's Cultural History Group. He maintains an active research interest in the print culture of northeast Scotland, and during the first half of 1999 was the MacCaig Visiting Fellow at the Scottish Centre of the Book, Napier University, Edinburgh.

**Maureen Bell**, Senior Lecturer in the English Department, University of Birmingham, has published work on women and the book trade in the sixteenth and seventeenth centuries; the provincial trade in the seventeenth century; and quantitative work on British book production 1475–1700. She is currently working on the Cambridge History of the Book in Britain vol IV (as Assistant Editor) and on A Chronology and Calendar of Documents related to the London book trade 1641–1700.

**Audrey Cooper** was formerly a librarian in the Arts Division of Warwick University Library. After retiring to her native Stourport she became interested in George Nicholson's connexion with the then new town, and hopes eventually to produce an account of his extensive output from Stourport for the Civic Society. Today Nicholson as a printer is relatively unknown, but in the nineteenth century he had acquired a considerable reputation and a recognized status in the book trade.

**Margaret Cooper**, bookseller and former Open University tutor, is continuing her study of the Worcestershire book trade, and also beginning work on the library of 12 000 volumes bequeathed to a Bristol independent school by the antiquarian C J Ryland.

**Diana Dixon**, who is now a freelance researcher, previously taught at the College of Librarianship Wales and at Loughborough University. She was co-author (with Lionel Madden ) of *The Nineteenth Century Periodical Press in Britain: a bibliography of modern studies 1901–1971* (Toronto: Research Society for Victorian Periodicals, 1975), and has been actively involved with Newsplan projects in the East Midlands and London & the South East.

**Jim English** has written and lectured on many aspects of the history of his adopted town and county, including the Gainsborough and Lincolnshire book trade. He is a retired public librarian.

**Stacey Gee** was the British Book-Trade Seminar Fellow for 1999, and is a graduate in medieval studies of the Universities of Birmingham and York. She has recently been awarded the PhD of York University for her study of the book trade of late fifteenth- and early sixteenth-century Yorkshire. She will be taking up a post in Derbyshire County Archives this year.

**Sarah Gray** is Assistant Librarian at Canterbury Cathedral Library. She is also employed by the University of Wales Aberystwyth to produce, with Dr David Shaw, a Rare-Books Module for the degree of the Department of Information and Library Studies.

**John Hinks** took early retirement in 1997 from the post of County Librarian of Leicestershire. His interest in the history of the book dates back to the 1970s when his part-time MLS studies at Loughborough University included research on the impact and use of print in the Regency period, and cheap series from 1827 to 1851. He has an MA in history from Leicester University, which included a dissertation on Ramsay MacDonald: the Leicester years (1906-1918). His current PhD research at Loughborough is on the history of the book trades in Leicester c1575-1850.

**Philip Henry Jones**, a lecturer in the Department of Information & Library Studies of the University of Wales Aberystwyth, has made a special study of the nineteenth-century Welsh-language book trade. He edited with Eiluned Rees *A Nation and its Books* (1998).

**Rheinallt Llwyd** is a Lecturer in the Department of Information & Library Studies of the University of Wales Aberystwyth, where he specializes in aspects of the historical bibliography of Wales, and sources and services for community history. A former editor of *Llais Llyfrau - Book News from Wales*, he has published numerous articles on aspects of the Welsh book trade, and edited *Gwarchod y Gwreiddiau* (1996), a collection of essays on twentieth-century Welsh publishing.

**Barry McKay**, an antiquarian bookseller who specializes in bibliography and the art and history of the book, has been, for several years, engaged in research on the book trade in Cumbria. He is joint editor of the *Print Networks* series.

**Brenda Scragg**, who now works part-time at the John Rylands Library, has published several catalogues of that library's exhibitions on nineteenth-century book arts and children's literature. Her book-trade research specializes on Manchester.

**David J Shaw** teaches French at the University of Kent at Canterbury. His special interests are the history of printing in fifteenth- and sixteenth-century France and eighteenth-century Canterbury. He is a Vice-President of the Bibliographical Society.

**David Stoker** is a Senior Lecturer in the Department of Information and Library Studies of the University of Wales Aberystwyth. He has been interested in eighteenth-century Norwich printing for thirty years and in Norfolk antiquarians for about twenty-five years.

**Richard Suggett** is a member of the staff of the Royal Commission on the Ancient and Historical Monuments of Wales, based in Aberystwyth, and head of the emergency recording team. He is particularly interested in the social (including architectural) history of the late medieval and early modern period, and has published articles on popular festivals, slander, and witchcraft in Wales, as well as a study of *John Nash, Architect* (1996).

**John R Turner** is a lecturer in the Department of Information and Library Studies at the University of Wales Aberystwyth. His main interest is the history of publishing in the nineteenth and early twentieth centuries.

# Editorial

IN AN AGE WHEN one of the fundamental freedoms, that of the press, is once again under threat, from either reactionary, political, theological, sociological or, perhaps worst of all, commercial forces it is well that we be reminded of the strengths of that humble piece of machinery, the printing press, *The Mighty Engine* which gives the title to this collection of papers from the seventeenth seminar on the history of the British book trade.

As one may expect from a conference held at Aberystwyth there is a strong element of study of the Welsh book but this is by no means parochial. Welsh-language publishing has a relatively short history but a not inglorious one, and its role in preserving and fostering that language, and its bardic traditions, is recognized by Rheinallt Llwyd, who discusses one particular publication which, as the author points out, 'stands apart from all the other [Welsh language] publications on account of both its content and typography'. At what is perhaps the other end of the scale Philip Henry Jones provides a fascinating insight into the problems of the publisher's traveller, albeit in a period rife with economic problems, and not only for a small Welsh-language publishing house.

Wales is not of course an entirely Welsh-speaking nation, and Chris Baggs reminds us that in Pembrokeshire – that little England beyond Wales – there was a flourishing English-language book trade which he profiles through the career of one family dynasty in Haverfordwest over the better part of a century.

Audrey Cooper's study of Nicholson's *Cambrian Guide* reminds us that the eighteenth and nineteenth centuries were a period when the Englishman began to understand and appreciate the beauties of his own country and its Celtic neighbours.

The role of the chapman and his fellow-travellers, hawkers and pedlars, in the distribution of print has in recent years begun to receive the attention it merits. Two excellent papers, by Richard Suggett on their place in early-modern Wales and by Maureen Bell on seventeenth-century attempts to control them, provide splendid examples of the use of documentary evidence to help our understanding of the lives of this sub-class of the book trade.

Passing just across the border into England Margaret Cooper, drawing on a small archive that survived by the most fortuitous circumstance, provides an unusual, if not unique, account of a small provincial bookseller at the end of the seventeenth and early eighteenth centuries.

At the other end of that century which encompassed the age of enlightenment Barry McKay draws on another significant archive to analyse one year in the life of Cumberland's premier bookseller and printer.

The place of the provincial newspaper and its importance in the financial affairs of the provincial press is becoming well-travelled ground. Research in recent years has shown the immense importance of the provincial newspaper in both a local and regional, and occasionally even national, context. Diana Dixon examines the newspapers of Huntingdonshire and highlights their often precarious existence.

London has always, and doubtless will always, dominate the English, if not the British, book trade. However, that domination is not total; it was very much two-way traffic. Jim English presents an account of that ubiquitous 'provincial' publishing house Mozleys of Gainsborough, and casts new light on the sometimes difficult problem of positively identifying certain London imprints. Kent is nearer to the Great Wen than Lincolnshire, or perhaps in an earlier period, just as far away, yet the Kent book trade, and that of Canterbury in particular, had country-wide connections which are minutely examined by David Shaw.

We are reminded that although its products were locally produced the provincial book trade was by no means invariably parochial in outlook by Iain Beavan, who makes imaginative use of the Oliver & Boyd papers to analyse the costs of advertising nationally, or rather internationally, and what returns were got from the outlay involved.

How often have historians in all fields wished for more contemporary observations; David Stoker has used those of the early press in Norwich to put this press into its context.

The period of change from the manuscript to the printed book in provincial England has received little attention. This lack is now most admirably corrected by the year's British Book Trade Fellow, Stacey Gee, whose paper on the early days of printing in York should become required reading for all interested in that period and that city.

The study of the book and the tracing of the spread of print becomes increasingly easy in this age of on-line catalogues, but John Turner reminds us that for all the benefits of on-line information we are still at the mercy of a library's cataloguing system and what it chooses to record in the way of imprint information, or perhaps not record. In consequence, even with these aids a true account of the volume of publishing in the provinces is still some way off.

Members of the provincial book trade were nothing if not flexible, commercially and socially. Brenda Scragg presents a lively account of William Ford though his cultural contacts with Edinburgh, while Sarah Gray examines the career of William

Flackton, perhaps the only provincial bookseller of the eighteenth century whose music is not only still played but still available recorded.

Flexibility of thought and deed is the theme taken by John Hinks in his examination of the radical book trade in Leicester, a town whose earlier record of corporate corruption stands second to none. His paper discusses the power of the press and reminds us that

> The mighty engine – the warrior whose name was 'legion'– which had taken so prominent a part and performed such deeds of strength in the great conflict of Truth and Justice with Error and Oppression.

The theme recurring though these papers is one of change and innovation, and of the book trade, throughout the centuries, responding to new challenges. Scholars of the history of the provincial book are as flexible and innovative, as these papers once again display.

*Barry McKay*, Appleby
April 2000

# 'Worthy of the poets and worthy of a gentleman':
# Publishing Gorchestion Beirdd Cymru *(1773)*

## RHEINALLT LLWYD

THE TOTAL OUTPUT of the Welsh book trade for 1773 as recorded in *Libri Walliae* amounts to forty-nine individual titles.[1] The majority of these, forty-three (88%) are in the Welsh language and most of them, thirty-six (74%) were printed in Wales. When we recall that the first official printing press was not established in Wales until 1718 at Trehedyn, Cardiganshire, and that the average annual output of Welsh books often did not exceed ten separate titles in the decades between 1720 and 1760, this figure of forty-nine for 1773 represents a considerable development.[2] Throughout the eighteenth century the demand for printed material grew continuously and rapidly, with the result that printing presses were set up in a number of the larger Welsh towns. Of the books listed for 1773, twenty-three were printed at Carmarthen, all by John Ross, thus representing 47% of the total annual output and 64% of those published in Wales. The other thirteen titles printed in Wales had been produced at presses in Brecon, Caerleon, Trefecca, Llandovery and Wrexham. But Welsh books and books relating to Wales were still being produced elsewhere, and the thirteen (or 26%) titles printed outside Wales in 1773 came from presses at Bristol [2], London [2], Dublin [2] and Shrewsbury [5] – with John Eddowes at Shrewsbury producing the most.

An analysis of the 1773 output reveals that the vast majority (some 90%) of these publications were religious in nature – published sermons, devotional and didactic texts, religious verse, collections of hymns, a Hebrew grammar, and a number of elegies to Howell Harris (1714–1773), one of the leaders of the Methodist Revival in Wales who died in July of that year. Nor surprisingly, the effects of the Methodist Revival, and the growth of literacy as a result of the remarkable success of the Circulating-Schools movement, were constantly fuelling the demand for more reading materials, and many of these religious publications were translations and adaptations from English texts. But lest we give the impression that the Welsh read nothing but wholesome religious books it must be remembered that another body of literature, in the form of ballads, almanacs, interludes and broadsheets were being produced by printers in Wales and beyond.[3] This category of literature is an interesting feature of the book trade in eighteenth-century Wales, and undoubtedly provides a more realistic and comprehensive picture of Welsh society at that time than the predominantly religious publications.

There is one volume produced in 1773 that does not fit into the above pattern. Indeed, it stands apart from all the other publications that appeared in that year on account of both its content and typography. Thomas Parry in his *A History of Welsh Literature* refers to it as 'one of the most beautifully printed books in the language',[4] and the entry in the *New Companion to the Literature of Wales* describes it as 'one of the most important collections ever made of Welsh poetry'.[5] That volume is *Gorchestion Beirdd Cymru: neu flodau godidowgrwydd Awen* (The Masterpieces of the Welsh Poets: or the most excellent flowers of the Muse).[6] Most of the anthology consists of the work of 'beirdd yr uchelwyr' (poets of the nobility), in particular those living during the fifteenth and sixteenth centuries. These poets flourished under the patronage of the landed gentry, and belonged to a professional guild, The Bardic Order, with its strict rules and regulations, jealously guarded by those who maintained and belonged to it.[7] There are also poems attributed (incorrectly in one instance) to two of the earliest known Welsh poets, Aneirin and Taliesin, poets who flourished during the late sixth century in the Old North of Britain and who are mentioned in Nennius's *Historia Brittonum* (*c*830). In all, the work of eighteen individual poets is represented in the *Gorchestion* and, the title-page informs us, they had been collected and selected 'O Gasgliad RHYS JONES o'r Tyddyn Mawr... yn Swydd Feirion' (from the Collection of Rhys Jones of Tyddyn Mawr... in the county of Merioneth). Better known as Rhys Jones o'r Blaenau (Rice Jones of Y Blaenau), he was a freeholder and a member of the minor gentry in Merionethshire. He could claim a connection on his mother's side with Robert Vaughan of Hengwrt (*c*1592–1667), the notable antiquary who had assembled the finest private library of books and manuscripts that Wales ever possessed.[8]

Rhys Jones had intended to pursue a career in law and, following initial schooling at the local grammar school in Dolgellau, he was sent to a Shrewsbury school, but on his father's death Rhys returned home at the age of eighteen to take charge of his small estate, to enjoy the pleasures of an eighteenth-century country squire, and play his part in the local government of his native county, Merioneth. Though he lacked university education he was an extremely cultured man and a poet of considerable standing. He mastered the intricate strict metres of medieval Welsh poetry, and a collection of his poems, *Gwaith Prydyddawl y diweddar Rice Jones o'r Blaenau, Meirion* (The Poetical Works of the late Rice Jones of Blaenau, Meirioneth), was published posthumously by his grandson Rice Jones Owen in 1818.[9] Rhys Jones had also been primarily responsible for establishing Y Gymdeithas Loerig (the Lunar Society) (*c*1750), a literary and debating society which met monthly on the occasion of the full moon at an Inn at Drws-y-Nant near Dolgellau. This was a society for local gentlemen and poets, and some of its activities have been recorded in a number of fascinating poems. Lewis Morris, the eldest of the famous Morris brothers of Anglesey,[10] in a letter to his brother William on 18 September 1757 says

Rhys Jones is a freeholder of about £50 a year just by Nannau, a great friend and follower of that family, a very ingenius good natured man about forty-five years of age. He is a better poet and hath prettier turns of wit than any of that country... My encouraging him and assuming him y gellid prydydd o hono [that he could become a poet] hath encouraged him to proceed, and he hath wrote very good things.[11]

Not only was Jones a poet but also a collector of poetry in both printed and manuscript format, and some of them have survived and are at the National Library of Wales.[12] In religious matters he was a staunch Anglican, and wrote a series of englynion (strict metre stanzas) satirising Methodists. One can imagine that few of the Welsh publications produced during 1773 would have appealed to Rhys Jones!

The only other name that appears on the title-page of *Gorchestion Beirdd Cymru* is that of the printer, Stafford Prys. He was a Welsh-speaking native of Montgomeryshire, and invariably used the Welsh version of his surname, Prys, as opposed to the more Anglicised Pryse, in his imprints. Fifty-six separate entries refer to him in *Libri Walliae*, ranging from 1758 (the year when he established his business) to 1780, four years before his death, though most of the publications were produced between 1758 and 1764. He also printed a number of Welsh ballads between 1758 and 1782.[13] He was apprenticed to Thomas Dunstan who, as Eiluned Rees points out, was 'the most prolific printer of Welsh books in Shrewsbury',[14] his career spanning from 1711 to 1764. Stafford Prys joined Dunstan as an apprentice on 21 November 1750 at the age of 18, and remained with him until 1758 when 'he was admitted a freeman of the Booksellers' Company – on 24 May 1758 on payment of a fine of 17s.4d.[15] All but one of the entries in *Libri Walliae* with Prys's imprint are for Welsh-language books, and it seems that he confined his attention as publisher and printer to materials in that language. In her analysis of Shrewsbury printing Eiluned Rees concludes that 'the Shrewsbury-printed Welsh books were not works of art',[16] and there are frequent examples of complaints against individual printers because of poor craftsmanship and numerous textual inaccuracies. One volume that came in for considerable criticism was an anthology of Welsh poetry *Blodeu-gerdd Cymry* (Welsh Anthology), edited by David Jones of Trefriw and printed by Stafford Prys in 1759. The following year another of the Morris brothers, Richard, wrote to Jones claiming

*There are many very good verses in your book, others that have little value. It is a pity, however, that the orthography is not more correct and that there are so many printing errors which detract enormously from the volume. More care should be taken with work that should last for ever, for the sake of the language.*[17]

Rhys Jones, in his preface, admits that there are numerous errors in *Gorchestion Beirdd Cymru*, some, he claims, because of his own incompetence and ignorance, others because he lived so far away from the compositor and never had the opportunity to correct the proofs.[18] Whatever its defects it is, typographically, an impressive quarto volume consisting of 300 pages of text and some 24 preliminary pages consisting of a dedication to William Vaughan, the squire of Corsygedol, and Nannau; an introduction in Welsh 'at yr hynaws ddarllenydd' (to the genial reader); a preface 'to the reader' (in English); a list of the bards (in English); Cynhwysiad y Llyfr (the book's content in Welsh); and a list of subscribers' names. The complicated make-up of the prelims is due to four inserted single leaves, and not all have been inserted in the same order in different copies that I have investigated. Could it be that some of the English sections such as 'to the reader' and 'a list of bards' were afterthoughts, since so many of the subscribers would be totally unfamiliar with the Welsh language? The text itself is nicely designed and printed, displaying a good typographical range and ingenuity, and it is often referred to in Welsh as Y Bais Wen (White Petticoat) on account of the particularly generous margins. In comparison to other eighteenth-century Welsh-printed books, and collections of verse in particular, it is 'beautifully printed' and the finest work produced by Stafford Prys. He could rightly be proud of his achievement.

*Gorchestion Beirdd Cymru* was also a considerable achievement for its editor, Rhys Jones, for the ideal of publishing a substantial anthology of medieval Welsh poetry had been comtemplated by many others over a long period of time. As early as 1547 William Salesbury was encouraging the poets to make use of the printing press in his *Oll Synnwyr Pen Kembro Ygyd* (The Whole Sense of a Welshman's Head). And in his Welsh grammar of 1592, *Cambrobrytannicae Cymraecaeve Linguae Institutiones et Rudimenta*, another leading Welsh Renaissance scholar, Siôn Dafydd Rhys, castigated the poets for their conservatism and in particular their refusal to see their works in print.

> *For they, and others, keep and hide their books and knowledge in chests and secret places;... And when the Poets die then all that beauty will go into the earth with them, and nothing more will be heard of it.*[19]

The Bardic Order, however, failed to adapt to the challenges of Renaissance learning, including making good use of the printing press. Hence the task of copying and compiling manuscripts and assembling collections in private libraries would remain a preoccupation in Wales until the beginning of the nineteenth century. We should also remember that Wales would remain a country without major national cultural institutions until the latter part of the nineteenth and early twentieth century. Its first university college was not established until 1872 and its National Library and National Museum not until 1907. Edward Lhuyd (1660–1709), the Celtic scholar and Keeper of the Ashmolean Museum at Oxford, realised the danger inherent in such a situation, and the catalogue of Welsh manuscripts and their location in private libraries which he published in his *Archaeologia Britannica* in 1707 would prove indispensable. Moses Williams, one of Lhuyd's ablest pupils and Wales's first bibliographer, intended to remedy the situation. Two years after the publication of his *Cofrestr o'r Holl Lyfrau Printiedig* (Register of all Printed Books, 1717) he published *Proposals* with the aim of

> Publishing a Collection of such MS Tracts as are now remaining in the Welsh Tongue (as well as Translations and Originals) to the beginning of the XVIth Century, with their various readings, referring throughout to the Books out of which they are taken.[20]

Williams was painfully aware that 'all manuscripts (whether in Public Places or in private hands) are liable to be embezzled or destroyed'. In the same year, 1719, an advertisement appeared in William Baxter's *Glossarium Antiquitatum Britannicarum*, a text edited by Moses Williams claiming

> There is preparing for the Press a Collection of writings in the WELSH Tongue, to the beginning of the Sixteenth Century, to be printed in several volumes in Octavo...
> N.B. No more Copies will be printed than are subscribed for.[21]

Williams failed, however, to secure sufficient support for his ambitious plan and it was abandoned, although he did manage to publish a Latin index to the works of Welsh poets, *Repertorium Poeticum*, in 1726.

Nine years later, in 1735, Lewis Morris (1701–1765), the eldest of the famous Morris brothers, produced on his recently acquired printing press at Holyhead *Tlysau yr Hen Oesoedd* (Gems of Past Ages). This was the first Welsh-language periodical and consisted of selections of poetry and prose copied from manuscripts. Morris realised the need to publish entertaining materials to arouse Welsh people's interest in their literary and cultural heritage. In his prefatory note 'To the English Reader' he claims

> It is intended to carry on this Collection of our British Antiquities, on the best Subjects handled by the Antients... Things which very few English Readers have any Knowledge of, except our Antiquaries, our MSS having never been made publick, and in a great measure destroy'd by the Folly of some, and Envy of others.[22]

Although Morris's plans came to nothing, since subsequent issues of the *Tlysau* were abandoned, it seems others were contemplating a similar scheme. In a letter dated October 1736 (to one Edward Samuel) Lewis Morris maintains that a Glamorgan poet and manuscript collector

> one John Bradford a Correspondent of mine... This man hath an Inclination to Publish some Poems of ye antients, and he says he can get subscribers Enough. I fancy he must mean some Balderdash stuff of ye last century[23]

5

Bradford also failed in his objective, although it is quite likely that what he had in mind was not dissimilar from what Rhys Jones published almost forty years later.

In 1751 the Cymmrodorion Society was founded in London by another of the Morris brothers, Richard, who became the first president and remained in post until his death in 1799. Although a London-based society it had corresponding members in Wales, and it was Lewis Morris who drafted the ambitious 'Constitutions' (published in 1755), which listed the aims. Its primary objective was to foster the Welsh language, its history, literature and cultural traditions. Among a number of interesting proposals 'The Society also propose to print all the scarce and valuable antient British manuscripts with Notes Critical and Explanatory'.[24] Only a few printed publications were produced during the first phase of the society's existence (1751–1787), and certainly none of them contained 'scarce and valuable manuscripts'. Yet the network of connections established by the Cymmrodorion Society, and the Morris circle, would prove important in the eventual appearance of *Gorchestion Beirdd Cymru*.

Although only two names appear on the title-page of *Gorchestion*, the editor Rhys Jones and the printer Stafford Prys, we know that two other individuals played a crucial role at various stages in the book's production. They are both listed in the 'Subscribers Names' one as 'Rev. Evan Evans, Curate of Tywyn Meirionydd' and the other as 'David Jones of Trefriw, Poet'. Evan Evans (1731–1788) was known during his lifetime as Ieuan Fardd (Evan the Bard) or Ieuan Brydydd Hir (Evan the Long Bard), and was the ablest Welsh scholar of his generation and the acknowledged expert on Wales's intellectual past.[25] Born in the parish of Lledrod, Cardiganshire, he was educated nearby at the reputable Ystrad Meurig grammar school, where he received an excellent classical education under the headmaster, Edward Richard.[26] Before going up to Merton College, Oxford, at the age of nineteen he spent some time in the employment of William Vaughan, the squire of Corsygedol and Nannau in Merionethshire 'as an apprentice household bard'. This is the same William Vaughan to which *Gorchestion Beirdd Cymru* is dedicated 'with the greatest respect' by the editor Rice Jones. William Vaughan (1707–1775)[27] was one of the most powerful men in his native Merioneth, representing the county as a Tory Member of Parliament from 1734 to 1768. He was also a Welsh speaker at a time when most of the gentry in Wales were abandoning the language, and he had wide cultural interests particularly in traditional Welsh poetry. There is some evidence that he was able to compose Welsh verse, and he certainly composed English poems and corresponded with other members of his social class, who had a dilettante interest in English literature. Vaughan became a valued member of the Morris circle, and, whereas Richard Morris became President of the Cymmrodorion Society when it was established in

1751, Vaughan became its 'Penllywydd' (Chief President)! There was also a distant family connection between Rhys Jones and the Vaughan family, and the minor squire of Blaenau composed numerous odes and poems to his more powerful and illustrious relative.

When Evan Evans became attached to the Vaughan household it is no wonder that Lewis Morris (who had himself moved to Cardiganshire in 1742) sent the aspiring young scholar and poet a list of 'instructions' on how to behave in 'a Gentleman's house' and the eighth instruction reads

> As I apprehend your chief Employment at first will be copying old Welsh manuscripts, If you meet with any dark passage or bad poetry, you had best leave blanks till you can compare it with other manuscripts, or write with a black lead pencil.[28]

Evans, during his 'apprenticeship' with William Vaughan, undoubtedly had access not only to the libraries of his master at Corsygedol and Nannau, but quite likely to the renowned Hengwrt libary and possibly that of Rhys Jones at Blaenau. It is more than likely that Evans and Jones would have met at this time.

Although Evan Evans enrolled at Merton College in 1750, he left a few years later before graduating. Ordained a priest in 1755, he never rose above the rank of curate, serving in a number of parishes in Wales and England. Despite his brilliance as a scholar and poet, he incurred the wrath of his superiors in the Anglican Church by attacking what he perceived to be the anti-Welsh attitudes and policies of the Welsh bishops of his day – the Esgyb Eingl (Anglo Bishops) as he called them. He was also addicted from an early age to drink. Lewis Morris in a letter to his brother Richard in 1752 claims 'He grows drunk and a mere poet in all respects'.[29] Evans would have been twenty-one at the time!

Despite his impoverished status and existence as a wandering curate his commitment to scholarship was total. From the mid-1750s onwards he was assiduously copying manuscripts. In 1757 he spent three months at Oxford copying sections of the Red Book of Hergest, and the following year he had the good fortune to see a copy of *Y Gododdin* (The Book of Aneirin), which was in the possession of Dafydd Jones of Trefriw. On 5 August 1758 Lewis Morris writes to Edward Richard, Evans's former master at Ystrad Meurig

> Who do you think I have at my elbow, as happy as ever Alexander thought himself after a conquest? No less a man than Ieuan Fardd, who hath discovered some old MSS lately that no body of this age or the last ever as much as dreamed of. And this discovery is to him and me as great as that of America by Columbus. We have found an epic Poem in the British called Gododin, equal at least to the Iliad, Aeneid or Paradise Lost.[30]

The ultimate result of this feverish period of manuscript copying was the appearance in 1764 of Evan Evans's *Some Specimens of the Poetry of the Antient Welsh*

*Bards*, published and paid for by a Welsh judge, Daines Barrington, who seems to have bought the text from Evans for £20. It was printed in London by Dodsley of Pall Mall. It is interesting to compare the layout and typography of the 1764 volume with *Gorchestion Beirdd Cymru* for there are many similarities, although they were produced by entirely different printers. *Some Specimens* was meant for the English market, and it brought Evans immediate recognition far beyond the boundaries of Wales and the acclamation of leading literary figures, such as Samuel Johnson, Thomas Gray and Bishop Percy. The work is divided into three main sections, the first consisting of ten Welsh poems in English; the second a Latin treatise *De Bardis Dissertatio*, a comprehensive survey of Welsh poetry; and the third a selection of poems in Welsh. Each section is dedicated to different individuals, and it is significant that the Latin text is dedicated to Gvlielmo Vaughan, the squire of Cors y Gedol!

While Evan Evans was producing his text of *Some Specimens* he was also thinking of producing an anthology of Welsh poetry in the original language. Among his manuscripts at the National Library of Wales are *Proposals* in his own hand for

printing by subscription a book of antient British poetry wrote by Bards who flourished from the beginning to the close of the fifteenth century, when they wrote correctest and best, and when as yet the language was free from any corruption occasioned since by our closer union & commerce with the English.[31]

The proposals claim that 'the publishers of this book… have skill in poetry themselves' before going on to praise the 'skill and learning' of the poets of old, and naming the most prominent ones to be included in the anthology. The proposals end with

CONDITIONS

1. The book will be printed on good paper and character and bound in calf skin in Qto, and will contain at least three hundred cywyddau and Awdlau.

2. Every Subscriber is to pay down two shillings at the time of subscribing, and two more at the delivery of the book.

3. The person to be employed for gathering subscriptions is to be David Jones of Trefriw near Llan Rwst. The Editor of the Blodeugerdd.

4. That the book be immediately printed as soon as we get a competent number of subscribers, and to be delivered if possible within half a year after the time of subscription.

5. The said David Jones above mentioned to have all the clear profits arising from the impression, for his trouble in gathering subscriptions and looking after the press.

6. That we our selves shall from time to time order the said David Jones to send us proof sheets of the work in order to see justice done by the printer.

7. That the Printer be Stafford Price of Shrewsbury.

8. That the said Stafford Price shall enter into articles with us, to do every thing according to our agreement with him.

Evan Evans Clerk Perpetual Curate of Llanvair Talhaearn
Rice Jones of Tyddyn Mawr at Blaenau Merionethshire.

NB To render this edition of British poems still more compleat we shall prefix a short tract of prosody, which will make those that are inclined apt judges of our measures, and of the nature of our poetry.[32]

It is obvious, therefore, that Evan Evans and Rhys Jones intended to be joint editors of the proposed anthology and in the manuscript the words 'Perpetual Curate of Llanvair Talhaearn' have been written above the crossed out 'curate of Trefriw Carnar',[33] suggesting that the proposals had been originally drafted before Evans left Trefriw for Llanfair Talhaearn at the end of June 1761. However, it was twelve years before *Gorchestion Beirdd Cymru* was published, and by then Evans was no longer joint editor. Unfortunately, no printed version of the proposals has survived, although there is evidence that they were produced. Richard Morris in a letter dated 15 June 1771 to a Mrs Penny of Bloomsbury Square claims

Inclosed is a proposal of a Merionethshire poet (Rice Jones of Blaenau) which I wish to see well executed: he has wrote me praying to assist in the publication, but I am not able to give any attention to it.[34]

It is interesting to note from the subscribers' names that 'Richard Morris, Navy Office, Esq' did in fact purchase fifty copies 'for the Use of the Cymmrodorion Society'.

Returning to Evan Evans it is difficult, however, to decide conclusively what part he did or did not play in producing the volume that claims Rhys Jones as the sole editor. Sections of 'to the reader', for example, have been taken verbatim from the manuscript 'proposals', and in 1783 Evans publicly claimed that he was the author of the English preface in the *Gorchestion*.[35] Even if he was not involved in editing the final anthology his involvement at the start would have been invaluable.[36]

Finally mention should also be made of David Jones (1703–1785) 'the person employed for gathering subscriptions'. A well-known figure of considerable importance in the context of eighteenth-century Welsh publishing, he had tried a variety of occupations, but is mainly remembered on account of his activities as a copyist and collector of manuscripts, publisher and printer.[37] David Jones had acted as agent for a number of Shrewsbury printers, often falling out with them on account of their lack of professionalism. He was particularly critical of Stafford Prys for failing to carry out his instructions when *Blodeu-gerdd Cymry* was published in 1759.[38] He also knew how crucial it was to secure subscribers, for without publication by subscription 'Welsh book-production would have been virtually non-existent'[39] in the eighteenth century.

And of all the subscribers' lists in eighteenth-century Welsh books none is more fascinating than the one in *Gorchestion Beirdd Cymru*. 505 individuals are listed subscribing to a total of 664 copies. We have already noted that Richard Morris ordered fifty copies for members of the Cymmrodorion, and others who ordered multiple copies included William Nannau of Maes y Neuadd and Maes y Pandy [8], William

Wynne of Penniarth [8], William Williams of Penniarth Uchaf [8], Sir Watkin Williams Wynne [6], William Lloyd of Rhiwaedog [6], Hugh Vaughan of Hengwrt [6], and William Vaughan of Cors-y-Gedol and Nannau [4]. These individuals represented the leading gentry families of Merioneth and North Wales, families with whom Rhys Jones was so familiar. Indeed he had written verse in praise of members of some of these families in the manner of the medieval poets. It is little wonder, therefore, that the highest strata of society is so well represented. Nor is it surprising that 21% of subscribers were members of the clergy – curates, vicars and rectors. Other professions are well represented, notably law and medicine. Along with barristers and attorneys-at-law there are a number of judges, 'His Majesty's Attorney-General Of North Wales', and, not surprisingly, 'The Honourable Daines Barrington, Chief Justice of North Wales', the publisher of Evan Evans's *Some Specimens* in 1764. He is one of a number of subscribers who can be directly linked to Evans, the other most notable being Samuel Johnson. No doubt Dr Johnson like many of the other subscribers would have found the text of *Gorchestion* entirely unintelligible, but without their support the volume might never have appeared.

Equally important, of course , was the support of the other less illustrious individuals listed, and it can be safely assumed that David Jones would have been personally responsible for securing the support of many of these. A wide range of occupations is represented including schoolmasters, inkeepers, shopkeepers, drovers, saddlers, grocers, booksellers, hatters, tanners, millers, skinners, mercers, students, timber merchants, miners, gardeners, and harpers. The list represents a remarkable cross-section of society from 'The Right Hon. Lord Grosvenor' to the humbler 'Mr Lewis Jones of Dolgellau, Skinner'.

Despite the gap of more than a decade between the drafting of the original 'proposals' and the appearance of *Gorchestion Beirdd Cymru*, its publication in 1773 was an event of note in Welsh scholarship. Not only had the editor realised a dream which had been so elusive to others, but he produced a text that was remarkably accurate. It provided the impetus for others, particularly Owen Jones (Owain Myfyr, 1714–1814)[40] and the Gwyneddigion Society to publish the contents of old Welsh manuscripts, and led to the appearance of *Barddoniaeth Dafydd ap Gwilym* (London, 1789) and *The Myvyrian Archaiology* of Wales (3 vols, London, 1801, 1807).

*Gorchestion Beirdd Cymru* also became the standard anthology for successive generations of Welsh men and women of letters, and I have seen very few copies that have not been marked with marginalia offering alternative readings or corrections – all invariably in ink! It became a standard text for aspiring scholars, and there are interesting examples of manuscript material being appended and bound with the printed text at some later stage. That it is still to this day very much a 'collector's item' is surely sufficient tribute to Stafford Prys the printer and in particular to the cultured country squire, Rhys Jones, who edited a volume 'worthy of the poets and worthy of a gentleman'.[41]

## NOTES

1. Eiluned Rees, *Libri Walliae: a Catalogue of Welsh Books and Books Printed in Wales 1546–1820* (Aberystwyth, 1987), 836. There are fifty-three entries for 1773. Some of these, however, refer to variant issues of the same work.

2. For the book trade in eighteenth-century Wales the following are indispensable: Eiluned Rees, *The Welsh Book-trade before 1820* (Aberystwyth, 1988); 'The Welsh printing house from 1718 to 1818', in *Six Centuries of the Provincial Book Trade in Britain*, [ed] Peter Isaac (Winchester, 1990), 101–24; 'The Welsh book trade from 1718 to 1820', in *A Nation and its Books: A History of the Book in Wales*, [ed] Philip Henry Jones & Eiluned Rees (Aberystwyth, 1988), 123–33.

3. Some of this popular literature such as 'periodicals, newspaper, ephemera and ballads' was outside the terms of reference of *Libri Walliae* and are, therefore, not recorded in the catalogue.

4. Thomas Parry, *A History of Welsh Literature*, tr H Idris Bell (Oxford, 1955), 275.

5. Meic Stephens [ed], *The New Companion to the Literature of Wales* (Cardiff, 1998), 270–1.

6. *Gorchestion Beirdd Cymru* has been variously translated as 'The Masterpieces of the Welsh Poets' in Parry, *History*, 275; as 'Exploits of the Welsh Bards' in Prys Morgan, *The Eighteenth Century Renaissance* (Llandybie, 1981), 81; and as 'The Triumphs of the Poets of Wales' in Stephens, *New Companion*, 270.

7. See Stephens, *New Companion*, 37–8.

8. *The Dictionary of Welsh Biography down to 1940* [hereafter *DWB*] (London, 1959), 1005–6.

9. Rice Jones Owen, *Gwaith Pryddawl y diweddar Rice Jones o'r Blaenau, Meirion* (Dolgellau, 1818). See Beryl H Griffiths, 'Rhys Jones (1713–1801) o'r Blaenau', *Journal of the Merioneth Historical & Record Society*, 11 (1990–3), 433–45.

10. The significance of the Morris brothers is briefly discussed in Stephens, *New Companion*, 511–12.

11. J H Davies [ed], *The Letters of Lewis, Richard, William and John Morris, of Anglesey, (Morrisiaid Mon) 1728–1765* 2 vols (Aberystwyth, 1907, 1909), 2, 16.

12. National Library of Wales [hereafter NLW] 3059D and NLW 7856D contain Rhys Jones's own poetry, and NLW 1246–7 are copies in his hand of poems written between the time of Aneirin and the end of the eighteenth century.

13. J H Davies, *A Bibliography of Welsh Ballads Printed in the 18th Century* (London, 1908–11). Twenty-three ballads with Prys's imprint are listed between 1758 and 1782.

14. Rees, *Welsh Book-trade before 1820*, xviii–xix.

15. Llewelyn C Lloyd, 'The book-trade in Shropshire', *Transactions of the Shropshire Archaeological & Natural History Society*, 48 (1935–6), 162.

16. Rees, *Welsh Book-trade before 1820*, xx.

17. Hugh Owen [ed], *Additional Letters of the Morrises of Anglesey (1735–1786)*, (Parts 1–2, London, 1947–9), 439–40. (Quotations in italics are the Author's translations from the Welsh.)

18. *Gorchestion*, vii: 'ag ynteu wedi printio amryw Lennau, heb im' erioed gael golwg arnynt i'w diwygio' (and he had printed many pages which I never had the opportunity to correct).

19. John David Rhys, *Cambrobrytannicae Cymraecaeve Linguae Institutiones et Rudimenta* (London, 1592); see Garfield H Hughes [ed], *Rhagymadroddion 1547–1659* (Caerdydd, 1951), 67.

20. Quoted in John Davies, *Bywyd a Gwaith Moses Williams (1685–1742)* (Caerdydd, 1937), 116.

21. Quoted in Aneirin Lewis,'Ieuan Fardd a'r gwaith o gyhoeddi hen lenyddiaeth Cymru', *Journal of the Welsh Bibliographical Society*, 8.3 (1956), 122.

22. Lewis Morris, *Tlysau yr Hen Oesoedd* (Ynghaer-Gybi, 1735), 2.

23. Quoted in G J Williams, *Traddodiad Llenydddol Morgannwg* (Caerdydd, 1948), 269.

24. R T Jenkins & Helen M Ramage, *A History of the Honourable Society of Cymmrodorion 1751–1951* (London, 1951), 236.

25. *DWB*, 229–31; also Gerald Morgan, *Ieuan Fardd* (Caernarfon, 1988), and Stephens, *New Companion*, 230–1.

26. *DWB*, 848–9.

27. M Rhiannon Thomas, 'William Vaughan (1707–75), Corsygedol', *Journal of the Merioneth Historical & Record Society*, 11 (1990–3), 255–71.

28. Owen, *Additional Letters*, 160.

29. Davies, *Letters of… Morris*, 1, 208.

30. Owen, *Additional Letters*, 349.

31. NLW 2024B, 89–92a; also Lewis, 'Ieuan Fardd', 144–7.

32. Lewis, 'Ieuan Fardd', 146–7.

33. NLW 2024B, 92a.

34. Owen, *Additional Letters*, 779.

35. G J Roberts, 'Robin ddu yr ail o Fon', *Bulletin of the Board of Celtic Studies*, vii (1933–5), 266.

36. The most comprehensive discussion of Evan Evans's possible role in the production of *Gorchestion Beirdd Cymru* is to be found in A Cynfael Lake, 'Rhys Jones: Y golygydd a'r Bardd', *Ysgrifau Beirniadol* 22 [ed] J E Caerwyn Williams (Dinbych, 1997), 204–26.

37. Stephens, *New Companion*, 370; Geraint H Jenkins, *Cadw Ty mewn Cwmwl Tystion* (Llandysul, 1990), 175–97.

38. Owen, *Additional Letters*, 627–9.

39. Eiluned Rees, 'Pre-1820 Welsh Subscription lists', *Journal of the Welsh Bibliographical Society*, 11 (1973–6), 85.

40. *DWB*, 4989.

41. Parry, *History of Welsh Literature*, 275.

# The Potter Family of Haverfordwest, 1780–1875

## CHRIS BAGGS

THE POTTER FAMILY operated as printers, publishers, booksellers and circulating-library owners in Haverfordwest, Pembrokeshire, between 1780 and 1875. There were other printers and publishers in both the town and county during this period, but the Potters proved the longest-lasting and most successful Pembrokeshire printing business until the rise of Richard Mason's firm in Tenby in the 1850s.[1]

Haverfordwest is an old town,[2] which probably received its first charter during Henry 1's reign, because of its strategic significance as a crossing point over the Western Cleddau en route for St David's and Ireland. It became the county town of Pembrokeshire in the sixteenth century and has enjoyed unique privileges, as a borough and county in its own right and the only town in Great Britain to have a Lord Lieutenant. With a population of some 4000 by the beginning of the nineteenth century, Haverfordwest was amongst the biggest towns in South Wales and its reputation was growing. Economically, it had become the premier market town in Pembrokeshire as well as its administrative and commercial centre. The 1821 edition of *The Cambrian Tourist* noted that Pembroke now lacked that 'trade and notice which Haverfordwest is deriving from its downfall'. Malkin in his *Scenery, Antiquities and Biography of South Wales* (1807) dubbed it 'the genteelest town in South Wales', whilst *Pigot's Directory* of 1822 stated that Haverfordwest was 'a very desirable and pleasing place of residence', which contained 'a considerable number of good houses, occupied by many families of fortune, professional persons, and tradesmen of respectability'. Haverfordwest had a long tradition as a centre for education, and in 1830 it boasted a grammar school, a bluecoat school and various boarding and day schools. In conjunction with the town's economic prosperity, its expanding population and social composition, it is not surprising to see the emergence, locally, of someone in the printing, publishing and book trades. An entry in the *Universal British Directory* for 1791 singles out one J T Potter, printer and bookseller.

Printing did not come early to Pembrokeshire, perhaps reflecting its remoteness and small population, although the proximity of Carmarthen may also have exercised a delaying effect. So, who brought printing and publishing to the county? Eiluned Rees in *Libri Walliae*, lists the first recorded work from Pembrokeshire as *A Serious Address to the Gentlemen, Clergy, and Freeholders of the County*, published in Pembroke around 1779 by William Wilmot. This was followed twelve years later by his *Catalogue of Books Belonging to the Pembroke Reading Society*,[3] once claimed as the earliest book printed in Pembroke in the *Journal of the Welsh Bibliographical Society* for 1913.[4] What of Haverfordwest?

An item in the same journal for 1912 quoted a former local newspaper editor as stating that 'the honour of establishing the first Printing Press in Haverford is attributed to Theophilus John Potter', who 'commenced the business of a printer about the year 1780'. This claim was based on 'old inhabitants who knew T.J. Potter' and who 'always asserted that he introduced the printing press'.[5] By 1925 this claim had grown, as Ifano Jones wrote that 'Pembrokeshire had its first printing-press about 1780, and at Haverfordwest'.[6] Jones based this on Brown's anecdotal *History of Haverfordwest*. But Brown had not been so definite, simply writing that 'old Theophilus John Potter' had settled in Haverfordwest as a printer, and had married locally in 1779.[7] This provided the approximate foundation date of 1780.

Unfortunately the position has been muddied by the Potter family itself, which claimed in 1868 that their ancestors 'had introduced the art of printing into this county about a century ago',[8] hinting at a date around 1770. *Kelly's Post Office Directory* for 1871 goes further by suggesting that Potter's reading room, another arm of the family business, had been established even earlier, in 1750. The exact date of the Potters' entry into the book trade remains unclear. But there is nothing in their surviving publications to substantiate the claim that John Theophilus Potter, as he is usually known, was the first printer in Pembrokeshire. Rees does list a Potter publication, but this was dated 1797.[9]

John Theophilus Potter was an Irishman, born around 1746, who had been an actor before settling in Haverfordwest. According to Cecil Price Potter visited Haverfordwest with a company of tragedians about 1775, where he settled 'very successfully as a printer'.[10] The links between the theatre and printing look tenuous, but there are relevant connections. At this period in the eighteenth century, there were many itinerant theatre companies, but these groups had to prove they were not bands of penniless travellers, in order to obtain the performance licences, required under the Licensing Act of 1737. One way to convince local authorities was to earn money through various sidelines, such as giving dancing lessons, fixing artificial teeth, or printing.[11] Boorman's study of Swansea as a seaside resort between 1780 and 1830 quotes a letter written in 1775 by Sir Herbert Mackworth of the Gnoll, Neath, recommending a troupe of players who wanted permission to perform in Swansea. Mackworth wrote 'their future views are, if they find encouragement sufficient, to set up their business of Stationary, Printing and Bookbinding, which I think might answer well and be a matter of convenience to us all'.[12] The ability to earn money by printing would be viewed positively by local magistrates, especially where a town had no printing business. The date of 1775 in the Mackworth example is interesting, as there was no printer in Swansea until the early 1780s.[13] Of more immediate practical value to a travelling theatre group however was that 'one member of a company was skilled enough... to print the playbills, which advertised their performances'.[14] A simple, portable press could have run off such playbills.[15] Perhaps John Theophilus Potter was one such skilled actor, who, having played Haverfordwest in the late 1770s, noticed its lack of an established printer and decided to change professions.

There is a second family example of this intriguing link between printing and the theatre. J W Potter, one of J T Potter's sons, pursued a theatrical career in south and west Wales during the 1820s and 1830s,[16] and according to a playbill preserved in Chepstow Museum, he gave a performance of *Romeo and Juliet* at the New Theatre in Chepstow in February 1822. The playbill's imprint reads 'printed by J. Potter, Theatre, Chepstow'.[17] Obviously he was practising both the family skills.

John Theophilus left the family business early in the nineteenth century, although it is not known precisely why or when. In 1803 the Potter press produced three notices informing the local population what to do in the event of a feared second invasion of Pembrokeshire by Napoleon.[18] These notices carried the imprint, J Potter. This was Joseph Potter, J T's son. Following the death of his first wife in May 1804, John Theophilus remarried in 1807 and moved to London, where he died, aged ninety-three, in October 1839.[19]

For much of the period between 1800 and 1819 another printer, James Thomas, who operated from premises in the High Street, looked far more likely to develop into the main publisher for Haverfordwest. Some nine items bearing his imprint appeared between 1802 and 1813, including in 1811 the first Welsh-language publication printed in Pembrokeshire, a sermon by Benjamin Davies.[20] By contrast, the printing firm of Joseph Potter remained very quiet. Perhaps he was concentrating on his other business activities, including selling books.

John Theophilus Potter had not been the first bookseller in Haverfordwest. A few items published between 1745 and 1781 were advertised as available in the town, via a Mr Alan, an Elizabeth Ayleway and others.[21] But none of these names appeared in the *Universal British Directory*, which listed only Potter as a bookseller. Early issues of *The Cambrian* newspaper provide more detail of this side of the family business, which Joseph Potter was probably also running by 1803. The newspaper's first issue for 28 January 1804 lists J Potter as an agent, and the third issue includes advertisements for three books, sold by Potter. Examining such advertisements in *The Cambrian* indicates the variety of books Potter offered for sale, and their prices. Items included Thomson's *The Family Physician*, for 6s; the *Gardener's Pocket Journal*, 1s.6d; Greig's *An Introduction to the Use of the Globes*, 2s.6d; and Ovid's *The Art Of*

*Love*, 10*s*.6*d*. Books were not the only articles available at Potter's. Like many other booksellers and stationers of the time, Potter sold patent medicines, including Barclay's 'Original Ointment', Taylor's 'Remedy for Deafness' and Newton's 'Restorative Tooth Powder'. Later the family sold tea, insurance, cigars and fishing tackle.

The Potters also opened a reading room and circulating library in Haverfordwest. J T's entry in the *Universal British Directory* does not refer to either, but two advertisements, in the *British Chronicle* in January 1786 and for a catalogue in the *British Journal* three years later, suggest that they were opened soon after the business was established.[22] By 1805 the local aristocracy was apparently frequenting the library. Reporting the Haverfordwest Races in 1805, *The Cambrian* for 3 August noted that 'Potter's Library was crowded daily with nobility'. Brown underlined the nature of the library's clientele noting that 'Potter's reading-room was only open to the elite of the town',[23] which is highly likely, given the charges made for borrowing books. These are listed on a plate from Potter's Circulating Library pasted in a copy of Depons's *Travels in South America* of 1807 held in the National Library of Wales. Terms varied: an annual subscription was a guinea, six months cost 12*s* and a quarter, 7*s*. Potter's Library was on a par with Oakey's in Swansea, but more expensive than other contemporary examples, such as Evans's or Jenkins's Circulating Library, both in Swansea, or Ross's in Carmarthen.[24] Unlike Evans, Potter offered neither a monthly rate nor a rate for borrowing a single volume. Other regulations were typical and included a restriction to one book at a time, a loan period of a week, fines for overdues, special provision for country subscribers, and no lending-on to non-subscribers. Visitors could borrow books, on depositing the value of the book.

By 1819 the Potters of Haverfordwest looked well established. The printing and publishing business was small-scale, and their main efforts seemed devoted to their bookshop and stationer's, and the fashionable reading room and circulating library. The 1820s saw an upsurge in their publishing activities, mainly linked to the Revd John Bulmer.[25]

Bulmer was born in Yorkshire in 1784 and came to Haverfordwest in 1812, where he was ordained the following year as Minister of Albany Independent Chapel on St Thomas's Green.[26] In 1813 James Thomas published a sermon by Bulmer, but Bulmer also exhibited literary pretensions and following the publication of some of his poetry in the *Carmarthen Journal*, a collection, entitled *Occasional Poems*, was published in 1820 for 1*s*. The printer and publisher was Joseph Potter.

Why had Bulmer switched allegiance? The introduction to *Occasional Poems* may contain a clue. It refers to a forthcoming work, 'larger and much more important', which Bulmer had had 'ready for the press a considerable time', but with which he was experiencing 'difficulties... in coming to any satisfactory agreement with Publishers'.[27] Perhaps Thomas was unwilling to deal with this 'larger' work, whereas Potter proved more amenable.

The 'much more important' work was Bulmer's version of Rhys Prichard's *The Vicar of Llandovery*, which appeared in 1821 under Joseph Potter's imprint. This subscription volume was the first major publication by the Potter press, and consisted of a preface and text with notes, totalling 260 pages. James Thomas, Bulmer's previous printer, had not produced a book of even a quarter that length, although in 1823 he did publish a volume of nearly 300 pages.

The years between 1820 and 1832 represent the Potters' most ambitious period of book publishing. In 1822 Joseph Potter published *Memoirs of Owen Glendower* by Thomas Thomas (another subscription volume of some 240 pages),[28] followed by three more items by Bulmer, two sermons in 1823 and 1824, and a biographical study in 1826 of Benjamin Evans,[29] one of Bulmer's predecessors. Later, in 1830 Potter printed a second edition of Bulmer's *The Vicar of Llandovery*, this time entitled *Beauties of the Vicar of Llandovery*,[30] and in 1831 Potter published the second edition of *A Dissertation on the Evidence of Christianity* by David Jones.[31]

Thereafter the Potters' publishing output became more spasmodic and lightweight.[32] Never again did they print anything over 100 pages, and apart from H L Williams's *An Authentic Account of the Invasion by the French Troops* published in 1842, their publications were either very parochial or theological, or both. They included various sets of rules and regulations, such as those for Haverfordwest Gaol, and the Pembrokeshire Agricultural Society, and occasional religious tracts and sermons, as well as two elegies in Welsh in 1846 and 1849. These represent the sum total of the Potter family's Welsh-language output in over fifty years of publishing. Their last traceable work was a pamphlet, published in 1859 by Jane Potter, Joseph Potter's wife, on a local religious dispute, B S Nayler's delightfully titled *Bones for Sabbatarians to Pick, Texts for Inquirers to Chew, Nuts for Mr. Woodman to Crack*.[33]

James Thomas published Bulmer's biographical study of Howell Harris in 1824, but this appears to be the last substantial work produced by Thomas, who also ran a bookshop, stationer's and religious-tract depository.[34] But there were other printers competing for business in Haverfordwest. William Perkins, who was still listed as a printer in *Kelly's Directory* for 1884, produced at least seventeen items between 1837 and 1863, and both David Evans and Edward Joseph published a few pieces, generally in Welsh, in the late 1840s and early 1850s. Evans also issued a newspaper, *The Principality*, between 1847 and 1850.

On 5 January 1844 the Potter family finally achieved an undisputed first in Pembrokeshire publishing history, when Joseph Potter sr published the first newspaper to be printed in the county, the *Pembrokeshire Herald & General Adver-tiser* priced 4*d*. Between then and 1872 the Potters published three different newspapers including the *Herald* – the aptly named *Potter's Electric News*, which ran from June 1855 to September 1869, and *Potter's Newspaper & General Advertiser*, which appeared between 1870 and 1872.[35]

Newspaper publishing seems to have particularly appealed to Joseph Potter jr. Officially he took over running the *Herald* when his father died in June 1846, but he had already assumed that role after his father's stroke the previous year. Nine years later it was Joseph who decided, following the abolition of newspaper stamp duty, to establish *Potter's Electric News* priced 1*d*. His close association with the newspapers is evident from a notice printed in the *Pembrokeshire Herald* at the end of 1858. This stated that whereas the *Herald* had previously been owned jointly by Joseph and his mother, Jane, this partnership was to be dissolved with Joseph henceforth becoming the sole owner. His sole ownership did not last very long.

In February 1860 the Herald carried a notice announcing that Joseph Potter had assigned all his effects and estate to two local tradesmen, William Llewelin and Thomas Whicher Davies. Thereafter the *Herald*'s imprint (and that of *Potter's Electric News*) was subtly altered to read 'printed and published, on behalf of the proprietors, by Joseph Potter'. Eight years later both newspapers were not only owned by Llewelin and Davies, but also 'printed and published' by them 'at their offices in the High Street'. It is not surprising that within eighteen months *Potter's Electric News* merged with the *Herald*. Both were Conservative in politics; neither enjoyed large circulation figures,[36] and the competition was fierce, especially from the Liberal *Haverfordwest & Milford Haven Telegraph*. But despite the demise of Joseph Potter jr the Potters had not finished with newspaper publishing. Perhaps it was family pride, or a rational decision to utilise the machinery that led his sister-in-law Elizabeth Potter to found the family's third newspaper venture, *Potter's Newspaper & General Advertiser*, in 1870. This enterprise was even less successful than the other newspapers, folding at the end of December 1872.

Close examination of the three Potter newspapers reveals much interesting detail about the family business and their lives over nearly three decades. Accounts published in the *Herald* show that income was regularly received by the firm's printing department and the newspaper itself for work done for local authorities, such as the County of Pembroke and Haverfordwest Town Council. In 1844 another family member, Henry E Potter, opened a general printing and stationer's business in Pembroke, but this ran into difficulties and was auctioned off in October 1848. Henry was to have another, equally futile experience with a similar venture in Haverfordwest between April 1852 and September 1853. In both instances his mother, Jane, who provided much-needed stability and continuity in the family business, stepped in to clear up the mess. When Jane retired in her mid-seventies in 1862, she handed over the remains of the business to yet another son, Edward J Potter.

The family newspapers are relatively short on information about two branches of the original business, selling books and the circulating library. There are some references to new consignments of almanacs, annuals, diaries, and the latest music, and local topographical prints were also available.[37] But few books are specifically named by title as being for sale, even though book parcels arrived from London three times a week. At Christmas time an assortment of unspecified elegant volumes, 'bound in the most approved and fashionable styles', were frequently advertised as making suitable gifts. There is also little, apart from the occasional general advertisement, to confirm the existence of the circulating library, until a notice in the *Herald* in September 1861. This announced an unreserved ready-money sale of Mrs Jane Potter's valuable circulating library of English literature, presumably signalling its end. Subsequent trade-directory entries suggest that the subscription reading room continued, as well as the more recently established billiards room.

Nor was their publishing business often mentioned. In the *Herald* for 30 May 1851 a notice announced a plan to republish Fenton's *Historical Tour through Pembrokeshire*, but nothing came of this idea, and apart from the occasional pamphlet, the Potters now seemed confined to general printing activities. When Edward Potter died aged thirty-seven in March 1868, his wife Elizabeth took over the business, concentrating on the stationery side, whilst 'experienced workmen' continued the bookbinding and printing departments. An advertisement in *Potter's Electric News* for 8 July 1868 provides an excellent résumé of the kind of printing that the Potters now undertook. It included pamphlets, broadsides, catalogues, society rules, prospectuses, circulars, reports and handbills. The period when they published books and other monographs had long gone. Indeed by now the firm's days were numbered. *Potter's Newspaper & General Advertiser* ceased publication at the end of 1872 and in July 1875 Elizabeth Potter died aged forty-two. There is no entry for the Potter family in either *Slater's Directory* of 1880 or *Kelly's Directory* for 1884.

The Potters of Haverfordwest provide an interesting case-study of a small-town family firm, which for nearly a century was occupied in numerous facets of the booktrade: bookselling, binding, printing and publishing; newspaper printing and publishing; and running a reading room and circulating library. On the surface their business ventures may not appear too successful. But, just how much business was there in the Haverfordwest area? What was the nature and extent of local competition? Were there simply too many fish in a small pond? According to *Kelly's Directory* for 1871, there were four printers, three booksellers and stationers, and two bookbinders in the town. In the High Street there was a printer at no 2, a bookseller and stationer at no 3, another general printer in Hill Lane, off High Street, and the Potters. Their premises at nos 8 and 9 housed a reading room, a billiards room, a bookseller and stationer, and their printing and publishing business. High Street Haverfordwest was clearly busy.

The Potters 'played an important part in the social, political and commercial life in Haverfordwest'.[38] John Theophilus was made a burgess of the town in 1787, an important privilege at that time, and in 1790 he was elected Sheriff. These were major achievements for a former actor, who had settled in the town only a decade earlier. His son Joseph went more than one better. Not only was he elected Sheriff on three separate occasions in 1814, 1834, and 1835, but he was also a town councillor, a trustee of local charities, a Gas Commissioner, and an occasional member of the town and county Petty Sessions. He became a freeman of the town, and in 1843 he was elected Mayor. Later family members were not nearly so successful politically, but they still played their part in town life. Joseph Potter jr was on the founding committee of the Haverfordwest Literary and Scientific Institute, and like other family members he contributed regularly to worthy causes. These included repairing and renovating local churches (and the town clock), establishing schools and a hospital, and responding to disaster appeals, such as the Irish famine and a fatal coal-mining accident at nearby Landshipping. On a less formal note male members of the family regularly played cricket for the town and county.

Neither Haverfordwest nor the Potters can be seen as seminal to Welsh book-publishing history, except that the family was amongst the earliest printers in Pembrokeshire. Their output was limited, of little subject interest and aesthetically dull. But their connections with newspaper publishing are of interest and not just because they produced three different newspapers in Pembrokeshire, including the very first. When John Theophilus Potter moved to London in 1807, his second family also entered the printing and publishing business, founding another local newspaper, the *Hackney & Kingsland Gazette*. According to an article in the *Pembrokeshire Herald* for 23 November 1896, and some more recent correspondence in the Pembrokeshire Record Office in Haverfordwest,[39] there were other family links with more distant newspaper publishing, including examples from southern Ireland and the United States. There would appear to be scope for more pottering about.

## NOTES

1. See Chris Baggs, 'Not just another local printer and publisher: Richard Mason of Tenby (1817–81)', *Welsh Book Studies* 2 (1999), forthcoming.

2. For information on Haverfordwest, see *Pembrokeshire County History. Volume 4 Modern Pembrokeshire 1815–1974*, [ed] David W Howell (Haverfordwest: The Pembrokeshire Historical Society, 1993); Brian John, *Pembrokeshire, Past and Present* (Newport, Pembs,

Greencroft Books, 1995); *Haverfordwest and its Story* (Haverfordwest: Brigstocke, 1882); and John Brown, *The History of Haverfordwest*, [rev] J W Phillips & Fred Warren (Haverfordwest: Brigstocke, 1914).

3. Eiluned Rees, *Libri Walliae* (Aberystwyth: National Library of Wales [hereafter NLW], 1987), 568 & 478.

4. Brief items on printing in Pembrokeshire appeared in the *Journal of the Welsh Bibliographical Society* [hereafter *JBWS*]. 'Haverfordwest printers', 1 (1912), 114–8; 'Pembrokeshire printers', 1 (1913), 152–3; 'Haverfordwest printers', 1 (1913), 153–5; 'Books printed in Pembrokeshire', 1 (1914), 198; 'Haverfordwest books', 1 (1914), 229; 'Haverfordwest books', 1 (1915), 259; 'Haverfordwest books', 2 (1920), 151–3; and 'Haverfordwest printing', 2 (1921), 233.

5. *JWBS*, 1 (1912), 114.

6. Ifano Jones, *A History of Printing and Printers in Wales to 1810* (Cardiff: William Lewis, 1925), 129.

7. Brown, *Haverfordwest*,123.

8. *Potter's Electric News*, 8 April 1868, 2.

9. Rees, *Libri*, 368.

10. Cecil Price, *The English Theatre in Wales in the Eighteenth and Early Nineteenth Centuries* (Cardiff: University of Wales Press, 1948), 13.

11. Price, *Theatre*, 13.

12. David Boorman, *The Brighton of Wales* (Swansea: Little Theatre Company Ltd, 1986), 27–8.

13. Rees, *Libri*, 457, no 3719.

14. Price, *Theatre*,13.

15. See James Moran, *Printing Presses* (London: Faber & Faber, 1973), 230, for an example dated 1769.

16. Price, *Theatre*, 128–131.

17. *Chepstow Broadsheets No 2* (Chepstow: Chepstow Society, 1972).

18. Later republished in *Pembrokeshire Antiquities* (Solva: H.W. Williams, 1897).

19. *Seren Gomer*, 22 (1839), 317.

20. *Dictionary of Welsh Biography* [hereafter *DWB*] (Oxford: Blackwell, 1959), 110–11.

21. Entries in Rees, *Libri*, under Allen, Ayleway, Sparks and Amos Thomas.

22. My thanks to Dr Keith Manley, Institute of Historical Research, University of London, for providing these references.

23. Brown, *Haverfordwest*, 142. He also reproduces a poem on books and reading, which he states was printed on the flyleaf of books in the library, 142–3.

24. Figures in Boorman, *Brighton of Wales*, 57 & 59; and Eiluned Rees, *The Welsh book-trade before 1820* (Aberystwyth: NLW, 1987), xxxix.

25. *DWB*, 59. The National Library of Wales contains some of Bulmer's publications.

26. *JBWS* 1 (1913), 155.

27. John Bulmer, *Occasional Poems* (Haverfordwest: Joseph Potter, 1820), iv.

28. *DWB*, 966.

29. *DWB*, 220.

30. Published in London by Holdsworth & Ball.

31. *DWB*, 452.

32. The author has found some thirty items, excluding newspapers and single sheets, printed by the Potters.

33. *Potter's Electric News*, 10 August 1859, 1. A copy has been located in the Library of Congress.

34. Thomas ceased being listed as a printer in Haverfordwest between *Pigot's Directory* of 1844 and *Slater's Directory* of 1850.

35. Much of the material included in the following paragraphs has been taken from these newspapers.

36. The *Pembrokeshire Herald* for 20 December 1861 gave the circulation of the *Herald* as 800 and of the *Electric News* as 1300.

37. The National Library of Wales has a few examples.

38. *Pembrokeshire Herald*, 13 November 1896, 2.

39. Copies of correspondence between Cork County Library and the Dyfed County Archivist in November and December 1982.

# Pedlars & Mercers as Distributors of Print in Early-Modern Wales

## RICHARD SUGGETT

THE THEME of this paper is seventeenth-century communications. I have borrowed this phrase from Margaret Spufford, who neatly used it to refer not only to the highways and by-ways which brought hawkers and pedlars to different communities, but also to the messages conveyed in the ballads and chapbooks they sold. Having finished a study of sixteenth-century itinerant entertainers, it seemed appropriate to have a look at new forms of communication in seventeenth-century Wales, and to follow Margaret Spufford, Tessa Watt and others on the trail of the distributors of popular print.[1]

### CONTEXTS OF PRINT

As Eiluned Rees and Geraint Jenkins have shown, a relatively small number of Welsh books were printed between about 1550 and 1700, perhaps an average of two titles a year.[2] But this does not mean that Wales was a print desert. Far from it – Wales was exposed to the flood of cheap print in English, and there were always cultural brokers who mediated between English and Welsh and literacy and illiteracy.

I think it true to say that the people of early-modern Wales in town and country, literate and non-literate alike, were surrounded by expressions of print culture. As an architectural historian by profession, I am acutely aware of this. Wall-paintings survive with designs that were clearly influenced by print. A gorgeous design of jewelled strapwork with classical motifs at Castell-y-mynach, Glamorgan, dated 1602, might have been influenced by continental (German) woodcuts, although the black-letter inscriptions are in Latin and English. This elaborate work is perhaps not unexpected in a gentry house, but a mid-seventeenth-century black-letter Latin inscription, recently found painted on the partition of a modest upland farmhouse in Montgomeryshire, gives the twentieth-century historian food for thought. Black-letter inscriptions in Welsh and English derived from the *Book of Common Prayer* abounded in Welsh churches. Some are still exposed, but many lie hidden beneath layers of whitewash.[3]

Discarded, lost or hidden books and papers, although often fragmentary, do actually turn up in old houses in process of restoration. However, I know from experience that this vulnerable material can be easily lost during radical repair schemes. Printed detritus is discovered behind wainscoting and under floorboards, and I have seen the remains of ballads and other printed ephemera pasted onto timber partitions in three farmhouses in Powys.[4] The point I am making, of course, is that Welsh men and women in the early-modern period – like English men and women – were increasingly surrounded in public and private contexts by visual images derived from print and by print itself.

## BOOKS AND CRIME

Print probably became ubiquitous in seventeenth-century Wales, but it is very difficult to know – even approximately – what sorts of books were in circulation, who owned them, and to assess the social range of literacy. Welsh probate records have proved a disappointing source of information about the world of book ownership, but criminal records can provide unexpected insights into the underworld of print culture.

Books, like other consumer goods, were stolen. In 1617 a Montgomeryshire servant-maid stole several items including books and papers from her master's chamber. She took the books home, but the household of three adults was illiterate. However, her visiting brother-in-law, Edward ap Hugh, a weaver, was able to read them and discovered they were 'three smale bookes of Latyne' and two deeds. There are several lessons here. Even if thieves were illiterate there would be someone within reach – a neighbour or relative – who was literate. In this particular instance a Montgomeryshire weaver, the brother-in-law of an illiterate woman, is shown to be able to read both the print of a Latin book and the script of a legal document. We have to remember that there was a range of reading skills; those who could read black-letter print would not necessarily be able to read what contemporaries called 'writing hand'.[5]

Large volumes, especially the Bible and the *Book of Common Prayer*, were stolen given the opportunity. We may note in passing that the Welsh *Book of Common Prayer* and the Welsh Bible, despite several editions, had probably become scarce by the early seventeenth century. This is suggested by the remarks of a minister and public preacher at Denbigh who, suspected of erroneous doctrine in 1615, explained how he was forced to translate from English into Welsh every Sunday because a Welsh Bible was not available in the church. *Books of Common Prayer* were stolen as soon as they appeared in the second half of the sixteenth century.[6] In 1568 a Montgomeryshire labourer broke into a house at Leighton and stole 'a booke of Comon prayers' (valued at 3*d*). In 1572 the *Book of Common Prayer* (valued at 8*d*) belonging to the parishioners of Llanyblodwell was stolen in Montgomeryshire.[7]

Why were religious books stolen? Of course, then as now, anything with a resale value, not nailed down or chained up, might be stolen, but it is not impossible that professional thieves formed a literate occupational sub-culture. It was certainly in their interests to be able to read. In certain circumstances a thief's life could depend on reading aloud a passage from a printed book. Felons convicted of grand larceny could escape hanging by claiming 'benefit of clergy', that is by demonstrating in open court their ability to read like a clerk. Those who successfully claimed benefit of clergy were discharged after branding on the brawn of the thumb; those who failed to read were executed. These public demonstrations of literacy or non-literacy were dramatic moments and sometimes produced unexpected results.[8] Numerous successful claims to benefit of clergy in Tudor and Stuart Wales suggest an unexpectedly high rate of literacy among thieves. Certainly some Welsh criminals seem to have been habitual book carriers. This might have been because they were keen to practise the so-called neck verses. However, another compelling reason for the possession of books was the binding nature of the oath when sworn on the gospels. Welshmen who had committed a robbery or an assault sometimes – rather unexpectedly – produced a book and forced their hapless victims to swear on the volume not to divulge the circumstances of the crime. There are several examples of these rather bizarre incidents including a case in 1578, when the book was identified as 'a boke of praiers' by a cleric who was forced to read several prayers from it before swearing that he would not identify his assailants.[9]

PEDLARS AS DISTRIBUTORS OF BOOKS

I want now to turn from stealers of books to the legitimate or at least not-so-shady vendors of cheap print, the pedlars and shopkeepers. Margaret Spufford has argued that numerous pedlars travelling all over England were the chief distributors of the chapbook, ballad, newsbook and woodcut to the poor alongside other consumer goods. The case is persuasive although specific references to pedlars as distributors of popular literature are quite hard to locate in documentary sources before the end of the seventeenth century.[10]

I want to try to establish whether a similar army of pedlars existed in Wales and, if so, to identify the types of goods they sold. This is easier said than done. As Margaret Spufford puts it, 'the pedlar is a very elusive figure indeed, not only because he or she was peripatetic… but also because many of them lived near the edge of society, on the vagrant fringe'.[11] But as pedlars were part of the vagrant fringe they often found themselves on the wrong side of the law, and there are many (but not necessarily representative) references to them in the seventeenth-century legal record which is abundant in Wales.

Firstly, it can be established that there were numerous pedlars in early-modern Wales, although it is not possible to estimate numbers before the end of the seventeenth century, when approximately 100 Welsh pedlars were licensed under the $169^7/_8$ Act.[12] As soon as the assizes and quarter sessions were established in mid-sixteenth-century Wales, pedlars made an appearance in their records. Gilbert Pedlar of Chester was indicted in 1542 (the year of the second Act of Union) for trading in the

Caernarfonshire boroughs to the annoyance of their burgesses. Gilbert was the first of many itinerant traders who appeared before the criminal courts. Significantly, the word 'pedler', a direct loan from English, first appears in the Welsh language in the mid-sixteenth century. William Salesbury in his interesting 1547 Welsh-English dictionary (one of the earliest printed Welsh books) defined a pedlar as 'dyn yn arwein waar', that is a man who carried about all sorts of wares [to sell] in contrast to the urban 'siopwr' or shopkeeper who traded from a shop or booth.[13]

Pedlars became numerous in the early seventeenth century along with the growing availability of consumer goods. The Denbighshire grand jury complained in 1631 that there were so many sturdy travelling beggar men and women carrying tobacco and other goods to sell that the country could not abide them. The distinctions between pedlars, tinkers, beggars and rogues became increasingly blurred. To be safe from arrest, a chapman needed a licence from the justices of the peace. But licences could be forged and pedlars with their networks were in a good position to acquire counterfeit passports. In 1634 a Denbighshire justice of the peace apprehended a pedlar named John Lewis – 'as daungerous a fellow as any that ever came before me', he noted – whose forged licence as 'coloured all his roguishness'. The licence declared that Lewis was a very honest man, descended from good parents, and brazenly demanded that the pedlar should be allowed to pass and repass without hindrance and given lodgings when required.[14]

What sort of goods were sold by itinerant traders? Pedlars can be divided into two types: those who bought and sold home-produced goods and those who imported consumer goods. Pedlars in Wales tended to be specialists rather than general dealers. Cuthbert Price of Merioneth, charged with theft at Denbigh in 1628, described himself as an 'ordinary chapman' who bought and sold Welsh knitted stockings and garters in fairs and markets. Other traders peddled home-made craft goods that included straw hats, beehives and wooden dishes. Glassware, knives made by cutlers, and Staffordshire pottery were carried into Wales by packmen. Tobacco, bought at Liverpool, was sold in the 1620s by hawkers and – yes – some pedlars carried books.[15]

In 1621 several itinerants described as 'tynkers', two from Radnorshire, were apprehended near Haverfordwest and committed to gaol on suspicion of dispersing 'popishe bookes'. Unfortunately the books are not further described. However, I think it probable that these pedlars were selling samples of small, 'godly' chapbooks, established as a new genre at precisely this period, and that this novel type of publication was not recognised by the arresting justice. Significantly, the pedlars were discharged at the following sessions.[16]

This is, I have to emphasize, the only case I have found of itinerants distributing books in the first half of the seventeenth century. Pedlars may have routinely carried small bundles of chapbooks, but documents rarely allow us to rummage retrospectively through a pedlar's pack. Margaret Spufford has traced a few chapmen's inventories, but books are not often listed in these documents. Several Welsh inventories have survived, but they are characteristically lists of textiles. Stock supplied to William Turberfield, chapman of Whitchurch, Pembrokeshire, listed in 1647, consisted largely of lace, thread, ribbons etc valued at £6. A pack stolen from Peter Marychurch of Haverfordwest, as he slept by the roadside in 1661, contained 280 yards of different fabrics worth £12. The contents of the pack carried by William Rawlinson, arrested in Shropshire on suspicion of theft in north Wales, was carefully inventoried by the common clerk at Shrewsbury in 1623. It was a classic mercery pack with lace, coloured silks, threads and buttons. Rawlinson refused to explain how he had acquired these wares, and with his wife was indicted at the Flintshire assizes for theft; William was found guilty and sentenced to be hanged.[17]

## MERCERS AS BOOKSELLERS

The Rawlinsons had stolen the goods from a shop at Holt, a small Flintshire borough. It is time now to examine, if we can, the stock carried by the shops which were to be found in most market towns and seem to have been fundamentally important for distributing consumer goods. Shopkeepers and mercers, like pedlars, appear in Welsh legal records from the mid-sixteenth century onwards, and were regular litigants in the actions for debt which fill the early-modern plea rolls. From this litigation we know that a nexus of debt linked town and country. Unlike the pedlar, the shopkeeper gave credit. It is clear from mercers' bills that some customers enjoyed extended credit although eventually a shopkeeper (or his executors) would call in the debts entered in a shop-book. The customer paid up on receiving a writ, but it was the end of a relationship. The customer moved on to another mercer and the cycle was repeated.[18]

There seem to have been shops in every town, but it is difficult to know – especially before the mid-seventeenth century – exactly what these shops stocked. However, persistent digging in the legal record has brought to light a shelf-by-shelf inventory made in 1634 of a mercer's shop in Llanidloes, a Montgomeryshire market-town. From this inventory it is clear that the mercer carried a stock of books amongst numerous other items. It is worth listing some of these items to show the range of goods available in a pre-Civil-War market town. Practical goods included combs, brushes, needles and pins, thimbles and buttons. Spices and groceries included: pepper, currants, raisins, green ginger, treacle, sugar candy, cumin seed, cinnamon and cloves. The books come between about fifty different sorts of textiles and useful artifacts like inkhorns, tobacco boxes, and curtain rings. The mercer had a total stock of 133 books, which are listed in the Appendix, besides half a ream of paper, sealing wax, and pasteboards. The most numerous items in his stock were hornbooks (13), ABCs, primers, catechisms, grammars of various sort, psalters and a dozen unspecified little Latin books. Beyond this there was a variety of religious and secular titles. Conduct books were represented by three copies of *The School of Virtue* compiled for children and youths 'to learn their duty by'. A copy of Aesop's *Fables* was inevitably among the stock, but more obscure items included *An Innovation of Germany* and three 'Bookes of Pedregree' valued at 1*s*.2*d*.[19]

In the absence of other inventories, one has to take this as representative of a mercer's selection of books in the first half of the seventeenth century. Several comments can be made about the range of books. The stock is heavily weighted to the requirements of those learning to read, presumably in the local schools. It illustrates the progression from the hornbook and ABCs to basic grammar-school texts. But for adults there were some instructive and entertaining books. All the titles listed are in English or Latin. If the mercer carried Welsh books they are hidden among the unnamed forty-one books which formed a third of his stock. The stock of 133 books was valued at about £2, a fraction of the shop's total goods which were worth £60.

The Welsh book trade in the first half of the seventeenth century seems to have been dominated by mercers who carried books as part of a general stock-in-trade. Once this is realised, one can browse through legal actions concerning mercers' bills and find books among the fabrics, buttons and thread supplied to country clients from the town. In 1606 Rees Jones, a Haverfordwest mercer, supplied 'one prognosticac[i]on' price 2*d* to a customer as well as 'fustian sleeves' and other goods; in December 1612 a mercer sold a copy of 'Esopps fables' at 1*s* to Richard Evans of Wiston, Pembrokeshire, perhaps for Christmas reading; 'one Welsh prymer' price 6*d* was delivered from Carmarthen to William Lloyd of Faerdre-fach, Cardiganshire, in 1634;[20] it is interesting that this book was delivered. A packcloth (valued at 2*s*), noted at the end of the Llandiloes mercer's inventory, suggests that shopkeepers would directly supply their country customers, presumably to the disadvantage of the pedlars.

The dominance of urban shopkeepers as suppliers of books (and other goods) becomes clearer in the second half of the seventeenth century. Geraint Jenkins has shown that Thomas Jones, the Welsh printer established at Shrewsbury in 1695, used a town-based network to distribute his almanacs in north and south Wales. There were book agents not only in principal market towns but in places that were little more than villages. Wherever there was a market there would be a shop, and this shop would generally sell some books.[21]

Several mercers' inventories survive for the period around 1700. They show that the value of books as a proportion of a mercer's stock can be surprisingly high. Books worth £58 represented about one-fifth of the value of Thomas Williams's stock at Pwllheli in 1681. Similarly, books priced about £25 were worth a quarter of the stock of Dawkins Gove, a prominent Carmarthen mercer, in 1692. The books stocked by these mercers were more varied than those carried by the mercer in Llanidloes fifty years earlier. The Llanidloes mercer seems not to have carried any Welsh books, but one or two generations later a fair proportion of a mercer's stock was made up of the Welsh devotional literature which was published in increasing volume after the Restoration. But popular secular material in English was also present among the Welsh mercers' stock at the end of the seventeenth century. Eiluned Rees has drawn attention to this item in a 1692 Carmarthen mercer's inventory: 'Item, a parcell of old paper [probably unbound] Bookes and Balletts'.[22]

It is really only in this period – the end of the seventeenth century – that one can find secure evidence for itinerant chapbook and ballad sellers in Wales. In 1691 some of Wrexham's townsfolk complained that they 'usually' (a significant adverb) received bad money from those who sold 'little bookes and ballads' there. One of these hawkers was arrested, and disclosed valuable details of his life history when questioned by the town's bailiffs.

John Hopkins, the pedlar, was relatively young, aged about twenty-five, and had led a mobile life in the Welsh Marches, west Midlands and Ireland. Born near Monmouth, he was apprenticed to a Bristol cutler, and subsequently served in Ireland where he had been wounded. After discharge from the army, he returned to England a sick man and lived with his wife in Coventry. Although a short-cutler by trade, he seems to have taken up business as a pedlar buying and selling in fairs and markets. Hopkins's speciality was buying old brass coin and silver lace, and selling small books. In autumn 1691 he set off on horseback on a long pedlar's itinerary travelling from Coventry to Lichfield and on to Cheshire. Finally he arrived in Wrexham where he announced that he would buy old brass money and silver lace. He also sold a little book with a long title carefully noted as 'The Dispairing Conscience xx or the Glory of the Gospel or the Flowing of Christ's Blood Freely to Sinners' which is not otherwise recorded. However, after complaints that Hopkins was giving customers bad money, he was committed to the house of correction and his 'yellow box' of wares seized. He was searched and his pockets emptied of twenty-three pieces of brass and 'cracked money' and a purseful of fourteen silver coins. Hopkins seems to have been buying old brass money cheaply, and then giving it in change to customers who bought his chapbooks with silver.[23] The precarious and marginal life of those who sold cheap print clearly emerges from this rare life history.

CONCLUSIONS

I have argued that Welshmen and women in town and country in the seventeenth century were increasingly surrounded by expressions of print culture. However, it is a challenge to establish who actually owned books and how they were distributed. Margaret Spufford has suggested that the pedlar was a key figure in the distribution of popular literature in seventeenth-century England. However, secure evidence for the pedlar as a distributor of popular literature in Wales is hard to find. I have found only one case before 1650. We are of course at the mercy of our sources. Pedlars in Wales might well have carried printed material along with other consumer goods, but the case is at best non-proven.

However, towns clearly emerge as centres of print distribution in early-modern Wales. Books were sold by urban mercers as part of a general stock-in-trade. One can trace in mercers' bills the distribution of books into the countryside alongside other consumer goods. However, I think it probable that townsfolk were the major purchasers of print in seventeenth-century Wales. This is certainly consistent with what is known about literacy in early-modern Wales. The evidence, such as it is, suggests that a high level of urban literacy coexisted with a low level of rural literacy.

Evidence for specialist chapbook and ballad sellers occurs only at the end of the seventeenth century. Although primarily an urban occupation, selling on market days meant that cheap print in Welsh and English reached into the heart of the countryside. Increased rural book consumption was certainly inseparable from increased rural literacy. The contribution of the charity and circulating schools to rural literacy is well established. They created a large market, but evidence for widespread book ownership is still hard to find in probate inventories. It is probable that cheap print was considered more or less valueless for probate purposes. The most poignant expression of widespread literacy I have found occurs in the inventories of insolvent debtors, a little-known source for details of personal goods. Here listed among the old tables and chairs, baskets and crockery are numerous bundles of books valued at a few pence. Clearly at the end of the eighteenth century books were among those personal possessions that were retained to the bitter end.[24]

I shall end with Robert Roberts's memorable description of the interior of an upland farmhouse kitchen in the early nineteenth century.[25] He describes how its whitewashed walls were adorned with several topical broadsides with woodcuts alongside two or three engravings of 'wonderfully ill-favoured' Nonconformist divines. In one or two shelves near the dresser rested a humble stock of books. The Bible is there, of course, and most of the other books are religious: *Taith y Perenin* and *Canwyll y Cymru*, and the other popular books whose publishing history has been chronicled by Geraint Jenkins and Eiluned Rees. There were also a few popular historical and literary volumes. However the point is that (apart from one stray volume) there were no English books; all the print in this farmhouse, broadsides and books alike, was in the Welsh language. In Wales during the long early-modern period, broadly 1550–1830, there was a movement from an urban and primarily English-language book culture to a rural print culture dominated by the Welsh language. Indeed, it can be argued that the vitality of Welsh as a spoken language in some ways depended on the vigour of the printed word.

## NOTES

1. Margaret Spufford, *Small Books and Pleasant Histories* (London, 1981); Margaret Spufford, 'The pedlar, the historian and the folklorist: seventeenth century communications', *Folklore*, 105 (1994), 13–24; Tessa Watt, *Cheap Print and Popular Piety, 1550–1640* (Cambridge, 1991). A study of vagabonds and minstrels is forthcoming in *Literacy and the Spoken Word*, [ed] Adam Fox.

2. Eiluned Rees, *Libri Walliae: a Catalogue of Welsh Books and Books Printed in Wales, 1546–1820* (Aberystwyth, 1987); Geraint H Jenkins, *Literature, Religion and Society in Wales, 1660–1730* (Cardiff, 1978).

3. Material on wall-paintings in the National Monuments Record for Wales (the public archive of the Royal Commission on the Ancient and Historical Monuments of Wales), Aberystwyth.

4. See *National Library of Wales Journal*, (1954–5), 32.

5. National Library of Wales [hereafter NLW], Great Sessions 4/143/1i/136–7.

6. NLW, Great Sessions 4/16/3/6–7.

7. NLW, Great Sessions 4/126/1/54; 4/127/5/108.

8. G Dyfnallt Owen, *Elizabethan Wales* (Cardiff, 1964), 224; see generally J H Baker, *An Introduction to English Legal History* (London, 1971), 281–2.

9. NLW, Great Sessions 33/1/1 (unnumbered examination of Robert Hughes).

10. Margaret Spufford, *The Great Reclothing of Rural England* (London, 1984).

11. Spufford, 'The pedlar', 14.

12. Spufford, *Great Reclothing*, 15 (map).

13. *Calendar of the Caernarvonshire Quarter Sessions Records, 1, 1541–1558*, [ed] W Ogwen Williams (Caernarvonshire Historical Society, 1956), 26–7; William Salesbury, *A Dictionary in Englyshe and Welshe* (London, 1547), under the words *pedler, sioppwr*.

14. NLW, Great Sessions 4/21/1/34; 4/21/3/19–20.

15. NLW, Great Sessions 4/18/5/10; see generally, Owen, *Elizabethan Wales*, 67–8.

16. NLW, Great Sessions 4/782/1/1. It is probably significant that these pedlars were working in English-speaking south Pembrokeshire, with its nucleated villages, rather than in upland Wales.

17. NLW, Great Sessions 13/30/4; Great Sessions 4/791/3/18,55; Great Sessions 4/17/5/21–5, 83.

18. See Conrad M Arensberg & Solon T Kimball, *Family and Community in Ireland* (Cambridge, Massachusetts, 1968 edn), chap 20, for the 'running account'.

19. See the Appendix.

20. NLW, Great Sessions 13/27/10; Great Sessions 13/28/8; Great Sessions 13/31/26; see also books supplied by Rees Gouch, Carmarthen, *c* 1650 to William Garlick, Laugharne: 3 Construing Grammars (6*d*), 1 Accidence (4*d*), 'one Bible booke' (1*s*) (NLW, Great Sessions 13/30/16).
21. Jenkins, *Literature*, 248–50.
22. Jenkins, *Literature*, 247–8; Rees, *Libri Walliae*, xvi–xvii.
23. NLW, Great Sessions 4/34/6/57–8.
24. Inventories of insolvent debtors are filed in the post-1750 prothonotaries' papers (NLW, Great Sessions P).
25. *The Life and Opinions of Robert Roberts a Wandering Scholar as told by Himself*, [ed] J H Davies (Cardiff, 1923), 16–18.

APPENDIX

The following books are listed in an inventory of the stock of a mercer's shop in Llanidloes in 1639 in an action for trespass upon the case for £60 between John Betton and John Walthall *v* Edward Lloyd and Richard ap Ieuan Morgan [NLW, Great Sessions 13/14/5].

The plaintiffs, who seem to have supplied the defendants, declared that on 21 July 15 Charles I [1639] at Llanidloes they owned the following goods:

| | |
|---|---:|
| 7 English books called 'Gramers' & | |
| 2 'Psaltar[s]' | 5*s*.1*d* |
| 3 books called 'Ovids' & | |
| 2 books called 'Fables & Castilians' | 4*s*.0*d* |
| 2 books called 'Mantuus' & | |
| 1 book called 'Derentius' | 18*d* |
| 1 book called 'An Inovation of Germany' | [no price] |
| 6 books called 'Accidentes' & | |
| 12 books called 'Primers' | 4*s*.1*d* |
| 13 books called 'Horne Bookes' & | |
| 1 dozen little Latin books | 2*s*.0*d* |
| 1 dozen books called 'A B Cs' [&] | |
| 1 book called 'A Construing Gram[m]er' & | |
| 1 book called 'Cordelius' | 1*s*.10*d* |
| 3 books called 'The Schoole of Virtue' | [no price] |
| 11 little books called 'Catachismes' | 10*d* |
| 4 other little books [in English ?– deleted] & | |
| 3 other books called 'Bookes of Pedregree' | 14*d* |
| 4 other books | 8*d* |
| 33 other books | 17*s*.3*d* |
| Total: 133 books valued at £1.18*s*.5*d* | |

# 'Business is Awful Bad in these Parts': New Evidence for the Pre-1914 Decline of the Welsh-Language Book Trade

### PHILIP HENRY JONES

ALTHOUGH THE 1911 Census indicated that the number of Welsh-speakers – about a million – was greater than it ever had been, from the early 1890s onwards many came to believe that Welsh-language publishing had entered upon a period of decline.[1] This view was shared both by members of the book trade and by outside observers. The former tended to regard the decline as a temporary phenomenon: as late as January 1914 a leading printer-publisher could state that, although the sale of Welsh books had steadily diminished in recent years, the firm trusted that the future would be brighter.[2] The latter – with some justice – accused Welsh-language publishers of complacency.[3] If one takes a broader view, the problems of Welsh-language publishing can be seen to derive from a period of economic, social, and linguistic change that was so rapid and far-reaching that a contemporary writer could maintain that Wales had experienced greater change during the generation preceding 1914 than in any previous century.[4] Many of these changes, notably an influx of English-speaking immigrants to the industrial areas of south Wales, and the economic crisis confronting the largely Welsh-speaking quarrying areas of north Wales as a result of the sudden contraction in the demand for slate, posed a challenge to Welsh-language publishers. The advent of new leisure activities (such as popular entertainments and mass spectator-sport, both of which were English in language and ethos) posed a more insidious threat. The most dangerous development of all was the sharp fall in the proportion of monoglot Welsh-speakers from over 30% in 1891 to below 9% in 1911 as state education promoted literacy in English.[5]

As a result of the current campaign to establish a printing museum at the premises in Denbigh occupied by the firm of Gee a'i Fab since the early 1830s, a small collection of material relating to the firm has come to light and has been transferred to the National Library of Wales. The documents include returns sent to the office by its traveller, Robert Williams, which cast light on the declining demand for Welsh-language material during the first decade of the twentieth century.

It was probably not until the 1860s that the major Welsh-language printer-publishers began to follow the example set by the English book trade a generation earlier by employing travellers.[6] As well as reflecting the growth of the Welsh-language book trade and the diversity of its retail outlets, this development may also have been a response to the aggressive canvassing techniques introduced into Wales by Scottish and English publishers of Welsh-language part-works.[7] By the later 1860s Joseph Roberts, traveller for one of the largest Welsh-language publishers, Hughes a'i Fab of Wrexham, visited twice a year every significant bookseller in Wales and in those English towns with large Welsh communities in order to publicise new books, receive orders, and collect money owed to the firm.[8] Hugh Humphreys, Caernarfon, advertised for a traveller in 1867,[9] and in 1870 P M Evans of Holywell was looking for a traveller in north and south Wales who would be 'experienced, a careful book-keeper, energetic and of a good character'.[10] Some time before 1870 (probably in the mid-1860s), Thomas Gee, the most enterprising and largest Welsh-language publisher of the second half of the nineteenth century, began to use his chief clerk, Robert Williams, as his firm's traveller. Born in Denbigh in 1840, Williams had entered Gee's employment before 1855 and remained with the firm until his death in 1916.[11] According to his obituarist, Williams was meticulous and utterly reliable. Although he might appear on first acquaintance to be stern and unbending, he was always prepared to give a sympathetic hearing to retailers who were experiencing difficulties. Following Thomas Gee's death in 1898 the firm came to rely increasingly on Williams's experience and judgement, and after the untimely death in 1903 of Gee's son, John Howel Gee, Williams was appointed manager and secretary of the family company which operated the business. Despite his additional responsibilities, Williams continued to act as the firm's traveller.

Williams made a spring and an autumn journey through both north and south Wales each year following a regular itinerary largely based on the excellent railway network Wales then enjoyed. The fact that the south Wales journey took considerably longer to complete than that through north Wales (six weeks as opposed to three) underlines the vital importance of the south Wales market to a firm located in north-east Wales.[12] Williams's journeys may have been rather lengthier than those of the travellers of other Welsh book publishers since the firm published a twice-weekly Welsh-language newspaper, *Baner ac Amserau Cymru,* which in 1913 enjoyed a weekly sale of some 13 000 copies and was sold by 827 retailers.[13] The north Wales journey could be covered by weekly circuits leaving Denbigh very early on a Monday (on 23 September 1907 Williams caught the 6.30 am train) and returning there on the following Saturday. Visiting the south meant spending ten weekends a year in commercial or temperance hotels, their bleakness possibly mitigated by the opportunity of sampling the sermons of local preachers.

To avoid carrying substantial sums of money while on his journeys, Williams normally banked the money he had received on Tuesdays, Thursdays, and Saturdays.[14] He would then send the office in Denbigh a completed pro-forma return noting the sum remitted and the number of orders he had gained. Williams also frequently noted on the verso his views concerning the state of the book trade locally and the various vicissitudes he had encountered during the past few days. Only one return from 1906 has survived (sent from Liverpool, 31 March 1906), but there is a complete sequence of returns for Williams's autumn journey in 1907, and (with one exception) for both his spring and autumn journeys of 1908 and 1909.[15]

As might be expected, a fair number of Williams's remarks give his opinion of the creditworthiness of retailers.[16] On 16 May 1908 he wrote from Swansea 'I hope you will not object to send Mr Dennis' order. He gave me a post-dated cheque for £10. In future he will be in a position to pay promptly'. When requesting the dispatch of a small order of books to Evan Williams Bangor, on 30 May 1908, Williams reassured the office that 'although there is a little balance still due on the old a/c please do not hesitate – as the money for it is safe'. Again, on 27 May 1909 he vouched for T Edmunds of Corwen 'He is alright and an old Customer of many years ago'. Other notes brusquely ordered the office to deal with problems concerning late or irregular delivery of the *Baner*. In October 1907, for example, Williams told the Office to keep a record of the forwarding of parcels to Aberdare: delivery to that town was so irregular that indignant retailers believed that their parcels were being stolen *en route*. Similarly, retailers in Pontypridd were 'much annoyed' and complained that 'there is much carelessness in the office', since they were receiving the Wednesday edition so irregularly that their customers were threatening to cancel their orders. On Saturday 15 May 1909 Williams had to remind the office of the importance of sending off all the parcels of the *Baner* for Swansea by the same train.

Several notes expressed Williams's frustration because retailers were not at home when he called. 'Somehow or other I am most unfortunate on this journey missing several customers' he wrote on 24 September 1907. 'Yesterday I missed three – one being at Llandrindod, one at L.pool and the other at the Cyf[arfod] Misol [monthly meeting of the Calvinistic Methodists] at Pentraeth. It is very annoying and worries me much.' Other customers were too unwell to see him or claimed that they could not place orders because they were moving to new premises. Writing on 9 May 1908 from Pontypridd, Williams described how a local customer was being compelled to move:

Mr M M Williams, who promised to be a good customer and was doing well... could not give me a line for the reason that he has received a month's notice to quit his shop, and his landlady (who is publican) states in her letter that the reason for her giving him notice is on account of him... taking part in a Procession in favour of the Licensing Bill.

Williams asked the office to draw the incident to the attention of Robert Griffiths, editor of the *Baner*, so that it might be publicized in the strongly pro-temperance newspaper.

The majority of Williams's comments, however, consist of complaints about poor trading conditions. Given his half-century of experience of the trade, these remarks provide an authoritative indication of the extent of the decline in the demand for Welsh-language material by the early twentieth century. The unspoken assumptions underlying his comments may also provide a partial explanation for that decline.

The sole surviving return from 1906 sets the tone. Although Liverpool then contained some twelve thousand Welsh speakers,[17] Williams noted 'There is no doubt about it. The Welsh Book Trade is getting low in L.pool'. On 20 September 1907, at the end of the second week of his autumn journey through north Wales, he noted 'Most wretched poor week's work. Yn wir y mae marweiddra y fasnach llyfrau bron iawn a'm lladd' (*Indeed the sluggishness of the book trade is very nearly killing me*). The switch in mid-sentence to Welsh in order to indicate emphasis or deep feeling is a characteristic feature of Williams's notes. On 17 November 1908 he noted that when he had left Cardigan that morning it was 'the first time in my life for me to do so without an order and a settlement of my account'.

The remainder of this paper traces the spring and autumn journeys made by Williams in 1909. The spring journey through north Wales began badly. Writing on Thursday 15 April from Llandudno, Williams noted that on the train that morning he had had an opportunity to tell D S Davies, Thomas Gee's son-in-law and the leading figure in the family company, 'what few orders I had on Tuesday and yesterday'. The note also provides an indication of the very long hours Williams worked, since he hoped to arrive in Bangor at 10.45 pm. A week later, on Thursday 22 April, having experienced various disappointments *en route* at Pwllheli and elsewhere, Williams arrived at Blaenau Ffestiniog. He immediately expressed a gloomy view of his prospects there: '[I] am rather afraid I shall not be able to do any business here – of course I will do as much as ever I can ond y mae pethau yn ddifrifol o wan yma ac yn wir yn mhob man yr wyf wedi bod ynddynt' (*but things are seriously weak here and indeed in every place I have visited*). For several years, Ffestiniog had been suffering the effects of a marked contraction in the demand for Welsh slate, and in October 1908 on his previous autumn journey Williams had noted that 'Business is in a serious state there and hundreds of people have gone and are still going to South Wales & America. That is the only reason some copies of the 'Baner' are stopped'. A year later Williams found that there had been no improvement: 'I am told that over 5000 people have gone from here to S[outh] W[ales] and other places and 400 men are to leave the Oakley Quarries next month so I must be very careful and it is not wise to push too much as things are at present'. A final plaintive note is struck by his remark 'Y mae yn anhawdd iawn ysgrifenu wedi cario y bag trwm yma' (*It is very difficult to write after carrying this heavy bag*). Williams returned to Denbigh (via Llanrwst) on

Saturday but had little time to rest since he summoned a clerk to the office after dinner to help him prepare for the south Wales journey. There was, of course, no question of working on a Sunday: in May 1908 Williams added a note to a letter written late on a Saturday 'If my letter will bear to-morrow's post mark... please do not draw wrong conclusions that I am writing on Sunday'.

The first week of the south Wales journey began badly. On Monday 26 April after a 'diwrnod gwlyb iawn a digalon' (*very wet and disheartening day*) Williams wrote from Corwen asking the office to send to the Bush Hotel, Merthyr, a sample copy of *Baner Gobaith* (The Banner of Hope) he had inadvertently left in the stock room. On arriving in Merthyr on Thursday via Wrexham and Oswestry, he submitted his 'little remittance' and complained of the number of post-dated cheques he had been compelled to accept. His wish 'I do hope there is some luck waiting me here – I shall do all I can and try to make up for the poor North Wales Journey' was soon to be disappointed. Despite being out until after 9.00 pm on Monday 3 May and 9.30 pm on Tuesday he did little business. On Thursday 6 May he wrote from Pontypridd:

> Business is awfully poor in this neighbourhood never worse they say. Mr John Evans Cilfynydd would have given me a bigger Order had he been able to pay me more money – You need not hesitate for one moment respecting him – He will I <u>know settle the whole with me on next journey</u>.

Williams's concluding remark that Evans 'is about removing to Pontypridd and has nearly settled for a splendid shop, but he will not give up the market' is an important reminder that, as in earlier centuries, Welsh books were still being sold by market traders – people who were not included in trade directories.[18] Despite all his efforts, trade continued to be so poor that on Saturday 8 May Williams complained

> I have had one of the most disappointing weeks I have ever had – Returning here late every night depressed and down hearted. Business in the Rhondda is in a most unsettled state, go where you will the cry is 'We are afraid we are going to have a Strike'. It pains me my returns are so miserable but I cannot help them. I do all I can but find it impossible to get orders or money.

These fears of a strike arose from the acrimonious negotiations concerning the implementation of the miners' eight-hour bill and were to be more than justified in 1910–11 by the protracted Cambrian Combine dispute and the riots at Tonypandy.

The following week, during which Williams visited Bridgend, Neath, and Swansea, proved to be equally disappointing. On Saturday 15 May he looked back over 'another week's hard work with very poor returns', noting in Welsh that he was '*having a very hard time indeed – very difficult to get money or orders*'. Things were no better when Williams moved via Llanelli (where over 77% of the population in 1911 claimed to be Welsh-speaking), Llandovery, and Carmarthen to the rural areas of mid-Wales. Writing from Newcastle Emlyn on Saturday 22 May, 'healthily tired as it has been such a hot day', he said he was

> sick and tired of this most poor journey and am very glad it is drawing towards the end and I shall be home again this day fortnight. I do not suppose I ever had such a very poor journey as this has proved to be – I have and am still doing all I can, but it is almost a matter of impossibility to get orders.

His one consolation was that next day he would hear one of the most popular preachers of the day, Evan Phillips (1829–1912), famous (in an era much given to lengthy sermons) as the 'twenty minute preacher'. The final fortnight, working northwards by way of Lampeter, Aberaeron, Aberystwyth, and Machynlleth proved to be no more successful. At Dolgellau on Thursday 3 June he reflected 'I don't know how it is but I cannot persuade Customers to Order and have to leave them with promises "cewch order y tro nesaf" &c. (*you will have an order next time*). I assure you I am not sorry that this fruitless journey is near the end'.

The autumn 1909 journey was equally disappointing. At the beginning of the second week of his north Wales journey Williams wrote from Bangor on Tuesday 12 October

> You will see that I am having very hard and disheartening time of it – Things are not improving one bit at Bethesda from where I have just returned and to make matters worse the weather is something cruel unfit to be out of doors still I am moving along and am quite well through all.

Bethesda, like Blaenau Ffestiniog, was a quarrying town hard hit by the slump in the slate industry. By Thursday 21 October Williams had reached Blaenau Ffestiniog, where he found that there had been no improvement since the spring: 'Business is seriously bad about here and the weather is most disheartening'.

The south Wales journey commenced badly, Williams commenting on Tuesday 26 October 'there is no business to be done in the places I visited yesterday'. Despite several days of hard work in the Merthyr area, he had to report on Saturday 6 November a reduction in orders for the *Baner*:

> Send six copies less of Sat *Baner* to Mr W James Bookseller Dowlais and six copies less of Sat *Baner* to Mrs Saint newsagent Merthyr Tydfil. Trade is awfully bad in Merthyr, Dowlais & neighbourhood and I am having very hard times of it. I am working hard and very long hours – I would not grumble if I could do some reasonable business.

For the whole of the following week Williams was based in Pontypridd where he found that trade in the mining valleys was as depressed as it had been on his spring journey. On Thursday 11 November he wrote: 'Everybody afraid of a Strike and are afraid to order – Mr John Evans Cilfynydd has just informed me that if he could only satisfy himself that a Strike would be avoided he would have more than doubled his

Order. On my last journey he promised me a big order on this occasion but he is afraid of venturing it'. Friday was no better; on Saturday, Williams wrote 'I was out yesterday from 8.30 in the morning until 9.35 last night and did no business – what little pickings I got was more from sympathy than otherwise'.

The following week provided further evidence of the declining demand for Welsh material. Writing on the 20 November from Swansea, Williams noted 'You will find Mr Fox's of Pontycymmer's returns are very heavy – I persuaded him some while ago to try and sell the *Baner*. He has done his best but failed'. At Swansea, he experienced a major disappointment. The leading Swansea booksellers, Morgan & Higgs, could not place a significant order with him on his spring 1908 journey because the firm was about to move to larger premises. Williams had, however, been led to believe that he could expect large orders in future. As he reported on Saturday 19 November, this was not to be since sales of Welsh books had been so poor. 'I spent some time with Messrs Morgan & Higgs but only got a small order – the bulk of my last order is still on hand.' Writing from Llanelli on Saturday 27 November, he replied (in Welsh) to a letter stating that all was going fairly smoothly at the office

*I am not surprised that few orders are being received since the book trade is ex-ceptionally depressed – Trash and nonsense go these days. So far I have had a hard and a very poor journey – some evenings almost breaking my heart after being out for many hours and returning late and weary and achieving next to nothing.*

A final disappointment awaited him in Machynlleth on Wednesday 8 December when, for the first time ever, he failed to meet one of his most reliable customers, the itinerant bookseller Richard Jones (1848–1915).[19]

One might legitimately ask whether the Welsh-language book trade was depressed as Robert Williams maintained. Travellers for other Welsh publishers shared his gloom: on 23 May 1908 Williams reported 'I met Messrs Hughes & Son's traveller the other day and he was complaining of bad trade &c'. On the other hand, the fig-ures for money remitted during the 1908 and 1909 journeys are remarkably similar, £1421.17*s*.3*d* being remitted in 1908 and £1424.16*s*.6*d* in 1909. The number of or-ders placed was also similar, 290 in 1908 and 286 in 1909. Other Gee records, how-ever, provide a context for Williams's observations. The General Ledger for 1897–1910 is of particular value in providing an overview of the firm's finances dur-ing this period.[20]

The first row of the table is probably the one that would have caused Williams most concern since it shows (apart from 1908) a gradual decline in the income from sales and advertising deriving from the mainstay of the firm, publishing the *Baner*. The full extent of the decline in sales is partly masked by advertising income since the income

| To | 1907 | 1908 | 1909 | 1910 |
|---|---|---|---|---|
| Baner income | £2647 1 9 ½ | £2660 8 3 ½ | £2567 0 6 ½ | £2549 7 6 ½ |
| N Wales Times | £ 561 13 11 | £ 517 16 6 ½ | £ 484 4 9 ½ | £ 470 19 4 ½ |
| Other income | £2035 18 9 | £1765 8 2 | £2107 3 11 | £1718 10 10 |
| Outgoings | £4537 10 10 | £4205 19 10 | £4256 5 11 | £4009 10 11 |
| Net profit | £ 707 3 7 ½ | £ 937 13 2 | £ 602 3 4 | £ 729 6 10 |

derived solely from *Baner* sales decreased steadily from £1909.16*s*.2*d* in 1905 to £1643.12*s*.5*d* in 1910. The income deriving from the firm's English-language weekly, the *North Wales Times* declined consistently. In so far as newspaper publishing is concerned, the conclusion must be that Williams's complaints were justified. The firm's reaction was to attempt to reduce its costs. The marked reduction in outgoings from £4537 in 1907 to just over £4000 in 1910 is the most striking feature of the table. Unfortunately, the reduction in outgoings was achieved at the cost of a decline in production standards[21] that did nothing to enhance the paper's sales appeal.

The General Ledger figures do not permit one to arrive at any firm conclusion concerning trends in the profitability of book publishing since the heading 'other income' lumps together income from book publishing, jobbing printing, lithography, and binding. Here one has to fall back on Williams's claims (and those of many other writers) that Welsh books were not selling. The basic problem – which Williams half recognised in his complaint that people now demanded 'trash' and 'nonsense' – was that the firm's products were becoming increasingly outdated, particularly for the growing number of bilingual readers who had the choice of buying more modern, more attractive, and often cheaper works in English. Thus on 14 May 1908 Williams wrote from Bridgend 'I had on my last journey two orders for the *Gwyddoniadur* – the two were staring me in the face yesterday but I was paid for them and had they been sold I would have had further orders'. Although a revised edition had been published between 1889 and 1895, this ten-volume encyclopaedia remained essentially rooted in the third quarter of the nineteenth century. New titles produced by the firm showed little recognition of the profound changes that were taking place. In 1909, with the south-Wales valleys in political ferment, less than three years before the appearance of the syndicalist pamphlet *The Miners' Next Step*, Williams's main concern was to persuade local booksellers to stock a scholarly new study of Calvin.

NOTES

1. An early expression of this anxiety can be found in John E Southall, *Wales and her Language* (Newport, 1892), 307.

2. National Library of Wales [hereafter NLW], Hughes & Son Donation 1958, Hughes letter-book 4, 1913–14 (409[b]), R Hughes & Son to W Llewelyn Williams, 7 January 1914.

3. See, for example, the critical remarks made in 1912 by E Morgan Humphreys reproduced in Philip Henry Jones, 'A Golden Age reappraised: Welsh-language publishing in the nineteenth century' in *Images and Texts: Their Production and Distribution in the 18th and 19th Centuries*, [ed] Peter Isaac & Barry McKay (Winchester: St Paul's Bibliographies; New Castle, DE, Oak Knoll Press, 1997), 137.

4. W Llewelyn Williams, *'S Lawer Dydd* (Llanelli, 1918), 5.

5. The 1891 figure probably exaggerates the number of monoglot Welsh speakers; the considerably more reliable figure for 1901 was just over 15%.

6. Graham Pollard, 'The English market for printed books: the Sandars Lectures, 1959', *Publishing History*, 4 (1978), 7–48 (40).

7. P H Jones, 'Scotland and the Welsh-language book trade during the second half of the nineteenth century' in *The Human Face of the Book Trade: Print Culture and its Creators*, [ed] Peter Isaac & Barry McKay (Winchester: St Paul's Bibliographies; New Castle, DE, Oak Knoll Press, 1999), 117–36.

8. NLW, Hughes and Son Donation 1958, Hughes letter-book 1, 1862–73 (69[a] & 70),R Hughes & Son to John Curwen, 2 December 1867.

9. *Herald Cymraeg*, 2 September 1867

10. *Goleuad*, 8 October 1870.

11. The main source for Williams's life is his obituary, *Baner ac Amserau Cymru*, 1 July 1916, 5.

12. It should, however, be noted that a week of the so-called south Wales journey was spent visiting border towns such as Wrexham and Oswestry.

13. NLW, MS 12156D (Morris T Williams MS 19), Sales Ledger for *Baner ac Amserau Cymru* 1913–16.

14. When Williams was unable to reach a bank he would transmit payment by postal order: he did this reluctantly, because it was more expensive than depositing cash and cheques at a bank.

15. The only gap in the sequence of numbered orders is for the period Friday–Saturday 26–27 November 1909.

16. Williams's comments are unfortunately less amusing than those noted in Bill Bell, '"Pioneers of literature": the commercial traveller in the early nineteenth century', in *The Reach of Print: Making, Selling, and Using Books*, [ed] Peter Isaac & Barry McKay (Winchester: St Paul's Bibliographies; New Castle, DE, Oak Knoll Press, 1998), 121–34.

17. Emrys Jones, 'The Welsh language in England *c*1800–1914, in *Language and Community in the Nineteenth Century*, [ed] Geraint H Jenkins (Cardiff, 1998), 231–59 ( 256).

18. Neither Evans, who ran the Cambrian Bookstall in Pontypridd market, nor another market trader mentioned by Williams, D N Jones of Carmarthen, is listed in the 1908 edition of *Kelly's Directory of Stationers, Printers, Booksellers, Publishers, Paper-Makers, &c.* The

directory also omits the important itinerant bookseller Richard Jones (see note 19). Rather less than half the identifiable traders referred to by Williams are listed in Kelly.

19. A Lloyd Hughes, 'Richard Jones, Aberangell (1848–1915*): Llyfrwerthwr Teithiol'*, *Journal of the Merioneth Historical and Records Society*, 8 (1980), 447–9.

20. NLW, Thomas Gee MSS, A1.

21. Williams complained from time to time that copies of the *Baner* sent to him on his journey were badly printed, and, perhaps more significantly, ordered the office to make sure that issues containing important advertisements were well printed with new type being used for the advertisements themselves.

# George Nicholson and his Cambrian Traveller's Guide

### AUDREY COOPER

THE SUBJECT OF this paper is George Nicholson (1760–1825), printer, author and bookseller, the extent and range of his output, but particularly his celebrated guidebook to Wales and the Marches, called *The Cambrian Traveller's Guide*. From 1807 to 1825 George Nicholson was printing at Stourport in Worcestershire, and it was there that he brought out the two editions of his guide to Wales. He had previously set up presses in Bradford, Manchester, and at two venues in Shropshire. In the old *British Museum Catalogue*, to distinguish his works as author from others of the same name, his entries were headed Nicholson, George, printer at Stourport.

I first came across George Nicholson over thirty years ago through acquiring by chance from a northern bookseller an 1808 guide to Wales by a then unknown printer, surprisingly, from my home town. Stourport had existed since the 1770s, when the place where the River Stour joins the Severn was chosen by Brindley to link up with the new Staffordshire and Worcestershire Canal, so becoming a busy and important part of an extensive waterways transport system. As it happened the prosperity of the new town was short-lived, and it lost something of its importance and trade when the railways came in the 1850s.

Local enquiries at the time came up with the possible location of a press connected wrongly with the name of Baskerville, who in fact was born and went to school in north Worcestershire. Then comparatively recently Nicholson surfaced again, when by an unlikely coincidence, an elderly friend produced a tiny book she had kept since a child, which turned out to be one of Nicholson's unique pocket-sized series of titles, the only known surviving copy in the county. By then, rather more was known about him, the local Civic Society had been interested for some time, and valuable research and evidence uncovered from as far back as the 1890s nationally and locally.

George Nicholson was an eminent, highly accomplished, innovative and amazingly industrious printer, author and bookseller. From a Yorkshire printing family background, over the length of his career he established presses and worked extensively in five places: in the 1780s at Bradford, from 1793 at Manchester, 1799 to 1807 at Ludlow and nearby Poughnill in Shropshire, finally from 1807 to 1825 at Stourport. He had established a considerable reputation in his own time, from an entry in a biographical dictionary of 1816, an obituary in the *Gentleman's Magazine* in 1825, to an article in the original *Dictionary of National Biography*, the volume dated 1894. That was written by one C W Sutton, then librarian of Manchester Public

Library; this article was, and still is, the starting point for research into his life and work. There is a great deal still to be learnt, especially about the early years, and though I am not competent to evaluate printing techniques and style, I can appreciate its range and excellence. It is, however, the content of his output, the range of subject matter, his ideals, educative zeal, seemingly tireless industry as editor, compiler, printer, that compel attention and admiration. I have still no tally of titles, but with multiple editions, different sizes and format, the total must be formidable, and compiling a complete checklist, even more contemplating a bibliography, is a daunting proposition.

It seems that George's father, John Nicholson, left Keighley, where George had been born in 1760, to start the first printing business in Bradford. This was about 1780, and by 1784 George with one of his brothers set up on their own account, printing, according to Sutton, mainly chapbooks and penny numbers. There is, however, record of work done for the new canal companies, and for other local concerns; one such is *An Explanation of the Plan of the Canal from Leeds to Liverpool* [by] John Hustler, Bradford, printed by George Nicholson, 1788. Copies of these pamphlets are still in existence.

From Bradford the ambitious George in 1793, by then with wife and two children, moved to Manchester setting up twice, first in Palace Street, later in Spring Gardens. There until 1799, from the range of important titles he put out, some of them as author, is demonstrated his particular brand of humanitarianism and radical idealism, the product of a Dissenting, likely Unitarian, background. He was a dedicated vegetarian, and surely one of the earliest declared supporters of animal rights, above all it seems, a didact, a born educator, particularly of the young, and in the fashion of that time, of the young female person; many moral and didactic tracts aimed at like targets are in the forefront of his titled output. At Manchester he started an ongoing series called *The Literary Miscellany: or, Selections & Extracts, Classical and Scientific; with Originals in Prose and Verse*. This covered eventually about eighty titles in twenty volumes. A volume was intended to collect three or four selections of related interest from works of proved reputation, for example, on subjects such as education, moral philosophy, selections from poets, story or song anthologies. Each volume had an overall title-page, with imprint and date, a heading and brief subject title, followed by individual title-pages for the ensuing parts, often with imprints of varying dates and locations, and usually decorated with engraved vignettes on title-page or, later, as frontispiece. For instance, one such collection is titled *Preceptive*, another *Elegiac*; the grave figured prominently as a feature of popular concern. The uniform size was duodecimo, and prices varied according to the number of pages; *The Juvenile Preceptor* in three parts cost 1s.6d, 2s.6d and 1s.

In a preface to the early volumes he extolled at some length the reason and aim of the series, starting as follows:

It is an evident and acknowledged fact that our most celebrated authors have their excellencies and defects; their admirable and less interesting compositions... We therefore have engaged in the task of selecting 'the valuable parts'. Subjects of utility, whatever can amend and humanise the heart, inform the understanding, correct the judgement and establish first, general and liberal principles; whatever can awaken attention to obvious and important truths, will be eagerly preferred. We shall avoid the adulation of power, the celebration of offensive achievements, and of savage and unmanly sports, absurd traditions, mythological fictions, unnatural allegories, visions and fables, and details of mad and violent passions.

Manchester 1797 saw the first publication of Nicholson's own commitment to vegetarianism, as part of his major work *On the Conduct of Man to Inferior Animals: on the Primeval State of Man; Arguments from Scripture, Reason, Fact and Experience, in Favour of a Vegetable Diet*. This work made four editions, the last from Stourport in 1819; so it had quite a following. The contents list of chapter headings is extremely emotive including 'Cruelty of a carter', 'On mutilating animals', 'Stripping of geese', 'Savage amusements and sports', and 'Caging of birds'. A few other titles from Manchester were *Ancient Ballads, Songs and Poems, Songs Descriptive, Moral and Pastoral, Humorous*, and the first edition of a title, often reprinted in various forms even to this day, *Pious Reflections for Every Day of the Month*, his version translated from the eminent French theologian Fénelon by a well-known Manchester cleric, John Clowes. One major compilation obviously close to his heart was *On Education* in two parts, listing topics under no less than 103 headings. Nor did he neglect the practicalities of living in favour of the mind and intellect, as evidenced in the pamphlets *On Clothing* and *On Food*, 1797.

In 1799, after a seemingly successful and profitable period in Manchester, Nicholson left his northern background to set up at Ludlow in the Welsh Marches, quite a different environment. Ludlow then was a very prosperous wool town, the population of country and county stock, largely well-to-do. There are few clues as to why Nicholson chose Ludlow, but some evidence from one Thomas Wright, a local academic and antiquary, writing some years later,[1] suggests that his father, also Thomas Wright, a printer, was once employed by George's father John Nicholson, later removing to Ludlow, whether with George Nicholson or to join him there is unclear. The younger Wright, in an account of Ludlow printers,[2] says of George Nicholson

His name belongs to the history of English printing in general and not specially to that of this town. George Nicholson... was a very remarkable man and whom I look upon as having greatly contributed towards an important revolution in the publishing trade in our country...

45

It seems obvious that from the start Nicholson was aiming for a national readership, by his contact with well-known London publishers as agents, naming them in imprints; for example, *Gothic Stories Containing Sir Bertrand, Sir Gawen, Edwin* [all from differing sources] has this statement 'Ludlow printed at the office of G Nicholson (from Manchester), sold by T Knott, 47 Lombard Street; and Champante and Whitrow, 4 Jewry Street, Aldgate, London, anno 1799'. There is no record of his placing advertisements for trade in the Shropshire press.

A number of titles originated from his base in Ludlow, an early ecclesiastical foundation called College. He stayed there for barely two years before removing to a rather isolated part of nearby Caynham called Poughnill. Several other printers already operated in Ludlow; the principal of them, Henry Proctor, became the friend and employer of the first Thomas Wright[3]. It is possible they could have resented the presence of a worthy, ambitious and industrious northerner, though he seemed to be offering no local competition. His output from Poughnill was astonishingly prolific lasting from late 1801 to 1807. There are only two properties he could have occupied; they are still habitable, at the end of a narrow farm road. Setting up a press and a trade from there seems logistically improbable, but a large number of single titles were printed, then issued later as part of the *Literary Miscellany*. A new innovative venture, the famous tiny pocket series set in 32mo, came out at the same time. Unfortunately, few copies still remain; Shropshire County Library has one, *Extracts from the Works of the Rev James Hervey*; I have one, *Pious Reflections* by Fénelon, and the British Library just a few, including *The Advocate and Friend of Woman* and *The Mental Friend and Rational Companion*. They were priced at 9d to 1s.6d in coloured boards, bound and lettered 3d each extra, later copies going up from 1s to 1s.9d. The range of titles from Poughnill include selections from poets, including Goldsmith, Pope, Gray, Milton and lesser-known versifiers like Nathaniel Cotton, competing with the great and famous Benjamin Franklin and Marcus Aurelius; popular religious and moral tracts such as *A Picture of the Female Character as it Ought to Appear when Formed* by Bishop Horne, *Letters on the Improvement of the Mind, The Advocate and Friend of Woman Compiled from Various Authors*. Then, in complete contrast, Nicholson's own manual *Stenography: a New System of Shorthand* made its first appearance from Poughnill.

During this time, Nicholson was commissioning the skills of well-known designers and engravers to produce frontispieces, title-page vignettes and tailpieces, even for the tiny pocket series. It is interesting to see styles changing and illustrations becoming larger and more elaborate in the later work. A favoured designer, the one most used, seems to be W M Craig, with various engravers like Chapman, Mackenzie, Hawkins or Nesbit, one of Bewick's best pupils. Another regular and quite

Title-page of Nicholson's *Select Pieces by Benjamin Franklin*(Poughnill, 1804) – reduced to 90%

recognisable hand is that of Richard Austin, known also as a type founder, though whether father or son of that name is not entirely clear. From Bradford in 1790

Nicholson started to commission work from Thomas Bewick. Later letters from Poughnill of dates 1801 to 1805 still exist, with transcripts kindly supplied by Iain Bain who is preparing an edition of Bewick's correspondence. The earlier letters show Nicholson upbraiding Bewick quite sharply for his failure to return designs in time, but later the tone is far more conciliatory until by 1805 he is writing at great length to offer advice on Bewick's dispute with Sarah Hodgson over her late husband Solomon's share of Bewick's *Quadrupeds*. However, he seems for once out of his depth by admitting 'I am certain you would not do what was palpably wrong and therefore I may leave the matter with you to determine. It is a situation in which it is difficult to advise.'

By 1808 Nicholson was in Stourport preparing *The Cambrian Traveller's Guide*, since both editions were printed there, the first in 1808, and the second, which increased the coverage beyond Wales to the neighbouring Marcher counties, in 1813. The third edition by his son Emilius Nicholson came out from London in 1840, fifteen years after Nicholson's death. By 1808 when Nicholson had arrived Stourport was already thriving, with a population of about 2000, and was a good base for business and trading. From the second edition of *Cambrian Traveller's Guide* in 1813 he describes Stourport as

> a place which has risen out of fields since the year 1770 to a mart of considerable business, a market and a post town. It abounds with docks and basins for the reception of trows [river sailing vessels], barges, etc from Worcester, Gloucester and Bristol and for canal boats from various quarters... Through this medium a direct and ready communication is formed between the north and west of England to and from Gainsborough, Hull and the eastern coast including many of the Midland counties. The place is indeed well calculated in every respect for carrying on, with facility, any extended business.

So he made a good choice in moving there, quite different from isolated Poughnill. He set up his press and bookshop in a house on the corner of Raven Street and Bridge Street, close to the canal basin and wharves. It is still there, but at present the lower half is sad and dilapidated. Until recently the ground floor was occupied by a similar-sounding but totally different trade, that of bookmakers.

The first edition of *Cambrian Traveller's Guide* came out in September 1808. At the beginning of the preface, Nicholson gives his reason for embarking on the Guide.

(*Opposite*) Title-page of first edition of Nicholson's *Cambrian Traveller's Guide* (Stourport, 1808) reduced to 94%, original page size 183x109 mm

# THE

# *CAMBRIAN*

# TRAVELLER'S GUIDE,

and

# POCKET COMPANION;

containing

THE COLLECTED INFORMATION OF THE MOST POPULAR
AND AUTHENTIC WRITERS,

relating to

THE PRINCIPALITY OF WALES, AND PARTS OF THE
ADJOINING COUNTIES;

augmented by

CONSIDERABLE ADDITIONS,
THE RESULT OF VARIOUS EXCURSIONS:

comprehending

HISTORIES AND DESCRIPTIONS OF THE

| CITIES, | MANSIONS, | INNS, | FERRIES, |
| TOWNS, | PALACES, | MOUNTAINS, | BRIDGES, |
| VILLAGES, | ABBEYS, | ROCKS, | PASSES, |
| CASTLES, | CHURCHES, | WATERFALLS, | &c. &c. |

ARRANGED IN ALPHABETIC ORDER.

Also,

DESCRIPTIONS OF WHAT IS REMARKABLE IN THE INTERMEDIATE SPACES,

as

| Solitary Houses, | Caverns, | Woods, | Tumuli, |
| Forts, | Rivers, | Fields of Battle, | Pillars, |
| Encampments, | Aqueducts, | Islets, | Druidic Circles, |
| Walls, | Lakes, | Cromlechs, | Works of Iron, Tin, |
| Ancient Roads, | Forests, | Carnedds, | Copper, &c. |

THE ROADS ARE DESCRIBED, THE DISTANCES GIVEN,
AND THE DISTINCT ROUTES OF

*Aikin, Barber, Bingley, Coxe, Donovan, Evans, Hutton, Malkin,
Pennant, Skrine, Warner* and *Wyndham,*

are preserved.

The whole interspersed with
HISTORIC AND BIOGRAPHIC NOTICES,
with
NATURAL HISTORY, BOTANY, MINERALOGY;

and with Remarks on the
COMMERCE, MANUFACTURES, AGRICULTURE, AND MANNERS
AND CUSTOMS OF THE INHABITANTS.

————◁◦▷————

## STOURPORT,

Printed and sold by George Nicholson, (from Poughnill). Sold also by Symonds, Lackington
& co., Champante & co., and Crosby & co., London; Stoddart & Craggs, Hull;
Knott & Lloyd, Birmingham; Houlstons, Wellington; and all other Booksellers.
1808.

49

Almost every tourist in Wales has found either the inconvenience of conveying and re-ferring to many volumes, or the want of a guide in every direction in a single book. To supply such desideratum has therefore been attempted in the present work'.

He goes on to state at length the wide range of subjects he intends to cover: cultural, historical, architectural, the natural sciences to name but a few, and how the text is to be planned and set out. As for the sources of all this information, he admits

> the aim of the compiler has been to include a larger portion of information and interest in a small compass than has hitherto appeared, yet whatever may be found in extracts should be considered only as outline to greater originals. He has avoided throughout to bedeck himself with borrowed plumes, giving to 'Caesar the things which are his, tribute to whom tribute is due' and if there had been one book existing which would have supplied the use of this, he would not have obtruded himself upon the public, who are superabundantly supplied with Welsh Tours, directories etc.

There exists a useful account and bibliography of travel and local guides to nine-teenth-century England, but not as far as I know, of Wales. However, Nicholson does enlarge upon 'the principal publications referred to in the present work' which are:

Thomas Pennant, *Tours through Wales*, 2 vols, 1784

Henry P Wyndham, *Tour*, 1781

Arthur Aikin, *Journal of a Tour through North Wales and Part of Shropshire*, 1797

Rev Richard Warner, *Walks through Wales*, 2 vols, 1798

Henry Skrine, *Tour through Wales*, 1798

Rev Richard Coxe, *Tour in Monmouthshire*, 2 vols, 1801

William Bingley, *Tour in North Wales*, 2 vols, 1804

Rev J Evans, *Tour in North Wales; Tour in South Wales*, 1804

John T Barber, *Tour through South Wales*, 1803

William Hutton, *Remarks on North Wales*, 1803

Benjamin Malkin, *Remarks on North Wales*, 1804

Edward Donovan, *Descriptive Excursions through South Wales*, 2 vols, 1805

finally referring to a new two-volume translation by Sir Richard Colt Hoare of Giraldus Cambrensis, *Itinerarium Cambriae*, which was published in 1806, to-gether with a new edition of the Latin original.

The preface continues with a section headed 'Modes of Travelling', that is, on foot, on horseback, or by carriage. Only one traveller, Dr Mavor, chose an open carriage and two horses, was accompanied by a female companion and two gentlemen, but found the attention and curiosity of the natives something of a handicap, if often pleasantly diverting. The compiler himself usually travelled on foot, but concedes that the principal objection to walking is that of carrying the luggage, a change or two of linen or stockings, a small compass, a prospecting glass, *Hull's Pocket Flora*, a portable press for drying plants, this interleaved Guide, a drinking horn and occasionally some provision more palatable than a penny roll. He concludes that the most desirable mode of travelling is certainly upon a strong little horse, which you can relieve by walking at intervals. A Welsh pony is recommended. He goes so far as to prescribe the right sort of shoes as described by him in No 47 of his *Literary Miscellany*, a useful plug, the wearing of fine soft flannel or woollen socks, and washing the feet with water before going to bed. Medication to cure blisters is added just in case. There follows a substantial tutor on the Welsh or British language and the pronunciation of Welsh letters taken from *Richard's Welsh Grammar*. The text of the *Guide* is headed alphabetically by principal towns or features, smaller places mentioned in italics appearing in the indexes; articles are prefaced by routes, with mileages and reference to the traveller consulted in each context, all printed in two numbered columns per page. The end of each article lists the tourists and the places where their routes began and ended, for instance

> Mr Pennant commenced his tour at Downing, his native place and residence and ended at Caerwys: he made two more excursions. Mr Aikin began his tour at Shrewsbury, proceeded to Llan-y-mynach and returned to Llangollen.

Now for a mind-boggling sequence of indexes, twelve in all. They are, exactly as headed:

1. Index of the plants after the arrangement of the *Flora Britannica* with their English names and times of flowering.

2. Index to the provinces, hundreds, districts, islets, promontories, peninsulas, vales, valleys, dingles, passes, roads, sands, plains, parks, moors, downs, fields, forests, woods, marshes.

3. Index to the mountains, hills, rocks, cliffs, caverns, caves and clefts.

4. Index to the fountains, rivers, estuaries, waterfalls, lakes, wells, bogs, aqueducts, creeks, bays, havens, ports, harbours, moats, ferries.

5. Index to the cities, towns, villages, hamlets, solitary inns and houses, bridges.

6. Index to the castles, forts, encampments, walls.

7. Index to the palaces, mansions, gentlemen's seats, villas.

8. Index to the Abbeys, Priories, Monasteries, Churches, Gorseddan, Reliquaries, antiques.

9. Index to the Tumuli, Carneddau or tombs, Cromlechs or monuments, pillars, Druid circles.

10. Index to works of iron, copper and tin; Potteries.

11. Index to miscellanies.

12. Names of persons which occur in the foregoing volume.

To describe the volume in loosely bibliographical terms; it is a small octavo 200x110 mm, iii–vii pages of prelims, being the preface, then numbered two-column pages totalling 720 columns. A present-day professional printer and traditional compositor judges the typeface to be 8 pt Baskerville in a contemporary version by Richard Austin. The skill of the typesetting seems in no doubt, the choice of the face gives a clear, easy-to-read capacity, the quality of the thin paper stands up well to the close printing impression, with little effect of bleeding. It has frontispiece designed by W M Craig, cut by R Branston, and a tiny tailpiece, but no other illustrations. There is no map, but in the preface Nicholson advises on the purchase of one, an excellent two-sheet map of the whole Principality by C Smith, price 7*s*. The title-page statement, which is illustrated earlier, is heroic, starting *The Cambrian Traveller's Guide and Pocket Companion*, and continuing the length of the page. No Welsh agents are quoted. The price was 7*s*.6*d* in boards.

It seems that the first edition was well enough received, though in need of some revision. This encouraged Nicholson to embark on a second version, which came out five years later in 1813. It proved to be much larger and of extended coverage, even so far as to include that unlikely Welsh border town, Birmingham, and its environs. In his preface Nicholson names journals with appreciative notices: *The British Critic, Monthly Review, European Magazine, Eclectic Review*, and *Literary Panorama*. He writes 'Encouraged by their candour I have laboured to render the present edition more complete. I have also received assistances, communicated in the kindest manner by several travellers'. He goes on to to justify the need for this larger volume:

> It is observable that the present edition is printed upon a larger paper than the last, and therefore more bulky, but it was not possible to fit into a smaller compass without rendering it less useful. I hope the important additions which have been made will more than compensate for the enlargement of the bulk and proportionate price.

The last paragraph of the preface turns from Wales to advertise 'A Caledonian Guide on the present plan [for which] considerable labour has already been bestowed on that design, and the work advancing by the rigid application of a part of every day on this pursuit'. However, so far as I know, Nicholson's Scotland never appeared in print. The critic of the *Eclectic Review*[4] had a little fun at Nicholson's expense by devoting twenty lines of his review to the lengthy title-page, remarking 'After copying the whole of this very instructive and amusing title-page, our account of the book may be short'. He concedes

> The plan appears to us not very judiciously chosen; but it has been executed with great diligence. The work is printed very closely on thin paper, and contains as much information as could possibly be comprised within the allotted space: it is very comprehensive without being bulky, and will be found to afford as much entertainment as can

ever be expected in a series of distinct articles of this kind arranged in alphabetical order. The second edition of 1813 is large octavo, 210x125 mm, set in 9pt Baskerville and again in double columns per page, in all 1470 numbered columns, without doubt much heavier than the first. The layout is similar, alphabetical by major place headings, each article prefaced by the best routes and mileages, with a note of those travellers whose reports were used in the compilation. The amount and content of information varies; present-day description, architecture, main houses and seats, history, folklore, trade, interspersed with individual travellers' tales and opinions of bed and board. Flora and fauna again are not neglected: under Anglesea [*sic*] are listed thirty-eight names of shellfish in the Latin and common forms, and thirty-five similarly of the plant species. For Amlwch on the north coast of Anglesey, a full account is given of the mining of copper and other mineral ores, the production, trade, transportation by sea to Swansea and Liverpool and current prices, all the work of the traveller William Bingley. As Pennant observed 'Nature hath been profuse in bestowing her mineral favours on this spot'.

Accounts of journeys by six extra travellers are incorporated in this edition, with the areas they covered, listed at the end of the guide as Manby, Gilpin, Lipscomb (accompanied by Nicholson from Worcester through south Wales and the Borders to Birmingham), Meyrick on Cardiganshire, Jones on Breconshire, and Fenton. If Gilpin is the well-known William Gilpin who wrote and travelled widely in search of the picturesque, and was parodied as Dr Syntax, he had died in 1804, but was not included in the first edition. Indexes are far fewer, four instead of twelve, being:

1. Index to the plants [12 columns]
2. Eminent persons [6 columns]
3. Index of places, inclusive of all named places, either as main headings, or those appearing in the text [81 columns, 3 per page]
4. Miscellaneous – This last index contains some very strange entries, for instance: Nails for the shoes in ascending mountains, described; Peasants, diet of; Story, a marvellous; Wreckers, their cruelties; Circumstance, a remarkable one.

The index to eminent persons is unreliable; obviously he could not include owners of all properties though scrupulously mentioned in the text. The River Wye is a main heading with a good fifteen-column article, but strangely not the Severn; it has only two or three references in the index, and nothing appears for the Severn Gorge with its great iron and china-clay industries working since the middle of the eighteenth century, now considered the cradle of the Industrial Revolution.

Unlike the first, this edition has the benefit of a map, or in one version, a map for each of north and south Wales. The title differs from the first edition in that it is considerably shorter, begins *The Cambrian Traveller's Guide in all Directions*, and is illustrated by a vignette cut down from the original frontispiece. At least two printed versions went out, differing only in the imprint's naming of particular publishers. One such reads 'Stourport, printed by the editor and published for him by Longman, Hurst, Rees, Orme & Brown; Sherwood, Neely & Jones; and R & R Crosby & Co; London, 1813'. The name of G Nicholson as printer only appears at the end of the volume. The price, at 18*s*, is more than twice that of the first edition.

The third edition of the *Cambrian Traveller's Guide*, edited by his son Emilius, rector of Minsterley in Shropshire, came in 1840, fifteen years after George Nicholson's death. The basic text must still be that of the earlier editions, and though the sources cited are the same, it seems to lack the appeal of its predecessors. Rightly, it is restricted to cover only the Principality; the text is page width and well set; it has a map and only one index: places, persons, plants in a single sequence, but adding a further category, paintings. The editor supplies his own lengthy, wordy preface. By leaving out the Border towns which by 1840 had guides of 'accuracy and merit' of their own,' 'an opportunity is gained of enlarging the articles strictly Welsh'. He admits

As others have availed themselves freely of this work, the Editor has occasionally taken advantage of theirs. The task of conveying the same ideas in other words when already happily expressed is but an unprofitable employment; many passages from recent writers are therefore quoted which it would have been tedious to acknowledge.

He enumerates the delights of Wales for the satisfaction of different categories of tourists, including 'The moralist will notice with a sense of satisfaction the marked difference which subsists between the dissolute habits of the English and the temperate socialities of Wales'. As for transport, he writes 'Now good roads and steam have almost annihilated time and space and London can be reached from Aberystwyth in twenty four hours, when formerly it required that time to accomplish the distance from Aberystwyth to Shrewsbury'. There is a map at frontispiece, but no other engraved illustrative matter. The edition was published in London by Longman, Orme, Brown, Green & Longmans, and printed in London by A Spottiswoode.

This contemporary review of the third edition from *Eddowes's Salopian Journal* of 20 May 1840[5] sums up the whole work. The critic writes

Our opinion of this book can be given in a few words. *The Cambrian Traveller's Guide* has long been a standard work. During the lifetime of its author it ran through two large editions, and has long been out of print. The present edition has the advantage not only of the author's last corrections, but the most careful revision on the part of his son, the editor. The information it communicates is thus brought down to the latest period and much original matter is added. The book is naturally devoted to topography but its scientific notices are good, and among the new matter in this edition is much that will be of material use to the angler in Wales...

For the remainder of his working career in Stourport Nicholson continued with additions to his famous pocket series and to the *Literary Miscellany*, which in 1812 had reached twenty volumes. He brought out new editions of old titles such as his *On the Conduct of Man to Inferior Animals*, and numerous new titles. One outstanding success was *The British Orpheus, being a Selection of two hundred and seventy Songs and Airs*, distinctive for including the music, printed from movable type known from research by Stanley Morison to have been cut by Richard Austin. Music became a Nicholson interest; several other titles on its art and practice emerged. He compiled a couple of spelling and pronouncing dictionaries, before later devoting his time to producing the works of local authors and poets in larger format, as well as the guide *A Description of Malvern* by a bookseller of that town, Mary Southall.

George Nicholson died in 1825. There is evidence that he was considered of some importance in his own time, with a brief entry in *A Biographical Dictionary of Living Authors*[6] of 1816. An obituary in the *Gentleman's Magazine* of November 1825 began[7]

> We cannot forbear some brief record of a man whose worth and talents entitle him a notice, whose name we hesitate not to place with the names of Dodsley and Baskerville... he has enriched our libraries with many valuable works. 'The Literary Miscellany' in 20 vols is a beautiful specimen of his ingenuity in the art of printing and of his taste and judgement as editor.

C H Timperley's *Dictionary of Printers and Printing*[8] quotes that obituary, and goes on to praise the 'accuracy of the "Cambrian Traveller", the humanity of "The conduct of man"' and enthuses that 'in short he possessed... strength of intellect with universal benevolence and undeviating uprightness of conduct'. A local Worcestershire article of 1897 by J R Burton,[9] still a reliable source, prints an appreciation in high terms by J C Hotten, the Victorian literary critic and essayist. An MP for Worcester in the later part of the century, Thomas Rowley Hill, who as a boy lived in Stourport and knew Nicholson, 'distinctly remembered him as a tall gaunt man. He was an author and printed chiefly by his own hands. He was a great scientific crony of my father'.[10] Nicholson is known to have been interested and involved in the affairs of Stourport, but there is so far no evidence of trade other than that in books from his shop in Bridge Street, though one imagines he would have dispensed, if not the traditional patent medicines, at least precepts and advice on most topics. His monument in the churchyard at Stourport reads 'The subject of this memorial was a man of strict integrity, expansive mind, devoted to the interests of literature, and a warm advocate of humanity'.

## NICHOLSON'S BOOKS

*The Cambrian Traveller's Guide and Pocket Companion*, [ed] George Nicholson, (Stourport: Printed and Sold by George Nicholson..., 1808)

*The Cambrian Traveller's Guide in Every Direction*, [ed] George Nicholson, 2nd edn (Stourport: [G Nicholson]; London: Longman, Hurst, Rees, Orme & Brown [and others], 1813)

*Nicholson's Cambrian Traveller's Guide in Every Direction*, edited and revised by Emilius Nicholson, 3rd edn (London: Longman, Orme, Brown, Green & Longmans, 1840)

*The Literary Miscellany; or Selections and Extracts Classical and Scientific*, [edited by George Nicholson], 20 vols (Stourport: G Nicholson, 1812)

George Nicholson, *On the Conduct of Man to Inferior Animals; on the Primeval State of Man...*, 4th edn (Stourport: G Nicholson; London: Sherwood, Neely & Jones, 1819)

NOTES

1. Thomas Wright, 'Printing and publishing in Ludlow', *Ludlow Sketches* (Ludlow: R Jones, 1867), 122–60 (147–8).

2. Wright, 'Printing in Ludlow', 147–8.

3. Wright, 'Printing in Ludlow', 149–50.

4. [Unsigned review] 'The Cambrian Traveller's Guide and Pocket Companion', *Eclectic Review*, 5, Art 23 (April 1809), 306.

5. [Unsigned review] 'Nicholson's Cambrian Traveller's Guide in Every Direction...', *Eddowes's Salopian Journal*, 20 May 1840, 4.

6. J Watkins & F Shoberl, *A Biographical Dictionary of Living Authors* (London: H Colburn, 1816), 251.

7. [Unsigned Obituary] 'Nov 1 Mr G Nicholson', *Gentleman's Magazine*, 95 (1825), 642.

8. Charles H Timperley, *Dictionary of Printers and Printing* (London: H Johnson, 1839), 896–7.

9. J R Burton, 'Early Worcestershire printers and books', *Trans. Worcestershire Architectural & Archaeological Soc*, 24 (1897–8), 197–213 (211–13).

10. Burton, 'Early Worcestershire printers', 212: quotation from a letter written to Alfred Baldwin, MP for the Bewdley Division of Worcestershire and father of Stanley Baldwin, later Prime Minister.

# William Ford and Edinburgh Cultural Society at the Beginning of the Nineteenth Century

## BRENDA J SCRAGG

AT THE END of the eighteenth century and the beginning of the nineteenth – from approximately, the death of Samuel Johnson in 1784 to that of Walter Scott in 1832 - Edinburgh, rather than London, was the intellectual centre of the kingdom.[1] During this period some dozen learned and scientific societies had been established.[2] Many of them maintained libraries or at least small collections of books. The directory[3] for 1820-1 & 22 lists some sixty booksellers and stationers, including such household names as Bell & Bradfute, Archibald Constable, William Blackwood and Oliver & Boyd. A number of well-established book collectors lived in and around Edinburgh, but above all the most prominent figure of the period was Sir Walter Scott, who gives further evidence of Edinburgh society when he writes in 1814

> On looking at the notes of introduction which Pleydell had thrust into his hand, Mannering was gratified with seeing that they were addressed to some of the first literary characters of Scotland "To David Hume, Esq."[4] "To John Homes, Esq." "To Dr Ferguson," "To Dr Black."[5] "To Lord Kaimes." "To Mr Hutton."[6] "To John Clerk, Esq. of Edin."[7] "To Adam Smith, Esq."[8] "To Dr. Robertson".[9]

In addition to the literary life, which largely revolved around members of the legal profession, Edinburgh was a thriving commercial centre attracting widespread admiration for its 'new town' architecture with elegant terraces and town houses. This society and atmosphere attracted William Ford to establish connections in Edinburgh. Timperley[10] gives us the earliest reference to Ford's being in correspondence with Sir Walter Scott. It is difficult to know when their first contact took place or indeed the degree of their friendship. When in Edinburgh Ford's letters are almost invariably sent from 'Mr Scott's Lodging' but whether he stayed there or only used it as an accommodation address we do not know. The tone of the correspondence is formal and does not indicate a degree of intimacy. Ford was certainly acquainted both socially and through business with the influential circle of lawyers and literary men who surrounded Walter Scott. Many of the members of Scott's circle who were in contact with Ford lived nearby having moved to the fashionable 'new town'.

Ford maintained his shop and residence in Manchester throughout his life and, while we know he did have a number of contacts in London, so far hardly any information about them has been forthcoming. Edinburgh and London are about equidistant from Manchester but I would imagine that then, as now, the journey would have taken twice as long to Edinburgh.

William Ford had been collecting books for some considerable time before starting his bookselling business in 1805. How and where he acquired his books is unknown, but the evidence seems to show that he was already known as a collector, at least in Scotland, before starting in business, as the following letter from Alexander Gibson Hunter to Archibald Constable dated 7 September 1806 shows: 'Supposing you have fixed the day of your sale, I wish much you would immediately write to Ford at Manchester and Robinson at Liverpool, and invite them to come down to it in the best way you can... I would like much if they – Ford particularly – should come'.[11]

Amongst the first book customers Ford is known to have been in contact with in Edinburgh are Robert Graham[12] and John Jamieson,[13] author of a number of books about Scotland. Jamieson purchased a number of items from Ford's 1810 catalogue and he asks Ford if he has an imperfect copy of *Polyolbion* as his lacks a few plates, and his copy of Coverdale's *Bible* wanted nearly all of *Genesis*. Some measure of the respect Ford commanded is evident as Jamieson writes 'I am always afraid of the booksellers here getting the start of me. But you always considered <u>authors</u> as your preferable customers and I have no doubt you will give me this indulgence'.[14]

In 1807 the Edinburgh bookseller William Laing[15] is writing to Ford concerning his translations of the classics, specially of Herodotus:

> My Herodotus is now finished. It sells for 56/- in boards. How many do you want? Are there such gentlemen as Dr Helme, Rev. H.B. Bayley, Dr Percival,[16] Wm. Hutchinson...[17] in Manchester? They are subscribers to my Gk. books. What can you give me Boydell's Shakespeare for?... Have you any of Dugdale's works, or Holingshed's Chronicles.[18]

Copies of his translation of Herodotus have not so far been traced or in fact any of his translations of Greek writers. The obituary in the *Gentleman's Magazine*[19] gives details of several of his classical translations including the Herodotus. Of the Manchester names mentioned both Percival and Hutchinson are known, but Dr Helme and the Revd Mr Bayley have not been identified.

An undated letter from David Laing,[20] the second son of William Laing, who had joined his father's business, addressed to Ford at Scott's Lodging shows that Ford continued to be a customer of Laing's bookselling business:

> I may add that the books you rec'd came to £1-18-6, discount off say 6/6 which leaves a balance in your favour of 8/- which I shall send you over – or such others as you may wish to have. I think that you said you desired to have an old 4to which came from Longmans, it cost us 9/- if you like for the balance you will herewith receive it, but I should mention that some parts of the vol. are not complete...[21]

In April 1814 Ford received a letter from Lord Buchan:[22]

> Your catalogue of books communicated by Mr. Vernon[23] It comprises many rare and interesting volumes & is worthy of the attention of collectors. This letter in the

Engraved portrait of William Ford by Henry Wyatt, 1824

meantime is meant to draw the attention of the good people of Manchester to Miss Feron, the daughter of the eminent Mr Feron, Veterinary Surgeon to His Royal Highness's 15th Regiment of Cavalry, who promises to be an actress and singer of the very fine order. I asked from Mrs Siddons[24] the Theatre Royal here for a night that I might see her perform in comic opera & hear her admirable voice so capable of being directed to the highest attainments in music. The result was that on Maundy Thursday the most unfavourable of all nights in the year the venue was well filled and the pit overflowing.[25]

One can only presume that Miss Feron was also coming to Manchester and that Ford might help to promote her.

The Advocates' Library which had been established at the end of the seventeenth century was, on occasion, a customer of Ford. The correspondence, much of it undated, is from David Constable who was in his own right a friend and customer of Ford. Robert Chambers writing in 1825 describing the Advocates' Library says 'besides this gentleman [Dr Irving, the Librarian] there are several assistant librarians whose kindness to strangers deserves public acknowledgement in a work of this nature'.[26] Writing from Park Place an undated letter, but perhaps of 1820, reads

I ought to have acknowledged your last kind note sooner why I did not do so was that I might at once finish the survey of the Italian books you were so good to send here and that I might make the note and the dispatch serve for all. In the first place. The manuscripts appear to me to be very reasonable at the price you mention & shall be kept. Secondly, – you will observe the books are divided into two parcels, the one, in green cloth, the other in brown paper. Those in the brown paper parcel are such, as appear to me to be the most desirable for the Advocates Library. Will you therefore have the goodness to make out a list of them in order that, it may be ascertained whether they are in the manuscript catalogues of the Library or not. – I observe they are not in the printed one. The best edition of 'Macaronica' I have kept a little longer in order to compare it with my own…[27]

A second letter, also undated but perhaps 1820, from Park Place refers to the same transaction:

I have been confined to the house since I last saw you otherwise I should have called to look at the original charters etc. which… are mentioned in your prospectus. If they are not very numerous will you send me a digest of them. You may send in the Italian books contained in the list you made out, (except the vol. of tracts) to the Adv[ocates] Library. I have not yet seen Dr Irving to learn whether they have any of them or not, but it is not very probable they have… You will of course favour us with your company to dinner to morrow at 1/4 to five. But I fear it will not be in my power to accompany you [on] our projected walk as…[tear] indisposed. P.S. You will charge them to the Advocates' Liby. advised by me.[28]

A further letter from David Constable dated 26 June 1820 begins 'I have received your two letters and must apologise for having delayed so long to acknowledge receipt of them…' Clearly the two letters are those just quoted above. The letter continues

> When your books, I mean the… parcel directed to my care, arrived at Park Place, I immediately sent a porter with them to the Advocates' Library and wrote a note addressed to the Librarian Dr. Irving[29] requesting him to pay the price to Messrs Ruthven & Sons as I think you desired in your letter… The Somme Rural, I thought had been only £2-12-6 in your catalogue. I should like to receive it as soon as possible with Dr Owen's tract on Quarles(?). Will you also send me the letters between Dr Wood and Bulstrode Whitelock…[30] If you send these to Messrs Longman & Co directed for me, they will be forwarded by the first parcel for Edinburgh.[31]

David Irving, in an undated note writes to Ford

> It was thought advisable to return the edition of Aldus's Anthology and we have this morning discovered a copy of the book on ecclesiastical discipline. All the volumes of the Neue Bibliothek der schoenen Wissenschaften must be delivered before the price can be paid. It will then be paid in any way that may best suit your convenience. I observe there is no reduction from the price of the MS. Your note will thus require so many corrections that I wish you would take the trouble of making out a new one, and on an entire sheet of paper.[32]

It has been noted elsewhere that Ford did not appear to use headed stationery, but simply wrote his invoices on any piece of paper which came to hand.

A copy of Constable's [Catalogue of] A *Collection of Rare Tracts, English and Scottish* is preserved in the National Library of Scotland. On the reverse of the title-page Ford has written 'This collection will be sold <u>entire</u> for six hundred guineas'. The catalogue claims that

> It forms an admirable nucleus for a very extensive systematic collection, and with regard to Scotland, more particularly contains things which it would require great expense and much time to bring together again and of past centuries also which might never again occur even to the most industrious and fortunate collector.

Ford had clearly asked David Constable for his opinion of this catalogue. On 19 May 1826 Constable writes from the Advocates' Library

> I also include a general view of the contents of the collection of tracts which I should be very happy to see preserved entire in the Cheetham [*sic*] Library… I am glad you agree with me that the price is not ridiculous which is often the case in such matters. It is always better to rise than to fall in one's estimate on such occasions. Should you succeed in disposing of them I would show a fair commission but the price cannot be lower than £600. Say 600 guineas. There are upwards of 8900 separate articles. None of these can be worth much less than 1/6 and a great proportion if sold by competition would bring much more. I have not yet had an opportunity of speaking with Lord Eldon on the subject of the two tracts you mention but I shall not forget to do so. The picture you give of Mr Edwards sale is gloomy indeed, but things cannot continue long in such a state of depression. I have no doubt we shall soon find them reviving.[33]

At the foot of this letter Ford added 'Send him an account of the author of the curious tract on Scotland entitled "A Modern Account of Scotland", 1679'.[34] This was published anonymously by Thomas Kirk and was a coarse satire presumably taken from the journal he kept during a three months' tour in Scotland undertaken in 1677.[35]

An undated (c1826) *Catalogue of Books in the Stock of the Sequestrated Estate of Archibald Constable* is to be found in the Manchester Central Library.[36] This contains 2765 items divided into ten sections. These were on sale at No 10 Princes Street, Edinburgh. Orders to be sent to Mr Cowan, the Trustee of Constable's affairs after their collapse. While I have not seen any list of purchasers or prices realised I have no doubt Ford would have been one of the customers.

In 1828 David Constable's own library was sold at auction by D Speare, Edinburgh.[37] The sale lasted twenty-two days and comprised more than 3000 lots including library furniture. As befits the library of an Advocate many of the items were legal documents, others related to Scottish history and a number of these were purchased by the Advocates' Library.

Another of Ford's important friends and customers in Edinburgh was Thomas Thomson,[38] who had an extensive and flourishing practice at the Bar; but his most important legacy to Edinburgh was the collecting and arranging of the Public Records and editing Acts of the Parliament of Scotland undertaken while he was Deputy Clerk-Register of Scotland. Aside from his legal and public duties Thomson was a close friend of Francis Jeffrey and other members of the circle involved in the publication of the *Edinburgh Review*. On occasion Thomson took over the editorship of the Review during the absence of Jeffrey. He contributed three papers to the *Review*.

In 1821 Ford had received a request for information from a Mr Pountrey about a rare tract concerning the second coronation of King Charles I at Holyrood House and of the ceremonies on the occasion, together with the grant of the title of Earl of Stirling to Sir William Alexander of Menstrie.[39] I have been unable to discover anything about Mr Pountrey, but he was clearly making the enquiry on behalf of someone else as he states that 'the object of these enquiries is of the first consequence and accuracy is indispensible'.[40] He offers to defray immediately any expenses incurred by Ford. Ford, unable to provide the answer, had appealed for advice to Thomson, who replied [41]

> I have never seen nor has Mr. C[onstable] ever seen a printed account of the coronation of Charles I in 1633. Though that such a tract may exist is not improbable… He has [seen an] account of some of the festivities which took place on that occasion but nothing of the ceremonial of the coronation or of the creation of the Earldom of Stirling…'

Thomson continues '…I hope your kind offices will procure for me a copy of Mr. Dibdin's work though I have not yet heard from him'. It is not possible to say which of Dibdin's works is refered to here. Following Ford's enquiry Dibdin hastens to reply '…I must look to this business immediately… I wish you much amusement in your proposed tour but don't calculate upon any trouvailles. Everything is denuded of book treasures abroad…[42] I have not so far discovered any details of foreign tours undertaken by Ford though this has clearly been the source of some of his stock.

Thomson was one of the founder members of the Bannatyne Club and on the death of Walter Scott became President. Ford was never a member but took a keen interest in their publications. From Thomson Ford received a number of gifts of books which he always carefully annotated, not only with the date of the gift but also often with his own opinion of the author. On the copy of Cranstoun and Browne *Disputatio Juridica* (1826), which Thomson gave him, Ford has written 'The author of this Thesis was the editor of Constable's Magazine – now qualifying for an Advocate. – A shrewd clever man with a long head as Mr T. described him.' George Cranstoun,[43] later Lord Corehouse, a lawyer with literary aspirations, was a friend of both Scott and Thomson from earliest times. Both Cranstoun and Thomson, together with Scott, were members of the 'Brotherhood of the Mountain', a group of young advocates who met for social and literary discussions.[44] Thomson also presented Ford with his *Life of James VI*, one of only a hundred copies printed with a very limited number for sale. Likewise Ford also received Thomson's *Collection of Inventories and other records of the Royal Wardrobe and Jewelhouse* (1815), and several publications of the Bannatyne Club.

Ford and Thomson continue their correspondence and on occasion when Ford visits Edinburgh they dine at each others houses. Ford's catalogues continue to be a source of interest. In November 1825 Ford's catalogue arrives when Thomson is away from home. On his return he says he is afraid to look in the catalogue as he feels he would be too late to add to his collection. 'There are many things I should have been delighted to possess but I endevour to console myself by thinking they are bad copies… I have continued to add a few articles to my collection since you were here & I should be happy to see you here again to show you my acquisitions…'[45]

The friendship between Ford and Thomson was such that, when Thomson learned of a projected visit of Ford to Edinburgh, he wrote to request Ford's assistance with what we can only speculate was some sort of court proceedings in which Thomson was concerned. An undated letter to Ford begins 'Besides what in particular can be obtained relative to the family of John Brown it is particularly desirable to know whether his youngest sister Julia Ellen married to Mr. Rachlen of Wolverhampton be alive, if dead when and where she died, and if the fact of her death be certainly known. Any other particulars of her history would also be desirable.'[46] The next letter, also undated, continues

If you are not asleep when you come to <u>Longtown</u> pray have the goodness to inquire if Colonel Bedingfield still lives at Kirklinton, in that neighbourhood – if he be there at present – if he is expected to continue to reside there this season – if he has been lately from home in <u>the North.</u> I dare say the ostler at the inn will be able to give you this information. Unless a very <u>favourable</u> opportunity should occur, it will perhaps be better to get the information from Mr. Ben Scott that you already have a note of. The risk is that Colonel B should be apprised that such enquiries were made. At the same time it would be of great importance to get the information alluded to if you find it can be done in a way not to excite suspicion.[47]

On the reverse of the first letter Ford has written 'Ask Mr Scott if the person who eloped with Col Bedingfield is still living – the mother and the sister are now living in Manchester'. No further information is forthcoming about this affair.

In 1821 Ford met in Edinburgh the Polish Count Zamoyski, whom he describes as 'a very amiable and accomplished young nobleman of considerable literary accomplishments, and travelling for improvement'. Zamoyski was endevouring to collect all the works printed in or relative to Poland and had apparantly had considerable success. He gave Ford a list in his own hand of items he was still hoping to acquire.[48] Some time later Zamoyski visited Ford's shop in Manchester but unfortunately Ford was not there. Zamoyski's collection must have been considerable but does not appear to have been sold at auction and its present whereabouts has not been traced.

While in Edinburgh in 1823 Ford was visited by John Clerk, Lord Eldin. There are no details of any purchases made but Ford's comment on the note announcing Clerk's visit is of interest:

Lord Eldin, one of the Lords of Session. Inventor of an important discovery in Naval Tactics For this His Majesty (tho' always in opposition to the administration) on his visit to Edinburgh created him a Lord of Session, but he will be always better remembered as one of the most celebrated advocates at the Scottish Bar and all the wits of Edinburgh at the head of whom he may very justly be placed.[49]

Scott's interest in many aspects of history and particularly that relating to Scotland is well demonstrated in an undated letter, but ascribed to July 1824, when Scott writes to thank Ford for sending him a needlework gift from Mrs Charlotte Birch of Manchester.[50] She had previously written to Scott requesting a copy of her father's last speech. Scott replies 'I remember her father's name well among the Manchester sufferers in 1745: and, amongst a large collection of things relating to that revolutionary matter, I have a copy of <u>his last speech</u>'.[51] Mr Birch, together with others, had had his head stuck up on a post in the Market Place in Manchester in 1745. The details of the incident have been reprinted by the New Spalding Club.[52]

Continuing the interest in the '45 rebellion Ford writes to Scott

As I know your interest generally about every thing which pertains to Prince Charles Stewart, generally called the Pretender I have sent you a copy of a curious document (lately in my possession) which most likely may be new to you. When on his march into this country he arrived at Manchester on Nov. 29th, and halted here the whole of the 30th during which he issued a printed proclamation to the inhabitants, of which this is one of the identical copies (probably the only one existing) as it was not known before the discovery of this, and it was supposed that his proclamation had been made by the bell-man of the town and this was the tradition which prevailed among the oldest inhabitants relative to it. The volume in which it had been preserved contained a number of the curious tracts relative to the same event; some of which are of extraordinary rarity and which I never met with before...The volume has passed from my hands but I have retained copies of the titles of the whole of them...It contained altogether about 14 tracts with a very curious small portrait of the Prince in his highland garb, as he then appeared, <u>which was engraved in Manchester</u>, coarse, rather, in its execution, but a very good likeness.

It has not been possible to trace the present whereabouts of these tracts, or to identify the portrait. The copy of the proclamation referred to above, written in Ford's own hand, is preserved in the National Library of Scotland.[53]

On 27 March 1829 Ford writes from 'Scott's Lodging' to Scott at Abbotsford

I took the liberty of addressing a letter to you through the Post Office on my arrival here but have not had the pleasure of seeing or hearing from you in advance, and as several gentlemen have informed me that you had left town and... that you were not expected to return for some time, I thought it better to forward the... parcel. I was the bearer of it from the Rev. Mr Greswell and have accordingly sent it to Messrs Constable & Co to forward to you. I shall remain here about a month longer... I regret that your arrangements have prevented you calling and looking at my collection, as, if I do not flatter myself, I had brought somethings that w'd have interested you.[54]

Another of Ford's Edinburgh customers was the Archdeacon of Leith whom Ford describes as 'An eminent literary character'. He writes to Ford at Scott's lodgings in April 1829[55] 'I am obliged to you for your note, & will take the books you have specified. The sum is 38/- which at 10% discount (I always being treated like a bookseller) comes to 35/-... I will give you the money if you can accede to my terms'.

While it is clear that most of Ford's sales in Edinburgh came from the wide distribution of his catalogues it seems that on his visits Ford also brought with him a selection of items which he felt most likely to interest his customers. There are a number of references which indicate that people came to his lodgings to examine his stock.

It should be remembered that Ford was also a dealer in prints. He had established considerable contacts in Edinburgh with artists and print collectors many of whom may also have been customers for his books. His most prolific contacts with Edinburgh were during the last decade of his life, when previous evidence had apparently shown a declining interest in business activity so it would seem that only his death in 1832 ended his Scottish connections.

## NOTES

I am grateful to the John Rylands University Library of Manchester for financing my visit to Edinburgh.

1. R. S Rait's introduction to W T Fyfe: *Edinburgh under Sir Walter Scott* (1906).

2. Website http://www.r.alston.co.uk/contents.htm

3. *The Commercial Directory, of Ireland, Scotland, and the Four Most Northern Counties of England, for 1820–21 & 22.* (Manchester: J Pigot, 1820).

4. David Hume (1711–1776), historian and political economist, Librarian to the Faculty of Advocates.

5. Dr Joseph Black (1728–1799), Professor of Chemistry, Glasgow University.

6. Dr James Hutton (1726–1797), geologist.

7. John Clerk (1757–1832), later Lord Eldin, a Scottish Judge.

8. Adam Smith (1723–1790), author of *An Inquiry into the Nature & Sources of the Wealth of Nations.*

9. *Waverley Novels,* vol IV, *Guy Mannering* (Constable, 1895), 124.

10. Charles Timperley, *Encycolpaedia of Literary and Typographical Anecdote* (Second edition, 1842).

11. *Archibald Constable and his Literary Correspondents. A Memorial by his Son Thomas Constable,* 1 (1873), 84.

12. Robert Graham (1786–1845), first Professor of Botany at Glasgow University, 1818; from 1820 Regius Professor of Botany at Edinburgh University.

13. John Jamieson (1759–1838), noted preacher came to Edinburgh in 1797; described by Sir Walter Scott as 'an excellent good man'.

14. National Library of Scotland [hereafter NLS], MS 18000, no 72.

15. William Laing (1764–1832), see *Dictionary of National Biography* [hereafter *DNB*], Chambers's *Biographical Dictionary of Eminent Scotsmen.*

16. Dr Thomas Percival (1740–1804), founder member of the Manchester Literary and Philosophical Society; from *c* 1787, became a member of the Royal Society of Edinburgh.

17. William Hutchinson is listed in Bancks's *Manchester and Salford Directory* (1800).

18. NLS, MS 5319, f 225.

19. *Gentleman's Magazine,* 102 (September 1832).

20. David Laing (1793–1878), first and only Secretary of the Bannatyne Club. For a memoir of Laing see David Murray, 'David Laing, antiquary and bibliographer', *Scottish Historical Review,* 11 (July 1914).

21. NLS, MS 18000, no 28.

22. David Stewart Erskine (1742–1820), 11th Earl Buchan, originated in 1780 the Society of Antiquaries of Scotland, established at a meeting held at his house 27 St Andrew Square.

23. Probably Thomas Vernon, print dealer of Liverpool, as Ford had started an additional book- and print-selling business in Liverpool in 1811.

24. Mrs Harriet Siddons, actress, sister of William Murray, and the daughter-in-law of the great Mrs Sarah Siddons.

25. NLS, MS 18000, no 44.

William Ford's transcription of the Young Pretender's proclamation (much reduced) –
reproduced by kind permission of the Trustees of the National Library of Scotland

26. Robert Chambers, *Walks in Edinburgh* (1825).
27. NLS, MS 18000, no 28.
28. NLS, MS 18000, no 27.
29. Dr David Irving, Keeper 1820–1849; see *DNB*.
30. I have been unable to identify these items in Ford's Catalogue.
31. NLS, MS 18000, no 29.
32. NLS, MS 18000, no 67.
33. NLS, MS 18000, no 26.
34. [Thomas Kirke] *A Modern Account of Scotland* (London, 1679) Wing K629.
35. See *DNB*.
36. Shelf mark G 017.4 Co4/2.

37. *Catalogue of the Library of David Constable, Esq. Advocate containing an extraordinary assemblage of rare and curious books and manuscripts… which will be sold… by D. Speare…* 1828.

38. The most extensive contemporary memoir of Thomson is that by Cosmo Innes, his successor as Deputy Clerk-Register, published by the Bannatyne Club in 1854.

39. See Cokayne, *Complete Peerage,* 12, 277.

40. NLS, MS 18000, no 51.

41. NLS, MS 18000, no 52.

42. NLS, MS 18000, no53.

43. George Cranstoun, 1771–1850; see *DNB,* also *Journal of Sir Walter Scott.*

44. MacCann, *Sir Walter Scott's Friends* (1909).

45. NLS, MS 18000, no 55.

46. NLS, MS 18000, no 56.

47. NLS, MS 18000, no 57.

48. NLS, MS 18000, no 47.

49. NLS, MS 18000, no 48.

50. For a discussion of Scott as an historical writer see James Anderson *Sir Walter Scott and History* (Edinburgh, 1981).

51. Transcript of the letter NLS, MS 851, f 169.

52. *A Plain, General, and Authentic Account of the Conduct and Proceedings of the Rebels, during their Stay at Derby, from Wednesday the 4th, till Friday morning the 6th December 1745.* Reprinted in James Allardyce [ed], *Historical Papers relating to the Jacobite Period 1699–1750,* 1 (New Spalding Club, 1895).

53. NLS, MS 3904, f 182 (see illustration on p 67).

54. NLS, MS 3908, f 162.

55. NLS, MS 18000, no 65.

# Advertising Judiciously:
## Scottish Nineteenth-Century Publishers and the British Market

### IAIN BEAVAN

A RCHIBALD CONSTABLE, William Blackwood, William & Robert Chambers, and Oliver & Boyd were all Scottish publishers of early- or mid-nineteenth-century origins, based, initially at least, solely in Edinburgh. As business enterprises, none saw its role as limited to publishing for the Scottish market (however defined). Indeed it has frequently been noted that they were able, with varying degrees of success, to challenge the dominance of London-based publishers.[1] London, however, remained in many respects the centre of the British book trade, and aspiring Edinburgh publishers acted accordingly. Constable opened a London office in 1809, albeit unsuccessful and short-lived. William & Robert Chambers, whose reputation was built on their *Chambers's Edinburgh Journal* and popular educational series, had a proportion of the print-run of the *Journal* produced in London, and Blackwood's London office opened in 1840. Oliver & Boyd differed in not expanding in quite the same way, in that along with their substantial publishing enterprises, the company became the largest wholesale house in Scotland.[2]

A measure of the extent to which these nineteenth-century Edinburgh publishers saw themselves as working within a British context, can be appreciated both in their titles published, and as importantly, in the edition sizes. The editions of Sir Walter Scott's writings are well-known examples (10 000 copies of *Rob Roy* reportedly sold in a fortnight[3]), but, less prominently, titles in Oliver & Boyd's newly commissioned, non-fiction monographic series, the Edinburgh Cabinet Library, were produced in initial print runs of between 2500 and 5000 copies – numbers which, given the content, make limited sense unless the enterprise was conceived of in British terms.

Robert Cadell, the Edinburgh publisher of Scott from the late 1820s, recognised the need for a reliable and committed wholesale agent in London, but rejected John Murray for the role, instead preferring Whittaker & Co. Cadell commented that Murray could not offer 'the facilities of a wholesale house' which were necessary in an 'agent in London for a Provincial Publisher'.[4] Provinciality here suggests a commercial fact of life. Edinburgh publishers were somewhat disadvantaged in that in order to succeed within a British context, a near-essential requirement was an agreement with a London wholesale house, whose contacts and networks could be used to mutual benefit. Arguably, those Scottish publishers who succeeded in trading within a British context, helped to accelerate the evolution of such specialist wholesale houses in London. The reverse is certainly true: London publishers' attempts to maximise their sales in Scotland, aided the consolidation of such roles in the Scottish book trade.

Potential readers, and members of the trade, needed to know what was to be published, and at what price. The single most effective medium available was the newspaper press, and there is much evidence to suggest a level of mutual dependency between advertiser and newspaper proprietor, as advertisements frequently represented a major source of profit.[5] J Cochran of the *Caledonian Mercury* was merely one of a number of proprietors who wrote to George Boyd (of Oliver & Boyd) expressing the hope that their particular newspaper would not be overlooked as a suitable medium for advertisements.[6]

The names of a publisher's wholesale agent and the publishers themselves were frequently locked together in advertisements in the same way in which they appeared on imprints, and for essentially the same reasons. However, there were exceptions. The role of wholesale agent grew in importance for Oliver & Boyd from the early 1820s, as their name started to appear with increased frequency in newspaper columns from that date, undoubtedly because John Murray had transferred his Scottish agency to Oliver & Boyd at the end of 1819 – an arrangement that was met with considerable surprise amongst the Edinburgh trade.[7] It is noticeable, however, that after only a few years as agent for Murray, Oliver & Boyd's name was frequently not recorded in advertisements in Scottish newspapers. The reason is unclear, but it may be that it became so well-known throughout the Scottish trade that Oliver & Boyd were Murray's agents, that the insertion of their name simply was unnecessary.

Normal practice was for the true publisher to have been responsible for the placement of advertisements in newspapers and magazines, but this function was sometimes delegated. In 1828 Oliver & Boyd contracted with Simpkin, Marshall of London to act as their agents, and specified that they, Oliver & Boyd, would be responsible for advertising.[8] Murray, on the other hand, was sufficiently confident of George Boyd's commercial acumen, to leave advertising in Scotland in the hands of the Edinburgh firm.[9] Similarly, William Blackwood instructed Johnston & Deas, of Dublin, to insert an advertisement for *Blackwood's Magazine* 'once in your best paper', but also to get extracts 'inserted in some of the Dublin papers and when they appear send me the papers', probably so that any complimentary review could be exploited in a subsequent advertisement.[10]

The wholesale agent was also frequently required to make sure that prospectuses were sent out to the trade. Murray expected Oliver & Boyd, as agent, to work for the privilege, sending them 600 Byron prospectuses, 1000 circulars, 100 boards, with the plea 'I beg you to be very liberal in the distribution of the prospectuses and let every bookseller have whatever number he thinks he can circulate'. And, because of the exertions Oliver & Boyd had previously made on behalf of Murray's titles in Scotland, 'the Volumes of Byrons works will be charged to you at Three & Seven Pence, Twenty Five as Twenty Four with an allowance of Ten per Cent instead of 7½'.[11] It is an arrangement which demonstrates clearly how a wholesale agent's profitability was intimately bound up with its promotion of a particular work. On occasion, agents were also expected to pass on to magazine publishers lists for insertion in a forthcoming issue.

Thus Constable to Hurst, Robinson, 'You will receive... 3500 advertisements of important Works... for... the Quarterly Review and such of the other periodicals as you may think most advantageous'.[12]

Constable appreciated the power of newspaper advertising. To Joseph Robinson (of Hurst, Robinson) he wrote, 'advertisements in the ordinary way, in newspapers, you may depend on it, always pay... advertise judiciously and you will never fail to reap the benefit'.[13] And as testimonial to his commitment, his papers contain a testy reply to an enquiry from Charles Gordon, clerk to the Highland [and Agricultural] Society, regarding that institution's published *Transactions*. Archibald Constable wrote[14]

> In reply to that part of your letter as to advertising we beg to state, that every exertion in our power shall be made to push the sale of the Volume... you must, we think, admit that we should be able to judge of the best mode of doing this, but we see no reason for incurring the charge of filing every Newspaper in which an advertisement appears, we think it an uncalled for Waste of Money...

And as a postscript:

> We think it proper to add, that were we to adopt literally your wish as to filing every advert. in which the vol. will appear – your table would have on all the Scots Newspapers, all the prominent London Papers – the Edinbr Review... Monthly Review – Monthly Mag... Gents Mag – Monthly Lity Advertiser – besides many others.

Where were advertisements to be placed? Publishers gave this much thought, and had access to information, either directly, or through advertising agents, on the circulation and coverage of newspapers throughout Britain. Advertising agents produced lists of newspapers then being published, and kept file copies of the same titles for consultation.[15]

Not unexpectedly, the textual content of any particular book was a significant influence on the geographical extent of the advertising. In the early nineteenth century, Oliver & Boyd dallied with the idea becoming literary publishers, and in 1819 started to promote *Robin Hood: a Tale of the Olden Time*. The novel was advertised in Edinburgh and the Scottish Borders, throughout northern England, and on into

Nottinghamshire, but seemingly not further south – at least not in the provincial papers.[16] Given that the legend places the supposed events in the English Midlands, Oliver & Boyd's tactics are unsurprising.

Any publishing enterprise of a serial nature imposed a practical time limit on the advertisements. It was in a publisher's interests to have largely completed the advertising of a volume in a particular series, or a journal issue, in time for the publication and announcement of a subsequent title, or number. Oliver & Boyd's papers relating to the advertising of their series, Edinburgh Cabinet Library, are sufficiently extensive to allow a number of useful insights into the mechanisms involved. The series of thirty-eight titles was published between 1830 and 1844. The programme, as originally conceived, was to publish a new volume every two months, on geographical discovery and history. Each volume – a small octavo – of $c$ 400 pages, with illustrations was priced at 5$s$.

The prospectus for the Edinburgh Cabinet Library struck a semi-apologetic tone for inflicting on the reading public yet another series, whilst simultaneously justifying its existence. It pleaded that 'the present age is honourably distinguished... by the avidity manifested for every species of useful knowledge, and by the successful efforts made to diffuse such knowledge among all classes of the community', and then, in equivocating over the usefulness of imaginative writing – 'works of fiction tend to exalt imagination and refine taste, but they may also betray the youthful mind into error, unless the impressions they make are corrected by a careful survey of the scenes and events of real existence' – it argued for the need for a series, combining amusement with instruction, on history and topography.[17] The phrase 'amusement with instruction' clearly echoes the sentiments behind the Library of Entertaining Knowledge published under the aegis of the Society for the Diffusion of Useful Knowledge, which was launched partly because of resistance to the remorselessly serious tone of that institution's Library of Useful Knowledge.

John Murray became anxious over Oliver & Boyd's series which bore some resemblance to the London firm's own Family Library. Murray approached the difficulty obliquely, and, in correspondence with George Boyd, denied – utterly disingenuously – being concerned by hints given to him that Oliver & Boyd might have had divided loyalties in not only being Scottish agent for the Family Library, but in also promoting their own series.[18] Murray might have had cause for disquiet. Competition for the 'useful-knowledge' market was intense, and publishers found themselves bringing out texts on the same subject at the same time. Patrick Tytler, historian, and a major contributor to the Edinburgh Cabinet Library, remarked in a letter to George Boyd, in which he discussed Murray's publications, 'The 2 vol of India... is to be abolished and India to be confined to the one volume already published. I suppose your India has the blood of this second vol of Gleig on its head.[19]

That works were published as part of a series was given prominence by Oliver & Boyd and other publishers in the wording of their advertisements. Drawing attention to the series title helped each constituent text appear as though part of a carefully conceived, extended programme; and, more importantly for profitability, it raised the hope that a systematic increase of knowledge of the subject domain (albeit very broad, and sometimes entirely artificial) addressed by the series, could indeed be apprehended by reading all volumes. The series title itself was not innovative, as many publishers were producing 'Library' series at the time.[20] Almost simultaneous with the launch of the Edinburgh Cabinet Library in autumn 1830, came Longman's Dr Lardner's Cabinet Library, monthly, also at 5s.

Moreover, the identification of a volume as part of a series could carry a suggestion as to the quality of the text. In 1832, the *Athenaeum* oozed over the first volume of Hugh Murray's *Historical and Descriptive Account of British India*, the sixth to appear in the Edinburgh Cabinet Library, and ended, 'the volume… is a worthy companion to those that have preceded it, and will help establish for the "Edinburgh Cabinet Library" the honourable distinction of being the best and cheapest series of volumes now publishing', and, significantly, noted that 'the publishers [Oliver & Boyd]… have no critical journal of their own, to trumpet forth their praise'.[21]

Records relating to the advertising of *The Lives and Voyages of Drake, Cavendish and Dampier*, the fifth volume of the series, published in 1831, are some of the most complete. Advertising started in October of that year, intensified in November and December, and finished in February 1832. In terms of British newspapers and magazines, the coverage was extensive, involving about 110 newspapers and magazines. The advertising stretched as far north as the *Inverness Courier*, and south to the *Plymouth Journal*.

A basic point to be made is that the wording of the advertisements (the copy text prepared by Oliver & Boyd) remained largely the same in each newspaper, though inevitably there was some typographical individuality exercised by the local press.

By 1831, Oliver & Boyd had settled into a regular (though not invariable) pattern for distributing advertisements. Richard Barker, advertising agent in Fleet Street, arranged for Oliver & Boyd's advertisements to be inserted in newspapers and magazines emanating from London,[22] Robertson & Scott, based in Edinburgh, handled the advertisements for the Scottish and English provincial papers, whilst Oliver & Boyd themselves dealt directly with the Edinburgh papers and magazines. Advertisements for the Irish press were attended to by Johnson & Co, and Curry & Co, with notices sent not only to Dublin, but also to Limerick, Cork and Waterford papers.

Oliver & Boyd's Irish agents consistently placed advertisements in those Dublin morning, evening and weekly papers with the highest circulations, suggesting that in general, another important factor in the placement of advertisements was the circulation size of any individual newspaper.[23]

It was presumably more efficient (in terms of time and accounting procedures) for Oliver & Boyd to commit their advertising, undertaken not only for their own titles, but also for those publishers for whom they acted as wholesalers in Scotland,[24] to the care of advertising agents, and pay commission, up to 5%. Not that the advertising agents lived off this margin alone, as they benefited from a discount of up to 10% on the notional price of the advertisements granted by newspaper proprietors. Publishers were also beneficiaries of increasing competition amongst the advertising agents: in 1833 Richard Barker offered to deliver Oliver & Boyd's advertisements into English provincial papers, at no commission.[25]

Merely placing advertisements was not all that was required of advertising agents. Like the wholesale agents in the publishing trade, they were sometimes paid to do a little more: in referring to the *Historical and Descriptive Account of China* (1836), Samuel Sutherland reported from London that 'I have nearly distributed the whole of the show boards of the "Edinb Cabinet", and upon going round a second time to most of the trade, find them displayed conspicuously in their windows & elsewhere'.[26]

Advertising costs could constitute a major element in overall publication costs. For the Revd Michael Russell's *Palestine* (1831), the fourth volume of the series, advertisements in London-based newspapers and magazines cost on average nearly 16*s*; in English provincial papers *c* 14*s*.; and in Scottish papers on average slightly over 9*s*. Essentially, then, the same advertisement was over 40% cheaper when placed in a Scottish newspaper – a set of facts which explains why George Boyd pored over his accounts annotating and questioning any individual amount that appeared disproportionately high. The cost of advertising *The Lives and Voyages of Drake, Cavendish and Dampier* was about £100, with expenditure on English and Scottish newspapers and magazines almost exactly equally split – *c* 46% each, with the remainder spent on the Irish press. However, it should be borne in mind that advertising became cheaper in 1833, as advertisement tax was lowered from a painful 3*s*.6*d* per advertisement to 1*s*.6*d*, though final repeal arrived only in 1853. Although advertising in itself became cheaper, Oliver & Boyd's records suggest no corresponding increase in advertising activity – at least within the newspaper press. The company was, however, part of a trade that witnessed, particularly from the late 1830s, the production of an increasing variety of magazines and periodicals, many of which offered advertising opportunities additional to those of the newspaper press.

John Boyd (junior) was sent to London to learn the trade, and, whilst acting as a proof reader with Spottiswoode,[27] was asked in 1840 to make an assessment for the benefit of his uncle, George, of the magazine market as vehicles for advertising. Respectability was (as might have been expected) the quality sought above all others, and secondarily a judgement was made as to how good a medium the magazine was. The *Gentleman's Magazine* (circulation given by Boyd as 1500 copies) was praised as 'highly respectable – good for miscellaneous [advertisements] only', whilst the readership of the *Evangelical Magazine* (15 750 copies) was described as aimed at the 'middle classes, &c. – good for miscellaneous'. The *Baptist Magazine* (4500 copies) was both very respectable and 'good for... school books'. However, John Boyd was less than effusive about the monthly parts of *Master Humphrey's Clock*, which, in spite of an estimated circulation of 20 000 copies, was described as appealing to 'various classes' and a 'very indifferent medium'.[28] In some contrast to newspapers, the circulation size of any particular magazine or serial was evidently insufficient to persuade Oliver & Boyd to place notices in it; its respectability, and its reputation and performance as a vehicle for advertisements were also relevant considerations.

Evidence suggests that the level of advertising adopted contributed towards the success of the Cabinet Library, as many titles therein went to third or fourth editions in runs of *c* 3000 copies. This financial commitment to promoting the Library was relatively high, as calculations based on production and associated costs for early volumes in the series, suggest that advertising was the second largest element of expenditure after paper.[29]

Newspaper and magazine advertising constituted only one, albeit central, operation in the marketing of books. From the early nineteenth century, publishers and wholesale agents had employed travellers to solicit orders from booksellers throughout the country. Recent research has shown that Oliver & Boyd had at least one traveller representing their interests in the Midlands and northern England from as early as 1811.[30] The market in Ireland was sufficiently important for Oliver & Boyd to arrange trade visits to Dublin, and in 1831 the firm received a lengthy report on the assiduousness of the wholesalers in promoting the Cabinet Library and other titles. Curry & Co came in for some criticism, as their stock on hand of Oliver & Boyd titles had, over the previous six months, actually increased. Consequently, an element of greater competition was suggested, 'Johnston has promised to get reviews in all the country papers... He says his influence in town [ie Dublin] is also strong, but he feels a little at not having the town advertising I do not know but our best way will be to let him have the whole in future, which will enable us to judge of what he can do'.[31]

Criticism of book reviews with only the thinnest veneer of objectivity was widespread. The authors of Oliver & Boyd's Cabinet Library were entirely typical in that they prepared reviews for, and composed suitable quotations to accompany, other volumes in that series. But the proprietorship of a literary review or magazine, was, if not *de rigueur*, then at least highly desirable. Oliver & Boyd never launched their own literary serial, though in 1846, they were presented with an opportunity to do just that. William Tait, Edinburgh publisher, wrote to Thomas Boyd[32]

> It is my purpose to retire from business in the course of next year, after 30 years nearly devotion to it.
>
> I delay my announcement from a wish to dispose privately of Tait's Edinburgh Magazine.
>
> It has been offered to one person only, a London gentleman, who has declined to give the sum asked, thinking an Edin. Magazine not transplantable, as he says... A Monthly Review would suit your House well. It affords a regular & large amount of printing; pays all its expenses and more; is a valuable medium for Reviews and Advertisements for your books; and is capable of great improvement and extension, in a New Series.

Oliver & Boyd refused the offer, for reasons as yet unclear, but which may be related to the company's inclination at the time to move towards more educational publishing. One of the more unexpected features of the advertising of books, is the speed with which advertising agent and publisher came together. Advertising agencies did not exist as business entities until the end of the eighteenth century, and as such constituted a relatively recent commercial phenomenon.

Oliver & Boyd – and there is no reason to assume that other publishers behaved differently – quickly embraced the services provided by advertising agents, with their contacts with the newspaper and magazine press. Oliver & Boyd began to deal with Newton & Co (a London advertising agency) as early as 1820, and that same year the Edinburgh firm was transacting business with Johnston & Co, general advertising and newspaper agency office, Dublin. One year earlier (1819) the newspaper agency of Robertson & Scott had started in Edinburgh, offering to give the commercial sector opportunities to advertise 'in every newspaper in the united kingdom';[33] and by the early 1830s Oliver & Boyd had opened an account with them. As publishers who were in business to sell throughout Britain and Ireland they, and those in commerce with them, were not prepared to ignore a more efficient way of furthering this aim. The book as commodity had indisputedly arrived.

## ACKNOWLEDGEMENTS

To the Scottish Centre for the Book, Napier University, for a MacCaig Visiting Fellowship, allowing opportunity to work on the Oliver & Boyd papers; to the Carnegie Trust for the Universities of Scotland, and to the Bibliographical Society for research grants; to the Librarian, Aberdeen University, for study leave; to Pearson Education Ltd for permission to quote from the Oliver & Boyd papers; and to the National Library of Scotland for permission to quote from material in their charge.

## NOTES

The Oliver & Boyd papers, deposited in the National Library of Scotland [hereafter NLS], are cited throughout as Acc 5000.

1. Eg John Feather, *A History of British Publishing* (London: Croom Helm, 1988), 122.

2. James Thin, *Reminiscences of Booksellers and Bookselling in Edinburgh in the Time of William IV* (Edinburgh: printed by Oliver & Boyd, 1905), 14. For an overview, see June B Cummings, *A History of Oliver & Boyd, 1778–1973* (Oxford: Oxford Polytechnic, 1973).

3. Quoted in Richard Altick, *The English Common Reader* (Chicago: University of Chicago Press, 1957; reprinted 1963), 383.

4. Cadell to Lockhart, 30 September 1832, NLS MS 21011, f.35, quoted by Jane Millgate, *Scott's Last Edition: a Study in Publishing History* (Edinburgh: Edinburgh University Press, 1987), 126.

5. Ivon Asquith, 'Advertising and the press in the late eighteenth and early nineteenth centuries: James Perry and the *Morning Chronicle*, 1790–1821', *Historical Journal*, 18 (1975), 704. Oliver & Boyd's announcements to the trade were primarily (though not exclusively) effected through *Bent's Literary Advertiser* and the *Publishers' Circular*. By late 1843 Oliver & Boyd had abandoned the former in favour of the latter.

6. Letter, Cochran to George Boyd, 27 April 1831. Acc 5000/196.

7. Fairbairn & Anderson had expected the agency. Letter, William Blackwood to Cadell & Davies, 12 January 1820. NLS MS 30002.

8. Letter-book: copies of letters of agreement, December 1828. Acc 5000/140, 252 *et seq.*

9. Letter, Murray to George Boyd, 7 December 1831. Acc 5000/196.

10. Letter, 26 March 1819. NLS MS 30301, 74–5.

11. Letter, Murray to George Boyd, 7 December 1831. Acc 5000/196. A 10% allowance was normal. See letters of agency agreement, Oliver & Boyd to Simpkin, Marshall, 'All works published by us on our own account to be sent to you on Commission... a Discount of 10 per cent from sale price to be allowed you on the Sales you effect – You always taking care to keep in stock a sufficient supply for the demand'. Acc 5000/140, 252 *et seq.* Similarly, standard agreements of Longman (1838), and Whittaker & Co (before 1828), which latter notes, 'MESSRS WHITTAKER & Co. cannot receive any Work but as the sole London publishers; and their imprint alone must appear as such on the title page'. Acc 5000/140, pasted to front endpaper.

12. Letters, 16 & 19 February 1823. Constable correspondence. NLS MS 792, 50–1, 55–6.

13. Thomas Constable, *Archibald Constable and his Literary Correspondents*, 3 vols (Edinburgh: Edmonston & Douglas, 1873), III, 341.

14. Letter of 14 July 1824. NLS MS 792, 309–10.

15. List of David Robertson, probably 1820s. Acc 5000/1109.

16. Acc 5000/51. Depending on the title, the British Isles was not always the limit of Oliver & Boyd's perceived market. Hugh Murray's *Historical... Account of British India*, and his *Account of China* were both advertised in the (London-published) *Indian Mail*.

17. Twelve-page printed prospectus, 1830, in Acc 5000/1423.

18. Letter, 18 February 1834. Acc 5000/197.

19. Letter, 12 September 1832. Acc 5000/196. G R Gleig's *History of India* was being published in Murray's Family Library at the same time as Hugh Murray's *Historical... Account of British India*, in the Edinburgh Cabinet Library.

20. Altick, *Common Reader*, 274. The incorporation of 'Library' into a series title has a long history. See Roger Chartier, *The Order of Books... * (Cambridge: Polity Press, 1994), 66–8.

21. *Athenaeum*, 26 May 1832, 329.

22. Simpkin, Marshall occasionally placed advertisements on Oliver & Boyd's behalf in the London literary magazines.

23. 'The provincial newspaper press', *Westminster Review* (January 1830), 87, estimated the cumulative circulation of Dublin's four daily morning papers at 2500 copies.

24. This explains the presence of Murray's titles in advertising accounts sent to Oliver & Boyd.

25. Account dated December 1832. Acc 5000/51.

26. Letter of 14 May 1836. Acc 5000/53.

27. The post was obtained after advice from John Dickinson, paper manufacturer, who had close business and personal contacts with Oliver & Boyd. Letter, John Boyd to George Boyd, 6 July 1838. Acc 5000/199.

28. Letter, 18 July 1840. Acc 5000/200.

29. A composite picture can be built up for some of the the earlier volumes in the series. First edition runs were for *c* 5000 copies. Production, paper and associated costs ran at *c* £380 (of which *c* £200 was expended on paper). Copyright was bought outright at £80–100. Cost book. Acc 5000/22.

30. Bill Bell, '"Pioneers of Literature": the commercial traveller in the early nineteenth century', in *The Reach of Print: Making, Selling and Using Books*, [ed] Peter Isaac & Barry McKay (Winchester: St Paul's Bibliographies; New Castle, DE: Oak Knoll Press, 1998), 121.

31. Letter, 26 September 1831, George Thornton to George Boyd. Acc 5000/196.

32. Letter, 7 October 1846. Acc 5000/203.

33. For Robertson & Scott, see David S Dunbar, 'The agency commission system in Britain'..., *Journal of Advertising History*, 2 (1979), 20.

# The Coming of Print to York, c 1490-1550

## STACEY GEE

CAN WE PUT a date to the advent of print in York? An easy answer might be 1509, the year in which Hugo Goes published the first known book with a York imprint, the *Directorium Sacerdotum*.[1] Another possible date is 1493, when John Hamman or Hertzog printed the earliest surviving edition of a service book of York use.[2] It is likely, however, that the inhabitants of York and the city's hinterland had heard of, and had probably come into contact with productions of the new technology of print a number of years before 1493. An indication of the number of printed books imported into the city on a commercial basis or acquired by individual readers is occasionally available, but how do we, or even can we, interpret these figures in order to assess the impact of print on the book trade of York? When did the scribes first realize the threat of print to their business? Was it after fifty, a hundred or a thousand books had been brought into or produced in the city? In this paper I shall attempt to discover how immediate and how dramatic were the consequences of print for the scribes of York.

In order to assess the impact of print on the York book trade a brief overview of the trade in printed books and the early printing industry in York will be given. Through an analysis of the freemen's register of York and other prosopographical details, an investigation will then be made of the manuscript copyists in the late fifteenth and early sixteenth centuries and how they might have been affected by the advent of print. The book artisans of York, like those of most other European cities, are not known to have directly protested against the use of printing technology, unlike, for example, the London stationer, Philip Wrenne, who complained in around 1487 that 'the occupation ys almost destroyed by prynters of bokes'.[3] Yet the lack of evidence of protest does not mean that the scribes meekly accepted the loss of their business for the sake of technological progress. The attempts of the producers of manuscript books to safeguard their livelihoods as revealed through their guild ordinances will be discussed.

It is likely that print first came to York in the form of woodcut pictures. Sheets of paper decorated with woodcut designs had been imported into Hull since the late fifteenth century. Important uses of the paper would have been as wall-paper or material for binding books.[4] In 1471-2, for example, Maynard Clauson brought a cargo of 120 painted papers into Hull.[5] In 1493, as we have already seen, the first service book of York use, a breviary, was produced in Venice. In the first decade of the sixteenth century, printed books began to be mentioned in Yorkshire wills and probate inventories in significant numbers. These included not only the wealthy and powerful ecclesiastics such as Martin Collins, treasurer of York Minster, who left at least fifty-three printed books at his death in 1508, but also some of the more humble clergy and laity.[6] An example is John Fell, a chantry priest of the Minster, who bequeathed 'a boyk in prynt with a blak coveryng' in 1506, and Jane Harper, the widow of a York merchant, who mentioned a printed massbook in her will dated 1512.[7]

An indication of the size of the trade in printed books by the early part of the sixteenth century is revealed by the large number of books imported into York by the stationer Gerard Freez or Wanseford. At Wanseford's death in 1510, a court case arose over his importation of 252 missals, 399 breviaries and 570 picas from France.[8] During this period, the trade in printed sheets also continued to grow. Painted papers, for example, were imported to Hull in 1511 by Clemence le Countay and in the next year by Harman Johnson, both times aboard ships from Dieppe.[9] London and Continental printers such as Pierre Violette, François Regnault, Richard Pynson and Wynkyn de Worde were also active in producing liturgical texts for the York market, sometimes in partnership with York stationers.[10] The most well-documented York stationer who financed the production of texts abroad, aimed at the York market, was John Gachet. At least six editions of service books were printed in Rouen and Paris and then sent to Gachet for sale in the city.[11] The surviving customs accounts of Hull record the importation of printed books by Gachet between 1517 and 1526.[12] Another York stationer, Neville Mores, is also known to have imported books through the port at Hull. Mores's probate inventory, made at his death in 1538, lists the 126 books in his shop at that time, valued at £3.3s.10d.[13] It is likely that this list of books is only a small indication of Mores's business as, on 5 August 1520, Mores is known to have paid customs dues on a cargo of printed books worth a higher value of £4.13s.4d.[14] Printed books were likewise imported through Hull by John Welles aboard the *Bonaventure* of Dieppe on 16 August 1526.[15] Welles can probably be identified as the same John Welles who became free as a bookbinder in York in 1519.[16]

It is possible that the first press in York was operated by Frederick Freez, the brother of the already mentioned Gerard Freez or Wanseford, and who became free of the city as a bookbinder and stationer in 1497.[17] In 1510, during the proceedings of the court case over the goods of Gerard Wanseford he was described as a 'buke prynter'.[18] Unfortunately none of his productions have survived. Probably at the same time as Freez was printing, a press was also operated at York by Hugo Goes. Goes is known to have printed three texts in York, but only copies of his 1509 edition of the *Directorium Sacerdotum* have survived.[19] Two grammar books printed by

Goes, a *Donatus* and *Accidence*, have been described by Christopher Hildyard in the seventeenth century but these texts are not known to have survived to the present day.[20]

Another press was operated in York from around 1513 by Ursyn Milner. In that year, Milner produced a supplement to the York breviary called the *Officia Nova*.[21] Another product of his press, a *Festum Visitacionis Beate Marie Virginis*, has been described by Joseph Ames, but there are no surviving copies.[22] The colophon of the *Festum* has also been found on two folio sheets used as endleaves to a printed copy of Joannes Gaufredus, held in Hereford Cathedral Library.[23] The colophons can be differentiated by minor variations in spelling, which suggest that the waste sheets had been used as proofs. The *Festum* was probably produced soon after 1513 when the feast was established by statute at York.[24] In 1516 Milner printed an edition of the grammar of Whittinton, of which only one copy has survived.[25]

The last known sixteenth-century York printer was John Warwick, who became free of the city in 1531.[26] In 1532 Warwick produced an edition of the grammar of John Stanbridge.[27] Warwick's probate inventory, made in 1542, itemizes the contents of his 'printing chamber'.[28] Inside the room was stored 'the prysse with iij maner of letters with brasse letters iij matteresses with all other thinges concernynge the prynthinge with glasse', valued at £8.5s. A stock of books, worth £22.10s.10d, is also mentioned.

We might expect the scribes to have viewed the coming of printed books and printing technology with dread and fear as the market for books in York was filled with cheap texts printed on paper. During the fifteenth century, there are indications that the craft of writing was becoming more professional. Not only were there increasing numbers of scribes obtaining the franchise, but also, more terms were being used to describe their trade. From the early fourteenth century, the York scribes were known as either 'clericus' or 'scriptor' in Latin, or 'clerk' and 'scrivener' in English. In 1419 the term 'writer' is first recorded in York to describe the trade of a new freeman, Thomas Lymber.[29] Other new freemen also used this term in 1452, 1456 and 1470.[30] In 1473 Richard Couke appears in the freemen's register as York's first 'textwriter'.[31] He was followed, in 1479, by the textwriters Thomas Lemyng and Henry Archer, and by William Sted and John Markynfeld in the early 1480s.[32] During this period, the number of scriveners who became free of the city also continued to rise. They included Thomas Benyt in 1478, John Calton in 1480 and Richard Riplyngham in 1484.[33]

The words 'writer', 'textwriter' and 'scrivener' may have been deliberately chosen to distinguish different areas of expertise. Evidence of the activities of the scriveners of York, for example, relates only to the production or authentication of administrative and legal documents. The scrivener Adam Gunby, for example, was paid 6*d* by the city chamberlains in 1449–50 for writing diverse bills concerning the justices of the peace of the city.[34] He also frequently appears as a witness to legal documents between 1446 and 1476.[35] In 1446 and 1475 he was appointed as an attorney.[36] John Wodd, who became free as a scrivener in 1486, is likewise known to have often written out the last wishes of testators.[37]

The textwriters or writers, in contrast, are likely to have specialized to a greater extent in the production of books. In 1487 the textwriters formed a guild with the other book crafts of the limners, noters, turnours and flourishers.[38] The ordinances of the guild refer specifically to the production of books. If a foreigner (that is, a person who was not a member of the franchise) wanted to sell books in the city, he was ordered to contribute to the upkeep of the guild's pageant in the Corpus Christi play. Evidence of a textwriter producing a book can be seen in York Minster Library MS Additional 30, a fifteenth-century missal of York use. The volume was produced by at least seven different hands. One of the scribes can be identified as Thomas Lemyng, a textwriter, who inscribed in the bottom margin of folio 132$^r$: 'Thomas Lemyng dwellyng in Yorke'.[39]

This theory that a distinction was made between the scriveners and textwriters is supported by a comparison with earlier developments in the London book trade. During the late fourteenth and fifteenth centuries, a specialist trade in writing books was developing in London. In 1357 the mayor and aldermen of London issued an ordinance which exempted the limners, barbers and scribes who wrote either court letter or text letter from serving on sheriffs' inquests. The distinction made between writers of court and of text letter is instructive: by the middle of the fourteenth century a contrast was being made in London between the scribes who wrote and witnessed wills and other legal deeds and those who produced books. A guild of the writers of court letter was formed in 1373 and in 1403 an amalgamated mistery of textwriters, illuminators and those who bound and sold books was formed. The formation of separate misteries emphasized the distinction between the two types of scribal activity. In other types of record, the separation of scribes into scriveners and textwriters took a while longer to come into general use. Yet, increasingly through the fifteenth century in London the term scrivener came to refer only to legal writers.[40]

With the advent of print, there would still have been a continuing need for the services of book scribes to write texts which had not yet been printed, or were not available in print locally. Manuscript books of music, for example, continued to be made throughout the first half of the sixteenth century. William Prince, a priest of York, was paid by the church of Louth to write song books in 1510 to 1513.[41] The fabric rolls of York Minster likewise include expenses to John Gibbons in 1518–19 for copying a number of hymnals.[42] In 1526, the church of St Michael, Spurriergate, paid a friar to write a sequence and later three mass books in 1536.[43]

Yet despite this demand for manuscript music books, it is clear that the printing of service books and grammar texts within the city of York, and the import of a wide range of other printed texts, particularly legal works, clerical manuals and vernacular books, seriously affected the trade of the scribes. The term textwriter quickly declined in York in the early sixteenth century. Fifteen textwriters became free in the period 1450–1499, compared with only two freemen between 1500 and 1549 and only one in the second half of the sixteenth century. A likely explanation for this trend is that a fall in the demand for manuscript books deterred new entrants to the craft of textwriting. Furthermore, some of the textwriters in the city seem to have decided to change their trade to scrivening. Henry Archer, for example, had became free as a textwriter in 1479.[44] But in his will, proved in 1520, he described himself as a scrivener.[45] Likewise, in 1483, John Markynfeld obtained the city's freedom as a textwriter, yet when he witnessed the will of Ninian Markenfeld, a knight, in 1528, he was called a scrivener.[46] Richard Middleton, who had become free as a textwriter in 1512, appears in a register of bonds as a scrivener in 1532.[47]

The craft of the scrivener continued to attract new freemen throughout the first three-quarters of the sixteenth century, which suggests that their trade was not greatly threatened by the advent of print. During the second half of the fifteenth century eleven scriveners became free of the city of York and a further ten in the first half of the sixteenth century. Demand for the copying and authenticating of wills, deeds, letters and other legal and administrative records continued. Nevertheless, there is evidence that the scribes' production of indulgences began to be usurped by the presses during the early sixteenth century. The York printer Ursyn Milner produced an indulgence for the York guild of St Christopher and St George in 1519, and an indulgence for the confraternity of St Mary of Mount Carmel in York was printed in around 1520 by Richard Pynson.[48] In 1527, widow Warwick was paid 10*s* in the city chamberlains' accounts for 'pryntyng of a thowsand breyffes'.[49] This printed brief can also be identified as an indulgence, as in the same year, 1527, the civic authorities were granted the right to issue an indulgence to raise funds for rebuilding the Ouse Bridge.[50] The production of a large number of indulgences was necessary, as they were intended for sale not just in York and its hinterland, but elsewhere in England. The register of Charles Booth, bishop of Hereford, refers to a licence to collect alms granted for the repair of the four bridges over the Ouse and Foss on 10 December 1527.[51] A commission by the mayor of York, dated 30 April 1528, appointed two citizens as messengers to collect gifts in the dioceses of Lincoln, Norwich and Ely for the bridges.[52] In 1530, indulgences were being sold to inhabitants of southwest

England by representatives of a York guild.[53] The advantage of printing technology for producing indulgences may also have been capitalized on by the Dean and Chapter of York Minster, who had made payments for the writing of indulgences during the fifteenth century. In 1469–70, for example, 17s.14d was paid for the writing of 312 indulgences.[54] The production of books was therefore not the only type of scribal activity that was affected by the new technology of print. The printing of indulgences in the early sixteenth century represents a significant loss of work and revenue for the scribes.

The freemen's register of York thus gives an indication of some of the changes in the book trade after the advent of print. Many of these changes can be dated to around the first decade of the sixteenth century, at approximately the same time as the first presses in the city were set up by Freez and Goes and as printed books begin to appear in wills and probate inventories. What the freemen's register does not give us, however, is an indication of how the scribes reacted to the threat of the new technology and how they might have tried to safeguard their livelihoods. In the final part of this paper I would like to put forward a suggestion that we can see a reaction against print at least twenty years before the establishment of the first York press. This reaction can be seen in the formation of the already mentioned textwriters' guild in 1487.

As we have seen, the ordinances of the textwriters' guild show a notable concern with the production of books. This preoccupation is absent from the previous ordinances of the guild of scribes called 'escriveners de tixt', which were registered in the early fifteenth century.[55] The late fifteenth-century ordinances reveal an anxiety about the production of books by unofficial part-time scribes and the consequent attempts of the guild members to establish a monopoly for themselves. This is shown in the guild's dispute with a chaplain, William Incecliff. In 148[6]/7 Incecliff was fined 8s for writing books without the freedom of the craft.[56] The tensions that this produced were revealed in 1487 when the textwriters Henry Archer, Thomas Lemyng and John Markyngton on one side and Incecliff on the other side were compelled to swear that they would do no bodily harm to each other.[57] An arbitration between the two parties decided that Incecliff should be allowed to finish the two books he was making, one of which was for his own use and the other for his chantry in the chapel of Foss Bridge.[58] He was also allowed to keep an apprentice and sell any books that the two of them made as long as it was for the upkeep of the apprentice and not for his own profit. Nevertheless, despite the settlement with Incecliff, the conflict continued. Revised regulations[59] of the guild of textwriters were presented to the civic authorities in 149[1]/2. The main changes concerned the fines, indicating that the guild was experiencing difficulties in asserting its authority. The fee for non-enfranchisement was raised from 3s.4d to 13s.4d; the fee to set up a business was doubled; the fine on aliens was raised from 20s to 40s; and, perhaps most interestingly, the fine on priests who wrote books without the freedom of the craft was increased from 13s.4d to 40s. It was agreed that no priest with a salary of seven marks or above would be allowed to exercise the craft or to take an apprentice.[60] In the conclusion of the dispute with Incecliff, he was allowed to finish the books he was writing, but he could not take an apprentice and henceforth he and other priests were only permitted to produce texts 'to ther awn proper use or to giffe in almose and charitie'.[61]

The production of books by part-time unofficial scribes such as Incecliff was not new in the late fifteenth century. Robert Wolveden, treasurer of York Minster, for example, bequeathed a book in 1432 which had been written by a notary public, John Arston.[62] In 1443/4 a priest was employed by the mercers' guild of York to rule lines onto sixteen pieces of parchment to make a register book.[63] A Dominican friar, John Roose, was also paid for sheets of organ music by the Dean and Chapter of York Minster in 1458 and 1469.[64] Why then did the textwriters begin to fight against the part-time production of books in 1487?

The anxiety with book production in the textwriters' ordinances suggests that the writing of books was becoming an increasingly important issue in the fifteenth century. The regulations can be related to a certain extent to a growing market for books during this period, which meant that the production of books formed a more important part of the scribes' work. A concern with the trade in books might also have been caused by the advent of print. The scribes would have heard reports of the new technology from travellers and small stocks of books might have reached the city by this date. Although as we have seen, the first known service book of York use was not published until 1493, printed books of Sarum use were produced from around 1475 and could be used without great difficulty.[65] It is possible therefore that the anxieties of the scribes were a response to the new technology of print. By 1487 the number of printed books brought into the city might already have been large enough for the professional scribes to suffer from a loss of business and they responded by attempting to gain a monopoly of the manuscript trade for themselves. Thus the ordinances seem to suggest that print was already a looming threat or menacing presence in York by the late 1480s, only a decade after Caxton produced his first book in Westminster. The history of the coming of print to York therefore does not start with the printing of the first service book of York use in 1493, or the establishment of the first York press, or the mention of printed books in Yorkshire wills, but with the self-protecting activities of the scribes in the late 1480s.

NOTES

1. *A Short-Title Catalogue of Books Printed in England, Scotland and Ireland and of English Books Printed Abroad*, [ed]. Alfred William Pollard & Gilbert Richard Redgrave, 2nd edn, revised by W A Jackson, F S Ferguson & Katharine F Pantzer (London: The Bibliographical Society, 1976–91), 16232.4 [hereafter STC].

2. STC 15856.

3. C Paul Christianson, *A Directory of London Stationers and Book Artisans 1300–1500* (New York: Bibliographical Society of America, 1990), 44n.

4. Wendy Childs [ed], *The Customs Accounts of Hull 1453–1490*, Yorkshire Archaeological Society Record Series, 144 (Leeds: Yorkshire Archaeological Society, 1984), 244; Nicholas Pickwoad, 'Onward and downward: how binders coped with the printing press before 1800', in *A Millennium of the Book*, [ed] Robin Myers & Michael Harris (Winchester: St Paul's Bibliographies; New Castle, DE: Oak Knoll Press, 1994), 61–106.

5. Childs, *Customs Accounts*, 163.

6. York Minster Library, L1(17)18.

7. York Minster Library, Dean and Chapter probate register, vol 2, fol $56^r$–$57^r$; York, Borthwick Institute of Historical Research [hereafter BIHR], probate register, vol 8, fol $98^v$–$99^r$.

8. York Minster Library, Pi (i) vii; E Brunskill, 'Missals, portifers and pyes', *The Ben Johnson Papers*, 2 (1974), 20–33.

9. Public Record Office [hereafter PRO], E 122/60/3, fol $4^v$; E 122/64/2, fol $21^r$.

10. A list of the York service books printed in the late fifteenth and early sixteenth centuries has been compiled by Gordon Duff, 'The printers, stationers and bookbinders of York up to 1600', *Transactions of the Bibliographical Society*, 5 (1899), 87–107 (107), and revised by William K Sessions, *Les Deux Pierres: Rouen, Edinburgh, York* (York: Sessions, 1982), 24.

11. STC 15858, 16135, 16221, 16223, 16250.5, 16251.

12 PRO, E 122/202/4, fol $18^r$; E 122/64/5, fol $3^r$, E 122/202/5, fol $4^r$.

13. BIHR, Dean and Chapter original wills, 1538; D M Palliser & D G Selwyn, 'The stock of a York stationer, 1538', *The Library*, 5th ser, 27 (1972), 207–19.

14. PRO, E 122/64/5, fol $21^v$.

15. PRO, E 122/202/5, fol $27^v$.

16. Francis Collins [ed], *Register of the Freemen of the City of York I: 1272–1558*, Surtees Society, 96 (Durham: Andrews, 1897), 241.

17. Collins, *Register*, 221.

18. York Minster Library, Pi (i) vii (8); Brunskill, 'Missals', 22.

19. STC 16232.4; Cambridge, Sidney Sussex College, Bb.5.17 and York Minster Library, XI.N.31.

20. British Library [hereafter BL], Harley 6115, 6.

21. STC 15861; Cambridge, Emmanuel College, 4.4.21.

22. Joseph Ames, *Typographical Antiquities* (London: Faden, 1749), 468.

23. STC 15861.3; Paul Morgan, 'Early printing and binding in York: some new facts', *The Book Collector*, 30 (1981), 216–24.

24. R W Pfaff, *New Liturgical Feasts in Later Medieval England* (Oxford: Oxford University Press, 1970), 59–60.

25. STC 25542; BL, 68.B.21.

26. Collins, *Register*, 250.

27. STC 23151; BL, C.70.bb.18.

28. BIHR, Dean and Chapter original wills, 1542.

29. Collins, *Register*, 128.

30. Collins, *Register*, 172 (Welles), 175 (Jameson), 190 (Letheley).

31. Collins, *Register*, 193.

32. Collins, *Register*, 200–1, 204, 206.

33. Collins, *Register*, 199, 201, 207.

34. York City Archives, C3:2; R B Dobson [ed], *York City Chamberlains' Account Rolls 1396–1500*, Surtees Society, 192 (Durham: Andrews, 1980), 67.

35. York City Archives, E20 (A/Y Memorandum Book), fol 309$^v$; E20A (B/Y Memorandum Book), fol 85$^r$, 96$^v$, 138$^v$, 156$^v$.

36. York City Archives, E20A, fol 132$^r$, 133$^r$, 137$^r$.

37. Wodd is named as the scribe in York, BIHR, Probate Register, vol 5, fol 402$^r$, 418$^v$, 472$^v$, 473$^v$ and also appears as a witness to thirteen wills, fol 378$^v$–481$^v$.

38. York City Archives, E20A, fol 149$^r$–150$^r$. The meaning of 'turnour' is ambiguous, referring in general to those who turn or fashion things, or, from the fourteenth century, a translator, and a 'noter' is a writer of musical scores: Robert E Lewis, *Middle English Dictionary* (Ann Arbor, 1956–1993), VI, 1098, XII, 1182.

39. A mid-fifteenth century date has been suggested for MS Additional 30, but as Lemyng became free of the city of York in 1479, it is more likely that it was written in the last quarter of the century. N R Ker & A J Piper, *Medieval Manuscripts in British Libraries* (Oxford: Oxford University Press, 1969–92), 4: 800; Collins, *Register*, 201.

40. Christianson, *London Stationers*, 22–3.

41. Reginald C Dudding [ed], *The First Churchwardens' Book of Louth 1500–1524*, (Oxford: Oxford University Press, 1941), 131, 148.

42. York Minster Library, E3/38.

43. BIHR, PR Y/MS/4, fol 61$^r$, 125$^v$; Dudding, *Churchwardens' Accounts*, I, 166, 179.

44. Collins, *Register*, 200.

45. BIHR, Probate Register, vol 9, fol 96$^v$–97$^r$.

46. Collins, *Register*, 206; BIHR, Probate Register, vol 9, fol 407$^r$–408$^r$.

47. Collins, *Register*, 235; York City Archives, F86, fol 17$^v$.

48. STC 14077c.84, 14077c.84A.

49. York City Archives, CC3, fol 188$^v$. I owe many thanks to Jennifer Kaner for this reference.

50. BIHR, Archbishop's Register, vol 27, fol 131$^r$.

51. Arthur Thomas Bannister [ed], *Registrum Caroli Bothe, Episcopi Herefordensis*, Canterbury and York Society, 28 (London: Canterbury and York Society, 1921), 358.

52. York City Archives, G24A.

53. Robert Whiting, *The Blind Devotion of the People: Popular Religion and the English Reformation* (Cambridge: Cambridge University Press, 1989), 113.

54. York Minster Library, E3/24.

55. York City Archives, E20, fol 21$^r$.

56. York City Archives, C4:1; Dobson, *Chamberlains' Account Rolls*, 178.

57. York City Archives, B6, fol 71$^r$.

58. York City Archives, B6, fol 150$^r$-150$^v$.

59. York City Archives, B6, fol 161$^r$.

60. Seven marks was the average annual wage of a chantry priest during the late fourteenth and early fifteenth centuries: Jenny Kermode, *Medieval Merchants: York, Beverley and Hull in the Later Middle Ages* (Cambridge: Cambridge University Press, 1998), 128.

61. York City Archives, E20A, fol 162$^v$-3$^r$.

62. York Minster Library, Dean & Chapter probate register, vol 1, fol 235$^r$-6$^r$.

63. York, Merchant Adventurers' Hall, Mercers' Guild draft account book 1443-5.

64. York Minster Library, E3/23, E3/24.

65. An example which illustrates the use of Sarum books in the diocese of York is the bequest of James Bathley, a chantry priest of Newark in 1517/8: 'also I gif and bequeth to the church of Hokerton ... a portouse of York use with an other of Salesbury use in prynt'; BIHR, Archbishop's Register, vol 27, fol 145$^r$.

# Sturdy Rogues and Vagabonds:
## Restoration Control of Pedlars and Hawkers

### MAUREEN BELL

A S WORK PROCEEDS on *The Chronology and Calendar of Documents Relating to the London Book Trade 1641–1700* a preliminary narrative history of the book trade in the second half of the seventeenth century is beginning to take shape.[1] Given the nature of the sources assembled, it offers a necessarily London-centred view of events and activities in the provinces, as seen from the perspective of the Stationers' Company, the King and Parliament, and the Secretaries of State.

A prominent feature of the Restoration period, judging by the material so far collected, was an anxiety about hawkers, pedlars and chapmen which gained momentum in the 1670s and 1680s. Anyone wishing to know about pedlars and chapman will turn immediately to Margaret Spufford's excellent studies of the subject in her *Small Books and Pleasant Histories* and *The Great Reclothing of Rural England.*[2] She has collected a great deal of evidence, much of it from local records, wills and inventories, and offers a vast amount of material about the petty chapman, his wares, his relative wealth, and his movement across the countryside and between town and country. In *The Great Reclothing* she summarizes the attempts at regulating and licensing the growing thousands of pedlars and chapmen; and in referring to the repeated attempts at Restoration legislation she suggests that

> The amount of parliamentary time spent on hawkers and pedlars after 1675, and [the] evidence that large sums of money were being raised to promote legislation against them is the most potent evidence that they were growing greatly in importance.[3]

The case she makes for the social and economic importance of pedlars and chapmen is surely unassailable, and it supports in its details the broad framework for the development of peddling in Europe conceptualized by Laurence Fontaine.[4] But I would like to set the parliamentary concern with pedlars and chapmen in a slightly different context, and to look at the preoccupation with regulating pedlars in the specific context provided by the *Chronology and Calendar*: that is to say, in the particular context of the London book trade, the Stationers' Company and governmental concern with the spread in the provinces of certain kinds of printed (and sometimes manuscript) writing.

A rising panic about hawkers and pedlars is observable in the *Chronology and Calendar* documents during the 1680s. From July 1683 to the summer of the following year the Secretaries of State received reports about an influx of 'Scotch pedlars'.

From York came a report that there were more 'Scotch pedlars' than usual, flocking to places remarkable for faction, selling 'godly bukes, as they called them'.[5] Orders against them were passed at Doncaster and Pontefract (1683) and at the Middlesex quarter sessions early the following year.[6] A report from Sotterley says that from mid-February to the beginning of May 1683 there were nearly forty 'Scotch pedlars' in Suffolk and Norfolk, with horses rather than packs.[7] They were prosecuted as vagrants. Scotsmen in London and Westminster petitioned for recognition, but the order that they were punishable by statute as rogues, vagabonds and sturdy beggars was reaffirmed by the Justices of Middlesex.[8]

The Stationers' Company joined in this general clamour for the suppression of hawkers but was interested principally in the situation as it affected their London trade.[9] An increased preoccupation with hawkers in London is apparent from the Stationers' Company Court Books when in June 1684 the Court ordered that an application be made 'to my Lord chiefe Justice or some other person in Authority for the subpressing all Hawkers'.[10] The Stationers' Company perspective was, unsurprisingly, conditioned by its own anxieties about maintaining its monopoly on selling books and pamphlets. In the *quo warranto* crisis of March and April 1684, when the Company had to surrender its Charter and negotiate a new one, the Stationers were presumably desperate both to please the King and to enforce the new Charter so as to protect themselves against encroachments on the trade.[11] The same June meeting of the Court agreed to summon 'Severall persons that are Printers Booksellers BookeBinders or dealers in Bookes in & about the Citties of London & Westminster, and not free of the Company' and decided to petition the Lord Mayor and Aldermen to order all such traders to be translated to the Stationers' Company.[12] The Company was also keen to pursue a number of stallholders and in particular Huguenot refugees dealing in books.

The matter of the suppression of hawkers and pedlars was at the same time being pursued through Parliament. Leave for bringing in a Bill 'to prevent Scotch Pedlars from coming into this Kingdom' was granted by the Commons in 1680, and from then on a sustained campaign of lobbying and attempts to formulate a bill and establish new licensing arrangements rumbled on well into the 1690s.[13] Concern about the situation across the kingdom was fuelled by complaints from citizens of provincial towns. As late as 1691, for example, a letter from Rochester in Kent complained of the prejudice to citizens of that city occasioned by hawkers, pedlars and itinerant chapmen and requested their suppression.[14] Petitions by merchants and traders of all kinds were presented to the House of Commons.[15] Eventually, an Act for the Licensing of Hawkers and Pedlars was passed in 1697 as a specific measure to raise funds for the Transport Debt, receiving its royal assent in 1698.[16]

Pedlars and chapmen had long been connected popularly and in the official mind with potential criminality and disorder. This general antipathy towards vagrants goes back (at least) to the sixteenth century and fuelled the Elizabethan legislation against them.[17] Increasingly in the seventeeth century, as Spufford and Fontaine demonstrate, the trading activities of pedlars gave particular cause for alarm: as pedlars became more numerous, acquired horses and began to settle in towns, they constituted a form of competition unwelcome to established town and city shop-keepers and the result was a vigorous campaign for their suppression by those whose trades were under threat. I should like here, however, to suggest that anxieties about pedlars in the post-Restoration period had to do with a more specific fear on the part of the authorities, which arose from the association of pedlars with the circulation of seditious pamphlets. In 1660, for example, Ekins's application for a grant of the office of licenser of pedlars acknowledged their usefulness but considered that 'if disaffected, they are of great prejudice, by dispersing scandalous pamphlets, etc...'[18] Reasons given for issuing a proclamation in May 1665 to advertise the patent which was granted on 3 May to Colonel Gray, Killigrew and others for licensing pedlars and petty chapmen included that the licensing of honest pedlars and the suppression of rogues would prevent the dispersal of Quaker and other sectarian books.[19] The order from the King in 1668 'that no Bookesellor or Printer shall lend or dispose anie Bookes whatsoever to Persons called Hawkers etc' and the list of hawkers' names made the same year and now preserved in the State Papers are evidence of the association of London hawkers with the circulation of seditious pamphlets.[20]

Anxiety about the distribution of seditious pamphlets and 'false news' runs through the State Papers of the Restoration period both in relation to London and, more tantalizingly, in relation to the country at large. Roger L'Estrange, Surveyor of the Press, was well aware that control of distribution in the provinces was vital if seditious material was to be taken out of circulation. In a letter to Secretary Jenkins in 1682 he stated that, from his experience, the process of detecting libels must begin from the country, since the stationers distributed first in the kingdom at large before dispersing them in London.[21] By placing pedlars alongside the other agents involved in the circulation of 'libels' in the country at large it can be shown that by the time of the Restoration the long-standing perception of the criminal potential of pedlars was explicitly connected with the circulation of printed matter offensive to the government.

Reports and investigations of the distribution of 'libels' in the provinces during the 1680s suggest something of the range of people and places involved. Provincial booksellers inevitably came under suspicion, but they were relatively easy to police. Some booksellers were apparently beyond reproach and, when sent a parcel of libels unsolicited, simply handed them over to the local justices. 250 copies of *Hunt's Post-scripts*, for example, which were delivered to Mr Fowler, a Northampton bookseller, were secured and 'discovered' by the bookseller himself.[22] Less obliging booksellers could be watched or questioned. For example the Earl of Sunderland, in a series of letters in February and March 1688, directed the examinations of Richard Lambert, a York bookseller; John Minshull, the Chester bookseller; Edward Gyles, bookseller in Norwich; Michael Hide of Exeter; Thomas Wall, bookseller in Bristol; Obed Smith, bookseller in Daventry; one Rose, bookseller in Norwich; Francis Hillyard in York; John Crosby and Henry Clements in Oxford; Henry Dickens and Richard Green in Cambridge; Jones and Evans in Worcester; and Thomas Clarke in Hull.[23]

Many of the seditious pamphlets circulating in the provinces, however, were distributed by those outside the book trade. The *Declaration* of James II, circulating shortly after his expulsion, was among a spate of libels reaching all parts of the country in the summer of 1688. Reports flooded in to the office of the Secretary of State that the *Declaration* and other libels were being distributed in Bristol, Chester, Cornwall, Plymouth, Cambridge, Durham and Newcastle.[24] Letters reporting the circulation and seizure of libels and 'declarations' were later received from Wressal and Dover; and Jacobite propaganda reportedly circulated throughout the next decade: in Cornwall, Cirencester, Warwick, Bath, Exeter (in the summer of 1693) and in Northampton, Nottingham and Dartmouth in 1695. Pictures of the pretended Prince of Wales were reaching Canterbury via Dover in March 1699.[25] At the height of the panic about James II's *Declaration* warrants were issued for searching the chambers and warehouses of carriers, waggoners, pack-horse men and hagglers leaving London on the main roads out of the city. The Earl of Shrewsbury thought that binding the carriers at the assizes to make them liable as accessories would encourage them to refuse to carry 'such pestilent ware'.[26]

The scale of dispersal in the provinces was impressive. Laurence Morris, committed to Ely gaol in 1681 for dispersing seditious pamphlets, was said to have disposed of the greatest part of 1400 copies of *Vox Populi, Vox Dei* which he had received from the bookseller Brooksby in London. Morris gave information that Laurence White rode about to fairs and markets, dispersing inflammatory pamphlets; whether White was himself a packman supplied with pamphlets by Morris is not clear.[27] White's activities are a reminder of the importance of fairs and markets in the distribution of seditious matter as well as legitimate goods. In 1683 at fair day in Bridgwater, Somerset, scandalous ballads were spread by the singing of 'a parcel of vermin' (though the Mayor 'laughed' when a complaint was made to him and refused to take action).[28] Fairs were, of course, one of the principal outlets for the ballads and penny chapbooks supplied on credit quite legitimately to pedlars and chapmen by the chapbook publishers who congregated around Smithfield market and on London Bridge, close to the major routes out of London. It would be surprising if the same distribution networks were not also sometimes used as a channel for the highly topical, scandalous and seditious pamphlets which would have been more profitable, if more risky, to carry.

As well as provincial booksellers and balladmongers at fairs, the authorities also expressed anxiety about the provincial coffee houses which, like London ones, were sites for gossip, political discussion and the exchange of news. John Kimbar's coffee house near the Tolsey in Bristol, for example, was the object of suspicion in 1681 because it was frequented by disloyal persons who were entertained there by 'false news' and 'lying and scandalous pamphlets'. A Quarter Sessions presentment asked for the suppression of the coffee house or an order that no printed or written news or pamphlets be allowed to be read or published there unless approved by the Mayor or Aldermen.[29] Other coffee houses under suspicion during the 1680s for the same reasons include Mrs Daye's coffee house and Fagge's coffee house, both in Oxford (1681); an unnamed coffee house in Leeds (1683); and the Dolphin coffee house in Chichester (1689).[30] Both printed and written material circulating via coffee houses were seen as equally dangerous and a considerable number of printed libels reached the provinces under cover of written newsletters. The wealth of information in the State Papers about the circulation of handwritten newsletters makes it clear that enclosures of *printed* matter were part of the bargain struck between country recipient and London-based newswriter. Thus, an anonymous newswriter in 1683 offered to supply a customer with his own written newsletters, with the *Gazette*, and with any other pamphlets that came out and were worth sending for £10 a year.[31] Professional newsletter-writers dealing also in printed pamphlets might target specific networks of country customers, catering for example to a particular religious interest. In 1683 James Harris, imprisoned in the King's Bench, gave information that a dissenter network was serviced by William Raddon and Thomas Parsons, who gathered their news from Francis Smith, the Baptist opposition bookseller, and in turn supplied 'scandalous and libellous news' to Baptists in Taunton, Dorchester, Lyme, Culliton, Axminster, Honiton, Tiverton and Exeter'.[32] A contemporary petition to Secretary of State Jenkins from aspiring newswriters, asking for permission to write newsletters to a few coffee houses in the country and in London, demonstrates the usual association of newsletter writers with printed sedition, in that the writers are careful to promise that they will not meddle with base pamphlets or in seditious matters.[33]

This brief sample of some of the documents being edited for the *Chronology and Calendar* brings into focus a new emphasis, specific to the Restoration period, in the general and long-running anxiety about pedlars and hawkers. Spufford and Fontaine have considered the activities of pedlars and hawkers in relation to retail distribution and certainly the reconciliation of competing trade interests is a primary issue. In this the Stationers' Company can be seen to have behaved very much like mercers, drapers and other established trading groups who saw pedlars and hawkers as unruly competitors. In attempting to suppress London hawkers and in joining in the lobbying for legislation, the Stationers were attempting, as ever, to maintain their retail monopoly. In much the same way they policed production, agitating about provincial printing, complaining of supernumerary presses at York and Chester in the 1680s and blocking the development of the provincial trade in general.[34] When in 1684, for example, Nathaniel Ponder proposed binding an apprentice with the intention of turning him over to a bookseller in the country, the Stationers' Court declared themselves to be 'against such ill presidents'.[35]

But seen from the perspective of those most concerned with the political control of seditious ideas and writing – L'Estrange, the Secretaries of State, Parliament and, ultimately, the monarch – pedlars and hawkers were part of a network with potential for inciting oppositional action. From this London perspective, pedlars and hawkers were moving fragments in a kaleidoscope of sedition. Pedlars, hawkers, carriers, country booksellers, balladmongers at fairs, provincial coffee-house keepers, individual recipients of manuscript newsletters with their printed enclosures were all, so it seemed, irritating agents in the spread of sedition across the nation. It is arguable, then, that while the anti-pedlar byelaws of provincial market towns certainly arose from concerns which were primarily about trade restraint, the London anti-hawker campaigns and the parliamentary drive for regulation of pedlars and chapmen were shaped as part of a specific anxiety to control the circulation of oppositional ideas in the provinces. Restoration attempts at legislation, therefore, should be seen not simply as the product of a concern with trade regulation, but as the culmination of complementary interests: in trade regulation, in the raising of tax revenue via licensing and, significantly, in the control of seditious material circulating in the provinces.

## NOTES

1. *The Chronology and Calendar of Documents relating to the London Book Trade 1641–1700*, [ed] D F McKenzie & M Bell (2 vols, Oxford: Oxford University Press, forthcoming) brings together in one sequence edited abstracts of documents from a range of sources: the MSS of the Stationers' Company Court Books; contemporary printed documents such as pamphlets and petitions; printed secondary sources (*Reports of the Royal Commission on Historical Manuscripts*; *Calendar of State Papers, Domestic Series*); and material from the printed *Journals* of the Houses of Lords and Commons.

2. Margaret Spufford, *Small Books and Pleasant Histories: Popular Fiction and its Readership in Seventeenth Century England* (London, 1981);*The Great Reclothing of Rural England: Petty Chapmen and their Wares in the Seventeenth Century* (London: 1984).

3. Spufford, *Great Reclothing*, 14.

4. Laurence Fontaine, *History of Pedlars in Europe* (Oxford: Polity Press, 1996), [trs] V Whittaker.

5. *Calendar of State Papers, Domestic Series* [hereafter *CSPD*] Chas II, v 428, n 75. *CSPD* references derived from *The Chronology and Calendar* are given as they appear there (ie as Public Record Office source numbers rather than *CSPD* page numbers) to facilitate direct access to the PRO documents.

6. *CSPD* Chas II, v 436, nn 37, 148.

7. *CSPD* Chas II, v 436, n 107.

8. *CSPD* Chas II, v 436, nn 148, 149.

9. A running battle between the Company and hawkers had been going on since the 1660s (see, for example, Stationers' Company, Court Book D, ff 143v, 147v, 154), but Company members were keen to use hawkers when it suited them (for suspicions about the Company, see, for example, *CSPD* Chas II, v 366, 263).

10. Stationers' Company, Court Book F, f 16$^{v.}$

11. The new Charter was dated 22 May. For a description of the process, see Cyprian Blagden, *The Stationers' Company* (London: George Allen & Unwin, 1960), 166ff.

12. Blagden, *Stationers' Company*.

13.*Journals of the House of Commons* [hereafter *CJ* ] ix, 683. This was not the first attempt at legislation; in May 1675 a bill achieved a second reading in the Commons (*CJ* ix. 328, 332, 335–6). See Spufford, *Great Reclothing*, 8–14, for an account of legislation and licensing arrangements. Between 1675 and 1695 more than ten bills were introduced into the Commons and the legislation ran into repeated difficulties for a variety of reasons, including repeated prorogations and opposition from the House of Lords.

14. *CSPD* William & Mary, v 3, n 86: William Lavender to Sir Joseph Williamson, 16 December 1691.

15. See, for example, *Reasons offered to the considerations of Parliament by the drapers, haberdashers, grocers, hosiers, glass-sellers, cutlers, and others of the great decay of their trades by the increasing numbers of pedlars, hawkers and petty chapfolks* (1691); *CSPD* William & Mary, v 3, n 96; 'A Petition of divers Merchants and Traders in and about the City of London...' (*CJ*, xi, 427); *CSPD* Chas II, v 370, n 293.

16. The Act was one of a number of bills receiving royal assent on 5 July 1698, including also 'An Act for granting...further Duties upon Stampt Vellum, Parchment, and Paper' and 'An Act for the more effectual suppressing of Blasphemy and Profaneness' (*Journals of the House of Lords*, xvi, 343).

17. The Elizabethan Act of 1597 against rogues, vagabonds and sturdy beggars had included references to 'Peddlers and Petty Chapmen wandering abroad' (Spufford, *Great Reclothing*, 8).

18. *CSPD* Chas II, v 25, n 94 (?December 1660).

19. *CSPD* Chas II, v 122, n 120.

20. *CSPD* Chas II, v 88, n 68 (*recte* 1668; misdated in *CSPD* as 1663); Stationers' Company, Court Book D, f 143v *CSPD* Chas II, v 251, n 196. See also Stationers' Company, Court Book D, ff 149v, 154.

21. *CSPD* Chas II, v 421, n 115.

22. *CSPD* Chas II, v 435, nn 3, 29.

23. *CSPD* Jas II, 44/56, 407, 410–11. My thanks to David Stoker for his identification of the Norwich bookseller as George Rose and to Margaret Cooper for identifying those in Worcester as John Jones (senior, freed 1668 or junior, freed 1670) and Sampson Evans.

24. *CSPD* William & Mary, Home Office [hereafter H O]. Letter Book (Secretary's) 1, 96, 121, 124, 125; *CSPD* William & Mary, v 1, nn 74, 79; and see *CJ* x 179, 187, 190.

25. *CSPD* William & Mary v 2, n 20; & H O Letter Books (Secretary's) 1, 228, 2 658, 660, & 3, 120, 137, 143; & Entry Books 100, 155; 272, 72; 99, 210, 619, 620–1.

26. *CSPD* William & Mary, H O Letter Book (Secretary's) 1, p121, 124 (4, 6 July 1689).

27. *CSPD* Chas II, v 415, n 122 (11 April 1681); the supplier was presumably Phillip Brooksby (bd 1662, fd 1670).

28. *CSPD* Chas II, v 422, n 122.

29. *CSPD* Chas II, v 415, n 142.

30. *CSPD* Chas II, v 416, n 120; v 428, n 53; William & Mary, v 1, n 126.

31. *CSPD* Chas II, v 433, n 89.

32. *CSPD* Chas II, v 429, n 184.

33. *CSPD* Chas II, v 437, n 115 (date uncertain: between April 1680 and April 1684).

34. Stationers' Company, Court Book F, f 47$^{\text{v}}$ (7 Dec 1685); ff 57$^{\text{v}}$-58 (7 June 1686); f 103$^{\text{v}}$ (2 July 1688); ff 166-166$^{\text{v}}$ (7 March 1692); f 215$^{\text{v}}$ (3 December 1694); f 263 (22 June 1697); *CSPD* Jas II, 44/236, 2; William & Mary, Warrant Book 34, 349.

35. Stationers' Company, Court Book F, f 20.

# Printing at the Red-Well:
## an Early Norwich Press Through the Eyes of Contemporaries

### DAVID STOKER

CHARTING THE HISTORY of an early provincial printing press is like doing a jig-saw puzzle where most of the pieces are missing. Concrete information is usually difficult, and sometimes almost impossible, to find. Typically, there may be a few surviving publications, perhaps a newspaper advertisement, or passing reference in a history of the locality. Searching local records may unearth the odd entry in a parish register or payment for a small printing job. But for most early provincial printers, that will be as much as is findable. Yet from time to time scraps of information may crop up in unexpected places.

This paper seeks to contribute a few pieces to a picture where the general outline is reasonably well known, but most of the detail is missing. It will examine the earliest eighteenth-century printing office in Norwich through the eyes of two unlikely commentators – Thomas Tanner and Humphrey Prideaux. Both men were cathedral dignitaries: Tanner was Chancellor from 1701 until he became Bishop of St Asaph in 1731; Prideaux was Archdeacon of Suffolk from 1688, and Dean of Norwich from 1702 until his death in 1724. Both were noted scholars, although with different temperaments. Tanner, an antiquary who published *Notitia Monastica* in 1695, aged twenty-one, was working upon the ambitious *Bibliotheca Britannico-Hibernica*, which appeared posthumously in 1748. He was a kindly, generous man who never forgot his modest origins. Prideaux had a reputation for pride and irascibility, particularly later in life. He was wealthy, and so was not constantly seeking promotion within the church, but had little sympathy for less-fortunate colleagues. He was a distinguished ecclesiastical historian and orientalist who published a *Life of Mohamet* in 1697, and was working on a history of the Jews. Neither would seem likely to have dealings with a fledgling local press, yet they both took a particular interest in its activities. Indeed the earliest references to its existence appear in their correspondence.

Writing to Arthur Charlett, Master of University College, Oxford, in April 1701 Tanner commented:[1]

> Here is a young Printer at present in this town who upon the encouragement of Dr Prideaux &c intends to bring down a new font of Letters from London and set up his press here. He proposes to print cheaper here than they can in London, by having paper at easier rates from Holland &c. I should be mighty glad if this project takes.

Three weeks later Prideaux received a letter from Bishop White Kennett confirming his encouragement of the plan.

> I am very glad to hear of the publick spirit for encouraging a press in Norwich, and hope that first fruits of it will be that excellent discourse of which I have seen a part, and which you ought no longer to deny the world.[2]

Francis Burges, the printer in question, set up his office, 'near the Red-Well',[3] during the summer of 1701, and his press continued in existence under the stewardship of at least nine printers, until its demise in 1718. He had been an apprentice of the prosperous London printer and Deputy Alderman, Freeman Collins, between November 1692 and December 1699.[4] Why he came to Norwich in April 1701, and how he attracted the attention of Dr Prideaux, is not known. Norwich was however the largest English provincial city with a rapidly growing population, and would remain so for thirty years,[5] an obvious place to set up a new press following the lapse of the 'Licensing Acts' in 1695.

Tanner also arrived in Norwich early in 1701. His scholarship had brought him to the notice of John Moore, Bishop of Norwich, renowned as the owner of one of the finest private libraries in England, and the father of two unprepossessing daughters. Moore appointed Tanner his personal chaplain, but employed him as researcher, book buyer, and writing master for his daughters. When early in 1701 Tanner married Moore's elder daughter Rose, the bishop showed his gratitude by appointing the young man Chancellor of his diocese.[6]

Once established Tanner took an interest in the local press. He sent a half-sheet 'combination paper' listing clergy due to preach at the Cathedral, to his friend John Bagford, who was collecting materials for a history of printing – thinking it was the first item printed by the press.[7] Bagford afterwards received an earlier publication, dated 27 September, written by the printer to forestall concerns about seditious printing, claiming to be the first item printed in Norwich. In *Some Observations on the Use and Original of the Noble Art and Mystery of Printing* Burges set out his reasons for establishing his press.[8]

> I likewise observed, when at London, how usfull it [printing] was to abundance of traders in divers respects, concluded this a fit place or as able to mantane a printing house as Exeter Chester Bristoll or York.[9]

In answer to charges that the press might promote the publication of libels, Burges promised his readers 'not to meddle with such'.

Burges is noteworthy for producing the first English provincial newspaper, *The Norwich Post*, in 1701.[10] Tanner followed the fortunes of the newspaper and mentions it several times. In August 1706, he discussed its origins with Browne Willis:

> The Norwich newspapers are the principal support of our poor printer here, by which, with Advertisements, he clears nearly 50s every week, selling vast numbers to

the country people. As far as I can learn, this Burgess first began here the printing the news out of London, since I have seen also the Bristol *Postman*, and I am told they print also now a weekly paper at Exeter.[11]

Few copies of the *Norwich Post* survive, but until the Norwich Library fire in 1994, there were twenty-six other publications surviving with his imprint, and thirty-two with anonymous Norwich imprints many of which might be attributed to it. Seven other works are known to have existed. These encompassed all types of small publications ranging from official notices for the Cathedral and Corporation, to almanacs, catechisms, and accounts of trials and executions. However most of his publications were religious works published by the local clergy. His two most prolific authors were both archdeacons: John Jeffery Archdeacon of Norwich, author of at least nine works printed by Burges, and Humphrey Prideaux.

Prideaux knew better than follow Kennet's suggestion of entrusting a major work to the press, but soon gave it some business: a handbook for the churchwardens in his Archdeaconry.

> The Doctor found in his Archdiaconal Visitations, that the Church-wardens of Suffolk,... instead of presenting what was amiss, as they are bound... usually gave in their presentments, as if all was right; and that for those parishes, where the contrary was most notorious. This afforded him... matter of melancholy reflection, that three or four hundred men should thus deliberately perjure themselves twice a year. In order to put a stop to this evil... he wrote his Directions to Churchwardens instructing them in all the branches of their duty... and exhorting and directing them faithfully and carefully to discharge their offices.[12]

*Directions to Church-Wardens* was the only known publication to emerge from the press in 1701 which extended beyond two printed sheets. Whether it was distributed freely by the author to those parishes in his charge, or was required reading, is not known. However, it was clearly a success, and due to Prideaux's reputation, it had an impact beyond his Archdeaconry. Nicholas Stratford, Bishop of Chester, asked him to send copies 'to some Bookseller here in London, that I may take some down with me into my diocese'.[13] Thus in 1704 Prideaux commissioned an enlarged edition from Burges, extended to four and a half sheets, and with two London booksellers and one from Norwich identified as distributors.[14]

An account tendered to Prideaux, dated 22 June 1704, apparently from one of these London distributors, indicates that copies of this work were being exchanged for 720 religious tracts, as part of a prearranged deal also involving Burges:

| | |
|---|---|
| 100 Xtian scholar | 1.00.00 |
| 100 Exercises for Sacrament | 1.00.00 |
| 100 Directions for spending a day | 0.06.00 |
| 100 Knowledge of religion | 0.10.00 |

| | |
|---|---|
| 100 Essay to make religion easy | 1.00.00 |
| 100 Instructions to young & ignorant | 1.00.00 |
| 120 Husbandman duty | 1.00.00 |
| Box and portage | 0.01.06 |
| | 5.17.06 |

'I have not yet received the Books as desired from your Printer at Norwich, I expect them and then you may please to account'.[15] These might have been intended for Burges's stock, as payment in kind to offset part of the cost of printing. Indeed it is clear from later newspaper advertisements that Burges's successors supplemented their business by supplying such works to chapmen and hawkers.

In common with other senior clergy Prideaux was periodically invited to preach before the Mayor, Sheriff, Aldermen and Common Councilors, to commemorate some anniversary. In December 1702 he preached a thanksgiving sermon for 'Successes vouchsafed to Her Majesty's Forces' in expedition against Vigo, in his usual outspoken manner, railing against popery and Jacobitism. The Mayor's Court approved so much that instead of merely thanking him, added a request that he should have his work printed. This seems to be the first occasion that such an invitation was given in Norwich. Prideaux did not like publishing his sermons, and sought the advice of his friend Sir John Holland whether he should have to comply.

> I am glad yr sermon took so well, I am suer you will always be valued when you have not those to deal withal who have more Passion than Brains. I should apprehend that you must comply in Printing, & cannot think it will be to your disadvantage, after what the Bp of Exeter has said before Q[ueen] L[ords] & Commons.[16]

The sermon was, therefore, printed by Burges with the prosaic, if accurate, title *A Sermon Preach'd 3 December 1702*, and included the request from the Mayor's Court that it be published. Thereafter several other sermons were published by the press specifically at the request of the Norwich Corporation, although after 1710 the practice becomes noticeably less common. In that year a glut of commemoration sermons was followed by a reluctance by the local trade to publish any more. Writing to Charlett in July Tanner commented:

> I wish I could make you some return from hence for the sermons the same way – but our Booksellers having been bit by 2 or more unsaleable ones, many that have been desired to be printed are dropt and our printers have furnish'd this place of late with nothing but stale news.[17]

On this occasion, but on no other, the Mayor's Court ordered that a printer's account should be paid for a sermon which they had requested to be printed.[18]

By 1706, Burges was established as the official printer for Norwich Cathedral and Corporation. In that year he printed a table of *The Bishops, Deans, and Prebendaries of Norwich* drawn up by Prideaux, the visitation articles for Tanner's father-in-law,

Bishop Moore, two commemoration sermons, and another work by Archdeacon Jeffery. He believed he had introduced printing to the city, but was mistaken. Soon after taking up office Tanner found evidence of an Elizabethan press in the Cathedral muniments, and Thomas Hearne discovered a broadsheet issued by it in the Bodleian Library.[19] However, by November 1706 Burges had died aged thirty, and his mistaken claim was engraved upon his gravestone in St Andrew's church. It was not until the 1740s when Francis Blomefield published more evidence that Burges's claim was generally discounted.[20]

That Francis Burges was successful is shown by events that took place after his premature death. Two further businesses were set up by a local distiller and a bookseller, neither of whom was aware of the other's plans, or that Burges's widow Elizabeth would remain in business. Each of the newcomers employed a printer and founded a weekly newspaper. The struggle among the three printing houses in Norwich over the next few years is well documented elsewhere.[21] The spectacle of the three printing houses in the city competing for business that had previously kept one in business gave rise to comment. Writing to Charlett 10 June 1709, Tanner comments 'what with Newspapers, Sermons & Ballads our three Printing Houses still keep up'.[22]

Elizabeth Burges continued the *Norwich Post*, and retained her husband's official position by printing various commemoration sermons and items for the Corporation, such as a catalogue of the city library. Yet this was only a small part of her business as a newspaper advertisement from May 1707 indicates

> These are to give notice to all country chapmen & others that at the Printing-house near the Red-Well, Norwich they may be furnish'd with all sort of history-Books, Song-Books, Broad-sides &c. There may also be had, Devotions for the Holy Communion. Price one penny. Likewise may be had a Book entitul'd a path-way to heaven: or, a sure way to happiness… Price one penny. The true description of Norwich, both in its antient & modern state… Price one Penny. Advertisements are also taken in there and carefully inserted in this Paper at very reasonable rates.[23]

However she did not survive her husband for long. Her rivals assumed that her death in November 1708 would mark the end of the Red-Well press, but this was not to happen for a further decade. Both the newspaper and other publications continued to appear, initially under the imprint of 'the Administrator of E. Burges', but in February a complaint from Henry Crossgrove one of the rival printers refers to the 'Printing-Office of Deputy Collins'.[24]

Freeman Collins had not lost touch with his former apprentice, and indeed in 1704 he had even printed a Norwich commemoration sermon – presumably because the Norwich press was unable to do so.[25] The transfer of the Red-Well press from the Burges family to Collins was, however a different matter, and raises two significant questions. Firstly, what was the connection between Elizabeth Burges and her husband's former master, which effected the transfer of the business? Secondly, why should a man such as Freeman Collins abandon a successful business in London, late in life, move to Norwich, and manage a near-bankrupt enterprise?

The answer to the first question must be speculation, but Collins had a daughter named Elizabeth and several sons. Francis Burges might have married his master's daughter, and Collins might then have financed their setting up in business in Norwich. Francis and Elizabeth Burges died childless and so Collins would have been the beneficiary of their business.

It is most unlikely that Freemen Collins ever moved to Norwich, especially as his business continued to operate on a much larger scale in London until his death in 1713. He rather sent trusted workmen or apprentices to manage the Red-Well press on his behalf. Certainly this was the case after 1711, when a notable apprentice named Edward Cave worked the press.[26] However, Cave did not arrive in the city until 1711, two years after beginning his apprenticeship. Yet between 1709 and the spring of 1711 there are several references in Tanner's correspondence to a printer named Collins working in the city.[27] This was probably Freeman, son of Freeman Collins, who was bound to his father 7 July 1707 immediately prior to Cave.[28] He was apparently sent to manage the Red-Well two years later, but by June 1711 had moved to Cambridge where he worked as a compositor at the University press for a few weeks before returning to London.[29]

1709 saw the publication of the most interesting of the publications from the press – Humphrey Prideaux's *The Original and Right of Tithes*.[30] This was somewhat more substantial than any work printed in the city previously, or indeed for many years afterwards, consisting of twenty-five octavo sheets. It was also a work of some scholarship; how it came to be printed in Norwich, rather than London, is explained in Prideaux's biography.

His design at first, was to give the History of Appropriations... and the treating of the *Original Right of Tythes* was intended... as a Preface... But when he came to write it, finding it swell to a bulk, beyond what he had expected, he thought it best, to publish separately, and reserve the rest for a second work... Whilst he was engaged in this undertaking, the unhappy distemper of the stone first seized him, which put a stop to all further proceedings: for in order to compleat the work... it was necessary for him to consult the Cotton library, the Tower of London, and other places, where antient Records are kept, which he could not do, but by taking a journey to those places; and being utterly disabled from bearing any such journey by his distemper, he was obliged to lay aside the whole design.[31]

Prideaux's painful disorder, inability to travel and suspicion that he might not have long to live were the reasons why the first part of the work was printed in Norwich. As he explained to John Ellis

Another part was intended when I began, wch would be much larger than this, but God hath pleased to disable me from proceeding any further by ye calamity wch is since fallen upon me.[32]

Tanner's correspondence provides a commentary on its nine-month progress in the press. In June 1709 he reported to Charlett 'Our Dean has got 9 or 10 sheets of his book of Tithes printed of here & the whole will be about as much more.'[33] In August Prideaux was

> very much indisposed above this month, there are symptoms on him either of an ulcer or stone in the bladder, which deject him pretty much... He complains sadly of his printer, who will not do a sheet of his book a week.[34]

During the autumn of 1709 Prideaux's condition worsened and he believed himself near to death. He wanted to air his views on a related subject whilst he still could, and decided to extend his work by adding a further five sheets, including 'A bill for restraining pluralities' dating from 1691, together with his commentary. This additional material had a separate title page and preface dated 10 October 1709, but was otherwise a component part of the work. The whole was issued mid-December by which time the author assumed he would be in the hands of his maker.

The work was clearly too specialised for the local market and was therefore issued twice: once with a Norwich imprint, and also with a misleading London imprint, each bearing the date 1710. Tanner commented that it was overpriced at 4s.6d and that 'Mr Collins might certainly afford it cheaper paying nothing for the copy, only 50 Books'.[35] The scholarship of the work was widely respected, but the outspoken tone of the Dean's additional material caused grave offence, particularly among curates and poorer clergy who were pluralists out of necessity rather than greed. As Tanner reported to Bishop Moore

> The Dean... shew me all the English History part of his Book of Tithes before it was printed, but I never saw the latter thing about the Act, till Mr Collins presented me wth the Book. I am no pluralist my self nor love it in others, where tolerable subsistence for the clergy can be had without them – but I can't see the necessity of Publishing all those things as we have upon the occasions of a project that will remedy but very few or none of the mischiefs wch equally arose from non-residence even on one living. But it has given most offence in some of those hard and scarce true expressions against curates, in wch most of the country clergy as having be so themselves at first, and think these passages design'd purposely to render them contemptible.[36]

The controversy was still smouldering in May, when Tanner again showed his disapproval in a letter to Charlett

> As for the business of Tithes, I think he has hit right – but his additional project of his Act of Parliament I never saw nor heard of till in print, where if I could have prevail'd it never should have been – for I fear there are many unguarded general expressions in it

against my friends the Curates, (who as little deserve those hard expressions as any other number of clergymen)…[37]

However, Prideaux did not die – he had a strong constitution, for, although in his sixties, he underwent an operation, 'to be cut for the stone', from which nobody thought he would recover. He lived until 1724, although perpetually thereafter in pain, and became yet more renowned for his bad temper. He had no more dealings with Norwich printers, but the elder Freeman Collins did print the third edition of his *Directions to Churchwardens* in London in 1712. Eventually in 1717 he quarrelled with the long-suffering Tanner.

> He having thought fit to break of all correspondence and good neighbourhood with me without any just offence by me given – who have pass'd by and covered many of his infirmities of mind & temper, out of regard for his learning and infirmities of body age &c.

After 1710 there appears to be no further reference to the press in the correspondence of either Prideaux or Tanner. However in 1712, Tanner did publish anonymously a tract for the use of his parishioners of Thorpe Hamlet,[38] but there is no indication which of the three Norwich presses was responsible. The active support given to the Red-Well press during its first decade seems to have dissipated. The last years of the press were somewhat less respectable without their patronage.

Edward Cave replaced the younger Freeman Collins in the summer of 1711. According to Samuel Johnson

> He was sent without any super-intendant to conduct a printing house at Norwich and publish a weekly paper. In this undertaking he met with some opposition, which produced a public controversy, and procured young Cave reputation as a writer.

The newspapers for the period have not survived and the nature of this controversy is not known, but other survivals from the press from 1712 and 1713 indicate that it was active and many of the productions were of a reasonable standard. The elder Freeman Collins died in January 1713, and was succeeded by his widow Susanna, whose name appears on Norwich imprints in the same year. Cave did not remain in the city for much longer, for he was 'unable to bear the perverseness of his mistress'. This accords with the surviving evidence, and Susanna seems to have handed over the operation of the Norwich business to her younger children in 1714. The newspaper was changed from the *Norwich Post* to the *Norwich Courant*, but no copies now survive. John Chambers saw a file of the *Norwich Courant* a century afterwards and gives a sorry account of the last years of the press.

> These papers are so wretchedly printed as to be scarcely readable. It is printed by S., afterwards by John Collins, and then by H. Collins, price three half pence, near the Red Well, St Andrew's, and has two slurred woodcuts of an express on horseback, and as rude a one of the city arms. It appears that the editor was a whig. At the end of

one paper, wretchedly spelt, the editor concludes in the following elegant style: - 'Note. An accident happening, the reader is desired to pardon all literal errors as it is not corrected'.[39] The quality of printing of the few surviving productions from this period confirms this account.[40]

Eventually the business was put up for sale in the autumn of 1717, and was taken over by Benjamin Lyon, yet another former apprentice of Freeman Collins.[41] Lyon was somewhat unfortunate, for within two months he was appearing before the Norwich Quarter Sessions charged with printing a libel, and within six months was out of business. He later turned up as the first printer in Bath in 1729.[42] Thus over an eighteen-year period, and due to a variety of internal and external circumstances, the Red-Well press declined from being a prosperous and respectable enterprise enjoying the support of the authorities, to an ill-equipped and poverty-stricken business operating on the edge of legality.

## NOTES

1. Bodleian Library MS Ballard 4, f 57.

2. Cornwall Record Office [hereafter CRO] PB 8/1/1-4, 17 May 1701.

3. The 'Red-Well' was at a junction of five roads, close to St Michael at Plea church; the press was situated at the north-western corner of this junction in St Andrew's parish.

4. D F McKenzie, *Stationers' Company Apprentices*, 2 vol (Oxford Bibliographical Society, 1974/8). Collins ultimately had nineteen apprentices, and operated five presses. Gwyn Walters & Frank Emery, 'Edward Lhuyd, Edmund Gibson, and the printing of Camden's *Britannia*, 1695', *The Library*, 5th ser, 32 (1977), 109-37 (128).

5. The population was 30 000 in 1700 and 42 000 in 1727.

6. Described unkindly by Hearne as a 'short squab dame… remarkable for drinking of Brandy', *Remarks and Collections of Thomas Hearne*, 11 vol (Oxford Historical Society, 1885-1918), 2, 9.

7. *Norfolk Preachers… 2 November 1701 to Trinity Sunday Following* (Norwich, 1701): British Library [hereafter BL] Harleian MS 5910.ii, f 152.

8. No copies have survived, but the text was reprinted in *The Harleian Miscellany*, 8 vol (London, 1745) 3, 148-51. Bagford transcribed extracts from Burges's preface and title page (Harleian MS 5910.ii, fol 152). Other extracts from the preliminaries are in John Chambers, *A General History of the County of Norfolk*, 2 vol (Norwich, 1829) 2, 1286-7.

9. BL Harleian MS 5910.ii, f 152.

10. See G A Cranfield, *The Development of the Provincial Newspaper 1700-1760* (Oxford, 1962), 13-14, and R M Wiles, *Freshest Advices: Early Provincial Newspapers in England* (Columbus, 1965), 463-5.

11. Bodleian Library Browne Willis MS xcv, f 259.

12. *The Life of the Reverend Humphrey Prideaux* (London, 1744), 100-1.

13. CRO PB 8/1/1-4, 26 March 1702.

14. R Simpson and J Nicholson in London, and Samuel Selfe in Norwich.
15. CRO PB 8/1/1-4, 22 June 1704.
16. CRO PB 8/1/1-4, 9 January 1702/3.
17. Bodleian MS Ballard 4, f 105.
18. Norfolk Record Office, Norwich Mayor's Court Book, 20 July 1710.
19. BL Harleian MS 5910.ii, f 147, and MS 5906, f 57.
20. Chambers, *History of Norfolk*, 1178, and Francis Blomefield, *An Essay towards a Topographical History of Norfolk*, 5 vol (Fersfield, Norwich & Lynn 1739-1775), 2, 210.
21. David Stoker, `The re-introduction of printing to Norwich: causes and effects 1660-1760, *Transactions of the Cambridge Bibliographical Society*, 8 (1977), 94–111.
22. Bodleian MS Ballard 4, f 95.
23. *Norwich Post* 3 May 1707.
24. *Norwich Gazette* 11 February 1710.
25. Thomas Clayton, *Unity of Worship Earnestly Recommended* (London, 1704).
26. Cave's obituary (by Samuel Johnson) in *Gentleman's Magazine* (February 1754), 55.
27. Bodleian MS Bodl 1013, ff 8–10, 23 January & 22 February 1709/10.
28. McKenzie, *Apprentices 1701–1800*, 82.
29. D F McKenzie, *Cambridge University Press 1696–1712*, 2vol (Cambridge: CUP, 1965), 1, 84; 2, 336.
30. Humphrey Prideaux, *The Original and Right of Tithes*, (Norwich, 1710).
31. *Life of Prideaux*, 115–17.
32. *Letters of Humphrey Prideaux... to John Ellis... 1674–1722*, [ed] Edward Maunde Thompson (Camden Society, 1875), 204.
33. Bodleian MS Ballard 4, f 95.
34. Letter to Charlett 10 August 1709, Bodleian MS Ballard 4, f 96.
35. Letter to Charlett 14 December 1709, Bodleian MS Ballard 4, f 99.
36. Letter to John Moore 22 February 1709/10, Bodleian MS Bodl 1013.
37. Letter to Charlett 15 May 1710, Bodleian MS Ballard 4, f 101.
38. *The First Principles of the Oracles of God, Made Plain to the Meanest Capacities... For Use of a Country Parish in the Diocese of Norwich* (Norwich, 1712). Tanner refers to this work in a letter to John Moore 21 March 1711/12, Bodleian MS Eng Lett c.570, fol 191.
39. Chambers, *History of Norfolk*, 1291. Evidence from other surviving imprints tends to confirm Chambers's account of the succession of printers. However the window-tax returns give a slightly different story. Susanna is listed as having paid for 1713/14, John for 1714/15, Samuel Collins for 1715/16, and Freeman Collins for 1716/17.
40. The complicated and often confusing evidence for the ownership of the Red-Well office is given in the entries for the Collins family in David Stoker, 'The Norwich book trades before 1800', *Transactions of the Cambridge Bibliographical Society*, 8 (1981), 79–125 (93–4).
41. *Norwich Gazette* 21 September 1717.
42. Stoker, 'Norwich book trades', 109.

# Canterbury's External Links: Book-Trade Relations at the Regional and National Level in the Eighteenth Century

## DAVID J SHAW

### CANTERBURY PRINTERS AND BOOKSELLERS TO 1800

AS BEFITS A TOWN With a major ecclesiastical establishment, Canterbury has a long history of commercial booksellers and stationers. Table 1 shows a summary list of Canterbury book trade personnel up to 1800. The eighteenth century saw a great increase in activity, especially with the establishment of James Abree's press in 1717 and the production of the first Canterbury newspaper, the *Kentish Post and Canterbury Newsletter*.[1] Sarah Gray outlines below the career of William Flackton as a successful bookseller, stationer, auctioneer and music-seller in the city and beyond in the mid-century. By the second half of the eighteenth century there were a number of competing firms of booksellers, printers and newspaper proprietors in the city, supplying what must have been a healthy local market.

It is well-known that many of the printers newly set up in provincial towns in the early eighteenth century had as their *raison d'être* the production of a newspaper.[2] This was intended to provide a more regular income than reliance on jobbing printing and production of the occasional book. The example of James Abree shows that even a town like Canterbury could not of itself provide a sufficient market to support a bi-weekly paper: Abree had itinerant newsmen who took the paper around the major towns in the county, a system which enabled him to obtain advertisements for the newspaper and to supply orders from his bookshop.

In addition to selling locally printed items, provincial printers and booksellers used their London connections both to obtain books to sell to their local customers and also to provide a wider distribution for the books which they themselves produced. Provincial booksellers maintained (or even depended on) good links with the centre of the English book trade in London. John Feather called the provincial newspaper owners 'a ready-made system of deep market penetration' for the London publishers, a system that also made them ideal agents for the wholesalers of patent medicines and insurance.[3] I hope to show that while this is largely true, it is not entirely true: there was a measurable trade at the national level in books printed in the provinces, though inevitably the Londoners had a large hand in it as wholesalers and distributors. Nicolas Barker has described the developments in transport which facilitated a national distribution system and the system of warehousing in London which supported it.[4] The Worcester booksellers' London connections and delivery methods have been examined by Margaret Cooper.[5] Let us examine these external trade links for some of the Canterbury figures of the period.

## THE EVIDENCE OF THE BOOKS

The evidence which I shall examine is drawn from the files of the ESTC project, thanks to data provided by colleagues in the British Library, London. I retrieved two sets of data:

1. books printed in Canterbury and also sold through booksellers elsewhere;
2. books printed in London and offered for sale in Canterbury.

A small number of these books are from the seventeenth century, mainly cases of Canterbury booksellers offering London publications by local authors, such as

*Cynthia: with the tragical account of the unfortunate loves of Almerin and Desdemona. Being a novel... Done by an English hand.* London: printed by R. Holt, for R. Fenner book-seller in Canterbury, 1687. 8°. Wing C7710A.

There is another small group in the first half of the eighteenth century, representing James Abree's commercial contacts with book-trade colleagues in nearby Kentish towns. By far the largest group of publications is from the second half of the eighteenth century.

It must be said that quite a number of the imprints in these lists are anything but informative. An imprint such as the following for an illustrated Bible

London: printed for C. Cooke; and sold by the booksellers of Bath, Bristol, Birmingham, Canterbury, Cambridge, [and 25 other towns in England] and by all other booksellers in England, Scotland, and Ireland, [1787?]. 2°[6]

tells us (according to John Feather's interpretation of the commercial significance of the precise wording of contemporary imprints in terms of wholesalers and distributors[7]) that Cooke is the copyright owner and financial backer for the work and that he anticipates wide national sales through his network of provincial distributors, but it is otherwise too unspecific to be of much use for investigating Canterbury's trading links.

Similarly, Daniel Prat's 1791 *Ode, on the Late Celebrated Handel, on his playing on the organ* has the imprint

Canterbury: printed and sold by Simmons, Kirkby and Jones, and all the booksellers in Kent

which tells us that Simmons hoped for sales throughout the county but gives us no details on specific colleagues with whom he was arranging distribution.[8] In fact, about one third of the books printed in Canterbury with indications of outside distribution give only a general phrase such as this showing an expectation of collaborative distribution throughout the county. A later example, which details only the Canterbury distributors, is:

Noyes, Robert. *An Elegy, (after the manner of Gray) on the Death of the Late William Jackson, Esq. of Canterbury,... By Robert Noyes.* Canterbury: printed by J. Grove, and sold by W. Bristow, Flackton, Marrable and Claris, and Simmons and Kirkby, and all other booksellers in Kent, [1789]. 4°.

Another category is where the book is published 'for the author'. For example, Daniel Dobel's *Plea for Infants Baptism, impleaded* has an imprint giving Dobel's house in Cranbrook as the main point of sale, together with the printing house in Canterbury:

Dobel, Daniel. *The Plea for Infants Baptism, impleaded: or, remarks on a piece, intitled, a plea for infants: or, the scripture doctrine of water baptism stated. By Daniel Dobel.* Canterbury: printed for the author, and sold by him at his house in Cranbrook; and at the printing-office, Canterbury, 1742. 8°.

This is clearly a case of private rather than commercial publication, though it must have represented useful business for the printer, James Abree, as Dobell used his services in the same way on a number of occasions.[9]

REGIONAL LINKS

Another example of private publishing shows a wider range of commercial distributors in London and East Kent, presumably involving the trade associates of the printer Joseph Grove:

*A Brief Vindication of the Appointment of God, against the inventions of men, in baptism, &c. in a letter to Mr. Wm. Kingsford, Canterbury.* Canterbury: printed for the author, by J. Grove, and sold by Mr. Scollick, London; Mr. Bristow, Messrs. Flackton, Marrable, and Claris, and Messrs. Simmons and Kirkby, Canterbury; Mr. Burgess, Ramsgate; Mr. Hall, Margate; Mr. Ledger, Dover; Messrs. Cocking and Son, Sandwich; Mr. Coveney, Faversham; and all other booksellers in Kent, 1789. 8°.

This imprint makes it clear that this is a privately produced book ('printed for the author') but it uses Joseph Grove's local and London trade connections to maximise its distribution. Several of the East Kent booksellers named here figure frequently in Canterbury imprints:

Burgess of Ramsgate 11 times,
Hall of Margate 13 times and
Ledger of Dover 5 times.

Others who appear frequently are Samuel Silver of Margate, Thomas Fisher of Rochester and his successor Webster Gillman, and Stephen Doorne of Faversham. The full list of Kentish booksellers acting as local distributors for books printed in Canterbury is given in Table 2. Most of these examples come from the second half of the century, with the firm of Simmons & Kirkby having particular prominence. The towns of Cranbrook, Smarden, Tenterden, which were involved in James Abree's partnerships in the first half of the century, do not figure later on; they are all at the further end of the county and no doubt developed their own more local links.[10] There were a few cases of books printed in other south-eastern towns distributed through one or more Canterbury booksellers: details of these are shown in Table 3.

## NATIONAL LINKS

The provincial book trade as described by John Feather was London-centred: 'The whole structure of the trade had evolved to take books from London to the provinces, not in the opposite direction'. It was a 'one-way flow of books' where the exception merely proves the rule.[11] While this is undoubtedly true as a generalisation, I hope to show that Canterbury was able to insert some of its own products into the national distribution system, and that this was also true for other provincial printing centres.

First of all, I shall look at the national pattern of distribution of Canterbury-printed books. A number of London booksellers acted as distributors; that is to say, they provided a central (London-based) facility for members of the trade in London and in other provincial towns to find out about and to place orders for Canterbury-produced books. There are a few cases of Oxford, Cambridge and York booksellers also acting as regional distributors,[12] but only as subsidiaries to a London tradesman. In this sense, it can certainly be said that the English book trade was centred on London. Many of these London figures acted only a small number of times for Canterbury colleagues, but a few had regular links with the Canterbury trade over long periods of time. Figure 1 shows the statistics for the major London distributors acting for Canterbury firms. I should like to look in further detail at the two principal cases, Joseph Johnson and Bedwell Law.

Figure 1

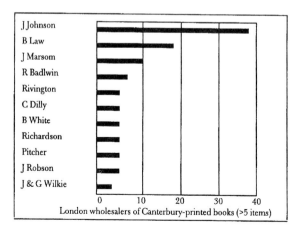

London wholesalers of Canterbury-printed books (>5 items)

Joseph Johnson is described in Plomer's *Dictionary* as 'one of the leading booksellers and publishers in London in the second half of the eighteenth century'. 'His shop became the headquarters of the book selling of Protestant Dissent.' Born 1738, he was apprenticed to George Keith, worked from premises in Paternoster Row from 1760 to 1770, and in St Paul's Churchyard from 1770 to 1809. He was gaoled for nine months in 1797 for publishing the political works of Gilbert Wakefield.[13]

Johnson handled three books for William Flackton (in 1774, 1785, and 1789), four books for the printer Joseph Grove (in 1789–92) and five books for William Bristow (in 1791–8), but it was the partnership of Simmons & Kirkby and its successors which used his services the most over a period of a quarter of a century (on twenty-eight occasions from 1774 to 1800). We can look at the earliest example: the first edition of William Gostling's popular guide book *Walk in and around the City of Canterbury*, 1774, which was handled in London by Johnson and by R Baldwin. William Flackton was also involved as a retailer of the book in Canterbury, and possibly also as a co-financer:

> Gostling, William. *A Walk in and About the City of Canterbury, with many observations not to be found in any description hitherto published. By William Gostling, ...* Canterbury: printed and sold by Simmons and Kirkby, and W. Flackton. Sold also by R. Baldwin and Joseph Johnson, in London, and by all the booksellers in the county of Kent, 1774. 8°.

Another more complex example is the fifth edition of George Berkeley's conservative sermon, *The Danger of Violent Innovations in the State.*

> Berkeley, George. *The Danger of Violent Innovations in the State, ... exemplified from the reigns of the two first Stuarts, in a sermon preached at the cathedral ... Canterbury, ... By George Berkeley, ... The fifth edition, with notes, historical and political.* Canterbury: printed and sold by Simmons and Kirkby. Sold also by Flackton and Marrable, and T. Smith, Canterbury; J. Johnson, J. Robson, and J. Debrett, London; Fletcher and Prince, at Oxford; T. and J. Merrill, Cambridge; Todd, York; and Elliot and Creech, Edinburgh, 1785. 12°.

This was distributed by Flackton and Smith in Canterbury, by Johnson and several other booksellers in London, and also in both University towns and in York and Edinburgh. Johnson had been the sole London distributor of several of the earlier editions. Altogether, Johnson handled forty books printed by his colleagues in Canterbury.

The second London bookseller to act as wholesaler for a Canterbury firm was Bedwell Law, bookseller and publisher in Ave Maria Lane, 1756–98.[14] Law acted for Canterbury publishers only half as often as Johnson in the same period of time (seventeen books in all). Interestingly, he acted only once for Simmons & Kirkby (in 1792) and only once for Joseph Grove (in 1798), both of whom seem to have preferred the services of Joseph Johnson. All of Law's other cases are for Thomas Smith & Son (1768–1785) and for William Bristow (1795–7). William Flackton appears on both lists as an additional Canterbury distributor.

The pattern suggested here is one of long-lived trade alliances between a successful provincial publisher and a specific London wholesaler. The question arises as to how typical this pattern is. Did printers in other provincial towns make regular deals with London booksellers to act as wholesale agents for appropriate items from their output? Did Johnson and Law favour Canterbury printers, or did they act in the same way for printers from other towns as well?

The answer to both of these questions is 'yes'. Both Johnson and Law had an enormous clientele for this sort of trade, drawn from all over the country. Table 4 shows that Johnson acted at least once as London wholesaler for printers in over thirty towns, and on a regular basis for a dozen of them. He seems to have particularly strong Midlands and northern connections, with Birmingham, Warrington and Leeds as his most frequent clients, but Canterbury's place in this list is a respectable fifth (with 6% of the total of these books handled by Johnson, to Birmingham's 19%, Warrington's 9% and Leeds's 8%).

Bedwell Law's scale of operations was not as large as Johnson's (perhaps one third of the number of books in this category), but it still amounts to nearly two hundred items. Law's geographic spread was much more southern and western than Johnson's, with the odd exception of Berwick which accounted for nearly 28% of the business which he did as wholesaler to provincial printers. Canterbury's proportion was just under 9%. Table 5 shows a comparison of Law's and Johnson's activities as wholesalers for the provincial press. They seem very rarely to have acted for printers in the same town. In fact, Canterbury and Exeter are the only significant cases where this is so and, in the case of Canterbury at least, this was because each dealt with a different printer or group of printers, Johnson with Simmons & Co and Law with Thomas Smith. The significance of Johnson's trade with Simmons & Kirkby is underlined by David Stoker's ranking of the Canterbury firm as one of the seven most important nationally in his ESTC sample of provincial booksellers for 1784–85.

Nor were Johnson and Law the only Londoners to engage in this aspect of bookselling. The firms of White & Son and Dilly both had a huge trade as wholesale distributors, though they handled only a half-dozen books each for Canterbury printers. J Marsom acted in only eighteen recorded cases, half of which were for Canterbury clients (the other towns being Henley, York and St Ives in Huntingdonshire). Pitcher is recorded as London wholesaler for nine provincial books, all of them printed in Canterbury, all anti-Unitarian tracts by George Townsend, for which

Pitcher does not appear to have been a very important outlet, coming rather towards the end of a typical imprint:

> Townsend, George. *A Word of Caution (or Advice) against the Socinian Poison of William Frend. Addressed to the inhabitants of Canterbury and its neighbourhood, ... By George Townsend, of Ramsgate.* Canterbury: printed and sold by Simmons and Kirkby. Sold also by Burgess, Ramsgate; Hall, Margate; and all the booksellers in Kent. Matthews; Pitcher, London; and the Rev. John Townsend, Rotherhithe, 1789. 8°.

This pattern of collaborative activity was not confined to England. Peter Isaac's recent article on the Edinburgh bookseller Charles Elliot shows Canterbury among the English towns with whose booksellers Elliot shared imprints: there are four cases, involving Simmons & Kirkby, Flackton & Marrable and Thomas Smith.[16]

<br>

## CONCLUSION

Throughout the early-modern period, no printing centre other than London itself had a self-sufficient market. Local newspapers had their sub-regional distribution areas. Locally produced books also needed the revenue from additional sales at the regional or national level. Provincial booksellers needed supplies from elsewhere to cater for the range of demand from their local market. The London wholesalers provided the mechanism for much of this trade, taking their percentage for warehousing and distributing books to provincial trade customers. This paper has tried to show that part of this wholesale trade provided facilities for provincially produced books to seek to find a national market. Specialist wholesalers built up long-standing networks of trade with the more important of their provincial colleagues. There is scope for further detailed work in the ESTC database to pursue the analysis of these commercial patterns.

<br>

## KEY TO TABLE 1

BAR: H R Plomer, 'The libraries and bookshops of Canterbury', *Book Auction Records*, 14 (1916–17).

Plomer: *Dictionaries of the Printers and Booksellers who were at Work in England, Scotland and Ireland, 1557–1775*, [ed] H R Plomer, and others (London: The Bibliographical Society, reprinted 1977).

Wiles: R M Wiles, *Freshest Advices: Early Provincial Newspapers in England* (Ohio State University Press, 1968).

Duff: E G Duff, *A Century of the English Book Trade* (London: The Bibliographical Society, 1905).

Dates for the late-eighteenth century are taken from imprints in books.

TABLE 1

A Summary List of Canterbury Book-Trade Personnel to 1800

| Name | Trade | Dates | Reference |
|---|---|---|---|
| John Barker | stationer | 1485 | BAR |
| William Ingram | binder, stationer | 1485-1489 | BAR |
| John Mychell | binder, printer | 1533?-1556 | STC |
| Thomas Kele | stationer | 1548 | BAR |
| Clement Bassock | bookseller, stationer | 1557, 1571-76 | Duff, BAR |
| Esdras Johnson | stationer | 1594 | BAR |
| Joseph Bulkley | bookseller | 1606-1622 | STC |
| Nicholas Johnson | stationer | 1638 | BAR |
| Rest Fenner I | stationer, bookseller | 1651-1711 | BAR, Plomer |
| Rest Fenner II | bookseller | 1681-1711 | Plomer |
| Enoch Fenner | bookseller | 1703-1734 | Plomer |
| Edward Burges | binder, bookseller | 1714-1740 | Plomer |
| James Abree | printer, bookseller | 1717-1769 | Plomer, Shaw |
| Thomas Reeve | printer (with Abree) | 1717-1726 | Wiles |
| Rest Fenner III | binder, bookseller | 1729-1741? | Plomer |
| W Aylett | printer (with Abree) | 1727-1737 | Wiles |
| William Flackton | bookseller | 1739-1798 | Plomer, Gray |
| Mrs Fenner | bookseller | 1732-1741 | Plomer |
| John Flackton | bookseller | 1738-1790 | Plomer |
| Thomas Smith | bookseller | 1746-1788 | Plomer |
| George Kirkby | printer (with Abree) | 1764-1768 | Plomer |
| Simmons & Kirkby | printer, bookseller | 1768-1791 | Plomer |
| Thomas Smith & Son | printer | 1772-1781 | |
| Simmons & Black | printer, bookseller | 1780 | |
| Thomas Smith II | printer | 1872-1787 | |
| Flackton & Marrable | bookseller | 1785-1789 | |
| Joseph Grove | printer | 1788-1794 | |
| Flacketon, Marrable & Claris | bookseller | 1789-1797 | |
| William Bristow | stationer, bookseller | 1789-1800 | |
| Simmons, Kirkby & Jones | printer, bookseller | 1791-1796 | |
| W Epps | newspaper | 1792-1795 | |
| Simmons & Kirkby II | printer, bookseller | 1795-1800 | |

TABLE 2
Kentish Booksellers acting as Local Distributors for Books Printed in Canterbury
in the Eighteenth Century

| Town | Bookseller | Date | Books | Canterbury Publisher |
|---|---|---|---|---|
| Chatham | M Towson | 1768 | 1 | Smith & Son |
| | J Towson | 1777 | 1 | |
| Cranbrook | J Maule | 1739 | 1 | Abree |
| Dover | R Brydone | 1777 | 2 | Simmons & Kirkby |
| | G Ledger | 1786-87 | 2 | Simmons & Kirkby |
| | | 1789-91 | 1 | Grove |
| | | 1794 | 1 | Bristow |
| Faversham | S Doorne | 1776 | 1 | Flackton |
| | | 1777-79 | 2 | Simmons & Kirkby |
| | Coveney | 1789 | 1 | Grove |
| Folkestone | T Page | 1777 | 2 | Simmons & Kirkby |
| Lewes | Burgess | 1794 | 1 | Bristow |
| Maidstone | Mrs Bailess | 1748 | 1 | Abree |
| | W Mercer | 1777 | 2 | Simmons & Kirkby |
| | Chalmers | 1794 | 1 | Bristow |
| Margate | J Hall | 1777-89 | 11 | Simmons & Kirkby |
| | | 1789 | 1 | Grove |
| | Crow | 1776 | 1 | Flackton |
| | S Silver | 1776 | 1 | Flackton |
| | | 1777-81 | 3 | Simmons & Kirkby |
| Ramsgate | P Burgess | 1788-92 | 9 | Simmons & Kirkby ( — & Jones) |
| | | 1789 | 1 | Grove |
| Rochester | T Fisher | 1772-79 | 4 | Simmons & Kirkby |
| | W Gillman | 1787-90 | 2 | Simmons & Kirkby |
| Rotherhithe | Rev J Townsend | 1788-89 | 7 | Simmons & Kirkby |
| Sandwich | J Silver | 1722 | 1 | Abree |
| | W Cronk | 1777 | 2 | Simmons & Kirkby |
| | Cocking & Son | 1789 | 1 | Grove |
| Smarden | J Brown | 1739 | 1 | Abree |
| Tenterden | T Winter | 1739 | 1 | Abree |

TABLE 3
Books Distributed by Canterbury Booksellers for Printers
in other Towns in the South-east in the Eighteenth Century

| Town | Printer | Date | Canterbury Bookseller |
|---|---|---|---|
| Chatham | Webster Gillman | 1782 | Simmons & Kirkby |
| Cranbrook | S Waters | 1791 | W Bristow |
| Dover | G Ledger | 1792 | Simmons, Kirkby & Jones |
| Lewes | W and A Lee | 1797 | |
| Maidstone | D Chalmers | 1796 | Bristow |
| Margate | J Warren | 1797-98 | Flackton & Co |
| Portsea | W Woodward | 1796 | Simmons & Co |
| Rochester | T Fisher | 1776-85 | Simmons & Kirkby |
| | T Fisher | 1781 | Smith & Son |
| | Webster Gillman | 1787-90 | Simmons & Kirkby |
| | Gillman & Etherington | 1792-93 | W Bristow |
| Tunbridge Wells | Jasper Sprange | 1785-1800 | Simmons & Kirkby |
| | | 1795-1800 | Bristow |

TABLE 4

Printing Towns for which Joseph Johnson acted as London Wholesaler

(omitting single occurrences)

| Books | Town | Dates | Printer |
|---|---|---|---|
| 134 | Birmingham | 1764-1800 | various |
| 61 | Warrington | 1774-1795 | W Eyres |
| 55 | Leeds | 1785-1796 | T Wright; J Binns; T Gill |
| 44 | Bristol | 1790-1798 | Bulgin & Rosser; N Biggs |
| 40 | Canterbury | 1774-1800 | Simmons & Kirkby; Grove; Bristo |
| 40 | Edinburgh | 1757-1800 | various |
| 37 | Bath | 1778-1798 | Cruttwell; Hazard |
| 32 | York | 1776-1800 | A Ward; & others |
| 29 | Cambridge | 1767-1797 | J Archdeacon; & others |
| 26 | Newark | 1787-1800 | Allin & Ridge |
| 20 | Taunton | 1781-1795 | T Norris; J Poole |
| 19 | Newcastle | 1758-1796 | T Saint; & others |
| 17 | Exeter | 1787-1796 | G Floyd; & others |
| 15 | Norwich | 1768-1797 | various |
| 11 | Salisbury | 1776-1781 | Collins & Johnson |
| 10 | Oxford | 1780-1795 | J Buckland; R Watts |
| 9 | Manchester | 1788-1800 | various |
| 9 | Shrewsbury | 1788-1795 | J & W Eddowes |
| 5 | Bradford | 1788-1800 | G Nicholson |
| 4 | Doncaster | 1795-1796 | W Sheardown |
| 4 | Glasgow | 1798-1800 | various |
| 4 | Hull | 1794-1796 | Rawson |
| 3 | Lancaster | 1785-1787 | various |
| 3 | Lichfield | 1780-1789 | J Jackson |
| 3 | Sherbourne | 1792-1796 | W Crutwell |
| 2 | Dublin | 1788-1796 | various |
| 2 | Derby | 1789-1798 | J Drewry |
| 2 | Huddersfield | 1794 | J Brook |
| 2 | Trowbridge | 1789-1790 | A Small |
| 2 | Wakefield | 1782 | T Waller |

TABLE 5

Comparative Figures for Printing Towns for which
Bedwell Law and Joseph Johnson acted as London Wholesaler
(omitting single occurrences)

| Town | Law | Johnson | Town | Law | Johnson |
|------|-----|---------|------|-----|---------|
| Berwick | 54 | | Norwich | 1 | 15 |
| Aldershot | 29 | | Edinburgh | | 40 |
| Eton | 19 | | York | | 32 |
| Canterbury | 17 | 40 | Taunton | | 20 |
| Plymouth | 17 | | Newcastle | | 19 |
| Southampton | 12 | | Oxford | | 10 |
| Exeter | 9 | 17 | Shrewsbury | | 9 |
| Bath | 4 | 37 | Bradford | | 5 |
| Birmingham | 2 | 134 | Doncaster | | 4 |
| Northampton | 2 | 2 | Hull | | 4 |
| Ipswich | 3 | | Glasgow | | 4 |
| Manchester | 3 | 9 | Lancaster | | 3 |
| Reading | 3 | | Lichfield | | 3 |
| Salisbury | 3 | 11 | Dublin | | 2 |
| Stafford | 2 | | Derby | | 2 |
| Warrington | 2 | 61 | Huddersfield | | 2 |
| Bristol | 1 | 44 | Sherbourne | | 3 |
| Cambridge | 1 | 29 | Trowbridge | | 2 |
| Leeds | 1 | 55 | Wakefield | | 2 |
| Newark | 1 | 26 | | | |

## NOTES

1. David J Shaw & Sarah Gray, 'James Abree (1691?–1768): Canterbury's first "modern" printer', in: Peter Isaac & Barry McKay [ed], *The Reach of Print: Making, Selling and Reading Books* (Winchester: St Paul's Bibliographies; New Castle, DE: Oak Knoll Press, 1998), 21–36.

2. John Feather, *The Provincial Book Trade in Eighteenth-Century England* (Cambridge University Press, 1985), 16.

3. Feather, *Provincial Book Trade*, 65, 83–5. On patent medicines, see also Peter Isaac, 'Charles Elliot and Spilsbury's Antiscorbutic Drops', *The Reach of Print*, 157–74, and his 'Pills and Print', in Robin Myers & Michael Harris [ed], *Medicine, Mortality and the Book Trade* (Winchester: St Paul's Bibliographies; New Castle, DE: Oak Knoll Press, 1998).

4. N J Barker, 'The rise of the provincial book trade in England and the growth of a national transport system', in F Barbier, S Juratic & D Varry [ed], *L'Europe et le Livre: Réseaux et Pratiques du Négoce de Librairie* (Paris: Klincksieck, 1996), 137–55.

5. Margaret Cooper, *The Worcester Book Trade in the Eighteenth Century* (Worcester Historical Society, Occasional Publications 8, 1997), 23–4.

6. *The Christian's New and Complete Family Bible: or, Universal Library of Divine Knowledge... Illustrated with notes... By the Rev. Thomas Bankes* (London: C. Cooke, [1787?]).

7. Feather, *Provincial Book Trade*, 59–62.

8. Daniel Prat, *An Ode, on the Late Celebrated Handel, on his playing on the organ: composed by Daniel Prat,... Printed partly on occasion of the grand musical festival at Canterbury, 1791...* Canterbury: printed and sold by Simmons, Kirkby and Jones, and all the booksellers in Kent, [1791]. 4°.

9. Abree printed books for sale by Dobell at his house in Cranbrook in 1742, 1743, 1744, 1745, having had a presumably unsuccessful attempt at wider commercial distribution in 1739: *The Seventh-day Sabbath Not Obligatory on Christians*. Canterbury: printed for the author, and sold by J. Noon, London; by the author, and John Maule in Cranbrook; Tho. Winder at Tenterden; James Brown at Smarden, 1739. 8°. Maule worked as a bookseller in Cranbrook from 1737–56 and had already published Dobell's *Seventh Day Sabbath* in 1737 (Plomer, *1726 to 1775*, 166).

10. Richard Goulden, 'Print culture in the Kentish Weald', *The Reach of Print*, 1–20.

11. Feather, *Provincial Book Trade*, 115.

12. T & J Merrill in Cambridge, Fletcher and Prince in Oxford, and Todd in York.

13. H R Plomer, *Dictionary of Printers and Booksellers, 1726 to 1775* (London: The Bibliographical Society, 1932), 141.

14. Plomer, *Dictionary*, 151.

15. David Stoker, 'The English country book trades in 1784–5', in Peter Isaac & Barry McKay [ed], *The Human Face of the Book Trade: Print Culture and its Creators* (Winchester: St Paul's Bibliographies; New Castle, DE: Oak Knoll Press, 1999), 25.

16. Peter Isaac, 'Charles Elliot and the English provincial book trade', in *The Human Face of the Book Trade*, 98, 114.

# William Flackton, 1709-1798, Canterbury Bookseller and Musician

## SARAH GRAY

IF YOU WERE TO browse through a recent edition of *The New Grove Dictionary of Music and Musicians*, in the alphabetical sequence for the letter F you would find between 'die Flachflote', a German organ stop, and 'Flagellant songs', an entry for William Flackton.[1] This might seem an unexpected place to find an eighteenth-century Canterbury bookseller, but as I hope to show, it is appropriate that Flackton's name should live on – even in this somewhat surprising company.

Born in the winter of 1709, William was the older son of John Flackton, bricklayer of St Alphege's parish in Canterbury. The family were 'antient and reputable',[2] but clearly of humble status. William's grandfather seems to have been employed in the works department of Canterbury Cathedral, whose records state that in July 1719, when William was a young child, it was

> ordered that John Flackton Senr take speedy care that the necessary house used by the Choristers & the Inhabitants of Mr Henstridge the Organist... be thoroughly cleansed.[3]

William's education was 'decent, though not learned', and he seems to have shown a musical ability from an early age. He was admitted as a chorister of Canterbury Cathedral in 1718,[4] and was joined by his younger brother John – later to become a partner in his business – in 1725.[5] As is often the case even today, the training of a chorister had a deep effect on the young William, and his love and talent for music began to develop.

When, in 1730, William Flackton took up his freedom and set up in business as a bookseller and stationer, Canterbury was already 'an urban island in the East Kent countryside'. Well-known as the seat of the Primate of All England, with its Cathedral and colourful history, Canterbury's position as a centre on the journey between London and the Channel coast gave it a cosmopolitan air.[6] The prosperity of the small cathedral city is indicated by the freemen's records from that time, which show the existence of 165 carpenters, 122 bricklayers, and 142 bakers. Given these figures, it is perhaps surprising that only six booksellers are listed (there being ninety-four peruke makers and 150 tailors suggests that it was easier to cater for the outer rather than the inner man).[7] There was a flourishing local newspaper, *The Kentish Post & Canterbury Newsletter*, founded by James Abree in 1717, and Flackton made good use of this to promote his growing business.

The bookselling business prospered. In 1738 William took his brother John into partnership, and in due course the business expanded to include John Marrable (1774) and James Claris (1784),[8] both of whom had served their apprenticeship with the firm. From the beginning the Dean and Chapter of the cathedral were loyal patrons – not only as customers for stationery products, but also for book buying and binding: Treasurer's Vouchers show accounts for 'Musick, Pens, &c. £2.13.6',[9] 'Pd Flackton for Com. Prayr. Books for ye Choir £7.8.6',[10] and 'To Wm. Flackton for binding Library-Books £1.3.6'.[11] Flackton's business was sufficiently successful to be involved in the publication of a variety of works: there are some sixty entries in ESTC[12] for books sold by Flackton and his partners, the earliest being a sermon preached by Isaac Johnson in September 1739, and the latest a treatise on *The Laws of Mechanics, as they Relate to Wheel Machines* in 1797, just months before his death. Perhaps the most important work he handled was Charles Seymour's *A New Topographical, Historical, and Commercial Survey of… Kent* in 1776.

In addition to selling books on publication, Flackton specialised in the second-hand and antiquarian book trade, dealing wherever possible with whole libraries of local book collectors. Many of his bulk purchases were from men of the cloth, and included the libraries of Revd Mr Manus, Revd Mr Leightenhouse, Revd Mr Gill, and many others. These sales could be substantial: in 1770 he published a catalogue of the library of the late Revd Isaac Johnson and others, which totalled 170 pages.[13] On occasion Flackton was able to combine his second-hand book trade with his interest in music: in 1789 he published a catalogue of the library of the late Revd Mr Airson, 'together with the entire musical library of a very judicious collector lately deceased'.[14] Flackton built a sound reputation for these kinds of sales, acquiring stock by word of mouth as well as advertising in the local press. A handwritten draft advertisement exists for a Collection of Hymns, arranged by Flackton, which continued with publicity material for the sale of the Library of Revd Mr Fremont and several other libraries lately purchased 'Containing a Large Collection of Books in Every Branch of Literature – Catalogues may be had gra[tis] at the place of Sale where may be had full Value for Libraries or Small parcels of Books'.[15] Many of his sales were advertised in the *Gentleman's Magazine*, and he built a reputation as a bookseller commanding great respect. His considerable knowledge of scarce and valuable books unfortunately suffered some ridicule when he sold a copy of 'The lamentable Tragedie of Queen Dido' for 2s later sold for 'an enormous price', and Flackton was on that occasion, rather uncharitably, dubbed 'the ignorant bookseller'.[16] Fortunately the occasion was rare enough for his reputation to survive relatively unscathed.

While Flackton built up his bookselling business, he managed at the same time to develop his musical skills. In 1735 he took on the job of church organist at

Faversham, a market town some eight miles from Canterbury, and remained in this post until 1752. His interest in music was not restricted to performance. In around 1735 he published a musical setting of Lord Lansdowne's ode 'To Celia',[17] and in 1743 the *Gentleman's Magazine* published a song he had written, 'On a young lady stung by a bee'.[18] Flackton's links with the cathedral, formed as a choirboy, remained strong, and his early interest in sacred music deepened, with compositions sung in the Cathedral and copied into the choirbooks there. While most of this music has been lost, a Morning Service, an Evening Service and two anthems are known.[19] A collection of manuscript sacred music, which he formed into three volumes, is now held at the British Library,[20] and a collection of verse anthems by Purcell stated to have been copied in 1783 from a manuscript 'in the possession of Mr Wm Flackton of Canterbury' is now in the Fitzwilliam Museum, Cambridge.[21]

Flackton's musical tastes were not restricted to the sacred. Canterbury during the latter half of the eighteenth century was fertile ground for musicians of varying tastes. The century had seen an explosion in many kinds of spare-time diversion for gentlemen, with clubs being formed for those with interests as diverse as archaeology, mathematics and different branches of the arts. In musical circles catch and glee clubs became very popular, with examples in Bath, Belfast, Dublin and other cities. A catch was a type of round song for three or more voices, such as 'Summer is icumen in'. The 'catch' was where each succeeding singer had to take up, or catch, his part in time. In due course the words were selected so that a comic effect was produced by the interweaving of the words in the different parts, and correct performance of the words and related comic gestures became a great skill. Flackton and some half a dozen other musicians began meeting regularly in a public house to sing glees and catches, and in 1779 the Canterbury Catch Club was established with the motto 'Harmony and Unanimity'. The success of the club was such that it lasted for almost a hundred years.

In its early days the club built up a loyal following and became well known in the county. A contemporary description of an evening at the club suggests that it was not all elegance and refinement:

> About half past 6. an overture was played by the band (in a small orchestra railed off at one end of the room) after which follow'd another glee & then a catch, which constituted the first Act; the second of w'ch after a short cessation began with another overture, next to w'ch Mrs Goodban [the publican's wife] generally made her appearance & sung a song, after which another glee & a catch or chorus concluded the concert. The generality of the audience & performers however commonly remained 'till 11 or 12 o'clock, smoking their pipes (which they did all the time of the concert, except during Mrs Goodban's song, immediately preceding w'ch the company were always desired by the president to lay down their pipes) during which time single songs were

sung as called for by the president. The price of admission to this club was only 6d. for w'ch besides the music an unlimited quantity of pipes & tobacco & beer was allow'd, in consequence of which many of the members, amongst the lower kinds of tradesmen etc. used... from 40. or 50. pipes (which was always enough to stifle a person at 1s. entering the room & was very disagreeable to the non smokers) there were 3 ventilators in the ceiling in order, in some degree to get rid of the smoke but the room was so low pitched & bad that notwithstanding this, it appear'd as if we were all in a fog there. – The terms of admission being so low it will naturally be wonder'd how the landlord co'd possibly help losing instead of profiting by it, but the fact was that every member of the Club (of whom there were 50. or 60) paid his 6d. whether he came or not & a great many were always absent (the club being on every Wednesday throughout the winter) besides which many that were present instead of drinking beer had spirits & water & particularly gin punch (w'ch Goodban was famous for making particularly palatable) w'ch were paid for extraordinarily.[22]

Flackton's interest in the club is demonstrated by his composition of a hunting catch, 'A glorious chase', in F major for three voices and horn, dated at around 1785.[23]

The music of the Catch Club is now held in the Cathedral Library, together with some of the later Minute Books. The collection is of interest not only to musicians, but also to print historians, since it represents the work of a wide selection of music printers. As might be expected, most of the music was published in London, but provincial centres such as Liverpool, Dublin, Lichfield and Salisbury are also included – surprisingly Canterbury does not feature. Most title pages, especially of the ephemeral items, refer to the popular concert or stage plays in which the music was first heard, in settings such as The Noblemen and Gentlemen's Catch Club, Drury Lane Theatre, Vauxhall Gardens or Ranelagh, and the performers' names are also recorded. The lyrics of the songs are of great interest in themselves, displaying as they do the predominant culture of the passing years: crude eighteenth-century drinking songs, bold patriotic songs during times of war, classical representations of the pastorale on recovery of peace. Topics over the years included such diverse themes as the cruelty of the press gang, perils of alcoholism, the English constitution, and how to eat onions – as well as specifically local themes such as Kentish cricket.[24]

Canterbury in the 1770s–1780s was home not only to the Catch Club but also to the Subscription Concerts, which were of a very different nature. These took place once a fortnight throughout the winter, alternating between 'public' and 'private'. The public events were held only on moonlit nights, and every subscriber had two tickets to give to ladies.[25] These seem to have been much more restrained events than meetings of the Catch Club, and Flackton is known to have been involved in both. He was at this time a pillar of the establishment, not only as a citizen and bookseller, but as a notable performer and published composer, whose works were well respected in London. The arrival in 1783, then, of another well-known musician and composer, who was immediately asked to take over the musical organisation of the city, is likely to have been less than welcome.

John Marsh (1752–1828), like Flackton himself, had received little formal musical training, and was also largely self-taught. He managed, however, to combine a career in the law with mastery of an impressive range of instruments including the violin, cello, oboe and organ, and he founded a small series of subscription concerts in his home town of Romsey, Hampshire. In 1776, Marsh moved to Salisbury where he soon became involved in the city's thriving musical life, and began to work on his compositions. When, in 1783, Marsh inherited a large family estate in East Kent, his fame had gone before him and he was offered, on arrival, the management of the Subscription Concerts in Canterbury. He set about reorganising the musical life of the city, while continuing to work on his compositions. There is no evidence of his relationship with William Flackton at the time, but a hint is given by the survival of a printed anthem based on Psalm 150, with a handwritten note in Flackton's hand 'These words set by John Marsh Esq. Not greatly to his credit – as some think'.[26] Perhaps fortunately, John Marsh found that the upkeep of his inherited family house was prohibitive, and in 1787, having achieved among other things the raising of the ceiling of the premises of the Catch Club, he moved to Chichester where he spent his remaining forty years, and successfully revived and organised the musical life of that city. Whatever Flackton's opinions may have been, the quality of Marsh's compositions ensured that even today some are available on compact disc.[27]

William Flackton's interest in music was such that it became an integral part of his bookselling business. His own works were published and sold by his firm, sometimes with subscriptions taken from as far afield as York, Norwich and Bath, as shown in an advertisement for *New Musick. Proposals for printing by subscription six sonatas in three parts for two violins*,[28] but his passion for music also led to other business deals. He had built up very friendly relations with the Young family of Bridge Place, near Canterbury, who were good customers of his business, and also appreciative of his musical talents. When Sir William Young, later to become Governor of Dominica, was travelling on the continent he was actively seeking sheet music on Flackton's behalf. On 2 August 1751, he wrote to Flackton from Marseille, regretting that he had been unable as yet to find Teparini's Sonatas, but acknowledging receipt of books sent by Flackton to his previous address in Paris. The books were editions of Herman Boerhaave's *Elements of Chymistry* and Brook Taylor's *Principles of Linear Perspective*. While these give some idea of the breadth of reading of a gentleman traveller and diplomat, it should perhaps be noted that Sir William's wife was the only child of the eminent mathematician Brook Taylor, and so possibly other motives came into play.[29] In his letter, Young thanks Flackton for delivery of the books, which had followed him to Marseille, and estimates the price at around £3. He writes 'as soon as I meet with any Musick that may be agreeable to you [I] will find some way of sending it you to that amount'. The letter goes on to state Young's plans to make the Grand Tour of Italy, and to 'endeavour to Hear Scarlatti play five Barrs, that I may not seem to Have Travell'd thro' Italy and lost the greatest Curiosity in It'. As an instructive sideline in Anglo-French relations at the time, he goes on to tell Flackton that

> Since I left Paris, I have had opportunity of seeing and hearing an Incredible Number of Jack-asses perform, and I assure you a French ass has something in his manner of Braying, very similar to the French manner of singing. I shall not at present enter into a disquisition on so Curious a subject: if I did perhaps I might be able to prove that [French people's] taste of vocal musick is natural to the air and soil of their country, and therefore proper here, 'tho not likely to Flourish in another land.[30]

Flackton's friendship with the Young family seems to have been based around music. Lady Young, her mother and her husband all agreed to stand as patrons for Flackton's compositions, and Lady Young was clearly an enthusiast for his music. She wrote a poem addressed 'To Mr Flackton on hearing his Chace Perform'd at the Canterbury Concert', and the opening words, 'Play on, while my attentive bibulous Ear, sucks the Divinely modulated air...' give some idea of its quality.[31] That Flackton was an enthusiast for Lady Young is demonstrated by his 'Elegy on Mrs Young [as she then was] set to music by WF' in 1747.[32] When Flackton wrote to her in February 1760, thanking her for standing as his patron, he was

> Sorry to say that most of our ladies and gents have a taste a trifle more for country dances or ballads. Good taste [in music] is acquired best by hearing a diversity of compositions of the greatest masters of the most musical and political courts in Europe (and you have experienced these).

Lady Young, in reply, writes in a letter dated 16 March

> I believe you have often heard me say in those pieces of music you have now publish'd there are more passages of Elegant Taste and Delicate expression than are scarcely ever found in our modern Compositions; I am but little skill'd in the Theory of Music and am apt to think that Harmony was rather meant to touch the soule than prove a labour to the Brain. You have certainly succeeded in the First...[33]

In another letter from Lady Young during that period she refers to Flackton's 'scholar' Betsy, and later Sir William comments on 'the merit of your performance and its utility to young practitioners', and it seems likely that Flackton taught their children music.[34]

As well as music, church matters formed a large part of Flackton's life, and he became friendly with many influential figures in the city's ecclesiastical circles – particularly with Bishop Horne who, while Dean of Canterbury, 'was often his visitor and esteemed him much'.[35] While actively involved with the cathedral in musical matters,

Flackton became churchwarden of St Andrew's church, whose rector at the time was poet and archaeologist John Duncombe (1729–1786). Flackton's tasks as church-warden included many administrative matters, such as maintaining lists of those pay-ing the Poor Rates, and nominating 'pitiable parishioners' for vacancies in the King's Bridge Hospital.[36] Children, too, seem to have been important to Flackton, though he himself never married. He was active in the development of Sunday Schools in Canterbury, and wrote or adapted hymns and psalms especially for children.[37]

Through his bookselling business and musical interests, Flackton made acquain-tance with many scholarly and cultured figures who were living in or visiting the area at the time. One of these who became a firm friend was the antiquarian and painter Francis Grose, whose wife came from the city, and who, 'like him, was possessed of a very happy vein of pleasantry and humour, bounded always with neatness and pro-priety'.[38] Grose has been described as 'a sort of antiquarian Falstaff... immensely corpulent, full of humour and good nature, and "an inimitable boon companion"'.[39] His wit was renowned, and Robert Burns wrote some verses about him as well as a rather coarse epigram.[40] Grose is perhaps best known for his *Antiquities of England and Wales*, which he completed in 1787: a set of four folio volumes of descriptions and drawings of notable archaeological sites. Grose himself was responsible for most of the illustrations, and his friendship with William Flackton is demonstrated by his gift of the original painting of the illustration of Saint Augustine's Monastery, Canter-bury.[41] A note in Flackton's hand reads 'This view of St Augustine's Monastery was drawn by Francis Grose and by him presented to his intimate friend Wm Flackton in the year 1771'.[42] A view of the cathedral painted by Grose in 1773 was 'taken from the NE end of a Garden the property of Wm F. in Broad Street... [and] presented to Mr Wm. Flackton as a testimony of many years friendship'.

Musical composition played an increasingly important role in Flackton's life, and during his later years he took on a new crusade and enthusiasm and 'nailed his colours to the mast on behalf of the viola'.[43] Until that time the viola, or tenor violin as it was often known, was considered to be an instrument of little individual merit. Flackton disagreed and believed that the viola deserved better recognition. He there-fore composed and in 1770 published a set of solos for viola,[44] prefaced by the note

> These solos are intended to shew that Instrument in a more conspicuous manner than it has hitherto been accustomed; the part generally allotted to it being little more than a dull Ripieno. If it happens to be heard but in so small a space as a Bar or two, 'tis quickly overpowered again with a crowd of Instruments. Such is the Present State of this fine toned instrument owing, in some measur', to the want of Solos and other pieces of music properly adapted to it. The publication of these Solos it is hoped may be productive of other works of this kind by more able Hands and establish a higher veneration and Taste for this excellent tho' too much neglected instrument.

According to musicians Flackton's music is very 'playable', and was much respected in the London circuit. In recent years his solos have been included as part of the Licentiate examination of the Trinity College of Music in London, and his viola solos are available on CD.[45] Flackton's viola playing is quite possibly the subject of one of a series of anecdotes published by Grose in 1793, where he relates the following

> A lover of music having bored a friend who called on him, with a number of sonatas, and other pieces on the fiddle, observed to his friend, that they were all of them extremely difficult; his friend, who did not love music, dryly replied, I wish they had been all impossible.[46]

Publishing and bookselling life in Canterbury during this time was not all harmony. When in 1768 James Abree, printer and proprietor of *The Kentish Post*[47] decided to retire, he announced his intention of resigning his business in favour of his partner, George Kirkby. Learning of this, however, a thrusting young Canterbury citizen, James Simmons, seeing an opportunity of stepping into Abree's shoes, proposed a partnership to Kirkby who refused, and what became known as 'The Canterbury Newspaper War' began. Simmons announced his intention of starting a new newspaper, and the city's booksellers (including Flackton) took fright. They 'regarded Simmons as a newcomer... a young upstart who might deprive them of some of their profits should he expand the scope of his printing business by selling books and stationery'.[48] A bitter dispute developed between Simmons and the city's booksellers, with acrimonious allegations appearing regularly in print. Flackton was present at many of the meetings which were held to try to reach some compromise, and it seems likely that the situation caused him much pain. Finally Simmons triumphed, launching *The Kentish Gazette* in September 1768 – the paper which still serves the city today. Whether this venture did in fact have an adverse effect on the booksellers' profits is not known. Flackton's business certainly continued to thrive, and he took on extra responsibilities, such as becoming agent for the Westminster Life Insurance Company in the 1790s.[49]

William Flackton died, aged 88, on 5 January 1798, having been a successful bookseller in Canterbury for almost seventy years. According to his obituary in the *Gentleman's Magazine*,

> If, to the witnesses of an exemplary life, spent in the practice of virtue and religion, it is an happiness to observe a death most truly comfortable, it was the lot of those who best knew him to be fully gratified. He departed this life, after a short illness... without a groan or struggle, beloved, esteemed, and regretted by all who knew him... possessing, till within a few hours of his death, his faculties, both of mind and body.[50]

His brother John and three sisters had predeceased him, and he represented the end of the 'antient and reputable family'. William's life seems to have been a full and happy one. He was known to be a great reader. His conversation was 'instructive, pleasant, and intelligent; and the chearfulness of his temper never left him till the lamp of his life was distinguished'.[50] Surely his grandfather John, while cleaning out the necessary houses of the cathedral precincts would have been amazed to consider that the young William, with his minimal formal education, would by the end of his life have reached the status of 'Gentleman' in the Canterbury Poll Book,[51] been friends with eminent scholars and diplomats, and composed music which would be still be performed two centuries later. Perhaps, though, William would have liked best to be remembered, as his obituary suggests, as 'a bookseller of the old school'.

## NOTES

1. *The New Grove Dictionary of Music and Musicians*, [ed] S Sadie (London: Macmillan, 1980), 622.

2. *Gentleman's Magazine; or Monthly Intelligencer*, 68 (1798), 170.

3. Canterbury Cathedral Archives [hereafter CCA], DCc/CA 6, f 79r.

4. CCA, DCc/TB 59, 25-6.

5. CCA, DCc/TB 60, 23-4.

6. David Knott, *The Book Trade in Kent. Working Paper: Canterbury Directory ca 1776-1832* (Privately printed, 1982), 1.

7. Anne Oakley, *Canterbury Freemen: Trades 1500-1835* (Typescript, Canterbury Cathedral Archives.

8. CCA, CC/AC9, 924 & 1111.

9. CCA, DCc/TB 88, f 56$^r$.

10. CCA, DCc/TB 68, f 76.

11. CCA, DCc/TB 68, f 78.

12. *English Short-Title Catalogue* (ESTC).

13. William Flackton, *A Catalogue of the Library of the late Rev. Mr. Isaac Johnson, of Canterbury, and of Several Other Libraries:... Which will be Sold... March [blank], 1770,... by W. Flackton, bookseller, in Canterbury...* ([Canterbury, 1770]).

14. Flackton, Marrable, & Claris, *A Catalogue, Including the Library of the late Rev. Mr. Airson, of Canterbury, and Several Other Valuable Collections of Books; together with the Entire Musical Library of a very Judicious Collector lately Deceased,... Which Will Begin Selling November, 1789, by Flackton, Marrable, and Claris,...* (Canterbury, [1789]).

15. CCA, Add MS 30/31. This and other items are contained in a scrapbook, Add MS 30, in Canterbury Cathedral Archives.

16. *Gentleman's Magazine*, 68 (1798), 170-1.

17. *The British Union Catalogue of Early Music: Printed before the Year 1801*, [ed] Edith B Schnapper (London: Butterworth, 1957), 339.

18. *Gentleman's Magazine*, 13 (1743), 47.

19. *New Grove*, 622.

20. British Library Add.30931-3 (as cited in *New Grove*, 622).

21. Fitzwilliam Museum, Cambridge, Mus 183 (as cited in *New Grove*, 622).

22. Canterbury Cathedral Library, MU97.

23. *The John Marsh Journals: The Life and Times of a Gentleman Composer (1752–1828)*, [ed] Brian Robins, Sociology of Music, 9 (Stuyvesant, NY: Pendragon Press, 1998), 302–3.

24. Christopher Cipkin, 'Catches in Canterbury Cathedral', *Canterbury Cathedral Chronicle*, 91 (March 1977), 53–6.

25. *John Marsh Journals*, 298.

26. CCA, Add MS 30/36.

27. *John Marsh Journals*. At the time of writing *John Marsh, Five Symphonies*, The Chichester Concert conducted by Ian Graham-Jones, Leader: Paul Denley is still available on CD and includes biographical information.

28. CCA, Add MS 30/32.

29. *Dictionary of National Biography* [hereafter *DNB*], 399.

30. CCA, Add MS 30/3.

31. CCA, Add MS 30/27.

32. CCA, Add MS 30/23.

33. CCA, Add MS 30/5/6.

34. CCA, Add MS 30/6,9.

35. *Gentleman's Magazine*, 68 (1798), 170.

36. Other items in CCA Add MS 30.

37. CCA, Add MS 30/30.

38. *Gentleman's Magazine*, 68 (1798), 170–1.

39. *Gentleman's Magazine*, 61 (1791), 660.

40. *DNB*, 273.

41. *The Antiquities of England and Wales*, [ed] Francis Grose (London, 1783), 3, 9 & 18.

42. CCA, Add MS 30/20.

43. Personal communication Anne Frazer Simpson 30 April 1999.

44. William Flackton, *Six Solos. Three for a Violoncello and Three for a Tenor, Accompanied either with a Violoncello or Harpsichord* (London, [1770]).

45. Bach sonatas for viola da gamba and cembalo and Flackton sonatas for viola and harpsichord, with Emanuel Vardi and Sir David Lumsden (Kingdom KCLCD 2026, 1991).

46. Francis Grose, *Olio* (London, 1796), 192.

47. For further information see David Shaw & Sarah Gray, 'James Abree (1691?–1768): Canterbury's first "modern" printer' in *The Reach of Print* [ed] Peter Isaac & Barry McKay (Winchester: St Paul's Bibliographies; New Castle, DE: Oak Knoll Press, 1997), 21–36.

48. David Rose,'Story behind the headlines of city's papers', *Kentish Gazette* 7 January 1977.

49. Knott, *Canterbury Book Trade Directory*, 9.

50. *Gentleman's Magazine*, 68 (1798), 171.

51. *The Poll of Freemen and Electors Entitled to Vote for Members to Represent… Canterbury* (Canterbury, 1835).

# Books Returned, Accounts Unsettled and Gifts of Country Food: Customer Expectations around 1700

## MARGARET COOPER

JOHN MOUNTFORT was fifty-four when he died in 1716. He had served his apprenticeship in Worcester with Sampson Evans, 'Bibliop.', and had been freed in June 1686.[1] On the evidence of the Mountfort Collection he was in business on his own by 1688.[2] In the following year he published *A Second Defense of the Government*, a sermon by Richard Claridge, and by June 1707 he had taken over his former master's premises in the High Street 'near the Town Hall', an ideal position, right in the commercial and administrative centre and close to the cathedral.[3]

Meanwhile Mountfort had married, had a family and apprenticed his eldest son and successor Samuel who, in turn, handed on the family business to his son Samuel in the mid-1750s.[4] The Mountforts were Worcester's leading booksellers for much of the century, stocking a tremendous range of books – many of them newly published, a significant proportion scientific and medical titles – and achieving considerable prosperity when measured by the number of houses owned around the city and the estate in Kempsey, a little to the south, for which Samuel senior commissioned a map from Joseph Dougharty, one of the well-known family of surveyors and map makers.[5] The premature death in 1760 of John Mountfort's grandson Samuel, still a bachelor, brought the business to an abrupt end.[6]

A decent profile of this family business which operated for over seventy years can be constructed from the usual spread of sources. A chance event in 1974, however, has given its founder a unique position in the history of the Worcester book trade – and probably a not insignificant one in the early history of the trade in general – for in October of that year a member of the public rescued a collection of material from a bonfire on Worcester racecourse. The rare insight the collection affords into the everyday business of a dealer in books around 1700 makes its retrieval a particularly fortunate one.

The Mountfort Collection consists of eighty-four separate items: sixty-five are letters or notes, most of them orders, nearly all written in the last two months of 1707; eighteen are receipts, most of these dated 1688 and 1689. One of the receipts is undated and so are eleven of the letters but it is possible from internal evidence to place four of the latter in late 1707. Between them, the letters and receipts bequeath two snapshots, one a vivid and detailed close-up of Mountfort's customers, the other a less focused view of his suppliers.

The volume of Mountfort's correspondence is striking: in the last two months of 1707 alone he received nearly sixty letters or notes. These show the bookseller dealing, like his successors, in a mixture of new and secondhand titles, some of the latter the collections of 'lately deceased' gentlemen.[7] His range, however, was nowhere near that handled by his son and grandson. Of the seventy-four identifiable titles (a further eleven are too abbreviated for recognition) nearly half are religious. There is very little literature, only one science book and nothing on law or the arts. On the other hand, Mountfort was already very involved in supplying schoolbooks, years before the mushrooming of educational institutions made these such an important market for booksellers. I have been working for some time towards producing an annotated edition of this correspondence which will list and comment on the titles ordered and cited by his correspondents. In this paper, however, I would like to concentrate on Mountfort's customers.

MOUNTFORT'S CUSTOMERS

The spread of Mountfort's customers, located in twenty-three different towns and villages over a distance of some fifty miles, is not too surprising. Though not quite the social and commercial magnet it was to become, Worcester was after all a large county town, situated on an important and navigable river, and serving a rich hinterland. By 1707 Mountfort was well established, his only real rival John Buttler, a fellow apprentice from the 1680s, and judging from Buttler's will there was clearly room for both to prosper.[8] The list of John Mountfort's customers and suppliers (at the end of this paper) shows that it has been possible so far to identify twenty-five of his forty-seven customers in this collection: thirteen clerics, six landed gentry, two schoolmasters, an attorney, a clothier and two students. The remaining twenty-two customers probably included a further five clerics, two landed gentlemen and two lawyers.

The high percentage of clergy is to be expected: the cathedral city demanded the attendance of this literate and on the whole financially secure group, and while they were there they could acquaint themselves with the booksellers and their stock. 'When I was last at Worcester I call'd at your shop,' writes one, 'and searching amongst your pamphlets, I found Bp. Reinolds funerall sermon, & a sermon of Dr Bates'; and another writes to order a 'wooden Sand-box' which he had seen at Mountfort's shortly before.[9] The bishop himself, the non-juror William Lloyd, was a very important customer. Six of the letters, written on his behalf of course, were orders 'for my Lord', all dated in the last two months of 1707.[10] This was good business, but did Mountfort wonder how much better it might have been if the bishop had spent more than his customary four or five months in the diocese? Still, Oxford and London, where he lived for most of the year, no doubt benefited, and it was a better state of affairs than later in the century when no-one from the Worcester book trade featured in the establishment of Bishop Hurd's great library at Hartlebury.[11]

The books ordered by the schoolmasters were bound for establishments well beyond the city and not, as one might have expected, for the ancient foundations within it. In the 1680s Mountfort's master had done some business with the Worcester Free School (later the Royal Grammar School), and Dean Hickes had attempted the 'rare' step of introducing geography into the King's School's curriculum, but no 'further payment for school books was made till 1850' and both schools were in decline.[12]

What did Mountfort's customers want from him and what were their expectations in terms of personal service? The largest group of letters, twenty-two, is concerned only with books, sixteen only with stationery and one only with patent medicine. There are seven orders for books and stationery, one for books and medicine, and one, written by the bishop's secretary on Christmas Eve, for books, stationery, medicine and snuff. Apart from an undated fragment listing eight book titles, the rest consist of sixteen letters or notes written for a variety of purposes: explanations about unpaid bills, reasons for returning books, a request for assistance in organising a loan, an offer of help to retrieve books not yet paid for, and expressions of thanks accompanying gifts of food.

The collection reveals the range of goods Mountfort was stocking – or prepared to obtain – and the services he offered. There are orders for all sorts of stationery – paper and parchment, plain and marbled, stamped and unstamped, ruled and unruled; quills, wax, sand and sand boxes, strips and boxes of wafers, warrants, bonds and a 12-inch 'Scale ... as cheap as you can' marked with 'Numbers, Artificial Lines and Tangents ... usefull in Trigonometry, Surveying, Navigation Dialling etc.'.[13] Two of the stationery orders are reminders that, whatever the century, bureaucratic muddle is never far away. William Hancock's clerk asked for forty-two highway warrants if, that is, Mr Dover had not already ordered them. A week later, on 30 December 1707, Mr Dover wrote in somewhat of a panic: if Hancock's clerk had not already ordered them he needed the warrants delivering to 'the Sessions' the following morning. One only hopes Jethro Daundecey had not already ordered the same forty-two warrants in his letter of 12 December 1707.[14]

Like those before and those who followed, he was also selling patent medicines: 'Peeks Pills' to Samuel Smart in Bromsgrove, who found them 'fine gentle Purging things'; two papers of 'the grand Cephalik or head-snuff', some pectoral tincture and 'Imperial eye water', all for the bishop's household.[15] More curious is Edward Hanford's request on New Year's Eve 1707 for 'a Small collar of Brawn ... and halfe a pound of Chocolate'; but perhaps this serves to show that at the edges of his business the bookseller was operating as a general mercer. There are requests for binding;

Mountfort was addressed as bookbinder on occasions and in an era where terminology was still fluid was described on his memorial as a stationer.[16]

The real importance of this collection, however, lies in what is revealed about his customers' expectations and his own daily working life. The condition of second-hand books, for instance, could give rise to dissatisfaction. Two days before Christmas 1707 Revd George Vemon of Hanbury found time to write a rather querulous letter which included a complaint about the condition of Du Pin's *A New History of Ecclesiastical Writers,* several volumes of which 'are much sullied and abused'. And a number of notes show that it was not uncommon to return books that had not only been examined but read, a practice which makes today's look-and-decide offers by book clubs seem quite puny. Thomas Bell, vicar of Tardebigge, who the year before had been refused ordination by the bishop on the grounds that he was not sufficiently acquainted with the kind of reading matter that would equip him to care for the souls of his parishioners and presented with a list of books to work on throughout the year in order to remedy this, sent back several books simply because he did not like them. Nor did he 'think fit' to buy Clarendon's *The History of the Rebellion,* but instead offered 'some allowance' for reading it.[17] Prideaux Sutton, vicar of Elmley Castle, wanted all Mountfort's new tracts via the bearer of his letter of 21 November 1707; he might keep some, he explained, but he would 'satisfy' the bookseller 'for ye reading' of others. If the time scale was as leisurely as that for payment it could have been months before such books were returned unwanted to the bookseller.

Francis Evans, who had followed the bishop as secretary from St Asaph to Lichfield and then to Worcester, returned a *Book of Common Prayer* which was 'useless in a manner as it is' because three sheets were 'misplaced'.[18] There was no question in Evans's mind that Mountfort would put this right for collection the following day. As well as personal visits to his shop a number of Mountfort's customers corresponded via servants or bearers, and on several occasions the bookseller was urged to make sure the bearers did their job properly: 'Rowl it not up But see he Buttons it under his wastcott next his shurtt that he may not lose it as formar[l]y'. This was Edmund Lane fretting about his stamped paper; and George Lench was equally anxious that his paper and parchment should be rolled up 'close and fast that the Bearer don't abuse it'.[19] In many instances, of course, Mountfort had to find ways of getting books and other stock direct to customers and some of these must have gone by packhorse or carrier. When the bishop's orders were not being collected by a servant he made use of the weekly 'clothboat' which carried cloth up the Severn to Hartlebury for fulling. Some deliveries, however, could be more complicated. An unsigned and undated note asked for a parcel of books to be directed 'to Mr Martons at Wolverhampton to be sent to Brewood to the Coffee house there'; and Revd

Ambrose Sparry, explaining that his 'Register for last June' had not arrived at the Swan, suggested Mountfort should try a route via another inn, the Crown.[20] There is a glimpse from one letter of the efforts Mountfort made to obtain a specific book, in this case soliciting the help of his nineteen-year-old nephew William Hook, a student at Merton College, Oxford. On 4 December 1707, apparently in response to his uncle's request for information, William advised that he had 'enquird after the Clarendons but am told they will not be finished before Christmas, and the price will be the same'; but then took the opportunity to tell him he had a new edition of 'Cowley's Works' which he would exchange for three titles about Dissenters by Bennett and would 'add another book' to make up the value if necessary. Mountfort must then have written about the reprint to Revd George Vemon, his customer, and offered a folio edition; but Vernon refused 'to go to the price', choosing instead to await the octavo reprint.[21]

A perennial problem for Mountfort centred on the price of books at a time when these were not fixed. A number of orders stipulate 'at the lowest price', but there was always the opportunity for the customer to decide it was not low enough when the book arrived at his home. Revd George Vernon, on the basis of this collection rather inclined to find fault, wrote on 2 November 1707 to say the books he had received were 'bound well enough' but 'something high priced': one is 'very dear at 5 shillings', another he would have but not at the price quoted. On 23 December 1707 he wrote again, this time to complain about the poor condition and high price of a set of books: 'I desire you w[oul]d use me like one that is, or may be a Tolerable good customer'. He is not alone. Revd Jonathan Cotton returned unwanted sermons by Tillotson and a book by Flavell and complained that the ones he had kept were dearer than expected.[22]

Sometimes Mountfort was paid for goods on the spot, more often he was not, typical of a leisurely approach to the settling of accounts. Revd Charles Sabery of Tenbury explained he could not pay that Christmas as he had no rents due until Candlemas, and although there was money owing him from 'down the Country' he was too 'Lame of the Gout' to stir.[23] William Ireland's reason for delay was an outbreak of smallpox among his scholars; Thomas Taylor would pay for the books he ordered 'when the opportunity arises'.[24] This low priority given to prompt settlement is most evident in a letter from Thomas Bell who, after returning several unwanted books, ordered a number of others while admitting he had had 'every design of coming out of ye debt, but had then ye good fortune of an occasion to apply it to another use'. Rather ominously, he continues: 'I must confess at p[re]sent 1 have agreed many waies for money but depend upon it I will honestly pay you were it a 100d tymes as much'.[25]

The problem became acute with the death of a debtor as three letters from Henry Jeffreyes illustrate.[26] Revd John Stanley of Clifton, a customer of Mountfort, had died in late 1707 and among his books were a number still not paid for. Jeffreyes, another customer and something of a gentleman scholar, was Stanley's patron, but in an act of friendship advised Mountfort that the parson had died over £200 in debt and the bookseller's bills were unlikely to be met out of the small estate. He had already put aside as many as he could of the books not paid for and suggested he should try to persuade the administrator to let Mountfort have these back, a much more profitable solution than any meagre amount he might eventually receive. The road to Clifton on the county's western edge would not have been the easiest of routes in winter and Jeffreyes wrote again to urge him not to make a 'dirty journey' just to check on the condition of the books and to supervise their packing – he could pack as well as anyone and the books, he assured him, were as good as new since the parson never lost a week in reading them.

A group of four letters shows Mountfort involving himself in the financial activities of Richard Barneby, a good but indisposed customer. The bookseller advances to Mr Blake and Mr Hall £100 delivered by Barneby's servant, witnesses the cancellation of six earlier bonds for £900, collects the overdue interest on these, draws up a new bond for £1000 – with a £2000 penalty – and, for good measure, pays Blake money Barneby owes for groceries. For his kindness in organising and witnessing these arrangements Barneby promises to 'gratify' him. 'The little Country fare against Christmas', writes Barneby days later, is 'scarcely worth yor acceptance.'[27]

## MOUNTFORT'S SUPPLIERS

The seventeen receipts for goods supplied, most from 1688 and 1689, are not quite such a rich vein.[28] With five of them, for example, it is impossible even to speculate about what had been purchased. Even so, together with two letters from suppliers and two of the orders for the bishop, they show the range of Mountfort's trade contacts.[29] From London he was getting wax, 'best' and 'hard', gold and silver (when gold was eight shillings an ounce) and patent medicines; and from two suppliers whose addresses are so far undiscovered he was buying paper and parchment. It is booksellers, however, who feature most among Mountfort's suppliers, eight, and possibly all nine, in London. One of six receipted bills shows that Francis Hubbertt had supplied a number of schoolbooks, including a small set of geography titles.[30] Locally Mountfort paid a mercer, possibly for binding materials, a watchmaker, and a carpenter who, among other items, invoiced for making frames for pictures and an almanac. Finally, in two respects the receipts from Mountfort's suppliers are like mirror images of his dealings with his customers. Like some of them, Mountfort sometimes benefited from long delays in settling accounts; and, just as he paid and collected money on behalf of some of his customers, so too others, including his married sister and Awnsham Churchill, the bookseller and later MP for Dorchester, performed the same services for him.

In terms of personal service and attention the expectations of Mountfort's customers were high. Perhaps he found encouragement in presents like John Mason's 'Gammon of Bacon'.[31] Even more, he must have welcomed the letters of Silvester Lamb, beautifully written, precise and detailed in their requests, and warmly appreciative; and the honest yearning of a genuine book lover, Revd Ambrose Sparry, who wrote on 15 October 1707:

> If I had a good Cargoe of money I w[oul]d write for a Cargoe of Books but I must make even with you before 1 have any more.

### JOHN MOUNTFORT'S CUSTOMER'S AND SUPPLIERS

ANON
Fragment listing 8 titles published between 1631 & 1684
ANON   Brewood
15 July ??: books order to be sent to coffee house via Wolv'hampton
BAKER Richard   Stourbridge
28 Nov 1707: stationery order written by son John
BARNEBY Richard   Brockhampton   ?Lawyer
15 Dec [1707], 18 Dec 1707, 5 Dec 1707, 30 Nov [1707]:
stationery order and request for help in organizing loan
BELL Robert   Clergyman, rector of two churches.
'Tuesday morn' [no date]: orders books and asks about his debt
BELL Thomas   Tardebigge   Clergyman, Vicar of Tardebigge
28 Nov 1707: returns and order books
BOW[Y]ER John   The Rose, Ludgate Street   Bookseller & Publisher
Receipt 22 Aug 1689: £3 paid by JM's sister to JB's servant
BRADLEY Samuel   ?Worcester   Watchmaker
Receipt 30 Dec 1707: 16/- paid by JM
BROWNE John   Hillend   ?Clergyman, ?ordained 1673
12 Dec 1707, 14 Dec 1707: stationery and books orders and part payment
CHURCHILL Awnsham   Black Swan, Paternoster Row, London
Bookseller & Publisher
Receipt 18 Feb 1689: £10 paid for JM by Henry Mowsell
     Account paid Gard (*qv*) For JM
CONYERS George
Receipt 22 Aug 1689: £5 paid by JM's sister

COTTON Jonathan  Clergyman, curate of Mitton, Kidderminster
  6 Dec 1707: returns books
COWCHER Richard  ?Little Malvern  Landed gentleman
  1 Jan 1707 [?8]: stationery order
COX Joseph  Kidderminster Attorney d 1737. Bought several Worcs manors
  12 Dec 1707, 28 Nov 1707: stationery orders
DAUNDECY Jethro  Poole
  12 Dec 1707: order for 42 warrants for supervisor, books and stationery
DOVER Jos
  30 Dec 1707: checking whether highway warrants ordered by Hill
DURANT Richard  Hagley  Clergyman, rector of Hagley
  3 Oct 1707, 9 Oct 1707, 1 Oct 1707: returns and orders books, owes JM money
EMPSON William
  Receipt 9 June 1688: £2.5s.9d paid by JM
EVANS Francis  Hartlebury  Clergyman
  13 Nov 1707, 24 Dec 1707: books and medicine order for bishop,
  stationery for self
EWIN Robert
  Receipt 22 Aug 1689: £1.10s.0d paid by JM's sister
FEANE J
  6 Nov 1707: books and stationery order
FRANCOMBE John  Worcester  Clothier, Mayor 1712, d 1722
  Receipt 21 Aug 1689: £22 collected by JM's sister
GARD Mr  ?London  Goldsmith
  Receipt ?1689: Paid £2.17s.0d by Mr Churchill for JM gold and silver
GOWER Thomas  ?Droitwich  ?Lawyer
  Receipt 10 Nov 1707: £18.15s.0d paid to John Nixon,
  G's administrator, for books
GREENE Tho. & John  ?London
  Receipt 11 Feb 1689: paid £8 by Henry Mowsell for JM
GRIFFITH John  ?Hartlebury  Clergyman
  [1707]: stationery and books order for bishop, books for bishop's wife,
  stationery for himself.
GRIFFITH William  Whitborn
  4 Nov 1707, 26 Nov 1707, [1707]: stationery orders
HANBURY Richard  ?Bromsgrove b Feckenham, bur Bromsgrove 1724 aged 60
  18 Nov 1707: stationery order

HANCOCK William   Bredon's Norton   Lawyer ?JP, founded school
23 Dec 1707: stationery order, checking warrants ordered by Dover
HANFORD Compton   Woollashall   Lawyer, Roman Catholic family
31 Jan ?1707: stationery and book order
HANFORD Edward   Hewell   Lawyer, son of above, inherited Woollashall 1711
31 Dec 1707: order for beef and chocolate
HIGGS John   ?Highly, Salop   ?Clergyman
5 Dec 1707: books order
HOOD Francis   Bromyard
22 Nov 1707: stationery order
HOOK William   Oxford   Student, JM's nephew, ordained 1711
4 Dec 1707: exchanging information and books
HUBBERTT Francis   London   Bookseller
Receipt 16 Aug 1689: £1.10s.3d paid by JM for 23 books including schoolbooks
IRELAND William   Ripple   Schoolmaster
16 Dec 1707: schoolbooks order
JEFFREYES Henry   Ham Castle   Lawyer, gentleman scholar
helps JM regain books
17 Nov 1707, 12 Dec 1707, 29 Dec 1707, 13 Dec [1707]:
books and stationery orders
KEMP Arthur   Parchment supplier
Letter [1707], receipt 20 Dec 1707: paid £3.9s.0d after disputed bill
LAMB Silvester   Hartlebury   ?Clergyman
13 Dec 1707, 23 Dec 1707, 29 Dec 1707, 20 Nov 1707: books and medicine
orders for bishop
LANE Edmund   Tenbury
30 Dec 1707: stationery order
LENCH George   Doverdale   Lawyer
6 Dec 1707: stationery order
LLOYD William   Hartlebury Castle   Clergyman,
Bishop of Worcester and prolific author
13 Nov 1707, 20 Nov 1707, 13 Dec 1707, 23 Dec 1707, 29 Dec 1707 [1707]:
books, stationery and medicine orders by S Lamb, F Evans, J Griffith
LOVEDAY W   Stationer
?Dec ?1707: ?reply to JM's order, draws bill on JM to pay others
MASON John   ?Clergyman, ?rector of Salwarpe
[Undated letter] Present of gammon

NASH George  Worcester  Mercer
 Receipt 22 Sept 1707: £2.17*s*.0*d* paid by JM
NOXON Joshua  Ipsley  Clergyman, rector of Ipsley
 8 Dec 1707: books order
RAYMUND  Ch  ?Lawyer
 19 Oct 1707: legal stationery order, including 'cartabells'
PETER Charles  Druggist
 Receipt 12 June 1688: 16/- paid by JM for 20 boxes of pills
REA Joshua  Carpenter
 Receipt 24 Dec 1707: £1.9*s*.4*d* for a variety of work
ROBERTSON R  Halesowen
 26 Dec 1707: books order, owes JM £10
SABERY Charles  Tenbury  Clergyman, vicar of Tenbury
 26 Dec 1707: reasons for inability to settle account
SALTER Humphrey
 Receipt: 6 June 1688: £7.4*s*.0*d* paid by JM
SEAGER Thomas  ?Kidderminster, ?BA King's College, Cambridge 1689
 28 Nov 1707: books order
SHARPE Joshua
 Receipt 29 Aug 1689: £8 paid by John Frankham for JM to Sharpe's servant
SMART Samuel  Bromsgrove, d 1732
 9 Nov 1707: pills order
SPARRY Ambrose  Eastham  Clergyman, Vicar of Eastham and son of ejected
 minister
 15 Oct 1707: books order
STANLEY John  Clifton  Clergyman, vicar of Clifton
 20 Dec 1707, 29 Dec 1707, 13 Dec 1707: died 1707 owing JM money for books
 (see Jeffreyes)
STOCKWOOD John
 [Undated] Stationery order
STRINGER John  Upton-on-Severn
 12 Nov 1707: books order
SUTTON Prideaux  Emley Castle  Clergyman with several livings
 21 Nov 1707: tracts order, account settled
TAYLOR Benjamin  Watling St, London  Wax chandler
 Receipt: 13 June 1688: £1.1*s*.2*d* paid by JM for 'best' and 'hard' wax
TAYLOR Thomas  ?Clergyman, ?curate of Enston 1703
 [Undated] Books order

TOMKINS George Martin Hussingtree Student, son of rector of Martin Hussingtree, BA Magdalen College, Oxford 1708
17 Dec 1707: books and stationery order
VERNON George Hanbury Clergyman, Hartlebury Grammar School, then rector of Hanbury
28 Nov 1707 23 Dec 1707: books and stationery order
WEAVER William Lichfield & Kidderminster Schoolmaster at Kidderminster, BA Pembroke College, Oxford 1706
12 Dec 1707, 28 Nov 1707, 14 Nov 1707: books order
WINBURY Thomas Upton-on-Severn
8 Dec 1707: books order

## NOTES

1. Worcester Record Office (hereafter WRO), W R Buchanan-Dunlop, *Monumental Inscriptions... of St Helen's Church*, Worcester, 128, 899:81 BA 1924/2; Liber Recordum 1685-86, X496.5 BA 9360.

2. WRO, Mountfort Collection (hereafter MC), letter dated 23 December 1707, 705:781 BA 7537/1.

3. *English Short-Title Catalogue*, C4435.

4. WRO, Worcester St Swithin's parish registers,14 April 1686, X985.6184. Evidence of Samuel senior's apprenticeship emerges in the record of his freedom on 29 March 1708, WRO A15 Box 3, folder 3.

5. For Samuel Mountfort junior's range see, for example, *Berrow's Worcester Journal*, 14 February 1760; for Samuel Mountfort senior's map see B S Smith, 'The Dougharty family: eighteenth-century mapmakers', *Transactions of the Worcestershire Archaeological Society*, 3 ser, 15 (1996), 260.

6. WRO, Worcester St Helen's parish registers, 942.456002.

7. Thomas Gower's, for example, in a receipt dated 10 November 1707.

8. Buttler was freed as an apprentice of Sampson Evans on 23 May 1684, WRO, Liber Recordum 1684-85; WRO, X900.87 BA 5346, will dated 3 July 1722.

9. WRO, MC, letters from John Higgs dated 5 December 1707, and from George Vemon dated 2 November 1707.

10. WRO, MC, letters dated 13, 20 November, 13, 23, 29 December 1707, and one undated.

11. Margaret Cooper, *The Worcester Book Trade in the Eighteenth Century*, Occasional Publication 8, (Worcester: Worcestershire Historical Society, 1997), 21.

12. *Early Education in Worcester* 1685-1700, [ed] Arthur F Leach (Worcester: Worcestershire Historical Society, 1913), 321, lxxvi-lxxvii. Perhaps the teaching of geography was not quite so 'rare' (see note 30.)

13. WRO, MC, undated letter from John Stockwood.

14. Surveyors of highways, appointed by warrant, had to be chosen in Christmas week, 22 Car 11, c 12 (1670), 3 W & M, c 12 (1691).

15. WRO, MC, letters dated 9 November 1707, 24 December 1707.

16. Equally fluid was the spelling of his name, nine variations being used in the correspondence.

17. Francis Evans, *Diary of Francis Evans 1699–1706,* [ed] Rev D Robertson (Worcester: 1903), 123–4; WRO, MC, letter 28 November 1707.

18. WRO, MC, letter dated 13 November 1707.

19. WRO, MC, letters dated 30 December 1707, 6 December 1707.

20. WRO, MC, letter dated 15 October 1707.

21. WRO, MC, letter dated 23 December 1707.

22. WRO, MC, letter dated 6 December 1707.

23. WRO, MC, letter dated 26 December 1707.

24. WRO, MC, letter dated 16 December 1707; Thomas Taylor's letter is undated.

25. WRO, MC, letter dated 28 November 1707.

26. WRO, MC, letters dated 13, 20, 29 December 1707.

27. WRO, MC, letters dated 30 November, 5, 15, 18 December 1707.

28. WRO,MC, receipt dated 21 August 1689 is for a payment to Mountfort by John Francome and thus the latter is a customer.

29. WRO, MC; letters from Arthur Kemp, parchment supplier, and W Loveday, stationer, are undated but certainly from 1707; letters from Silvester Lamb and Francis Evans are dated 13 and 24 December 1707.

30. WRO, MC, receipt for '4 Cluverins Geo. 0 - 3 – 4', dated 16 August 1689.

31. WRO, MC; Mason's letter is undated.

# Newspapers in Huntingdonshire
## in the Eighteenth and Nineteenth Centuries

### DIANA DIXON

ALTHOUGH Huntingdonshire was one of the smallest English counties, its three principal towns, Huntingdon, St Ives and St Neots all date back to medieval times, with St Ives boasting one of the busiest fairs in England. The Great North Road and the London-Edinburgh railway pass through the county and this meant that in the nineteenth century the towns of St Neots and Huntingdon grew faster than St Ives. The 1801 census recorded populations of 2099 in St Ives, 2035 in Huntingdon, and 1752 in St Neots.

The story of the first newspapers in St Ives is well documented.[1] However, it is interesting to look at this small town, which, within the space of four years, saw three different newspaper titles emerging. As with all early newspapers, their existence depended on an entrepreneurial local printer rather than any considerations of town size. In 1717 John Fisher of Tedd's Lane printed *St Ives Post*, a title which survived for only a few issues. Little is known of Fisher, except that he appears to have flourished from 1716 to 1751 and that this was his only venture into newspaper publishing. He is also known to have operated from premises in St Ives Lane, where he produced books and pamphlets, and it seems likely that his business failed in 1718 or 1719.

Perhaps it was the publication of this newspaper that brought Robert Raikes to St Ives in 1718. Born in Hessle, Raikes had been apprenticed as a printer and worked briefly in Lambeth, York and Norwich before settling in St Ives. Norris believes that he probably purchased the *St Ives Post* from Fisher. Shortly afterwards, Raikes published the *St Ives Post Boy, or the Loyal Packet*. Raikes took William Dicey into partnership, and together they issued the *St Ives Mercury, or the Impartial Intelligencer being a collection of the most material occurrences foreign and domestic together with an account of trade*. Like its predecessor, it was priced at 1½d, and it was 'printed by William Dicey near the Bridge where all sorts of books are printed'.[2] It is possible that the *St Ives Mercury* might have continued to flourish in St Ives had it not been for the fact that its printers were allegedly prosecuted by Sir Edward Lawrence for printing 'something that did not please or suit the times, nor please a certain king'.[3] As a result, Raikes and Dicey abandoned St Ives and moved to Northampton, where they started the *Northampton Mercury*. Its first number in May 1720 contained a reference to the *St Ives Mercury*:

With what care and exactness, we shall acquit ourselves of this Undertaking, has already been premised in the St Ives Mercury of the two preceding weeks.[4]

Certainly the woodcut of Fame appearing in the *Northampton Mercury* is identical to one in the *St Ives Mercury*, and there is also a statement that 'Advertisements taken by printers hereof, and also at the printing office in St Ives, Huntingdonshire'. The Dicey family continued to have links with St Ives and William's younger brother, Cluer, was printing in St Ives in 1732.

For the next ninety years Huntingdonshire had to rely on newspapers produced in the neighbouring towns of Cambridge, Stamford and Northampton. However, on 25 September 1813 the first issue of the *Huntingdon, Bedford & Peterborough Weekly Gazette* appeared. Its opening editorial claimed

Faithfully to narrate the intelligence which may weekly arrive from these diversified fountains, without any mixture of partiality or of rancour.[5]

Initially, the paper was printed in London at Great New St, Gough Square, for its proprietors George Ecton Jones and Weston Hatfield, and it was only in 1815 that it was actually printed in the town of Huntingdon itself. The Hatfield family had business interests in London and Cambridge, and were probably happy to avail themselves of the most economical place to conduct their printing business. On the enlargement of the paper, following its move to Huntingdon in 1815 an editorial proclaimed

We shall avail ourselves of the opportunities of part of our proprietors being owners of an extensive printing establishment in London, resolved that if by the kindness of our professional friends, we occupy a considerable number of columns weekly by advertisements.[6]

The imprint of the early issues of the paper indicates that its publishers were G E Jones & C H Merry, Bedford, Weston Hatfield & Thomas Lovell, Huntingdon, and T Newby, Cambridge. From 1 January 1814 'Weekly' was dropped from the title, and on 14 October a subtitle 'Northamptonshire General Advertiser' was added. The paper was clearly successful and in an editorial in April 1815 the editor proudly asserted

the proprietors of this paper again obtrude upon the public. By an extraordinary union of exertion and success, they have been enabled, within the short space of eighteen months, to obtain for their Journal, a circulation and a degree of acknowledged respectability, which not only outstrips the usual experience of proprietors of newspaper property, but have far exceeded the expectations of their own naturally sanguine expectation.[7]

*(Opposite)* Front page of the *St Ives Mercury* of 16 November 1719

Vol. I.

Num. 6.

## St. IVES

# Mercury:

OR, THE

# Impartial Intelligencer.

BEING

A COLLECTION of the moſt MATERIAL OCCURRENCES,

# Foreign *and* Domeſtick.

Together with

# *An Account of Trade.*

MONDAY, *November* 16, 1719. [*To be continued* Weekly.]

Sr. IVES, *in* Huntingdonſhire :
Printed by *William Dicey*, near the Bridge, where all ſorts of Books are
Printed, [*Price* Three Half-Pence.]

It boasted a wide circulation in the neighbouring counties, extending as far as Leicestershire, Lincolnshire, Norfolk and Suffolk. The list of agents was equally widespread, extending to Boston, Aylesbury and Ipswich. The paper soon attracted readers from as far away as Woburn: in the light of which 'we have resolved to establish a principal office for the paper at Bedford, for the more ready accommodation of our friends in that district'.[8] This is confirmed by a sharp rebuke to a would-be correspondent 'We think Mr C of Woburn is obliged by our not publishing his illiterate letter'.[9] By November 1816 the paper's imprint stated it was published at Huntingdon, Bedford, Cambridge and Peterborough for the proprietors Hatfield & Twigg. Weston Hatfield was assisted by his brother William, and later by his son James. William later became proprietor of the *Northampton & Leamington Free Press*, and James was a printer in Huntingdon and later in St Neots.

Weston Hatfield was a radical man with Whig sympathies who believed firmly in parliamentary and municipal reform and campaigned through the pages of the paper for

> the exposure of and correction of the many abuses that exist both in and out of Parliament, to the subversion of the best interests of the public.[10]

In 1819 the paper was moved to Cambridge, possibly at the instigation of one of its publishers, where it was printed, published and edited by Weston Hatfield at Market Hill until his death in 1837. His son James succeeded him. The paper benefited from its new location, and in 1839 it became the *Cambridge Independent Press*, adopting its subtitle as the main title. An imprint for the paper in June 1838 still stated that it was published at the offices at Huntingdon, Bedford, Peterborough and Cambridge, but by then it was to all intents and purposes a Cambridge newspaper.

The second truly Huntingdon paper appeared in February 1825 and was founded on Tory principles. This, the *Huntingdon, Bedford & Cambridge Weekly Journal*, was owned by H G James, and was printed and published for the proprietor by A P Wood at the Journal Office, Huntingdon. Despite its claim

> that under the circumstances of its being the only political paper in this quarter, has given it an ascendancy which it could not otherwise have obtained,[11]

it never really attracted many advertisements, and it ceased publication in 1828. The printer, Andrew Page Wood, had a long career as a printer from 1822 to 1866, and died only in 1877, having enjoyed forty-five years in printing. However, he did not return to printing newspapers.

It was not until after the repeal of the newspaper stamp tax in 1855, that the towns of Huntingdon again had their own newspapers. The removal of this impediment encouraged the rapid appearance of the *Illustrated St Neots Chronicle & Pictorial Newspaper* in June 1855:

the removal of the Newspaper Stamp – that last restriction on the freedom of the press – enables us to issue the first number of the St Neots Chronicle...[12] The paper was lavishly illustrated, with the Crimean war the main topic of the pictures. In all some eight illustrations were provided, one of which, depicting the capture of the Mamelon tower, occupied a full page. There was plenty of supporting text, and the paper claimed 'We shall, therefore, always court in our columns, the expression of intelligent opinion'. The paper was printed by Frederick Topham, High Street, who had been apprenticed to his cousin James from 1842. The *Chronicle* was not Topham's first venture into newspaper publishing in St Neots, as in November 1853 he had started the *St Neots Advertiser*, a free single sheet of advertisements, which was the predecessor to the *Chronicle* and was incorporated into it. From November 1855 it continued as the *St Neots Chronicle* until 1872, when it was bought by another prominent St Neots printer, David Richard Thomson.

Thomson was predominantly a book and pamphlet printer, but he, too, had ventured into journal publishing with the illustrated monthly paper *St Neots Family Paper* (1854–6). He was not particularly interested in the *Chronicle* and sold it to Messrs Evans & Wells, but retained the copyright which he later sold to the *Hunts County News* in 1886. He preferred monthly publications and began the *St Neots Monthly Advertiser* in September 1878. Enjoying modest success, this paper continued until 1885, when it became the weekly *St Neots Advertiser*. In November 1898 Mr D S Wycroft, of the Cross Printing Works started the *St Neots Free Press* which lasted only until 1902.

After a gap of 135 years, St Ives had a newspaper again. This, the *St Ives Reporter Metropolitan Record & Huntingdonshire Record*, survived for only a few issues in October 1855. It appears to have developed out of a monthly magazine, 'and we venture to hope that as our *Monthly Miscellany* has been well received by the public in this town, the same patronage will be bestowed upon its successor'.[13] Rather pompously the proprietor, George Skeeles, a local printer, invited his readers to decide upon the benefits of a weekly paper for St Ives. He clearly failed to convince them, as only three issues of this title survive in the Norris Museum in St Ives.

Two years later a jobbing printer Samuel Deadman Cox founded the *St Ives & Huntingdonshire Gazette & General Advertiser* in 1857. Cox operated from Crown Street, St Ives, where he both printed and published the paper, and was also responsible for letting rooms at the Public Institution. The paper got off to a rather shaky start with at least four of the advertisements on the front page being inserted by Cox himself. The rest of the page carried the local railway timetables. Cox did not own the *Gazette* long, and it was taken over firstly by William Ainsworth Cooper and then by

James Jaffray, printer of the *Peterborough Times*, who succeeded him from 1865 to 1870.

An attempt to rival the *Gazette* was the rare *St Ives, Hunts & Cambridgeshire Examiner*, of which only a single issue survives. This saw the light in March 1863, and was printed and published by William Lang at the St Ives Printing Works, Crown Street. The tentative tone of the opening address may have been justified in view of the short life of the paper:

> It is with some hesitation that we make our first bow to the reading public of Huntingdonshire and Cambridgeshire; but having summoned the resolution, we hereby beg leave most respectfully to do so.[14]

St Ives continued to be the home of newspapers, and in 1870 the *Hunts Guardian* was launched by its printer and proprietor, Edward W Foster. It soon became an established and successful title and, by August of the same year, it boasted

> The Hunts Guardian is acknowledged on all hands as a newspaper full of news, and as a well printed and most respectable journal. Its weekly intelligence from all parts of the County and Cambridgeshire is ample and its growing and ample circulation strongly commends it to the notice of Advertisers.[15]

These claims were justified, as the paper survived until 1893, having changed its title to the *Hunts County Guardian*, and also its printers before being sold to the new *Huntingdonshire Post*. Before its incorporation into the new title, it had changed ownership in 1885 to H Gilbert Stringer, and again in 1886 to Sydney Gardnor Jarman & Alfred Thomas Gregory. Its final issue announced

> If our successor, the 'Huntingdonshire Post' can open up a larger circulation for the advocacy of the same cause, it will be a change welcomed not only by us, but by all Conservatives in the County.[16]

The new paper, the *Huntingdonshire Post*, was well endowed with advertising, with the whole of pages one and four carrying advertisements from local tradesmen and property for sale and to let. It began confidently, asserting that

> Looking at the present condition of Huntingdonshire in respect of its newspapers, we think it is hardly necessary to give reasons for our appearance or to justify our existence. That a county returning two members in favour of the Conservative and Unionist Party should have no recognised local newspaper for the whole county to support those principles seems an anomaly on the face of it. Apart from politics, it is our object to provide a readable paper for all classes; which will reflect not only the local life and interests of the whole district, but which will deal with all topics and subjects of interest in an agricultural county.[17]

The sentiments were justified as the *Hunts Post* celebrated its centenary in 1993 and continues to survive. Sydney Thomas Smith bought the paper for £680 in 1898, and in 1898 it passed into the hands of Henry Butterfield. Its liberal counterpart, the

*Hunts County News* was older but succumbed in 1926. The *Hunts County News*, under William Goggs, its proprietor and printer, began in 1886. From 1888 to 1896 it was printed and edited by W F O Edwin, and after his death it was sold to R Winfrey MP, who moved it to Peterborough. Its editorial tone was decidedly pompous:

> We have a distinct object in view – political in its methods and patriotic in its intent. We value party government as a means to an end. That end is the welfare of the whole community. Thus we shall advocate the ascendancy of liberal opinions... The programme of the *County News* in pursuing will be to be a faithful and impartial reporter, a fair critic and guide.[18]

The Cambridge series of newspapers published by the Cambridge Newspaper Co, Regent St, Cambridge, circulated throughout Cambridgeshire and the surrounding counties, and launched the *St Ives Chronicle* in May 1889 and the *Ramsey Herald* in 1899.

> We publish today the *St Ives Chronicle*, which is issued in connection with the *Huntingdon Chronicle* and is the latest addition to the Cambridge series of newspapers, which has also affiliated newspapers at Royston, Ely, Newmarket and Cambridge... Probably no county papers have ever obtained the same popularity and the same circulation in so short a time. What makes our success so gratifying is that the circulation is increasing every week.

The editorial continued

> The *St Ives Chronicle*, like the other papers will be thoroughly independent. Politically we shall lean neither to one party nor the other, and we shall give all a fair hearing. The grievances of the poor will be as freely ventilated in our columns as those of the rich.[19]

Complementary to this was the *Huntingdonshire Times* series. The first issue appeared on 18 March 1896 and saw itself as a mid-weekly village reporter, which did not intend to usurp the position of the *Hunts County News*. The *St Ives Times* in the series was printed and published for the proprietor William F Edwin of 137 High St, Huntingdon, and published at Huntingdon, St Neots and St Ives.

Unlike many English counties, Huntingdonshire has been fortunate in preserving so many copies of its newspapers. The Norris Museum in St Ives holds a number of unique titles and stores them in ideal conditions. Access to the collection is offered freely and willingly and warm thanks are due to the Curator and Trustees of the Museum.

Huntingdonshire provides an excellent microcosm of the history of English journalism, with a varied and lively newspaper press. Nonetheless a number of issues still have to be resolved. Why was Huntingdon a more appropriate place for Weston Hatfield to launch a newspaper in 1813 than its more populous neighbour, Cambridge? Why was 1819 a suitable time for Weston Hatfield to move the paper to Cambridge? What led Robert Raikes and William Dicey to begin their newspaper publishing activities in St Ives, and what was it that they published that caused them to migrate so hastily to Northampton in 1720?

## NOTES

1. H Norris wrote extensively on printing in Huntingdonshire. The two main sources on St Ives are *History of St Ives* (St Ives: Hunts County Guardian, 1889), and 'St Ives Huntingdonshire, booksellers and printers' in *Notes and Queries*, 10 ser, 5 (1909), 201–2.

2. *St Ives Mercury*, 6 November 1719, 1.

3. Norris, *St Ives*, 68.

4. *Northampton Mercury*, 2 May 1720, 4.

5. *Huntingdon, Bedford, Cambridge & Peterborough Weekly Gazette*, 25 Sept 1813, 1.

6. *Huntingdon, Bedford, Cambridge & Peterborough Gazette*, 8 April 1815, 1.

7. The same.

8. *Huntingdon, Bedford, Cambridge & Peterborough Gazette*, 30 November 1816, 4.

9. *Huntingdon, Bedford, Cambridge & Peterborough Gazette*, 3 June 1815.

10. *Huntingdon, Bedford & Peterborough Gazette*, 24 February 1816.

11. *Huntingdon, Bedford & Cambridge Weekly Journal*, 26 February 1825.

12. *St Neots Chronicle*, 30 June 1855, 1.

13. *St Ives Reporter, Metropolitan Advertiser & Huntingdonshire Advertiser*, 6 October 1855, 1.

14. *The St Ives, Hunts & Cambridgeshire Examiner*, 27 March 1863, 1.

15. *Hunts Guardian*, 1 January 1870, 1.

16. *Hunts Guardian*, 11 November 1893, 5.

17. *Huntingdonshire Post*, 18 November 1893, 5.

18. *Hunts County News*, March 1886, 8.

19. *The St Ives Chronicle & Cambridgeshire Weekly News*, 25 May 1889, 4.

## APPENDIX

### PRINCIPAL EIGHTEENTH- AND NINETEENTH-CENTURY HUNTINGDONSHIRE NEWSPAPERS

HUNTINGDON

*Huntingdon Bedford & Peterborough Weekly Gazette* September 1813 to May 1839, then *Cambridge Independent Press* 1839–1981
*Huntingdon Bedford & Cambridge Weekly Journal* February 1825 to April 1828
*Hunts County News* March 1886 to December 1926
*Hunts Weekly News* April 1889, then *Hunts Chronicle & Cambridgeshire Weekly News* April 1889 to December 1900
*Hunts Post* November 1893–date
*Huntingdonshire Times* March–April 1896

ST IVES

*St Ives Post c*1717 to 6 June 1718
*St Ives Post Boy or Loyal Packet* 16 June 1718 to February 1719
*St Ives Mercury* 1719–1720
*St Ives Reporter Metropolitan Record & Huntingdonshire Record* October 1855
*St Ives, Hunts & Cambridgeshire Examiner* March 1863
*St Ives & Huntingdonshire Gazette & General Advertiser* September 1857 to February 1859, then *Eastern Counties Gazette* February 1859 to January 1860, then *Huntingdonshire News & Eastern Counties Gazette* January 1860 to December 1873
*St Ives Chronicle & Cambridgeshire Weekly News* May 1889 to February 1901
*Hunts & Cambs Observer* October 1890 to October 1893
*Hunts Guardian* 1870 to November 1893
*St Ives Times* March–April 1896

ST NEOTS

*St Neots Advertiser* November 1853 to June 1855
*Illustrated St Neots Chronicle & Pictorial Weekly Newspaper* June–November 1855, then *St Neots Chronicle* November 1855 to March 1886 *St Neots Monthly Advertiser* September 1878 to June 1885, then *St Neots Advertiser* 1885–1979
*St Neots Free Press* 1899–1902

# Chapbooks & Primers, Piety, Poetry & Classics: the Mozleys of Gainsborough

## JIM ENGLISH

IT IS A SOBERING thought for me to realise that I first spoke about Gainsborough printing some thirty-six years ago to the History Society of the local grammar school, and produced a duplicated list of some locally printed books,[1] and that it was about five years later that I slogged through the county directories to produce a type-script county book-trade listing;[2] it was never published, but has been incorporated into the British Book Trade Index. I retained an intermittent interest in the subject, especially in the Mozleys, and have fitfully added to my notes over the years without really doing anything very practical with them.

It all began in 1962 when I went to Gainsborough as Librarian and found a number of locally printed books in the local collection;[3] these caught my imagination and I began making a study of them and the local book trade. The pattern was a familiar one: building up a card catalogue (more recently transferred to disk) of titles, starting with those at Gainsborough and in local libraries, in booksellers' catalogues, finding additional editions in the British Museum Catalogue – you know the kind of thing: you see reference to a book printed in York or Bath or wherever and think 'I wonder whether my man did an edition'. I had great help from colleagues in libraries country-wide, and from people like the late Peter Wallis, with whom I exchanged letters and information back in the 1960s and early 1970s. Later, searches of ESTC produced many more titles – including some for other Lincolnshire towns whose book trade I have studied much more discursively[4] – and more lately searches of the CD-ROMs of the Biography Database and of Nineteenth-Century Short-Title Catalogue have been fruitful; the latter has thrown up many post-1800 probable Mozley titles which are still to be checked with the holding libraries. Then very recently there has been fruitful contact with Indiana University Library which holds several Mozley titles.[5] Thomas Mozley's autobiography[6] contains information on the family and the business (not all of it fully reliable); and the histories of the Derby firm of Bemrose[7] were also useful as the founder, William Bemrose, was apprenticed to Henry Mozley. I was privileged to borrow William Bemrose's manuscript memoirs many years ago through the good offices of Clive Bemrose. I also had a brief exchange with a surviving member of the Mozley family, but their family traditions did not always accord with established fact. There are, of course, many sources still to be explored.[8]

What, then, of the Gainsborough book trade and the part that the Mozleys played in it?

## THE EARLY GAINSBOROUGH BOOK TRADE

Locally it was thought for a long time that the earliest book printed in Gainsborough was issued in 1776, and *The School of Wisdom* was usually cited.[9] In the absence of bibliographical evidence to the contrary, and despite printers' having appeared in the town's parish registers before that date, I accepted this although I always thought it unlikely that a 324-page book would be the first product of a local press in a small provincial town. Other 1776 Mozley-printed books include *The School of Arts Improved* (156 pages), and an edition of more than 400 pages of *The Pilgrim's Progress*, but no earlier work printed by John Mozley has so far been discovered, a 1770 edition of *The Pilgrim's Progress* listed in ESTC being, I am sure, a misdating of the 1776 edition.

The earliest printer recorded in the Gainsborough parish registers was Henry Thompson in 1754, although stationers, booksellers and a bookbinder appeared before that date. The only example of his work I have found is an edition of *The History of Adam Bell, Clim of the Clough and William of Cloudeslie*.[10] It is undated, but the imprint reads '*Gainsbrough*: Printed by H. THOMPSON, where all manner of Printing is perform'd', and it is tempting to speculate that John Mozley took over this printing business. If he did he might have found the printing presses inadequate for his purposes, as he sent for a new press from Edinburgh which was lost in a gale at sea; he subsequently acquired an even better one. Many of the other book-trade names in the parish registers are, I believe, those of journeymen working for Thompson, the Mozleys, and other printers and booksellers and stationers in the town, some of whom, like Thompson and Oswald Carlton, are worth further investigation.

## THE MOZLEY FAMILY

The founder of the firm, Henry Mozley, was, according to his great-grandson Thomas Mozley, the son of a Yorkshire weaver; he was born about 1721 in Conisborough and came to Gainsborough in the early 1740s. He had begun his working life as a ploughboy, working and going to school on alternate days, and was sufficiently educated to gain employment in a Doncaster attorney's office where, it is said, 'he became an exquisite penman. He was also a good accountant, and he must have been a great reader'.[11] How and why he came to Gainsborough is not known but, to quote Thomas Mozley again,

My great-grandfather seems to have had a good many irons in the fire, trying first one employment, then another, all apparently with success. He kept a school long enough to have scholars that did him credit and were grateful. He was an accountant and as such was frequently consulted by tradesmen in difficulties, and invited to arbitrate in disputes. He made many wills dealing with considerable properties... For some time he was a grocer. For a longer time he had a windmill for the crushing of linseed... Finally, my great-grandfather started bookselling to which his son John added printing.[12]

Both father and son were astute businessmen and both invested in the companies set up to build the toll-bridge over the River Trent at Gainsborough (opened in 1791 and still carrying today's infinitely heavier traffic) and the turnpike from Gainsborough to Retford.

As an example of Thomas Mozley's unreliability, he says 'I have no knowledge of the retail part of the business, if ever there was a retail part. There was none within my recollection',[13] yet William Bemrose wrote in his memoirs[14]

> By this time [1811] I had attained a great proficiency in my business. Mr. B. Booth, a journeyman in the office, undertook voluntarily to teach me to play the flute... Mr. Robert Popple gave me a German flute... His father conducted the retail business for Mr. Mozley...

Also the subscription lists on the two Biography Database CD-ROMs so far issued show that in 1788 John Mozley probably subscribed to David Young's *Agriculture, the Primary Interest of Great Britain* (Edinburgh & London, 1788), and certainly subscribed in the same year for seven copies of the first volume of *Prolegomena to the Dramatic Writings of William Shakespeare*; in 1796 J & H Mozley subscribed for a copy of E T Jones's *English System of Bookkeeping by Single or Double Entry* (Bristol, 1796), although this might have been for use within the firm, and as late as 1814 the younger Henry Mozley subscribed to Joseph Toulmin's *Historical View of the State of the Protestant Dissenters in England*, although this might have been for his own use as he had, according to his son, an excellent library. As further proof of their retail trade, in a newspaper advertisement of 1815 Henry Mozley refers to himself as a bookseller and printer.[15] I have so far found no references to the Mozleys' selling patent medicines or any of the other stock-in-trade items sold by most provincial booksellers.

When John Mozley died in 1788 at the age of 43, his father appears to have taken over the business again, and when he died in 1790 the business fell to John Mozley's son, another Henry Mozley who was only about seventeen years old at the time; three of his brothers apparently worked with him, but his elder brother, John Meggitt Mozley, died in 1796. Again, according to his son, the young Henry Mozley 'had brothers, but their tastes clashed. It was a case for undivided management, and my father, if not quite autocratic, was always disposed to be single-handed. One brother went into the army, another into the mercantile navy'.[16] Because of these deaths and family partings the sequence of Mozley imprints is rather confused, especially as several of their publications were undated, but the main imprints seem to have been:

| 1776–1788 | John Mozley |
|---|---|
| 1787–1793 | Henry Mozley |
| 1787–1796 | Mozley's Lilliputian Book-Manufactory |
| 1791–1792 | J M Mozley |
| 1792–1794 | J M Mozley & Co |
| 1792–1800 | Mozley & Co |
| 1795–1798 | Henry Mozley & Co |
| 1797–1800 | H & G Mozley |
| 1798–1815 | H (or Henry) Mozley |
| 1804–1809 | H (or Henry) Mozley with Brambles, Meggitt & Waters of London |

Little more is known of the first Henry Mozley, apart from entries in the local parish registers. John Mozley's personal life can be briefly summed up: in 1768 he married Ann Meggitt of Gainsborough, by whom he had at least six children; she died and was buried in June 1777. Five months later John Mozley married Ann Wroot, also of Gainsborough, by whom also he had at least six children, the last being baptised eight months after her father's death. Between 1776 and 1788 John Mozley was involved in the publication of about forty volumes, some of which were printed in Gainsborough. Several were published in association with London booksellers, but some of these look suspiciously like false imprints, for they do not correspond with known members of the London book trade, the surnames but not the initials being listed in the standard sources. (How widespread was this practice of fictitious imprints, and why did they do it?) In addition to these, between 1788 and 1793 the Mozleys printed books, which were variously sold by J Edwards of Pall-Mall, William Miller of Old Bond-Street and C Elliot of Parliament-Square, Edinburgh.[17]

Apart from more substantial works John Mozley started printing children's books and chapbooks, a tradition carried on in later years by his sons, although this is an aspect of their work seemingly overlooked by chapbook historians, for the only study that I have traced is a dissertation for a Leeds BA degree.[18] In the late 1780s and early 1790s several items were issued from Mozley's or Mozley & Co's Lilliputian Book-Manufactory including such titles as *Three Day's Chat: Dialogues between Young Ladies and their Governesses* (1790?, 102 pp), *The History of Giles Gingerbread* (a 32-page chapbook dated 1791), and *The Easter Gift*, the title-page of which proclaimed that it was 'Published for the Amusement of all the Little Gentlemen of Christendom'. Other titles from their Lilliputian Book-Manufactory included *Sinbad the Sailor*, *Dick Whittington* and *Tom Thumb*, and little books by authors such as 'Solomon Sobersides', 'Sir Gregory Greybeard' and 'Tommy Trapwit'. Not all were little chapbooks as I had at first suspected – only five of the twenty so far discovered are of about 32 pages – but even those with 150 or more pages are only about 100 or 110 mm tall. Chapbooks issued by Henry Mozley around 1802 include *Charlotte and Francis*, *The Slaves*, and *The Hat; or, Gratitude Rewarded*. Perhaps the most unusual of their productions was *The Bible in Miniature; or, A Concise History of the Old and New Testaments*, published by H & G Mozley in 1798 with pages measuring only 41x33 mm; according to the title-page it cost 'Sixpence in neat Gilt Covers'.[19] Of all their imprints perhaps the most fantastic is that for *Tommy Trapwit's Pleasant Tales, Entertaining Stories, and Merry Jests, recommended to the perusal of the Little Gentry of this Kingdom*, which (in its ESTC record RCN N047035) reads 'Alexandria [ie London?] printed for the author, and sold by all the booksellers of Europe, and by John Mozley, Gainsbro, 1733'. (The date should probably be 1783.)

In the last decade of the eighteenth century their real or apparent London and countrywide trade connections led to a newspaper partnership with the Doncaster printer William Sheardown, the 1795 announcement reading:

DONCASTER, MARCH 27.

W. SHEARDOWN, encouraged by the success his Paper has already experienced, and determined to spare no pains or expense in extending the circulation, and rendering it still more advantageous to his advertising Friends, and interesting to his Readers, has made the same a joint concern between himself and Messrs. J. & H. MOZLEY, *Gainsborough*, from whose extensive connections throughout the Kingdom, he trusts it will soon rank with any of its Contemporaries. The Partnership commencing on Saturday the 4th of April, it will be published on that Day, under the title of The DONCASTER, RETFORD, AND GAINSBOROUGH GAZETTE AND UNIVERSAL ADVERTISER.[20]

Some twenty-one months later, after the death of John Meggitt Mozley, the partnership was dissolved by mutual consent:

DISSOLUTION OF PARTNERSHIP

NOTICE is hereby Given, That the Partnership between WILLIAM SHEARDOWN, of Doncaster, in the County of York, Printer, and JOHN MOZLEY, late of Gainsborough, in the County of Lincoln, deceased, and HENRY MOZLEY, of the same place, Printer, and Executor of the said JOHN MOZLEY, deceased, in the Printing and Publishing the Doncaster, Retford, and Gainsborough Gazette, will be dissolved by mutual consent on the 31st day of December instant...[21]

It would be interesting to discover whether the Mozleys advertised in the paper, whether there was any increase of Lincolnshire (and especially Gainsborough) news and advertising during the partnership, and also whether any new Lincolnshire advertisers carried on using the paper after the connection was broken – a project for some future date.

Henry Mozley the younger seems to have been a man of principle and character, and a respected businessman. He was, too, a man of some learning for, as his son wrote,

From my earliest recollection we had a very good library... The books were many; they were on all subjects... Ours was no casual library... My father had collected it with a special view to the wants of a large family...[22]

His business activities were wide and varied. Between 1795 and 1815, when he moved the family business to Derby, he was involved with at least 130 works, printing and publishing some, and being listed on the title-pages of others as a cooperating bookseller. He printed at least three catalogues (bound in the back of books he printed in 1811, 1812 and 1815); they list 60, 106 and 58 titles respectively of works 'just published' by him, which from time to time I have tried to identify, but with only varying success. He had some trade connections with Bewick and also with Thomas Wilson of York with whom he 'acted in concert, maintaining a position shared by no other country booksellers in England, and somewhat antagonistic to the London trade, then ensconced in very close lines of circumvallation'.[23] He almost certainly had business dealings with William Davison in Alnwick, although neither Peter Isaac nor I can now remember where this idea arose as, apart from a Mozley-printed book with a Davison cancel title-page,[24] and a cryptic note to me from the late David Fleeman, we cannot pin it down.[25] Certainly Henry Mozley travelled in Scotland, where he was graciously received and entertained by the Edinburgh booksellers in 1801,[26] and also in the north of England where in 1808 he saw a Stanhope press in South Shields of which he wrote to his wife 'I really am so pleased with the principle, I could dwell on it a good hour'.[27] About 1814 he was employing a traveller, Mr Phipps, who was at the supper that William Bemrose gave when he completed his apprenticeship.[28]

In 1815 Henry Mozley moved the firm to Derby, as he thought it more central than Gainsborough and he wanted to expand his already substantial business. His property in Gainsborough included a three-storeyed house in the Market Place, with a counting house behind and stable accommodation adjoining, and three buildings in Little Church Lane used as a printing office, a warehouse and a binding shop, together with two 'excellent dwelling houses' in the same thoroughfare.[29] According to William Bemrose, over a hundred people – employees and their families – migrated to Derby, many of them, with their goods and chattels and the firm's goods and stock, going by canal and up the Trent.[30] It is interesting that two of Mozley's employees, William Bemrose (a compositor) and Thomas Richardson (a binder), went on to found successful businesses in Derbyshire, and Mozley's business itself was carried on by his family until the 1860s.

THE

# ECONOMY

OF

## HUMAN LIFE.

IN TWO PARTS.

NEWLY REVISED AND CORRECTED.

London:

PRINTED FOR J. BRAMBLES, A. MEGGITT, AND J. WATERS,
BY H. MOZLEY, MARKET-PLACE, GAINSBOROUGH.

1803.

*The Economy of Human Life* (Gainsborough, 1803),
showing the fictitious London imprint – slightly enlarged

What, then, was produced by this substantial Gainsborough printing business? Henry Mozley followed his father's practice of using dubious London imprints, and went even further by inventing the wholly fictitious London booksellers 'J Brambles, A Meggitt & J Waters' – his wife's maiden name was Brambles, his mother's was Meggitt and his mother-in-law's was Waters. Between 1804 and 1809 at least twenty volumes were produced using this imprint, and again one wonders about his reasons.

Little of their jobbing work seems to have survived beyond the odd theatre poster, but they produced several works for local authors – books of verse, sermons for local clergy and booklets such as *The Village Rambler: a Topographical and Sentimental Excursion, Descriptive of the Town and Vicinity of Gainsborough.*[31] They published editions of the classics – at least nine of *The Pilgrim's Progress* between 1776 and 1813; Oliver Goldsmith's histories; Cervantes's *Don Quixote*; four editions of James Thomson's *The Seasons*; fables by Aesop and John Gay; a stereotyped edition of Sterne's *Sentimental Journey* in 1812, and also one of Gessner's *Death of Abel* in the same year; children's books and chapbooks; educational works such as Anne Fisher's *Practical New Grammar*, Daniel Fenning's *Universal Spelling Book*, Francis Walkinghame's *Tutor's Assistant* and Falconar's *Key to Walkinghame's Tutor's Assistant*; anthologies such as *Elegant Poems* (which included works by Pope, Gray and Goldsmith), and William Enfield's *The Speaker; or, Miscellaneous Pieces Selected from the Best English Writers… [for] the Improvement of Youth in Reading and Speaking*; the three-volume edition of Jane Harvey's *Memoirs of an Author* was printed in 1812 'By and for Henry Mozley, and sold by Longman, Hurst, Rees, Orme and Brown', and a four-volume edition of *Arabian Nights' Entertainments* printed in Gainsborough 'by and for Henry Mozley' was published in 1811. Then there were practical books – editions of Elizabeth Raffald's *Experienced English Housekeeper* in 1808 and 1814, for example, Elizabeth Moxon's *English Housewifery* (1789) and a 332-page edition of Culpeper's *English Physician Enlarged* in 1813; books for tradesmen included *The Complete Ready Reckoner, in Miniature* (1807, 202 pp, 110mm) and J Thompson's *A New, Correct, and Complete Ready Reckoner… for the Accommodation and Assistance of Merchants and Tradesmen* (1810); religious works like *A New Week's Preparation for a Worthy Receiving of the Lord's Supper*; Richard Baxter's *Saint's Everlasting Rest*; explanations of the church catechism by the Revd Thomas Adam (1789) and by John Lewis (1804); *The Whole New Duty of Man*, and editions of hymns and other works by Isaac Watts. In 1793 they started publishing a monthly journal, *The Country Spectator*, which ran to thirty-three numbers; it contained general essays in the tradition of *The Tatler* or *The Rambler* and was written by the local curate, Fanshawe Middleton, who went on to become Bishop of Calcutta. There were also miscellaneous works such as *Memoirs of a Printer's Devil* (1793), *The Jovial Songster, or Sailor's Delight; a Choice Collection of Chearful* [sic] *and Humourous Songs* (1792) and *The Humorist; or, Droll Jester, a Dish Calculated to Please Every Palate, and to Drive Dull Care Away* – a book of humorous anecdotes, but not ones to appeal to present-day humour.

None of their books are outstanding examples of typography, although many are competent productions, and they very rarely printed above octavo, but in all nearly 300 titles and editions which the Mozleys printed, published, or were associated with in some way have been discovered – a substantial and varied output over a period of thirty-nine years for a firm in a small provincial town of about 5000 inhabitants.

## NOTES

1. J S English, *Some Gainsborough Printers: Books Displayed at a Talk Given to the Queen Elizabeth's Grammar School History Society, 27th October 1964* (Gainsborough Public Library, 1964).

2. J S English, *The Lincolnshire Book Trade from the County Directories 1826–1861* (1967, unpublished typescript).

3. The collection has been added to, particularly in the years up to 1974, and now numbers some sixty items.

4. J S English, 'The Lincolnshire booktrade', in *Lincolnshire Places and People: essays in honour of Terence R Leach*, ed Christopher Sturman (Lincoln: Society for Lincolnshire History & Archaeology, 1996), 198–203.

5. I am grateful to the staff of The Lilly Library, Indiana University, Bloomington, Indiana, for the help they have given me and for the photocopies of Mozley title-pages they have supplied, also for permission to quote from their catalogue entries relating to items of Mozley interest.

6. Thomas Mozley, *Reminiscences Chiefly of Towns, Villages and Schools*, 2 vols (London: Longmans, Green, and Co, 1885).

7. H H Bemrose, *The House of Bemrose 1826–1926* (Derby: The Bemrose Press, 1926) ; A E Owen-Jones, *The Romance of a Century 1826–1926* (Derby: The Bemrose Press, 1926).

8. For example, the resources of the Lincolnshire Archives Office have scarcely been touched, and the Derbyshire Archives Office has still to be investigated for any Mozley records.

9. The imprint reads GAINSBROUGH: Printed by JOHN MOZLEY; and Sold by J. F. AND C. RIVINGTON, Booksellers, St. Paul's Church-yard, LONDON. 1776.

10. I am grateful to the Houghton Library, Harvard University, for supplying a photocopy of this chapbook which they date *c*1760.

11. Mozley, *Reminiscences*, 1, 57.

12. Mozley, *Reminiscences*, 1, 61-2.

13. Mozley, *Reminiscences*, 1, 64.

14. William Bemrose manuscript memoirs.

15. *Hull Rockingham & Exchange Gazette*, 28 January 1815.

16. Mozley, *Reminiscences*, 1, 64. Notice that the partnership between Henry and George Mozley was dissolved by mutual consent on 12 November 1800 was published in the *London Gazette* 15–18 November 1800.

17. Since delivering the lecture I was interested to discover from Peter Isaac's paper on Charles Elliot, read at the 1998 seminar, that some Elliot/Mozley correspondence survives in the John Murray Archive; also that John Mozley received Elliot's sale catalogues which again suggests a probable retail trade. See Peter Isaac, 'Charles Elliot and the English provincial book trade', in *The Human Face of the Book Trade*, ed Peter Isaac & Barry McKay (Winchester: St Paul's Bibliographies; New Castle, DE: Oak Knoll Press, 1999), 115.

18. Caroline Bowditch, *Popular Literature and Literacy: a Study of Gainsborough in the Late Eighteenth Century*; presented as part requirement for the Degree of BA (Hons) at the University of Leeds, 1982/3. It is largely based on the Mozley chapbooks in the Gainsborough Library Local Collection.

19. I have subsequently learned that The Lilly Library at Indiana University have Mozley editions of the work dated 1795 and 1797; their catalogue entry for a French version, published in Guernsey in 1797, states that it is translated from part of the Old-Testament portion of a 1782 Mozley thumb Bible which I have so far been unable to identify.

20. *Yorkshire, Nottinghamshire & Lincolnshire Gazette & Universal Advertiser*, 28 March 1795.

21. *Doncaster, Retford & Gainsborough Gazette*, 31 December 1796.

22. Mozley, *Reminiscences*, 1, 118–20.

23. Mozley, *Reminiscences*, 1, 153. Despite this apparent close partnership I have at present no record of any joint imprints for them alone, although their firms appear together on the title-pages of books printed, for example, in Oswestry, Ulverston, Bath, and Macclesfield – further instances of the range of the Mozleys' widespread book-trade relationships.

24. Peter Isaac, 'William Davison in name only?', *Quadrat*, 6 (November 1997), 12–16.

25. In a letter dated 4 July 1965 David Fleeman wrote 'It was nice... to know that my little note on the Mozley-Davison link at Alnwick and so on, wasn't a wild goose chase for you.' Unfortunately the note referred to has not survived.

26. Mozley, *Reminiscences*, 1, 150–1.

27. Mozley, *Reminiscences*, 1, 155.

28. Bemrose, *House of Bemrose*, 17.

29. *Hull, Rockingham & Exchange Gazette*, 28 January 1815.

30. Bemrose, *House of Bemrose*, 19.

31. The imprint reads *Gainsbrough*: PRINTED BY MOZLEY AND CO. FOR THE AUTHOR. 1794. PRICE SIXPENCE.

*John Ware, Printer and Bookseller of Whitehaven:*
*a Year from his Day-Books, 1799-1800*

### BARRY McKAY

JOHN WARE father and son were for half a century the best-known printers in the town of Whitehaven, Cumberland. The elder Ware was born in about 1728 and died in 1791. The whereabouts of his birth and any book-trade activity before his arrival in Whitehaven in, or shortly before, 1770 remains a mystery. However a writer in the late nineteenth century recorded that he had been informed 'that they belonged to York'.[1] If this is true I have been unable to substantiate it; neither the International Genealogical Institute (IGI) nor the British Book Trade Index can offer any help on the matter. One suggestion put to me was that they were from Dublin but neither Munter nor Mary Pollard[2] can offer any firm evidence of this.

There were two John Wares operating in Dublin earlier in the eighteenth century: John Ware (1698-1713) bookseller and publisher of High Street, whose business was perhaps continued in one form or another by his widow until 1715, and John Ware, printer of Dublin (active 1726) whose name is known only from a single imprint. A son born to this second John Ware in 1728 who later moved to Whitehaven, perhaps via York, is a possibility but at the moment it remains only the most slender thread of conjecture and, as Michael Sadleir reminds us 'imagine leads to lies in bibliography'.

The elder John Ware of Whitehaven married a woman called Mary (1731-1787) but again the IGI offers no clue to the place of the marriage, nor has the date of birth of John Ware junior been discovered. What is beyond doubt is that they were in Whitehaven, a thriving port and the dominant town on the west coast of Cumberland, by 1770.

Between that year and the death of John Ware junior in 1820 the firm, to a greater or lesser degree, dominated the book trade in Cumberland. During the period they printed at least twenty-eight books and fourteen pamphlets or catalogues together with eight 'ghosts' of which I have been unable to locate copies. The ghosts include that notorious – indeed perhaps legendary – rarity, the second edition of Malton's *Complete Treatise on Perspective* (1780). They also printed some editions of the *Bible* and *Book of Common Prayer* in Manx between 1771 and 1808.

Bishop Wilson of Sodor and Man had produced a Manx version of the *Testament* in 1722 which his successor, Bishop Hildesley, completed. The manuscript of this translation was sent from Douglas to Whitehaven in 1770 in the charge of one

Reverend Mr Kelly, but the ship on which he was travelling was driven ashore near Harrington (a few miles from Whitehaven). However the resourceful Parson Kelly is reputed to have 'broke open his trunk, secured the precious [manuscript], and, holding it up with one hand swam ashore with the other'.[3] Or, according to another version of the tale, the manuscript was 'held for five hours above the breaking sea, and was one of the few things saved from the wreck of the vessel'.[4]

The Ware's problems with the Manx *Bible* did not end in getting the manuscript safely into the printing office. In 1806 Ware junior donated a copy to the Durham Cathedral Library and in a covering letter apologised for the delay in fulfilling his promise to send them a copy which had been caused by

> a person, who said he came from Suffolk – had visited several foreign Universities – was deeply engaged in the Study of Celtic – (and to whom in the course of a few Weeks, I had lent several Books) – took the opportunity of borrowing the 3 Vols of the Octavo Manks Bible – and marched off, – leaving me only the Copy which I am now packing up for you.[5]

The *Bible* Ware junior sent to Durham was a copy of the quarto edition of 1775, of which the *English Short-Title Catalogue* (ESTC) records that 500 copies were printed. It is no mean piece of work for a provincial printer of that time. Set in three columns it remains, perhaps, as the finest monument to Ware's skill.

Together with his book and jobbing printing Ware also produced *The Cumberland Pacquet, or Ware's Whitehaven Advertiser*, which first appeared on Thursday 20 October 1774. A four-page four-column weekly originally published on Thursdays priced 2½d; by 1799 it was published on Tuesdays and priced at 6d. It was the second newspaper to be published in Whitehaven, indeed the second in Cumberland in general, and passed through several changes of ownership before ceasing production in March 1915.[6]

The *Pacquet* seems to have been a well-respected provincial newspaper with a wide circle of agents in the region and elsewhere throughout England and lowland Scotland. In the early years it was extremely well-supported by advertising from the London publishing houses, though by the year under review their contribution, while still not insubstantial, was noticeably less. However there is a much greater proportion of local advertising for all manner of goods and services, notices and the usual material which makes reading a two-hundred year old newspaper so fascinating.

So much for an extremely brief survey of the careers of John Ware, father and son. I now turn to the day-book of John Ware junior.[7] The day-books consist of two vellum-bound narrow folio volumes of some 1200 pages, which cover the period from August 1799 to July 1802, and from August 1802 to June 1805. Within their pages is contained a wealth of information about Ware's business, who his customers were, what they were buying, and who was supplying him. Transcription has now been completed for the first year from Friday 9 August 1799, when John Hartley & Sons, merchants and bankers of Coat's Lane, Whitehaven, purchased 'two quires of Elephant paper and a quire of Blue Paper' for 7s, to Tuesday 29 July 1800 when David Fletcher, Rope Maker of Bowling-Green, Workington, paid Ware £1 off his account. The intervening pages offer a fascinating insight, not only into the book trade of the town, but also to its social and business life in general.

I can make no claim to any understanding of late eighteenth-century bookkeeping practices (indeed a copy of Woodhaugh Thompson's *The Accomptant's Oracle,* Whitehaven: John Ware for the Author, 1771, is high on my 'wanted books' list). In this primary attempt at an analysis of the business I have concentrated exclusively on debtor transactions. A breakdown of these reveals that Ware's 'shop' sales (of printing, book sales, binding commissions, stationery and proprietary medicines) amounted to a fraction under £400. Of this figure the sales of books and serials accounted for 47% of turnover, printing 21%, binding 5%, stationery 21%, and proprietary medicines 5%. In fact the stationery and binding turnover is a little misleading as sometimes accounts for the binding of say a ledger will be broken down into cost of paper, ruling, the insertion of an alphabet and binding (allowing for a more accurately account of the component parts of the transaction), while on other occasions it is given as a complete figure. I have classified such instances simply as 'stationery'.

WARE'S 'SHOP' SALES

(9 August 1799 to 29 July 1800)

| | | | |
|---|---|---|---|
| Printing | £ 84 | 4s | 4d |
| Books | £145 | 0s | 0d |
| Part-books | £ 13 | 11s | 0d |
| Serials & almanacs | £ 29 | 3s | 1d |
| Binding | £ 21 | 4s | 5d |
| Paper | £ 47 | 6s | 11d |
| Other stationery | £ 38 | 16s | 10d |
| Medicines | £ 20 | 2s | 9½d |
| Total | £399 | 8s | 4½d |

*The Cumberland Pacquet,* and Ware's business outside Cumbria, apparently accounted for over £854, or more than two-thirds of his apparent turnover. This is slightly misleading as some of the monies debited to London booktrade debtors and miscellaneous must include payment for newspaper advertising. Equally the figure for newspaper sales must be on the low side. I trust that as transcription of the later years of the day-books progresses it will become clear which credit amounts relate to sales made in the preceding year (or years) and which is a pre-paid subscription to the *Pacquet* for subsequent year or years.

WARE'S 'OTHER' SALES

| | | | |
|---|---|---|---|
| Newspaper sales & subscriptions | £ 104 | 0s | 5d |
| Advertisments | £ 581 | 12s | 0d |
| London trade debtors | £ 360 | 0s | 0d |
| Miscellaneous | £ 168 | 0s | 8d |
| Total | £1214 | 1s | 1d |

Total suggested turnover        £1613  9s  5½d

What is obvious is that advertising accounts for over one-third of Ware's entire suggested turnover, and more than all his 'shop' sales put together.

My method of arriving at the advertising figures is perhaps open to deeper scrutiny. Four times in the year under review Ware paid an advertising tax of 3s per advertisement to William Wilkins, Stamp Collector of Appleby, Westmorland. Ware seems to have charged most adverts out at 6s each. Based on annotations in the file copies of the *Pacquet* in the Cumbria Record Office (Carlisle) some advertisementswere were charged at 5s, others at 6s, while others were 6s.6d. Therefore for the purposes of this exercise I have worked on the basis that each advert was charged at 6s and simply doubled up on the tax paid to arrive at the figure shown. Analysis of the advertisements in the *Pacquet* awaits further investigation but on completion should give an indication of the real sphere of influence of the newspaper.

London book-trade debtors accounted for £360 in a series of periodic payments, invariably in regular round sums, mainly from W J & E Richardson, booksellers of Cornhill, and William Knight Cullum of Bolt Court, both agents for the *Pacquet* and long-time trade contacts of Ware.

The 'miscellaneous' figure includes payments received from other of Ware's trade contacts throughout England including: Solomon, and later Sarah, Hodgson in Newcastle; Wilson & Spence, and Tesseyman in York; and Inman in Lancaster. Within the area of Cumbria (and it should be borne in mind that in 1799 Cumbria consisted of the counties of Cumberland and Westmorland, and parts of Lancashire and Yorkshire) Ware had dealings with roughly a third of the members of the contemporary 'Cumbrian' book trade: John Soulby in Ulverston (Lancs) Anthony Soulby in Penrith (Cumb) Michael Branthwaite, and William Pennington in Kendal (West) W Halhead, Francis Jollie, and Benjamin Scott in Carlisle (Cumb), Peter

Walker in Cockermouth (Cumb); and William, and later Mary, Eckford in Workington (Cumb). However it is not Ware's trade contacts that are principally under review for the purposes of this paper, it is the day-to day activity in his bookselling, stationery and printing business in King Street, Whitehaven.

The day-books suggest a debtor customer base for the year of some 428 'accounts'; of those whose place of residence can be identified with certainty or strong conviction, 245 were in or very close to Whitehaven itself and 115 in the rest of Cumberland; 18 were in London, 18 on the Isle of Man and 57 elsewhere in the United Kingdom.

As we have seen stationery sales accounted for just over one-fifth of his shop turnover. The information given in the day-books allows this to be broken down a little more accurately. Paper sales, either by the sheet, quire or ream, amounted to £47.6s.11d. Ware stocked a wide range of papers including silk paper (1s per quire), blotting paper (10s per quire), marbled paper (2s ?a sheet), brown paper (10d per quire) and mourning post was 8d per half quire while folio mourning paper was £1.4s.0d per quire. Of white 'printings' and the like, prices ranged from 1s per quire for pot (though a ream resulted in a 10% bulk discount as it was charged out at 18s) to elephant paper at 3s per ream. Best foolscap was 8d a half quire, 1s.4d a quire, or £1.4s.0d a ream.

Of other stationery goods: sticks of sealing wax were 6s each, wafers 6d per ounce (equivalent to 8s per pound), but again a bulk purchase could be had as 'best' wafers either white, red, or black, were 6s.8d per pound. At least three sorts of quills were stocked: common at 1s.6d per hundred, clarified at 4s.6d per hundred, and Dutch at the same price. Pencils (and pencil manufacture is a long-established Cumberland industry) were 6d each. Black ink powder was 5½d per paper, while red was 10d. Skins of parchment, of which Ware sold several throughout the year, were 3s or 3s.6d each. Finally several customers paid 1s.8d for '100 maguls'.

Ware did a fair amount of bespoke binding for his customers; part of it was for the binding of ledgers and the like, but much was the binding up of books and serials. A half-binding on a copy of Hutchinson's *History of Cumberland* 4to, was 3s.6d while similar binding on the *Botanical Magazine* 8vo was 1s or 1s.6d full bound, while the *Philosopical Magazine* 8vo in calf, gilt extra, was 1s.9d. The Whitehaven Subscription Library was a good and frequent customer. Ware was not only founding secretary, but printed catalogues and books of rules for them on several occasions. Where title and style of binding can be compared, Ware seems to have allowed the Library a modest reduction on the prices charged to other customers. A half binding on an octavo was charged at 10d to the Library. At least one example of Ware's binding is known, the file copies of the *Pacquet* in the Cumbria Record Office at Carlisle. This is perhaps similar in style (half red morocco, marbled paper boards) to the binding executed on the *Pacquet* of 1799 for the Reverend Mr Wood of Maryport at 2*s*.6*d*.

Printing, apart from the weekly edition of the *Pacquet*, accounted for 21% of Ware's turnover. I do not know how many men were working for Ware in 1799, but in 1803 he had three journeymen, George Clark, Thomas Nicholson and William Steel, each of whom was paid 15*s* a week. And he presumably filled the post of an apprentice which he advertised in the *Pacquet* on 15 October 1799.

During the year under review Ware printed 232 commissions. The majority of these were single-sheet productions: hand bills, notices, indentures, and the like. As *ESTC* records only a handful of single-sheet printing by Ware between 1771 and 1800 and we have no reason to think that his business was, in 1799, in any way in decline, it is an interesting observation that only the two books printed by Ware in the period have been recorded as surviving. In short the survival rate of his jobbing printing for the period covered by this first year would seem to be zero per cent.

The map (*opposite*) indicates the distribution of Ware's cutomers in the area of modern-day Cumbria. It shows that his main area was principally on the west coast and along the valley between the central fells and northern fells of the Lake District, in effect along the line of the present-day A66, together with a smattering of places elsewhere in the county. What is most noticable from the identifiable commissioners of printing work is that the area from which he drew work is much smaller than that for other sales. Presumably the printers in Carlisle, Penrith, Kendal and Ulverston took such trade as there was in the other areas.

Print runs varied widely for the jobbing work from one copy of a 'Notice About Strangers' printed for the Whitehaven Subscription Library at 6*d* to '5000 [?turnpike] tickets 84 to a sheet on common pot' at 4*s*.6*d* for Messrs Raven & Barnes of Grey Southern.

Among Ware's 'passing' trade during the year was the famous pugilist Daniel Mendoza. On 27 August 1799 the *Pacquet* reported that

> Mr Mendoza, who with his brothers has lately exhibited to respectable Audiences in many of the first Towns of England, and in the principal Theatres, proposes visiting Whitehaven, in the course of the present week. His performances at Penrith, Carlisle, &c. have been well attended, and his Skill and Dexterity in the Pugilistic Art, are the Subject of general Admiration and Applause.

This piece in the *Pacquet*, positioned in the local intelligence section, has the figure of 5*s* inked over it in the file copy; not being an 'advertisement' in the strict sense of the word it was not subject to tax and was presumably among the payments made to

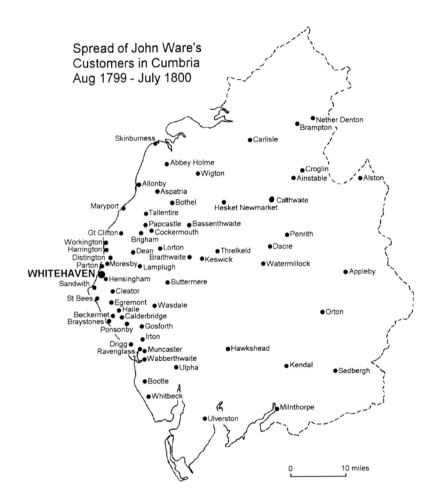

Spread of John Ware's
Customers in Cumbria
Aug 1799 - July 1800

Ware by Mendoza on 29 August. At the same time he ordered, and apparently paid for, 200 handbills each for the nearby towns of Maryport, Workington and Cockermouth. The *Pacquet* carried an advertisment for Mendoza's performances in Whitehaven in the edition of 3 September, performances which were to take place on 4 and 6 September (front seats 2*s*, back seats 1*s*). On the 4th Mendoza bespoke a further 500 handbills, presumably to drum up an audience for these performances. He was back, the first customer of the day, on the 6th for Steer's Opeldoc, one of Mr Newbery's nostrums, at a price of 2*s*. And that, for a time, is the last we hear of Mr Mendoza. He does not appear to have paid the bill outstanding to Ware which may explain a small report in the *Pacquet* of 18 March 1800:

> Mendoza, [*note the lack of a Mr on this occasion*] the celebrated *pugilist*, who has been confined there [Carlisle Gaol] upwards of six months, for a small debt, has obtained his enlargement. – One of his *friends*, straining a compliment to the keeper of the prison, (whose conduct, we doubt not, has been very porper) describes the exquisite *feelings* of the *Israelite*, in the following words:– "Instead of expressing that *satisfaction*, usually attendant on the recovery of liberty, he declared, that from the generous and lenient conduct," &c "he quitted prison with the most *painful sensations!*" – Some people may think this *grateful* effusion rather too much, – if it has flowed even from the pen of a *Brother Jew*.

A search of the quarter-sessions papers failed to reveal if Ware had the great pugilist brought to book over the trifling matter of an unpaid bill for 500 handbills and a bottle of medicine, but Mendoza's incareration in Carlisle Gaol was due to his having failed to settle an account with a Hull wine merchant.[8]

Ware was more fortunate in his dealing with another exotic character. On 24 September Count Boruwlaski[9] (described in the *Pacquet* as a Polish gentleman aged fifty-eight years old and only three feet three inches high) announced that he had 're-moved from his lodgings to Mrs Steel's in King-Street ..[and would be] ... happy to receive company from 11 to 4, admittance 1/-'. Furthermore the diminutive Count proposed to have 'a concert of music at the Assembly rooms in Howgill-Street on 1 October'. But this was later announced as being unavoidably delayed until the 10th. Tickets were available at 2*s*.6*d* and after the concert there would be a ball. Ware printed the Count 200 handbills, presumably for this event, and a further 400 handbills and 150 tickets, of which he retained twenty-four for sale, succeeding in disposing of sixteen by the 10th. The band of the recently formed Regiment of the Isles, stationed at Whitehaven and which brought Ware a modicum of trade from the officers, played at the Count's concert which was deemed to have been a great success. Finally the Reverend Mr Allott of Whitehaven seemed so enchanted by the Count that he had a copy of the Count's *Memoirs* bound up in November.

One steady customer for printing was Mr William Howgill, organist, of Addison's Alley, Whitehaven. On 12 February he was debited for the printing of fifty 'Proposals for Sacred Music, fine quarto post' at 7s, on the 18th he had a further sixty which now, with presumably no compositorial costs, were only 5s. Mr Howgill had a further number of his proposals printed on 25 February, 3, 7, 11 and 20 March. On the 27th he had a further thirty printed but with the addition of subscriber's names; a further 2s was charged for this additonal service. And again more proposals were printed on 5 & 12 April, 23 May, and 6 June. On 13 March he was debited £2.18s.0d for advertisements for his 'Sacred Music' in Gore's *Liverpool General Advertiser*, Billinge's *Liverpool Advertiser*, the *York Herald*, and the *Star*. In the *Pacquet* of 11 February Howgill advertised that he proposed to publish by subscription an
Original Anthem and two voluntaries for the organ or piano-forte with a selection of thirty-eight Favourite Hymn Tunes to be published on 1 June 1800 at half a guinea to subscribers, subscriptions to be taken in by booksellers in London, Oxford, Cambridge, York, Newcastle, Durham, Liverpool; Lancaster, Preston, Kendal, Carlisle, Penrith, Cockermouth, Ulverston
and of course by Ware in Whitehaven. On the 1 April he announced that publication had now been delayed until 4 June. On 13 July Howgill essayed £2.10s.0d on $4^1/16^{th}$ of a lottery ticket. Perhaps in the hope of being able to pay the printing and advertising bill! I have been unable to locate a copy of Mr Howgill's *Sacred Music*, nor, in the period so far examined, does the *Pacquet* offer any advertisments of the 'this day is published' variety for Mr Howgill's anthem.

Ware printed two books in the year (and for the purposes of this exercise I am defining a 'book' as being more than a single-section octavo of sixteen pages). One of these is the Reverend John Brockbank of Wasdale Head's *Two Sermons* which, at twenty pages, just makes it into my questionable definition of a book. On 1 October 1799 Ware debited the Reverend Mr Brockbank with the sum of £2.18s.0d for '200 copies of Sermons, 1½ sheets, Fine Foolscap, Pica, 30 Lines in each page, folded, and Sewed'. On the 3rd Ware noted in the day-book that he had kept fifty copies of the *Semons* for sale. There is no further mention of the *Sermons* in the day-books for the year. One copy has survived in the British Library and it is tempting to suggest that the other 199 are still lining the attic of Wasdale Vicarage.

Bookselling as we have seen accounted for almost half of Wares 'shop' turnover and the bulk of this was for what I must term 'real books' (is there a better one?). He had regular subscribers to several serials: the *Army*, and *Navy Lists*, *Gentleman's*, *Commercial, Botanical*, and *Copperplate Magazines*, and so forth. Part-books also accounted for a modest amount of turnover. Ware had one subscriber to Wright's *New and Complete Family Bible,* which had been advertised in the *Pacquet* in October, Hall's *Dictionary,* and the *English Encyclopaedia* which found one subscriber in the Bishop of Sodor and Man.

Advertising titles in the pages of the *Pacquet* does not seem to have been a great aid to sales. Admittedly a more detailed analysis of the advertisements is awaited, but only four titles seem to have had any discernible effect. Fry's *Pantographia* was advertised on 20 August 1799 and several other occasions, Ware subscribed to six copies but, infuriatingly, the amount columns of the day-books are blank for this entry. Perhaps terms were generous and the sum paid to Fry will be revealed at a later date. However we can be sure that three copies were promptly sold to Sir W Lawson, Mr E L Irton, and the Reverend Mr Barnes of St Bees at £1.11*s*.6*d* each. Claverigg's *New Complete Parish Officer* was advertised on 12 November 1799 and six copies sold over the next six months, while Hogg's *New and Complete Universal Letter Writer* advertised on 11 March 1800 saw two copies sold in May.

If these figures of sales from advertisements are hardly dramatic the same cannot be said for an advertisement which first appears on 27 August 1799. It was for Butterworth's *Writing Master's Assistant,* while the advertisement also drew attention to the same author's *Piece of Ornamental Penmanship with the Portraits of the Admirals Bowe, St Vincent, Duncan and Nelson.* Ware supplied eighteen copies of the *Writing Master* at 7*s*.6*d* and fifty-one copies of the *Admiral's Portraits* at 5/-, a number of which were previously subscribed. In June 1800 Ware had six copies of the fourth edition of Bewick's *History of Quadrupeds* in royal 8vo from Sarah Hodgson in Newcastle, at 12*s*.6*d* a copy; two copies sold fairly readily at 15*s* each.

The works of song-writer Charles Dibdin, who visited the county in May 1800, found a ready market. Ware credited £12.10*s*.0*d* to Dibdin in May for 'sundries', and a further £20.3*s*.0*d* in July for 'goods on return'. These goods would seem to have been copies of his individual songs and other works. Ware sold copies of Dibdin's *History of the Stage,* 5 vols, at £1.17*s*.6*d*; *The Younger Brother* 3 vols, at 19*s*.6*d* and *Hannah Hewitt* 3 vols at 13*s*.6*d*; all in boards. He also supplied copies to other Cumbrian booksellers: Benjamin Scott of Carlisle, Anthony Soulby of Penrith, and John Soulby of Ulverston at £1.8*s*.0*d*, 11*s*.6*d*, and 9*s* respectively. Ware paid Dibdin £1.6*s*.9*d* for the *History of the Stage,* 10*s*.6*d* for the *Younger Brother,* and 8*s* for *Hannah Hewitt.* His terms to trade colleagues would seem to have been generous indeed when compared to what he had received from Hodgson for the Bewick. He also supplied Scott with four dozen of Dibdin's various single songs at 8*s* the dozen, two dozen to John Soulby, and six and one-half dozen to Anthony Soulby, including one song which eventually was to find its way into a Soulby chapbook.

This has, so far, been a somewhat discursive and highly selective trawl through the potential riches of the Ware day-books and before finishing I will examine one other title in slightly more detail as it provides further clues to Ware's pricing, services and trade relations.

On 14 January 1800 the *Pacquet* carried an advertisment announcing that the Reverend David Williamson of Whitehaven's book *Some Observations on Mr. Sike's Creed for October 1799* was to be published in about a month. On 1 February Ware printed for Williamson 'halfsheet, A, of The Doctrine of the Churches, &c., Demy, Longprimer, 8vo' but with no price noted. This was perhaps some form of prospectus. On 1 April the *Pacquet* announced that 'The Doctrine of Churches is to be published in 5 April, sold by the author and also to be had of Ware, Scott in Carlisle, Soulby in Penrith, Walker in Cockermouth, Eckford in Workington, Pennington in Kendal, Walmsley in Lancaster and Soulby in Ulverston.' On 7 April Ware debited the Reverend Mr Williamson for

Printing 600 Copies of "The Doctrine of the Churches," &c. viz.

| | |
|---|---:|
| Longp. 28 by 52, - Compositers Press work, Folding, & sewing | £3 15 3 |
| Wove Demy. 4 ¼ Reams, at 2/- | 4 9 3 |
| Blue Demy 6 Qrs | 4 6 |
| | £8 9 0 |

The author took 284 copies ; Scott of Carlisle, Walker of Cockermouth, Soulby of Ulverston, and Eckford of Workington were each supplied with twenty-four copies on return at 10*d* , while Bell of Wigton had twelve on the same terms. During the course of the month Ware sold four copies retail at 1*s* each and on 10 April Williamson had two copies bound up in calf, gilt at 1*s*.6*d* each. No payments for any of the copies to the trade can be accounted for in the year under review. I rather hope healthy sales and payments will show up in the next year's accounts, for I have become very fond of David Williamson, a notable divine, perhaps wasted on Whitehaven, who emigrated to America where he died shortly after arriving.

These day-books have much yet to reveal and I feel sure that the complete transcription and their eventual publication will be of great value both to historians of the book trade and to local historians of the town of my birth.

NOTES

1. [R L] Ferguson, 'On the collection of chap-books in the Bibliotheca Jacksoniana, in Tullie House, Carlisle, with some remarks on the history of printing in Carlisle, Whitehaven, Penrith, and other north country towns' (Kendal: *Transactions of the Cumberland & Westmorland Antiquarian & Archaeological Society,* xiv.1 (1896) , 35–6.
2. Robert Munter, *A Dictionary of the Print Trade in Ireland 1550–1775* (New York: Fordham University Press, 1988). I am also grateful to Mary Pollard of Marsh's Library,

Dublin, whose dictionary of the Dublin book trade is in the press with the Bibliographical Society.

3. Ferguson, 'Chap-books', 36.

4. William Canton, *The Story of the Bible Society* (London,1904), 31.

5. Letter of John Ware to librarian of Durham Cathedral Library, 13 April 1806, inserted in CIIIB.11.

6. F Barnes & L J Hobbs, *Handlist of Newspapers Published in Cumberland, Westmorland and North Lancashire* (Kendal: Cumberland & Westmorland Antiquarian & Archaeological Society Tract ser XIV), 199.

7. I am grateful to Anne Dick of the Cumbria Record Office and Local Studies Library in Whitehaven who brought to my notice the notebooks of Daniel Hay, former librarian and historian of the town (MS 282). These notebooks recorded the existence of the day-books in the Cumbria Record Office in Carlisle. In equal measure I owe much to the perseverance of David Bowcock for locating them in an uncatalogued collection (now DA box 277) and for arranging for them to be microfilmed, and to Newcastle University for defraying the costs of microfilming.

8. 'From Liverpool I proceeded to several places in the north of England, and in 1799, returned to Carlisle, where unfortunately I was arrested for a debt contracted with a wine merchant at Hull.' Paul Magriel [ed], *The Memoir of the Life of Daniel Mendoza* (London: Batsford, 1951), 101.

9. See *Dictionary of National Biography*.

# Some Radical Printers and Booksellers of Leicester c1790–1850

## JOHN HINKS

IN 1832 THE *Leicester Chronicle* reported on a great procession to celebrate the passing of the Reform Act. The centre of attention was a portable printing press, fitted up in a colourful cart bearing the mottoes 'Liberty', 'Education' and 'Reform'. People flocked to see what it was:

> it was soon understood to be the mighty engine – the warrior whose name was 'Legion' – which had taken so prominent a part and performed such deeds of strength in the great conflict of Truth and Justice with Error and Oppression.[1]

The production and distribution of the printed word were crucial to the advancement of the cause of reform. For about sixty years, in Leicester at least, book-trade people of a radical persuasion held centre-stage in the long and bitter struggle for democracy and freedom.

The story begins around 1790, a time when the English ruling classes looked with horror at events in France. There were fears of a revolution here, and many expected a French invasion of England. The Government, seeing a Jacobin around every corner, introduced a battery of repressive legislation, including the suspension of *Habeas corpus*. Harsh measures were taken, not only against those who spoke or wrote anything which might be construed as revolutionary, but also against those who printed or distributed books, pamphlets or newspapers of a 'seditious' nature.

Leicester had been governed since Tudor times by the Corporation, an oligarchy dominated by Tory and Anglican interests. In the years leading up to its demise, following the Municipal Reform Act of 1835, the Corporation was not only undemocratic, as it always had been, it was also blatantly corrupt – Leicester was 'a national symbol for corporate corruption'.[2] But the town was also a major centre of both religious dissent and radicalism – and the two are by no means unconnected – so the political life of Leicester between c1790 and 1850 was usually turbulent, and sometimes violent. Leicester's book-trade people held a variety of religious and political views – a few were members of the Corporation – but the majority were those of a radical persuasion, often attracted to the book trades in order to promote their opinions.

An early example is Richard Phillips, who came to Leicester in 1788, at first owning a small commercial academy, then a hosier's shop – hosiery manufacture being the main industry in the town. In the summer of 1790 he turned his hand to the book trades, selling stationery, books, music, prints and patent medicines. He soon added a printing press and a circulating library. It was said of Phillips that he had an 'absorbing desire to act as "guide, philosopher and friend" to the public at large, if they would but buy from him all they required for the equipment of their minds and the doctoring of their bodies'.[3]

Phillips was openly radical and his shop was well-stocked with 'advanced democratic literature of the revolutionary epoch'.[4] In 1792 he established the town's first radical newspaper, the *Leicester Herald*. He also founded the Adelphi Society, ostensibly for philosophical and scientific study, but which soon turned to radical politics. This brought Phillips to the attention of the Corporation, which had 'allowed itself to become alarmed at the thought of a few intellectuals reading "left" literature, and welcomed the [Government] proclamation of 1792 against seditious publications'.[5]

Like many booksellers in Leicester and elsewhere, Phillips stocked the radical works of Tom Paine, but in 1793, a paid informer bought a copy of *The Rights of Man* from Phillips, who was convicted of selling seditious literature and sentenced to eighteen months imprisonment. But he continued to conduct correspondence and even edited the *Herald* while he was in prison.[6] Also in 1793, the Adelphi Society was forced to disband when the Corporation expressed its concern over their experiments with electricity, thought to be at least as dangerous as their politics.[7]

Shortly after Phillips's release from prison in 1794, there was a disastrous fire, which completely destroyed his business: his shop, printing office and circulating library were all burnt down. His enemies thought that the fire was deliberate, though it had started in his neighbour's premises, which were also destroyed, and his insurance claim was quickly paid in full, suggesting that the fire was accidental. After the fire, Phillips resumed business for a time in Leicester, but by the summer of 1796 he had moved to London and was trading in St Paul's Churchyard. His later career is beyond my scope but, briefly, he became a prolific publisher, mostly of textbooks, which he often wrote himself under various pseudonyms. He was Sheriff of London in 1807 and was knighted the following year by George III.

Richard Phillips is a fascinating character. He was a strict vegetarian – a very eccentric habit in those days. He was described as 'earnest-minded, energetic, and warm-hearted – his friends, and even his servants, loved him with an affection as intense as the hatred of his enemies, and he had many of both'.[8] The *Dictionary of National Biography* gives a fair assessment of Phillips's achievement: 'His chief importance was as a purveyor of cheap miscellaneous literature designed for popular instruction, and as the legitimate predecessor of the brothers Chambers and of Charles Knight'.[9]

Richard Phillips was not overly modest. He wrote of himself that 'politics appeared as profitable an article as he could deal in; and with that alacrity which has ever distinguished the acts of able men, he established the newspaper called *The Leicester Herald*.[10]

Not surprisingly, the newspaper publishing business attracted a number of prominent radicals. (Important though the newspapers were, I can mention them only briefly here.[11]) Richard Phillips's *Herald* was for a time one of two radical newspapers in the town. From 1792 to 1793, Thomas Combe published and edited the first of two papers to be called the *Leicester Chronicle*. Combe was a noted figure in the life of the town. In addition to his activities as newspaper proprietor and editor, bookseller, printer and circulating librarian, he was a popular speaker – 'an oracle on literary subjects' – who also taught reading and grammar at the Misses Simpsons' Boarding Academy for Young Ladies.[12] Combe seems to have been Leicester's leading bookseller for many years, and was a publisher of some local importance.

The second *Leicester Chronicle* ran from 1810 to 1864, owned at first by a committee of radicals, then by Thomas Thompson, later joined by his son James, who became a distinguished local historian. The Thompsons each edited the paper for many years, but its editor and printer from 1812 to 1813 was George Bown, a prominent radical book-trade figure who had been a member of Richard Phillips's Adelphi Society. He was also secretary of the Constitutional Society, and was charged, though unsuccessfully, with organising seditious meetings. James Thompson records that members of the society addressed each other as 'citizen' and had to declare their revolutionary principles as a sort of password to gain admittance.[13]

Another very radical printer in Leicester was John Pares,[14] who has the distinction of having been arrested three times on account of his politics. In 1798, while he was taken to London for questioning, his house was searched and his papers seized in the hope of finding evidence of treason. Apparently none was found, as Pares was released after being held for a fortnight.[15] He was less fortunate in 1802 when he was convicted at Leicester Quarter Sessions of publishing 'a song of seditious tendency', for which he was imprisoned for twelve months.[16]

John Pares was one of the leaders of the Leicester Hampden Club, founded in 1816, a time when Hampden Clubs were expanding rapidly in the provinces, enabling radicals to meet together for political debate and readings. The Corporation regarded the Leicester Hampden Club as a hot-bed of revolutionary activity and the Town Clerk paid a spy to infiltrate their meetings. This led to Pares narrowly escaping prosecution in 1816 for publishing two seditious pamphlets which had been read out at a meeting of the Club.[17]

The following year, the Town Clerk reported Pares to the Home Office as 'a dangerous fellow' who would be 'better out of the way'.[18] This was a time of further repressive legislation – *Habeas corpus* was again suspended – and many Leicester radicals, including John Pares, were arrested. He was charged with publishing a 'seditious, blasphemous, and malicious libel'.[19] Although Pares was acquitted, he was almost ruined by the expense of the case.[20]

Isaac Cockshaw and his sons Isaac and Albert were important figures in the Leicester book trades. Isaac Cockshaw senior, an engraver and drawing master, opened a circulating library in 1800. After he died in 1818, the library seems to have been carried on by his son Isaac. His other son, Albert, opened a second library in 1824 and later added a reading room, where the London morning papers could be read the same evening. The Cockshaws were a prominent radical family. Isaac (the father) – described as 'the doughty radical printer and engraver'[21] – printed radical pamphlets and election addresses, and Albert was well known for his extremely radical views.

In Leicester, as elsewhere, radical activity was refocused, rather than ended, when the Reform Act was passed in 1832. A measure of parliamentary reform might have been achieved, but attention now turned to local government. In 1833 the commissioners arrived in Leicester to begin their investigation of the Corporation. At about the same time, the Corporation prosecuted Thomas Thompson, the *Chronicle* editor, and Albert Cockshaw for printing and distributing a pamphlet alleging maladministration of justice and misuse of public funds. The case was dismissed, but only on a legal technicality.[22]

In 1836 yet another radical newspaper, the *Leicestershire Mercury*, was established. Albert Cockshaw was both proprietor and printer for its first four years. The *Mercury* in Cockshaw's time was notoriously radical. It was sympathetic to Chartism, and also supported the disestablishment of the Church of England – a cause dear to the hearts of many of Leicester's nonconformists.

Nonconformists had long played a leading part in Leicester's radical politics. Originally the Unitarians had been in the forefront of local religious and political dissent, but by this time the Baptists had taken the lead. In particular, three Baptists were openly expressing extremely radical views. They were Albert Cockshaw, the Reverend J P Mursell (who had a very strong influence over the *Mercury* during Cockshaw's time), and another important book-trade person (who was also a Baptist minister) Joseph Foulkes Winks.

Winks was a very active printer, bookseller and publisher – 'a fiery little gamecock of a man who was always thirsting for a fight in the name of justice and liberty'.[23] He came to Leicester from Loughborough in 1830, and quickly immersed himself in the

(*Opposite*) Advertisement for Albert Cockshaw from Thomas Combe's *Leicester Directory* (1826)
Reproduced by permission of the Record Office for Leicestershire, Leicester & Rutland

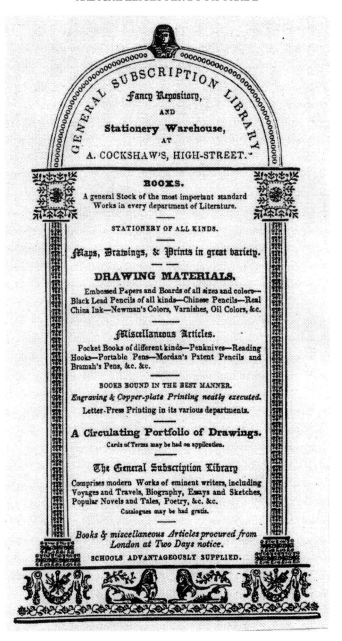

town's radical politics. He was a leading light of the Leicester and Leicestershire Political Union, which campaigned *inter alia* against newspaper duty, the dreaded 'taxes on knowledge'. Winks became a thorn in the Corporation's side, speaking in public about their abuse of charitable funds and the partiality of the magistrates.[24]

Many Nonconformists at this time refused on principle to pay Church Rates and this became a major issue in Leicester. On one occasion, when Winks refused to pay, eleven reams of his paper were seized and sold.[25] He was certainly energetic; in addition to his duties as a Baptist minister and his work as one of Leicester's leading printers, he was also the publisher for the General Baptist Union and personally edited no less than five monthly magazines.[26] Winks was a leading radical who campaigned vigorously not only for parliamentary and municipal reform but also for many other causes.

One cause that Winks is said to have won single-handedly, was the ending of the practice of gibbeting – the public exhibition of the bodies of executed murderers. A rather bizarre book-trade link is that Winks's campaign focused on the notorious case of one James Cook, a Leicester bookbinder who murdered and dismembered a commercial traveller in 1832. As a result of Winks's crusade, Cook was the last person to be gibbeted in England.[27]

Joseph Winks had been brought up in Gainsborough, where he set up a mutual-improvement society. Although it closed down when Winks left Gainsborough, the society left a lasting impression on one of its members, a seventeen year-old who had helped Winks run a Sunday school teaching poor adults to read.[28] His name was Thomas Cooper, and he was to become one of the leaders of the Chartist movement, and would also write a detailed autobiography, giving us a unique insight not only into Leicester's radical politics but also its book trades.

When Thomas Cooper arrived in Leicester in 1840, to take up a job as a journalist with the *Leicestershire Mercury*, he was delighted to be reacquainted with his old friend Joseph Winks. Cooper's *Life* records several conversations with Winks, one of which took place when Cooper was planning to leave Leicester to look for another job. He had begun openly to advocate Chartism and had written articles for the Chartist penny weekly paper, *The Midland Counties Illuminator*, edited by the veteran radical George Bown. This was not to the liking of Collier – the new manager of the *Mercury*, which had become more moderate – and Cooper was told to leave. A Chartist deputation asked Cooper to stay in Leicester as paid editor of the *Illuminator*, because Bown wanted to give it up. 'Have nothing to do with them, Tom,' said Winks, 'you cannot depend on 'em. You'll not get the thirty shillings a week they have promised you'.[29]

Cooper ignored his old friend's advice, though he knew he was right about the thirty shillings. After being paid in full for the first week but only half the second week, Cooper bravely offered to take the paper over, including its debts, and he arranged with Albert Cockshaw to print the *Illuminator* on larger and better-quality paper.[30] This arrangement worked well, until Cockshaw suddenly told Cooper that he could no longer print the paper, although he 'was not at liberty to tell the reason'.[31] Cockshaw, despite his radical politics, was printer to the Corporation, and Cooper assumed, probably correctly, that the Corporation was behind his sudden unwillingness to print the *Illuminator*. No other printer was willing to print it, except Thomas Warwick, a Tory-voting small printer, whose meagre facilities fell far short of Cockshaw's standard; so Cooper decided to start a more modest paper called the *Chartist Rushlight*.

He opened a newspaper office in the High Street, which soon became a shop, selling the Chartist *Northern Star* and other radical newspapers and pamphlets. The little shop became a popular meeting place for working men and, when Cooper was evicted, he managed to lease better premises, with two large coffee rooms also used for meetings. He also began to sell bread, although by 1842 he was giving it away or selling it on credit because of the slump in the hosiery industry, a time of terrible poverty, which horrified Cooper. He had to close down an adult school he had been running, and was saddened by the attitude of a few of the men who said 'What the hell do we care about reading if we can get nought to eat?'[32]

Cooper was elected secretary of the Leicester Chartists, but before long they followed the national trend and split into two factions, advocating 'physical force' and 'moral force' Chartism. Cooper became leader of the more militant group, who called themselves the 'Shakespearean Chartists'.[33] They were so named because they met in the Shakespeare Rooms but it was a nicely appropriate name for a group led by Thomas Cooper, who had learned to read at the age of three. As a young man 'he read everything he could lay his hands on; and his memory was remarkable'.[34] He lectured passionately on literature, science and many other topics and could quote huge tracts of Shakespeare and other writers without difficulty.[35]

Thomas Cooper's support for the use of force got him into trouble with the law in 1842. While he was travelling through Staffordshire, on the way to a Chartist convention in Manchester, his name was linked with an uprising in the Potteries, where there had been scenes of great violence and arson. From the book-trade angle, it is interesting to note that, when Cooper was questioned in Burslem, he was asked why he described himself as a commercial traveller when he was really a Chartist lecturer. 'I have not told a lie,' he said, 'for I am a commercial traveller, and I have been collecting accounts and taking orders for stationery that I sell, and a periodical that I publish, in Leicester'.[36]

Cooper was allowed to return to Leicester, but was soon arrested and sentenced to two years' imprisonment. After his release, he returned not to Leicester but to London, where he had briefly worked as a young man in journalism and bookselling.[37] He achieved in his later years some success as an author and lecturer. Tom Cooper's time in prison made him much less militant, and he finally broke with the Chartist movement in 1846. He turned from politics to religion and spent some years as an itinerant Baptist preacher. He visited Leicester in 1859, when he was baptised on Whit Sunday by none other than his old friend Joseph Winks.[38]

It is an interesting coincidence that Joseph Winks had also baptised the young Thomas Cook, back in 1826, when they both lived in Melbourne, in Derbyshire, where Winks was Baptist minister and had his first printing press. When Winks moved his press to Loughborough, Cook was briefly apprenticed to him.

Thomas Cook's fame rests on his achievements in the travel industry, and his life is well documented.[39] But he was for some years an important printer and publisher in Leicester. In 1841 Cook ran his famous pioneering railway trip to a temperance rally in Loughborough. This led to excursions further afield and ultimately to the establishment of a large international travel business which became so successful that Cook gave up his book-trade activities in 1854.

Although Cook held radical political views, much of his energy was devoted to the cause of temperance and his forays into political action were relatively rare, although he and Winks both attended a great Chartist meeting in Leicester in 1848.[40] This was shortly before the so-called 'Bastille' riots in Leicester. The local workhouse, nicknamed the 'Bastille', was the focus of opposition to the new Poor Law, culminating in three days of serious rioting in May 1848. Cook joined a committee which was set up to gather evidence against the actions of the police and specials during the riots.[41] But Cook usually kept his distance from the Chartists; he was a moderate radical who deplored the 'physical force' Chartism advocated by Thomas Cooper. Another book-trade Chartist was John Seal, who ran a small newsagency and bookselling business. He and his brother Richard were prominent 'moral force' Chartists and leading lights of the Leicester Working Men's Association. John Seal's rather stirring advertisements told 'the friends and admirers of cheap political knowledge' that he sold newspapers and pamphlets 'advocating the just rights of the wealth-producing millions and opposing the aggrandisement of the non-producing few'.[42]

Historians often remark on the difficulty of identifying a tradition of radicalism in this country. There was never a cohesive, or continuous, radical movement. But one important study of the years 1760–1848 concludes:

Nevertheless the tradition of native British radicalism is real enough, with links forged by men who survived to join successive organisations, and by a literature which ensured the transmission of ideas and the accumulation of a body of radical thinking which each generation could savour and to which it could add new insights.[43] Literature really was the lifeblood of radical politics. As we study book-trade history, let us give a prominent place to those who held to their radical principles, often risking their personal liberty. By producing and distributing the printed word, they made a crucial contribution to the unity and continuity of the long struggle for democracy.

I end as I began, with the *Leicester Chronicle*'s comments on the procession of 1832:

> Men of England! while you are celebrating your achievement of the Reform Bill as one great step in the cause of Freedom, crowd round the Printing Press – bear it on your shoulders – cherish it in your hearts – without it the Reform Bill would never have been yours... Ever remember that the Printing Press is your dearest treasure and its Liberty your noblest right.[44]

ACKNOWLEDGEMENT

This paper derives from my current research into the Leicester book trades up to about 1850, for a PhD of Loughborough University under the supervision of Professor John Feather. I am happy to place on record my appreciation of his expert advice and enthusiasm.

NOTES

1. *Leicester Chronicle*, 25 August 1832.
2. Derek Fraser, *Power and Authority in the Victorian City* (Oxford, 1979), 123.
3. Frank S Herne, *An Old Leicester Bookseller (Sir Richard Phillips)* (1893), 5.
4. *Dictionary of National Biography*, 45, 210.
5. R W Greaves, *The Corporation of Leicester 1689–1836*, 2nd edn. (Leicester,1970),110.
6. Herne, *Leicester Bookseller*, 7.
7. James Thompson, *The History of Leicester in the Eighteenth Century* (1871), 213.
8. Herne, *Leicester Bookseller*, 3.
9. *Dictionary of National Biography*, 45, 210.
10. 'A Citizen of London', *Memoirs of the Public and Private Life of Sir Richard Phillips* (1808), 27–8.
11. Newspapers are thoroughly surveyed in Derek Fraser, 'The Press in Leicester c1790–1850', *Transactions of the Leicestershire Archaeological & Historical Society*, 42 (1966/67).
12. *Leicester Journal*, 20 January 1792.
13. Thompson, *History*, 212.
14. Not to be confused with another John Pares, a Leicester banker.

15. A T Patterson, *Radical Leicester: a History of Leicester 1780–1850*, 2nd imp, (Leicester,1975), 97.

16. *Leicester Journal*, 16 July 1802.

17. Patterson, *Radical Leicester*, 109.

18. Burbidge (Town Clerk) to Lord Sidmouth, 16 March 1817 (Home Office ref H O 40/6), quoted by Patterson, *Radical Leicester*, 118.

19. The offending work was an extract from Volney's *The Ruins of Empires*, entitled 'A Dialogue between the Privileged Class and the People.'

20. Patterson, *Radical Leicester*, 118.

21. *Victoria County History of Leicestershire*, 4, 138.

22. Patterson, *Radical Leicester*, 199; *Leicester Corporation Hall Book*, 24 March 1834.

23. Patterson, *Radical Leicester*, 188.

24. For example in March 1833 (*Leicester Chronicle*, 30 March 1833).

25. Patterson, *Radical Leicester*, 250.

26. Fred M W Harrison, *It All Began Here: the Story of the East Midland Baptist Association* (1986), 54.

27. *Carley 1823-1973*, [a history of Carley Evangelical Baptist Church] (Leicester, 1973), 8; Michael Tanner, *Crime and Murder in Victorian Leicester* (1981), 11.

28. Thomas Cooper, *The Life of Thomas Cooper* (1872, reprinted Leicester, 1971), 46.

29. Cooper, *Life*, 46.

30. The timing and details of Cooper's takeover are disputed by R Barnes, 'The Midland Counties Illuminator', *Transactions of the Leicestershire Archaeological & Historical Society*, 35 (1959).

31. Cooper, *Life*, 151.

32. Cooper, *Life*, 172.

33. J F C Harrison, 'Chartism in Leicester', *Chartist Studies*, [ed] Asa Briggs (1959), 144.

34. G D H Cole, *Chartist Portraits* (1965), 189.

35. Cooper, *Life, passim*.

36. Cooper, *Life*, 202.

37. Cooper, *Life*, Chapter 12.

38. Cooper, *Life*, 380.

39. A good biography is Piers Brendon, *Thomas Cook: 150 Years of Popular Tourism* (1991). Leicester's links with Cook are ably surveyed in Derek Seaton, *The Local Legacy of Thomas Cook* (Leicester, 1996). I am most grateful to Derek Seaton for information on Cook and Winks, and for alerting me to sources of Baptist history which I might otherwise have missed.

40. *Leicester Chronicle*, 8 April 1848. (The meeting was attended by 3000 people.)

41. *Leicester Chronicle*, 10 June 1848.

42. *Leicestershire Mercury*, 31 December 1836.

43. Edward Royle & James Walvin, *English Radicals and Reformers 1760-1848* (1982), 181.

44. *Leicester Chronicle*, 25 August 1832.

# Book Publishing from the English Provinces in the Late Nineteenth Century: A Report on Work in Progress

### JOHN TURNER

THE GENERAL PATTERN OF the development of book publishing in England appears to fall into three main periods; (1) confined to London from the earliest times until the beginning of the eighteenth century, (2) very gradually spreading out to the provinces from the eighteenth to the early twentieth century, and (3) the provincial spread going into reverse and publishing retracting to London again after about 1918. Scotland, Wales and Ireland, of course, had their own separate developments. In England, London always remained far and away the most important centre, but by the late nineteenth century several independent and completely successful publishing firms were operating in the provinces. Why did successful provincial publishers disappear?

Less work has been done on nineteenth-century English publishing than that of earlier periods and further progress has been hampered by two factors, (a) the vast increase in nineteenth-century publishing output and (b) by the lack of a modern searchable short-title catalogue for the nineteenth century. An obvious starting point would be a list of titles and publishers from various provincial towns, and at first sight there appears to be plenty of sources which would provide such a list for, say, publications from Bradford between 1850 and 1919. Even if a complete list were not possible, surely a representative sample could be obtained? On-line Public-Access Catalogues (OPACs) of several large research libraries, including the British Library, are available, but the problem with OPACs is that none of them supports searching over a range of dates.

CD-ROMs, however, do permit searching over a range of dates and are available for the British Library, the Bodleian Library and the *Nineteenth Century Short Title Catalogue* (*NSTC*). Unfortunately, the Bodleian Library catalogue includes the place of publication but not the name of the publisher, and therefore their CD cannot produce anything more detailed than a grand total of publications from Bradford between 1850 and 1919. *NSTC* includes the name of the publisher and the place of publication, but searches are possible only on place of publication. Thus, as with the Bodleian CD, a list of publications from Bradford could be extracted, but analysis by publishers could be done only by reading each title individually to find the publisher. Even the British Library CD does not include the name of the publisher in about half the entries, presumably at the whim of earlier cataloguers.

Another possibility would be to use On-line Computer Library Center (OCLC) which would allow exactly the kind of searching required, but this is still heavily based on holdings of libraries in North America. It was therefore considered that a more representative sample of English provincial publishing would be obtained from holdings of British libraries.

Thus, only the British Library CDs can be used to produce even a partial list of titles published in a given provincial town and then broken down by publisher. Using these CDs all titles published between 1850 and 1919 can be extracted. Searching can then be limited by place and then by publisher. It was decided to pursue this line of enquiry by including (a) all towns in England with populations of more than 50 000 in the 1851 census, (b) county towns (marked with C in the following table), and (c) any others known to have had an involvement in the book trade, particularly publishing, such as Halifax and Aldershot. This gave a total of sixty-one towns.

All these decisions, of course, affect the findings and in particular it must always be borne in mind that subsequent remarks are based on only those publications which have happened to survive in the British Library. The full list of towns with their populations in 1851 and the number of titles surviving from each town in the British Library, is shown in Table 1.

The grand total of publications between 1850 and 1919 from all sixty-one provincial towns is 44 241. The total for London between 1850 and 1919 is 355 745 and thus, on these figures, provincial publications constitute 12.44%.

A problem becomes apparent even at this stage and arises from the words used in the imprints of the original copies. For example, Newcastle upon Tyne had several active publishers during this period and the total of 1007 titles for the town is far too low. Walter Scott (the most prolific of the Newcastle publishers) had their editorial and production departments in Felling on Tyne, which strictly speaking has never been part of Newcastle, although for many years 'Felling, Newcastle-on-Tyne' was the recognised postal address.[1] However, Scott also had a London office in the Paternoster Row district and their imprints either mentioned only the London office: 'LONDON: | WALTER SCOTT LTD., | PATERNOSTER SQUARE. | 1895', or gave prominence to London: 'LONDON | Walter Scott, 24 Warwick Lane, Paternoster Row | and Newcastle-on-Tyne | 1887, or THE WALTER SCOTT PUBLISHING CO., LTD., | LONDON AND FELLING-ON-TYNE. | NEW YORK: 3 EAST 14TH STREET'. Scott's London office was little more than a warehouse, but the British Library cataloguers could not be expected to tease out the intricacies of company history hidden behind every imprint. Furthermore, it was not a case of Scott and others trying to hide their provincial origins, just that it was easier to sell books from a London trade counter.

TABLE 1

## Towns and their Surviving Titles in the British Library

| Town | Pop. 1851 | Pub. 1850-1919 |
|---|---|---|
| Aldershot* | 875 | 105 |
| Appleby (C) | 709 | 2 |
| Ashton u Lyme | 56959 | 33 |
| Aylesbury (C) | 6081 | 91 |
| Bath | 52240 | 682 |
| Bedford (C) | 11693 | 146 |
| Beverley (C) | 8915 | 44 |
| Birmingham | 232841 | 2638 |
| Bodmin (C) | 4327 | 24 |
| Bolton | 61171 | 198 |
| Bradford | 103778 | 486 |
| Brighton | 65569 | 939 |
| Bristol | 137328 | 1722 |
| Bury | 70143 | 55 |
| Cambridge (C) | 27815 | 6606 |
| Carlisle (C) | 26310 | 217 |
| Chelmsford (C) | 7796 | 104 |
| Chester (C) | 27776 | 236 |
| Derby (C) | 40609 | 592 |
| Dorchester (C) | 3513 | 85 |
| Durham (C) | 18334 | 194 |
| Exeter (C) | 32818 | 625 |
| Gloucester (C) | 17572 | 261 |
| Guildford (C) | 4835 | 173 |
| Halifax | 33582 | 476 |
| Hereford (C) | 12108 | 163 |
| Hertford (C) | 6605 | 206 |
| Hull | 50670 | 506 |
| Huntingdon (C) | 3882 | 26 |
| Ipswich (C) | 32914 | 330 |
| Lancaster (C) | 14378 | 289 |

| Town | Pop. 1851 | Pub. 1851-1919 |
|---|---|---|
| Leeds | 172270 | 1399 |
| Leicester (C) | 60584 | 479 |
| Lewes (C) | 9097 | 161 |
| Lincoln (C) | 20393 | 323 |
| Liverpool | 433733 | 2633 |
| Maidstone (C) | 20801 | 109 |
| Manchester | 186986 | 6491 |
| Newcastle (C) | 87784 | 1007 |
| Northampton (C) | 26657 | 260 |
| Norwich (C) | 68195 | 698 |
| Nottingham (C) | 57407 | 550 |
| Oldham | 52820 | 132 |
| Otley | 4522 | 86 |
| Oxford (C) | 24398 | 7504 |
| Plymouth | 52221 | 462 |
| Portsmouth | 61767 | 350 |
| Preston | 68557 | 224 |
| Reading (C) | 22174 | 268 |
| Rochdale | 80241 | 131 |
| Salford | 63423 | 73 |
| Salisbury (C) | 11657 | 326 |
| Sheffield | 135310 | 548 |
| Shrewsbury (C) | 19681 | 178 |
| Stafford (C) | 11829 | 64 |
| Stoke on Trent | 57942 | 35 |
| Taunton (C) | 13119 | 201 |
| Warwick (C) | 10973 | 86 |
| Winchester | 13704 | 337 |
| Worcester (C) | 29339 | 366 |
| York (C) | 36303 | 505 |

* In 1851 Aldershot was not yet an army camp

As a comparison for the outputs from provincial towns, the outputs of four London publishing houses of varying sizes were checked:

|                  | Publications 1850-1919 |
|------------------|------------------------|
| Henry Vizetelly  | 160                    |
| Charles Rivington| 810                    |
| Smith, Elder     | 1955                   |
| John Murray      | 3398                   |

Comparisons can also be made using data obtained from the Bodleian and NSTC CDs despite the limitations mentioned above. The simple total for the number of titles recorded for each of these 61 towns can be used as a check on the figures from the British Library. Figures from the three CDs are shown in Table 2.

TABLE 2

**Towns and their Titles Recorded on 3 CD-ROMs**

| Town            | Bodl  | NSTC | BL    |
|-----------------|-------|------|-------|
| Aldershot       | 31    | 58   | 105   |
| Appleby (C)     | 2     | 1    | 2     |
| Ashton u Lyme   | 22    | 27   | 33    |
| Aylesbury (C)   | 50    | 83   | 92    |
| Bath            | 464   | 816  | 682   |
| Bedford (C)     | 104   | 114  | 146   |
| Beverley (C)    | 36    | 34   | 44    |
| Birmingham      | 1431  | 2224 | 2638  |
| Bodmin (C)      | 7     | 19   | 24    |
| Bolton          | 180   | 172  | 198   |
| Bradford        | 320   | 350  | 486   |
| Brighton        | 569   | 776  | 939   |
| Bristol         | 1517  | 1214 | 1722  |
| Bury            | 42    | 47   | 55    |
| Cambridge (C)   | 6227  | 5285 | 6606  |
| Carlisle (C)    | 122   | 188  | 217   |
| Chelmsford (C)  | 59    | 74   | 104   |
| Chester (C)     | 159   | 227  | 236   |
| Derby (C)       | 324   | 790  | 592   |
| Dorchester (C)  | 55    | 54   | 85    |
| Durham (C)      | 183   | 211  | 194   |
| Exeter (C)      | 502   | 486  | 625   |
| Gloucester (C)  | 294   | 236  | 261   |
| Guildford (C)   | 144   | 175  | 173   |
| Halifax         | 258   | 385  | 476   |
| Hereford (C)    | 136   | 132  | 163   |
| Hertford (C)    | 164   | 241  | 206   |
| Hull            | 343   | 388  | 506   |
| Huntingdon (C)  | 12    | 17   | 26    |
| Ipswich (C)     | 230   | 409  | 330   |
| Lancaster (C)   | 47    | 69   | 289   |

| Town            | Bodl  | NSTC | BL    |
|-----------------|-------|------|-------|
| Leeds           | 1124  | 1049 | 1399  |
| Leicester (C)   | 371   | 348  | 479   |
| Lewes (C)       | 122   | 115  | 161   |
| Lincoln (C)     | 248   | 175  | 323   |
| Liverpool       | 1992  | 2023 | 2633  |
| Maidstone (C)   | 76    | 103  | 109   |
| Manchester      | 5679  | 4065 | 6491  |
| Newcastle (C)   | 671   | 890  | 1007  |
| Northampton (C) | 240   | 219  | 260   |
| Norwich (C)     | 459   | 619  | 698   |
| Nottingham (C)  | 416   | 398  | 550   |
| Oldham          | 105   | 90   | 132   |
| Otley           | 42    | 103  | 86    |
| Oxford (C)      | 12447 | 6752 | 7504  |
| Plymouth        | 295   | 301  | 462   |
| Portsmouth      | 290   | 141  | 350   |
| Preston         | 155   | 178  | 224   |
| Reading (C)     | 283   | 155  | 268   |
| Rochdale        | 116   | 90   | 131   |
| Salford         | 43    | 43   | 73    |
| Salisbury (C)   | 2     | 231  | 326   |
| Sheffield       | 362   | 452  | 548   |
| Shrewsbury (C)  | 177   | 174  | 178   |
| Stafford (C)    | 44    | 63   | 64    |
| Stoke on Trent  | 34    | 26   | 35    |
| Taunton (C)     | 169   | 175  | 201   |
| Warwick (C)     | 70    | 77   | 86    |
| Winchester      | 281   | 240  | 337   |
| Worcester (C)   | 150   | 178  | 366   |
| York (C)        | 289   | 424  | 505   |

In general the totals increase from Bodleian to NSTC to British Library. NSTC is a conflation of several large library catalogues including the Bodleian and the British Library and therefore the NSTC total, it would seem, ought to be highest. However, the British Library catalogue includes publications which were excluded from NSTC, such as first issues of periodicals.[2]

Not much more can be deduced from these figures because they are simple totals with no indication of which titles are common to all three catalogues. It seems likely that there would be some degree of overlap in the holdings, but it is theoretically possible that, for example, the 230 titles in the Bodleian with Ipswich imprints are completely different from the 330 Ipswich imprints in the British Library. Large discrepancies have been double-checked but, just like the consistencies, for the most part remain unexplained. The two outstanding problems are Lancaster (with 289, 69 and 47) and Salisbury (with 548, 231 and 2). Some of the other anomalies between the three catalogues are perhaps easier to understand. It is not particularly surprising that in almost every case the total for the Bodleian is less than the British Library, although rather more surprising is the Oxford total, not so much because the Bodleian has more Oxford imprints (12 447) than NSTC (6752) or the British Library (7504), but because the Bodleian total is so much higher than the other two. It would be interesting to compare the survival rate of Cambridge imprints in Cambridge University Library.

Another check on the British Library figures is to arrange the three lists for the Bodleian, NSTC and the British Library in numerical order. This also confirms the general reliability of the British Library figures because the order of the towns is roughly similar and towns with low, medium or high outputs, apart from the exceptions mentioned above, remain in the same area of the lists.

Despite all the drawbacks of being forced to rely solely on the British Library catalogue, useful information can be extracted. Exact figures for the publications from a particular town are desirable but not absolutely necessary. The names of the publishers are probably the most important information and it is unlikely that the output of any significant publisher, active only about a hundred years ago, has disappeared completely. Similarly, the relative importance of the business of publishing to such towns as Bodmin (total surviving output four) and Brighton (total 939) is also probably unaffected by the lack of definitive figures.

The most remarkable fact to emerge from these totals for 1850–1919 publications simply in terms of numbers, however, is the clear supremacy of Manchester. The totals for Oxford and Cambridge are higher, obviously due to their long-established university presses,[3] but in all three catalogues (BL, Bodleian, NSTC) Manchester (6491, 5697 and 4065) is in third place, the next town below Oxford (7504, 12 447 and 6752) and Cambridge (6606, 6227 and 5285). Manchester also has about double the number of publications of the next town below in fourth place, either Liverpool (2633, 1992 and 2023) or Birmingham (2638, 1431 and 2224).

Another unexpected result was the utter lack of importance of county towns as centres of publishing. County towns were included on the assumption that public information connected to local government could have attracted printers and publishers in the late nineteenth century. A few county towns were important centres of publishing, but none owed its publishing importance to its county status. It seems that the governing factor was the size of the population and, as always in any form of trade, there had to be the possibility of commercial transactions; there had to be a sufficiently large local market before a local publisher appeared.

A cursory, and very subjective, view of the range of titles being published was then taken. Some of the titles are quite predictable, and probably the least surprising are sermons by the local vicar. On the other hand, the results of overseas missionary work sometimes make a more unexpected appearance. For example, there are eleven books on the Yoruba published in Exeter by James Townsend, or there is Henry J Prince *How You May Know Whether You ... Believe on Jesus Christ* published jointly in Bath by T Noyes and in Vizagapatam by the Mission Press. Similar to the sermons are tracts and books by a local enthusiast, often simply published by 'The Author', but also from commercial publishers. Occasionally publication by the author leads to a more permanent business arrangement; a good example of this is James Kear of Bristol who, between 1889 and 1910, published eight books and four periodicals on the game of draughts.

Other obvious local publications are reports of meetings, sometimes by national organisations, held in the area, for example, the handbook of the 1911 meeting of the British Medical Association published by Allday of Birmingham, where the meeting was held. Freemason lodges, too, appear to have published large amounts of material, for example, *A History of the Lodge of Fidelity... Leeds* (Leeds, 1894), *Some Notes on the History of the Apollo Lodge* (Birmingham, [1906]), and at least three histories of lodges in Bolton.

Two categories of books with no clear provincial connections but which are nevertheless well represented are education and medicine. In education one firm in particular, E J Arnold of Leeds, went on to become very successful and remained in business until 1988. In medicine there were two outstanding firms, Cornish Brothers of Birmingham and John Wright of Bristol. In both these subjects publishers were providing texts for national, rather than provincial, use. For example, Howard E Ward, *Helpful Notes on Nature Study* [1908], and Horace J Bower, *Hints on English Composition* [1912], both from E J Arnold; David C L Owen, *Elements of*

*Ophthalmic Therapeutics* (1890) from Cornish; Patrick W Williams *Diseases of the Upper Respiratory Tract* [1894] from Wright.

Perhaps related to medical books, some with and some without provincial connections, but which appear more frequently than expected, are biological classification schemes. For example, Louis C Miall, *Summary Notes on the Classification of Brachiopoda* ({Bradford: William Byles, 1866); John W Ellis, *Coleopterous Fauna of the Liverpool District* (Liverpool: Turner, Routledge, 1889); and Thomas Hick, *Synopsis of... British Flowering Plants* (Manchester: J E Cornish, [1891]).

Another feature of the list as a whole is the poor showing of literature. There do not appear to be many original novels, apart from the output of J W Arrowsmith, and few reprints of standard works, apart from those of Walter Scott of Newcastle. However, there is plenty of verse on every conceivable subject by local authors, often published at the author's expense. There is also a good showing of local stories and folk lore. Both Abel and John Heywood of Manchester had an interest in this topic; Abel published a large series of Lancashire dialect sketches by the pseudonymous, 'Ab o' th' Yate', while John appears to have taken a more scholarly approach, for example, Edmund Bogg, *The Old Kingdom of Elmet* (1902). Other publishers and other localities were involved, for example, Ella M Leather, *The Folk-Lore of Herefordshire* (Hereford: Jakeman & Carver; London: Sidgwick & Jackson, 1912).

Another line of enquiry still at the planning stage is to compare the data from a series of single years, say, 1860, 1880, 1900 and 1914. So far only 1914 has been attempted.

First, a list of titles for 1914 on the British Library CDs was printed out. There were 401 titles, and each one was then checked against the *English Catalogue* for 1914. Only seventy of the 401 British Library titles were listed in the *English Catalogue*. Next, the *Publishers' Circular* and the *Bookseller* for 1914 were searched for any mention of a provincial publication, either an advertisement by the publisher or a notice by the periodical. The weekly lists of publications in the *Publishers' Circular* were used at this time to compile the *English Catalogue* and so the weekly lists were ignored for the present exercise.

There were eighty-six provincial titles mentioned in the *Publishers' Circular* for 1914 and thirty-two in the *Bookseller*. The extra titles in the *Publishers' Circular* (eighty-six) to the *English Catalogue* (seventy) could be accounted for by announcements in the *Publishers' Circular* of forthcoming titles. The *Publishers' Circular* titles break down as follows: forty-five from Milner of Manchester, thirteen from Arrowsmith of Bristol, six from Wright of Bristol, five from E J Arnold of Leeds, four from Jarrold of Norwich, three from Scott of Newcastle and from Young of Liverpool, and one each from Baker of Bristol, Barnicott & Pearce of Taunton, Cornish of

Birmingham, King of Oundle, the North British Academy of Arts of Newcastle, Phillput of Weston super Mare, and Thurnam of Carlisle.

The thirty-two *Bookseller* titles were eleven from Arrowsmith, seven from E J Arnold, four from Wright, two from Philip of Liverpool, and one each from Barnicott & Pearce, Brown of Hull, Combridge of Brighton, Gale & Polden of Aldershot, Mackay of Chatham, the Tapestry Studio of Stratford on Avon, and Tillotson of Bolton.

Some titles are mentioned in both *Publishers' Circular* and the *Bookseller* but most appear only in one periodical; sixty-eight in *Publishers' Circular* were not mentioned in the *Bookseller*, and fourteen in the *Bookseller* were not mentioned in *Publishers' Circular*.

More work needs to be done, but of the 401 titles on the British Library CDs for 1914 only a small percentage was included in the standard book-trade announcements. It would seem that most provincial publishers relied on local publicity. Furthermore, there is an indication that the publishers taking advantage of national announcements were the most accomplished, such as J W Arrowsmith and E J Arnold.

However, the situation is complicated by joint publications. The publication details given by the British Library CD-roms and the *English Catalogue* do not always agree and what appears to be a title from a single publisher turns out to be a joint publication when both the British Library and the *English Catalogue* are checked. For example, Henry Lethbridge Jessep's *Anglo-Saxon Church Architecture in Sussex* was published only by Warren & Son of Winchester according to the British Library, but only by Simpkin Marshall of London according to the *English Catalogue*. Two more Warren titles, and three titles from John Wright of Bristol are given similar listings with Simpkin Marshall as the sole publisher in the *English Catalogue* but sole provincial publishers by the British Library. Simpkin Marshall must have had a hand in these titles and it seems likely that, in these cases, Simpkin Marshall was acting as the wholesaler. It also looks as though Simpkin Marshall informed the *Publishers' Circular* that the books were published. Some provincial publishers who used London wholesalers or who were partners in joint publications therefore left it to the London house to provide details for the *Publishers' Circular* and *English Catalogue*. The British Museum, quite separately, would prepare catalogue details from a copy of the finished, printed book, sent in by the provincial publisher. The *Publishers' Circular* was working from a note from a London publisher, the British Museum was working from the book itself.

Finally, some work has been done on other aspects of joint publications. Using the data from the British Library CD-roms and despite the discrepancies in recording joint publications mentioned above, of the total 44 241 provincial publications, 1948 (or 4.4%) were published by some form of partnership. Most of the partnerships were between a provincial and a London publisher, with Simpkin Marshall taking by far the largest number. In 1889 Simpkin Marshall & Co. merged with Hamilton Adams & Co, and with Kent & Co, but unfortunately after the merger the firm was still often referred to simply as Simpkin Marshall. There are ninety-five partnerships with Hamilton Adams alone, and eight with Kent alone, and if all these are included with the Simpkin Marshall figure of 542 partnerships, a total of 645 is achieved, or 33.11% of all joint publications (1948).

The partnerships entered into by Arrowsmith of Bristol and Brown of Salisbury have been investigated a little further. Arrowsmith published 380 titles under their name alone between 1861 and 1914, and sixty-five jointly with a London publisher: fifty-eight with Simpkin Marshall between 1885 and 1914, two with Griffith & Farran in 1875 and 1884, and one each with Freeman in 1855, Tweedie in 1855, Partridge in 1859, Longman in 1867, and Trübner in 1885. Brown published seventy-two titles under their name alone between 1850 and 1914, and thirty-nine jointly with a London publisher: twenty-eight with Simpkin Marshall between 1857 and 1910, five with Rivington between 1850 and 1869, three with Longman between 1894 and 1906, and one each with Macmillan in 1862, Hunt in 1868, and the Churchwoman Office in 1902. As well as showing the clear supremacy of Simpkin Marshall, the figures show both Arrowsmith and Brown settling down to arrangements with Simpkin Marshall after more random arrangements in the early years of their business histories.

Two of the titles published by Brown and Simpkin Marshall also had a third partner in W P Aylward (like Brown, also from Salisbury) in 1868 and 1870. Other examples with three partners are found, some with two London and one provincial publisher: both P H Chavasse's *Advice to a Mother* and *Advice to a Wife* were issued from London by Longman and Simpkin Marshall, and from Birmingham by R Davies.

In fact, all combinations were possible, and besides the above examples, there were partnerships of two provincial publishers: William H Bailey, *The 'Bradshaw' of Shakespeare* (Birmingham: Cornish Brothers; Manchester: Sherratt & Hughes, [1904]), and more surprising because a Yorkshire dialect book was being published in Lancashire: William Cudworth (of Bradford), *Yorksher Speyks* (Bradford: W H Brocklehurst; Manchester: John Heywood, 1906). Sometimes, like Aylward and Brown, the two partners were from the same town: Thomas Trocke, *Life's Short Day: a Sermon* (Brighton: H S King; Curtis & Co, 1851), and sometimes there were three publishers from the same town: *Bulgarian Horrors and England's Duty*

(Manchester: J E Cornish; John Heywood; A Ireland, 1876). Partnerships could occasionally be with overseas publishers and Alf Cooke of Leeds published several titles with Frederick A Stokes of New York.

Once a partnership was seen to be working there would be little point in changing the arrangement. Simpkin Marshall and others must have offered attractive terms, but there would also have been an element of avoiding change for the sake of change. It seems as though word of mouth also operated among provincial publishers; for example, the London publisher Elliot Stock had arrangements with three separate publishers in Bradford and only one in Leeds.

One remaining question is how close the late nineteenth-century system was to the eighteenth-century system for joint publications? Certainly some of the imprints were similar, for example, Robert M Willcox, *An Appeal for Peace: a Sermon* (London: sold by John Mason; Leeds: H.W. Walker, 1855), and Henry R Crewe, *A Letter to John Smedley* (Printed by W. Rowbottom, Derby; sold by Hamilton Adams & Co., London, 1855). But both these examples are very early, and more books need to be examined before any conclusions can be reached. The great majority of imprints as recorded on the British Library CDs simply give the names of the publishers involved with no indication of the details of the agreements, such as 'sold by' 'printed for' and so on.

Ideally, records of actual agreements between publishers need to be discovered and, despite the frequency of joint publications, the survival rate of such records appears to be low. The most interesting, of course, would be the Simpkin Marshall archives, but they were all destroyed in the air-raid of 30 December 1940 which obliterated most of the area round Paternoster Row. There are a series of pre-printed forms in the Longman archive,[4] the earliest of which is dated June 1865 and headed, 'Messsrs. Longman & Co.'s Terms for Publishing Books on Commission, for Authors, Publishers, Etc.' and which in brief states that all production expenses and advertising are to be paid by the 'Proprietors of the Books' and Longman will then take 10% of the trade sale price on all copies sold. The form went through nine revisions until June 1904, but it is only this 1865 version which mentions books on commission for other publishers. The first revision in 1874 sets out terms 'for Authors, Booksellers, Etc.' and after that the forms are simply headed 'Terms for Publishing Books on Commission'. The main purpose of the forms seems to be for agreements with authors. Furthermore, all the examples are blank and presumably the terms set out, especially for other publishers, would be starting points for negotiation rather than the final agreement. Another clause on the form which remains constant through all the revisions after 1874 is that only Longman's name is to appear on the title-page.

In conclusion, there was clearly plenty of publishing activity in the English provinces between 1850 and 1919. A large part of the output was of no interest outside its own area. Many of the publishers produced only a small number of titles, but there was a rising scale of output which culminated in businesses which were as prolific and competent as any in the capital.

Similarly, at the bottom of the scale, publishers sold their books locally, but the most successful (firms like Walter Scott, J W Arrowsmith, Jarrold of Norwich, and Bemrose of Derby) sold nationally and internationally. These firms were general trade publishers, but specialists (E J Arnold for education, and John Wright for medicine) could also succeed nationally and still be based in the provinces.

The pattern is complicated by addresses used in imprints after provincials opened London offices,[5] a factor which is almost certainly lowering the true figure for provincial publications. Inconsistencies in contemporary methods of recording joint publications may also be masking the extent to which partnerships were used. Similarly, details of partnerships could be hidden in the wording of imprints; in some cases at least, Longman insisted their name only should appear on title-pages, while Simpkin Marshall seem to have been partners for books in which their name is not mentioned at all.

At some point after 1914 (although exactly when is unknown) provincial publishing went into decline. The reasons were the toll taken by the First World War and the slump which followed, combined with the established strength of most London publishers. E J Arnold managed to thrive in Leeds, but the firm was secure by 1914 and education is not affected by trade recessions. The simple fact that London was the traditional centre of publishing and the book trade was always a threat to the provincials.

Misfortune also played its part. The two most successful provincials and the equals of most London houses were both, by complete coincidence, brought down within three years of each other. Sir Walter Scott died in April 1910 and James Williams Arrowsmith in January 1913. Neither man had made sufficient provision for a successor and their businesses never recovered.

## NOTES

1. Felling became part of Gateshead in the local government reorganisation of 1974 and before that it was under the administration of County Durham.
2. The holdings for some towns are remarkably consistent in the three catalogues, for example, Bolton with 198, 180, and 172; Cambridge with 6606, 6227, and 5285; Durham with 211, 194, and 183; Guildford with 175, 173, and 144; Northampton with 260, 240, and 219; and Shrewsbury with 178, 177, and 174. The holdings for other towns show discrepancies, for example, Bath with 816, 682, and 464; Birmingham with 2638, 2224, and 1431;

Derby with 790, 592, and 324; Halifax with 476, 385, and 258; Lancaster with 289, 69, and 47; Oxford with 12447, 7504, and 6752; Portsmouth with 350, 290, and 141; Salisbury with 548, 231, and 2; and Worcester with 366, 178, and 150.

3. The output of private firms in Oxford and Cambridge, mainly Blackwell and Heffer, have not been distinguished because, like the University Presses, they were not typical provincial publishers.

4. *Archives of the House of Longman, 1791–1914,* Chadwyck-Healey, 1978, Reel 64, 'Commission Agreement Forms and Letters 1840–1904'.

5. Gale & Polden began in Aldershot in 1892, opened a London office at 2 Amen Corner which by 1914 was advertised for some publications as their only address. However, the Aldershot office was still operating during the Second World War.

# Index

Aberystwyth, National Library of Wales, 3,4, 8,16,33

Abree, James (printer), 107,108,109,121,128

Advertisements, in newspapers, 70–76,97, 101,147,148,155,164,165,166,170,171,172

Aldershot, book trade at, 192,196

Alexander, Sir William, 62

Almanacs, printed, 1,19,28,99

Ames, Joseph, 81

Aneirin, 2,7

Archer, Henry, 81,83,84

Arnold, E J (publisher), 190,191,192,195

Arrowsmith, J W (publisher), 191,192,193, 195

Arston, John, 85

Austin, Richard (engraver and typefounder), 47,52,55

Aylward, W P (publisher), 193

Bagford, John, 98

Baggs, Chris, vii,ix,13-22

Bain, Iain, 48

Baker (publisher), 191

Baldwin, R (printer), 111

Ballads, printed, 1,3,23,25,29,30,92

Bangor, book trade at, 35,38

Baptists, printing for, 180

Bardic poetry, 3,4,6,8

Barker, Nicolas, 107

Barker, Richard (advertising agent), 191, 192

Barneby, Richard, 136

Barnicott & Pearce (publishers), 191,192

Barrington, Daines, 8,10

Bath, printing at, 105

Baxter, William, 5

Beavan, Iain, vii,ix,69-78

Bell, Maureen, vii,ix,89-96

Bell, Thomas, 134,135,173

Bell & Bradfute (publishers), 57

Bemrose, William (printer/publisher), 153, 155,158,195

Benyt, Thomas, 81

Bewick, Thomas (engraver), 48,158,172

Bibles, printed, 24,30,58,164

Bingley, William, 53

Birmingham, book trade at, 112,190,192,193

Blackwood, William (publishers), 57,69,70

Blomefield, Francies, 101

Bolton, book trade at, 192

Boruwlaski, Count (dwarf), 170

Bown, George (printer), 177,180

Boyd, George (publisher), 70,72

Boyd, John (publisher), 75

Boyd, Thomas (publisher), 76

Bradford, printing at, 43,44,47,193

Bradford, John, 5,6

Branthwaite, Michael (bookseller), 166

Brecon, printing at, 1

Brighton, book trade at, 192,193

Bristol, book trade at, 1,190,191,195

Bristow, William (printer), 111,112

Broadsides, printed, 1,19

Brockbank, Revd John, 171

Brown (publisher), 192,193

Buchan, Lord, 58

Bulmer, Revd John, 16,17

Burges, Elizabeth, 101

Burges, Francis (printer), 98,99,100,101

Burgess (printer), 109

Butterfield, Henry, 148

Buttler, John (bookseller), 132

Byron, Lord, 70,71

Cadell, Robert (publisher), 69
Caerleon, printing at, 1
Calton, John, 81
Cambrensis, Giraldus, 50
Cambridge, book trade at, 110,111,189
Canterbury, book trade at, 107–130
Canterbury Catch Club, 123–125
Carlisle, book trade at, 166,172,192
Carmarthen, book trade at, 1,16,28,29
Cave, Edward (printer), 102,104
Chambers, John, 104
Chambers, Robert (publisher), 60,69
Chambers, William (publisher), 69
Chapbooks, trade in, 23,25,26,27,29,30,44, 92,93,156-162
Charlett, Arthur, 97,100,101,103
Chatham, printing at, 192
Chester, printing at, 94
Churchill, Awnsham, 137
Claris, James (printer), 122
Clarke, Thomas (bookseller), 92
Clauson, Maynard, 79
Clements, Henry (bookseller), 92
Cochran, J, 70
Cockermouth, book trade at, 167,173
Cockshaw, Albert (printer), 178,181
Cockshaw, Isaac sr & jr (printers), 178
Coffee houses, 93
Collins, Freeman (printer), 98,101,102,103, 104,105
Collins, John, 104
Collins, Martin, 80
Collins, Susanna, 104
Combe, Thomas (bookseller/printer), 177,178
Combridge (publisher), 192
Constable, Archibald (publisher), 57,58,62, 65,69,70,71
Constable, David (book collector), 60,61,62
Cook, James (bookbinder & murderer), 180
Cook, Thomas (publisher), 182
Cooke, Alf (publisher), 194
Cooke, C (publisher), 108

Cooper, Audrey, vii,ix,43–56
Cooper, Margaret, vii,ix,108,131-142
Cooper, Thomas (radical journalist), 180,181, 182
Cooper, William Ainsworth, 147
Cornish Brothers (publishers), 190,191-192, 193,194
Corwen, book trade at, 35
Cotton, Revd Jonathan, 135
Couke, Richard, 81
Cox, Samuel Deadman (printer), 147
Craig, W M (designer), 46,52
Cranstoun, George, 63
Crosby, John (bookseller), 92
Crosby, R & R (publishers), 54
Crossgrove, Henry (printer), 101
Cullum, William Knight (bookseller), 166
Curry & Co (advertising agents), 73,75
Cymmrodorion Society, 6,9

Davison, William (printer), 158
Derby, printing at, 153,155,158,195
Dibdin, Charles, 172
Dibdin, T F, 62–63
Dicey, Cluer (publisher), 144
Dicey, William (publisher), 143,144,149
Dickens, Henry (bookseller), 92
Dilly (bookseller), 112
Dixon, Diana, vii,ix,143–151
Dobel, Daniel, 109
Dodsley, Robert, 8
Doorne, Stephen (printer), 109
Dougharty, Joseph (mapmaker), 131
Dover, printing at, 109
Dublin, book trade at, 1,70,73,74,75,163
Duncombe, Revd John, 127
Dunstan, Thomas (printer), 3

Eckford, William (bookseller), 167,173
Edinburgh,
— Advocates' Library, 60,61,62
— Bannatyne Club, 63

Edinburgh,
— book trade at, 111,156
— 'Edinburgh Cabinet Library' series, 72–73
— literary life at, 57–68,69
— National Library of Scotland, 61,65
Eddowes, John (printer), 1,54
Edwin, W F O, 149
Eldin, Lord, 64
Elliot, Charles (bookseller), 113,156
Ellis, John, 102
English, Jim, vii,ix,153–162
Evans, Benjamin, 17
Evans, David (printer), 17
Evans, Revd Evan, 6,7,8,9,10
Evans, Francis, 134
Evans, P M (publisher), 34
Evans, Sampson (printer), 131
Exeter, book trade at, 112,190

Faversham, printing at, 109
Feather, John, 107,108,110,183
Fell, John, 80
Fisher, John (printer), 143
Fisher, Thomas (printer), 109
Flackton, John, 121,128
Flackton, William (bookseller), 107,111,112,
   113,121–130
Fontaine, Laurence, 89,91,93
Ford, William (bookseller), 57-68
Foster, Edward W, 148
Fowler, Mr (bookseller), 92
Freemasons, printing for, 190
Freez, Frederick, 80,84
Freez, Gerard, (or Wanseford), 80,84

Gachet, John (stationer), 80
Gainsborough, book trade at, frontispiece,
   153–162,180
Gale & Polden (publishers), 192
Gee, Stacey, vii,ix,79–88
Gee, John Howel, 34
Gee, Thomas (publisher), 34,39,40

Gibbons, John, 82
Gillman, Webster (printer), 109
Goes, Hugo (printer), 79,80,81,84
Goggs, William, 149
Gorchestion Beirdd Cymru ('Masterpieces of
   the Welsh Poets'), publication of, 1–12
Gove, Dawkins, 29
Graham, Robert, 58
Gray, Sarah, vii,ix,107,121–130
Gray, Thomas, 8
Green, Richard (bookseller), 92
Gregory, Alfred Thomas, 148
Griffiths, Robert (newspaper editor), 35
Grose, Francis, 127,128
Grove, Joseph (printer), 109,111
Gunby, Adam, 82
Gwyneddigon Society, 10
Gyles, Edward (bookseller), 92

Halhead, W (bookseller), 166
Hall (printer), 109
Hamilton Adams & Co (publishers), 193,194
Harper, Jane, 80
Harris, Howell, 1
Harris, James, 93
Hatfield, James, 146
Hatfield, Weston (publisher), 144,146,149
Hatfield, William, 146
Haverfordwest, book trade at, 13-22,26,27,28
Hearne, Thomas (antiquary), 101
Hengwrt, library, 2,7,10
Heywood, John (publisher), 193,194
Hide, Michael (bookseller), 92
Hill, Thomas Rowley, 55
Hillyard, Francis (bookseller), 92
Hinks, John, vii,ix,175–184
Hoare, Sir Richard Colt, 50
Hodgson, Sarah (bookseller), 48,166,172
Hodgson, Solomon (bookseller), 48,166
Holland, Sir John, 100
Holyhead, printing at, 5
Hook, William, 135

Hopkins, John, 29
Hornbooks, 28
Horne, Bishop, 126
Hotten, J C, 55
Howgill, William, 171
Hubbertt, Francis (bookseller), 136
Hull, book trade at, 79,80,192
Humphreys, Hugh (publisher), 34
Hunter, Alexander Gibson, 58
Huntingdonshire, newspapers in, 143-151
Hurd, Bishop, 133
Hurst, Robinson, 71

Incecliff, William, 84,85
Indulgences, printing of, 83,84
Inman (bookseller), 166
Ipswich, book trade at, 189
Ireland, A (publisher), 194
Ireland, William, 135
Irving, Dr David (librarian), 60,61
Isaac, Peter, 113

Jaffray, James (printer), 148
James, H G, 146
Jamieson, John, 58
Jarman, Sidney Gardnor, 148
Jarrold (publishers), 191,195
Jeffery, John, 99,101
Jeffrey, Francis, 62
Jeffreyes, Henry, 136
Jenkins, Geraint, 23,28,30
Jollie, Francis (bookseller), 166
Johnson, Harman, 80
Johnson, Joseph (bookseller), 110–111,112
Johnson, Dr Samuel, 8,10,57,104
Johnson & Co (advertising agents), 73
Johnston & Deas, 70,75,76
Jones, Dafydd, 7
Jones, David, 3,6,8,9,10,17
Jones, George Ecton, 144
Jones, Owen, 10
Jones, Philip Henry, vii,ix,33–42

Jones, Rees, 28
Jones, Richard (bookseller), 39
Jones, Rhys (or Rice), 2,3,4,6,7,8,10,11
Jones, Thomas, 28
Jones & Evans (booksellers), 92
Joseph, Edward (printer), 17

Kear, James, 190
Keith, George (printer), 111
Kendal, book trade at, 166
Kennet, Bishop White, 98
Kimbar, John, 93
King (publishers), 192
Kirk, Thomas, 62

Laing, David (bookseller), 58
Laing, William (bookseller), 58
Lamb, Silvester, 137
Lambert, Richard (bookseller), 92
Lancaster, book trade at, 166,173,189
Lane, Edmund, 134
Lang, William (printer), 148
Law, Bedwell (bookseller), 110,111,112
Lawrence, Sir Edward, 143
Ledger (printer), 109
Leeds, book trade at, 112,190,191,194
Leicester, book trade at, 175–184
Lemyng, Thomas, 81,82,84
Lench, George, 134
L'Estrange, Roger, 91,94
Lewis, John, 26
Lhuyd, Edward, 4
Libraries
— circulating, 16,19,167,176,177,178
— learned societies', 57
Liverpool, book trade at, 36,189,192
Llandovery, printing at, 1
Llanidloes, book trade at, 27,28,29
Lloyd, William, 10
Lloyd, Bishop William, 132-133
Llwyd, Rheinallt, vii,ix,1-12

London,
— book trade at, 89,90,93,99,110,111,112, 113,136,156,166,176,185,188
— British Library, 46,171,185,186
— false imprints, 156,159,160
— printing at, 1,54,102,103,144
— publishers, 69,111,188,194,195
— scribes at, 82
— Stationers' Company, 89,90,93
Longman (publishers), 54,160,193,194
Ludlow, printing at, 43,45,46
Lymber, Thomas, 81
Lyon, Benjamin, 105

Mackays (printers), 192
Mackworth, Sir Herbert, 14,15
Manchester,
— bookselling at, 64
— Central Library, 62
— Chetham's Library, 61
— printing at, 43,44,45
— publishing at, 189–190,193,194
Manx language, printing in, 164
Margate, printing at, 109
Markenfeld, Ninian, 83
Markynfeld, John, 81,83
Markyngton, John, 84
Marrable, John (printer), 122
Marsh, John (musician), 125
Marsom, J (bookseller), 112
Marychurch, Peter, 27
Mason, Richard, 13
McKay, Barry, vii,ix,163–174
Mendoza, Daniel (pugilist), 168,170
Mercers, in Wales, 27,28
Methodism, in Wales, 1,3
Middleton, Richard, 83
Milner, Ursyn (printer), 81,83
Minshull, John (bookseller), 92
Moore, Bishop John, 98,101,103
Mores, Neville (stationer), 80
Morgan & Higgs (booksellers), 39

Morris, Laurence, 92
Morris, Lewis, 3,5,6,7
Morris, Richard, 3,6,7,9
Morris, William, 3
Mountfort, John (bookseller), 131
Mountfort, Samuel, 131
Mozley, Henry sr & jr (printers), 153,154, 155,156,157,158,160
Mozley, John (printer), frontispiece, 154,155, 156,157
Mozley, Thomas (printer), 153,154,155,156
Murray, John (publisher), 69,70,72,188
Mursell, Revd J P, 178
Music printing, 124,125

Nannau, William, 9
Nennius, 2
Newcastle, book trade at, 166,186,191,195
Newsbooks, printed, 25
Newspapers, see periodicals
Newton & Co (advertising agents), 76
Nicholson, Revd Emilius, 48,54
Nicholson, George (printer), 43–56
Nicholson, John, 44
Norwich, printing at, 97–106,195

Oliver & Boyd (publishers), 57,69,70,71,72, 73,74,75,76
Oundle, book trade at, 192
Oxford,
— Bodleian Library, 185,188,189
— book trade at, 110,111,189

Pares, John (printer), 177-178
Parsons, Thomas, 93
Patent medicines, trade in, 133,136,175
Pedlars, as distributors of print, 23–32,89–96
Pedlar, Gilbert, 25-26
Percy, Bishop, 8
Pembroke, printing at, 13,14
Pennington, William (bookseller), 166,173
Penrith, book trade at, 166,172,173

Periodicals:
- *Army List*, 171
- *Athenaeum*, 73
- *Baner ac Amserau Cymru*, 34,35,38,39,40
- *Baptist Magazine*, 75
- *Blackwood's Magazine*, 70
- *Bookseller*, 191,192
- *Botanical Magazine*, 171
- *British Chronicle*, 16
- *British Critic*, 52
- *British Journal*, 16
- *Caledonian Mercury*, 70
- *Cambrian*, 15,16
- *Cambridge Independent Press*, 146
- *Carmarthen Journal*, 16
- *Chartist Rushlight*, 181
- *Commercial Magazine*, 171
- *Copperplate Magazine*, 171
- *Country Spectator*, 160-161
- *Cumberland Pacquet*, 164,165,166,168,170, 171,172,173
- *Doncaster, Retford & Gainsborough Gazette*, 157
- *Eclectic Review*, 52
- *Edinburgh Magazine*, 76
- *Edinburgh Review*, 62
- *Eddowes's Salopian Journal*, 54
- *European Magazine*, 52
- *Evangelical Magazine*, 75
- *Gentleman's Magazine*, 43,55,58,75,122, 123,128,171
- *Hackney & Kingsland Gazette*, 20
- *Haverfordwest & Milford Haven Telegraph*, 18
- *Huntingdon Chronicle*, 149
- *Huntingdon, Bedford & Cambridge Weekly Journal*, 146
- *Huntingdon, Bedford & Peterborough Weekly Gazette*, 144
- *Huntingdonshire Post*, 148
- *Huntingdonshire Times*, 149

Periodicals:
- *Hunts County News*, 147,149
- *Hunts Guardian*, 148
- *Illustrated St Neots Chronicle & Pictorial Newspaper*, 146
- *Inverness Courier*, 73
- *Kentish Gazette*, 128
- *Kentish Post & Canterbury Newsletter*, 107, 121,128
- *Leicester Chronicle*, 175,177,178,183
- *Leicester Herald*, 176,177
- *Leicestershire Mercury*, 178,180
- *Literary Panorama*, 52
- *Master Humphrey's Clock*, 75
- *Midland Counties Illuminator*, 180,181
- *Monthly Review*, 52
- *North Wales Times*,40
- *Northampton & Leamington Free Press*, 146
- *Northampton Mercury*, 143
- *Northern Star*, 181
- *Norwich Courant*, 104
- *Norwich Post*, 98-99,101,104
- *Pembrokeshire Herald*, 18,19,20
- *Peterborough Times*, 147
- *Plymouth Journal*, 73
- *Potter's Electric News*, 18,19
- *Potter's Newspaper*, 18,19
- *Principality*, 17
- *Publishers' Circular*, 191,192
- *Ramsey Herald*, 149
- *Quarterly Review*, 71
- *St Ives Chronicle*, 149
- *St Ives Mercury*, 143,144,145
- *St Ives Post*, 143
- *St Ives Post Boy*, 143
- *St Ives Reporter*, 147
- *St Ives Times*, 149
- *St Ives, Hunts & Cambridgeshire Examiner*, 148
- *St Ives & Huntingdonshire Gazette*, 147
- *St Neots Advertiser*, 147

INDEX

Periodicals:
- *St Neots Chronicle*, 147
- *St Neots Family Paper*, 147
- *St Neots Free Press*, 147
- *St Neots Monthly Advertiser*, 147
Perkins, William (printer), 17
Philip (publisher), 192
Phillips, Richard (bookseller/printer),
 175–177
Phillput (publisher), 192
Pitcher (bookseller), 112,113
Plomer, H R, 111
Ponder, Nathaniel, 94
Pontypridd, book trade at, 35,37
Potter, family (Haverfordwest printers), 13–22
— Edward J, 19
— Elizabeth, 18,19
— Henry E, 18
— Jane, 17,18,19
— J T, 13,14,15,16,20
— J W, 15
— Joseph, 15,16,17,18,20
Poughnill, printing at, 43,46,47,48
Price, Cuthbert, 26
Prideaux, Humphrey, 97-99,100,102,103,
 104
Prince, William, 82
Proctor, Henry (printer), 46
Prys, Stafford (printer), 3,4,6,8,9,11
Pynson, Richard (printer), 80,83

Raddon, William, 93
Raikes, Robert (printer), 143,149
Ramsgate, printing at, 109
Rawlinson, William, 27
Regnault, Francois (printer), 80
Rees, Eiluned, 3,13,23,29,30
Religious/devotional publications, 1,17,29,99
Rhys, Sion Dafydd, 4
Richard, Edward, 6,7
Richardson, Thomas (bookbinder), 158
Richardson, W J & E (booksellers), 166

Riplyngham, Richard, 81
Rivington, Charles (publisher), 188
Roberts, Robert, 30
Robertson & Scott (advertising agents), 73,76
Robinson, Joseph, 71
Rochester, printing at, 109
Roose, John, 85
Rose, George (bookseller),92
Ross, John (printer), 1

Sabery, Revd Charles, 135
St Ives, newspapers at, 143–150
Salesbury, William, 4,26
Salisbury, book trade at, 189
Schoolbooks, trade in, 132,136,160,194
Scott, Benjamin (bookseller), 166,172
Scott, Sir Walter, 57,63,64-65,69,173
Scott, Walter (publishers), 186,191,195
Scragg, Brenda, vii,ix,57-68
Seal, John, 182
Seal, Richard, 182
Seditious literature, distribution of, 91,92,93
Shaw, David J, vii,ix,107-119
Sheardown, William (printer), 157
Sherratt & Hughes (publishers), 193
Sherwood, Neely & Jones (publishers), 54
Shrewsbury, printing at, 1,3,9,28
Simmons & Kirkby (publisher), 108,109,111,
 112,128
Simpkin Marshall (wholesalers), 192,193,194,
 195
Skeeles, George (printer), 147
Smith Elder (publishers), 188
Smith, Francis (bookseller), 95
Smith, Obed (bookseller), 92
Smith, Sydney Thomas, 148
Smith, Thomas (printer), 112,113
Society for Diffusion of Useful Knowledge, 72
Soulby, Anthony (bookseller), 166,172,173
Soulby, John (bookseller), 166,172,173
Southall, Mary (bookseller), 55
Sparry, Revd Ambrose, 134-135,137

Speare, D (auctioneer), 62
Spottiswoode (printer), 54
Spufford, Margaret, 23,25,27,30,89,91,93
Stanley, Revd John, 136
Sted, William, 81
Stock, Elliot (publisher), 194
Stoker, David, vii,ix,97–106,112
Stourport, printing at, 43,45,48,55
Stratford, Bishop Nicholas, 99
Stringer, H Gilbert, 148
Suggett, Richard, vii,ix,23–32
Sutherland, Samuel, 74
Sutton, Prideaux, 134
Swansea,book trade at, 14,15,16,35,39

Tait, William, (publisher), 76
Taliesin, 2
Tanner, Thomas, 97-98,100,101,103,104
Taunton, book trade at, 191
Taylor, Thomas, 135
Tenby, printing at, 13
Tesseyman (bookseller), 166
Thomas, James (printer), 16,17
Thompson, Henry (printer), 154
Thompson, James (printer), 177
Thompson, Thomas (printer), 177,178
Thomson, David Richard (printer), 147
Thomson, Thomas, 62,63
Thurnam (publisher), 192
Tillotson (publisher), 192
Timperley, C H, 55,57
Topham, James (printer), 147
Topham, Frederick (printer), 147
Trefecca, printing at, 1
Trehedyn, printing at, 1
Turberfield, William, 27
Turner, John R, vii,ix,185–196

Ulverston, book trade at, 166,172,173

Vaughan, Hugh, 10
Vaughan, Robert, 2

Vaughan, William, 4,6,7,8,10
Vernon, Revd George, 134,135
Viloette, Pierre (printer), 80
Vizetelly, Henry (publisher), 188

Wales, book trade in, 1–56
Walker, Peter (bookseller), 167,173
Wallis, Peter, 153
Walmsley (bookseller), 173
Ware, John sr & jr (printers), 163–174
Watt, Tessa, 23
Wanesford, see Freez, Gerard
Warren & Son (publishers), 192
Warrington, book trade at, 112
Warwick, John (printer), 81
Warwick, widow (printer), 83
Welles, John (stationer & bookbinder), 80
White, Laurence, 92
White & Son (booksellers), 112
Whitehaven, book trade at, 163-174
Whittaker & Co, 69
Wholesale agents, 69–76,191–195
Williams, Moses, 5
Williams, Robert, 33–40
Williams, Thomas, 29
Williams, William, 10
Williamson, Revd David, 173
Wilmot, William, 13
Wilson, Thomas (bookseller), 158
Wilson & Spence (bookseller), 166
Winchester, book trade at, 192
Winfrey, R, 149
Winks, Joseph Foulkes (bookseller/printer),
    178,180,182
Wodd, John, 82
Wolveden, Robert, 85
Wood, Andrew Page (printer), 146
Woodcuts, trade in, 25,30,79,14
Worcester, book trade at, 107,131-142
Worde, Wynkyn de (printer), 80
Workington, book trade at, 167,173
Wrenne, Philip (stationer), 79

INDEX

Wrexham, book trade at, 1,29,34
Wright, John (publishers), 190,191,192,195
Wright, Thomas (printer), 45,46
Wyatt, Henry, 59
Wynne, Sir Watkin Williams, 10
Wynne, William, 10

York:
— book pedlars at, 90
— book trade at, 110,111,166
— printing at, 79-88,94
— scribes at, 79,80,83,84-85
Young, Edward, frontispiece, vi
Young, Sir William, 125–126
Young, Lady, 126

Zamoyski, Count, 64